# Prepossessing Henry James

The novels of Henry James are filled with ghosts, but most of them escape dramatic treatment. These elusive specters are the voices of precursors that haunt his narratives, compromising their constitutive freedom. *The Strange Freedom* is an examination of the ways James's fiction is prepossessed by some major voices of the English literary tradition: those of Shakespeare, Richardson, Fielding, Gibbon, Thackeray, and Dickens. This subtextual arrogation sets constrains to the unfolding, in James's narratives, of liberal and romantic freedom—it places limits both to the absolute exemptions of aesthetic interest and to radical Bohemian abandon. But these constrains and limits can be regarded, dialectically, as the enabling conditions of the very liberty they imperil. Drawing on recent research on the spectral dynamics and indirections of literary influence by scholars like Adrian Poole, Philip Horne, Nicola Bradbury, Tamara Follini, and Peter Rawlings, but also on earlier deconstructive work by John Carlos Rowe, *Prepossessing Henry James* offers a speculative account of the way James is simultaneously resourced and restrained by his sources. Along the way, we discover how Hamlet's ghost instills in James a fantasy of mental autonomy, or how he adapts Gibbon's Enlightened narrative to inhibit civic liberty with images of female sacrifice. We see the governess in *The Turn of the Screw* possessed by the specter of Richardson's *Pamela*, exposing social freedoms with liberal brutality. We encounter Gray, in *The Ivory Tower*, striving to obtain personal freedom by repressing Dickensian "figures, monstrous, fantastic." And, finally, we recognize how much *The Ambassadors* owes to the ambiguous manner of Thackeray.

**Julián Jiménez Heffernan** (Ph.D. Bologna, Italy) is Professor of English and Comparative Literature at the Universidad de Córdoba, Spain. He has authored three books on Shakespeare, co-edited the collection *Community in Twentieth-Century Fiction* (2013), and published many essays on Renaissance philosophy, deconstruction, and modern fiction—from Samuel Richardson to Nadine Gordimer. He is currently working on a book on Karl Marx and William Thackeray.

# Routledge Studies in Nineteenth Century Literature

**The Vampire in Nineteenth-Century Literature**
A Feast of Blood
*Edited by Brooke Cameron and Lara Karpenko*

**Wilkie Collins**
The Complete Fiction
*Stephen Knight*

**Jane Austen and the Ethics of Life**
*Brett Bourbon*

**The Significance of Fabrics in the Writings of Elizabeth Gaskell**
Material Evidence
*Amanda Ford*

**Cultures and Literatures in Dialogue**
The Narrative Construction of Russian Cultural Memory
*Elena Bollinger*

**Memory in German Romanticism**
Imagination, Image, *Reception*
*Edited by Christopher R. Clason, Joseph D. Rockelmann and Christina M. Weiler*

**Keats and Scepticism**
*Li Ou*

**Prepossessing Henry James**
The Strange Freedom
*Julián Jiménez Heffernan*

For more information about this series, please visit: www.routledge.com/Routledge-Studies-in-Nineteenth-Century-Literature/book-series/RSNCL

# Prepossessing Henry James
## The Strange Freedom

Julián Jiménez Heffernan

Routledge
Taylor & Francis Group
NEW YORK AND LONDON

First published 2023
by Routledge
605 Third Avenue, New York, NY 10158

and by Routledge
4 Park Square, Milton Park, Abingdon, Oxon, OX14 4RN

*Routledge is an imprint of the Taylor & Francis Group, an informa business*

© 2023 Julián Jiménez Heffernan

ISBN: 978-1-032-05865-8 (hbk)
ISBN: 978-1-032-05866-5 (pbk)
ISBN: 978-1-003-19956-4 (ebk)

DOI: 10.4324/9781003199564

Typeset in Sabon
by Apex CoVantage, LLC

The OA version of chapter 3 was funded by Universidad de Córdoba.

For Pilar, Julián, and Marisa

# Contents

# Foreword

This book started as a deconstructive examination of intertextual belatedness, openly indebted to Bloom, and indirectly to de Man. But it soon got bound up with two additional theoretical strands: an ontological redescription of the historical vocabularies of liberalism along aleatory-materialist lines, and a Lacanian demand on the ineliminable priority of social-sexual inconsistency. Whether and how these three lines of argument can be seen as successfully converging is something the reader is invited to decide by herself. Although the present book rests largely on poststructuralist assumptions, I certainly don't believe anything can do. I abide by the rule of prudence stipulated decades ago by John Carlos Rowe when he questioned the boundlessness of "happy pluralism," "indeterminacy," and "undecidability" (*Theoretical* 21, 145). Ned Lukacher's sharply observed two years later that "the task of reading James is one of remembering that although there is a right track, we are not going to be on it" (*Primal Scenes* 123). What is shocking in this observation is the serenity with which it presumes that *there is a right track*. I believe Rowe and Lukacher are right. There is a limit, therefore, to the contingency, in this book, of my subtextual choices (*Hamlet, The Decline and Fall of the Roman Empire, Pamela, Joseph Andrews, Amelia, Denis Duval,* and *Our Mutual Friend*) and my theoretical commitments (Derrida, Deleuze, Badiou, Žižek). But I presume their *rightness* in leading us to James's *right track*.

# Acknowledgements

*Prepossessing Henry James* draws on my own previous research on Henry James, which has materialized in four articles: " 'Constructed to Revolve': Interest in Henry James," *The Henry James Review* 38.2 (2017); " 'On the Outer Edge': The Temptation of Bohemia in Henry James," *Studies in American Fiction* 44.1 (2017); "Two New Sources for *The Tragic Muse*," *ANQ* 29.3 (2016); " 'The Hard Worldly Basis': History and Infrastructure in Henry James's 'Julia Bride,' " *Arizona Quarterly* 74.4 (2021). Given the antagonistic coloration of some of the claims I put forward in these four essays, especially those dealing with German idealism, aesthetics, materialism, and homosexuality, I was forced to engage heavily with Jamesian criticism. In the present book I have in part dispensed with the scholarly obligation to cover exhaustively the existing Jamesian criticism on each of the topics I discuss. I only allude to research that has a direct bearing on my central arguments. However, I would like to acknowledge the debt I have incurred with the invaluable work of some scholars from which I have learnt more than I can assess, whose arguments inform some of my claims, and whom I have perhaps cited less than they deserve. These scholars are Peter Brooks, J. Hillis Miller, and Eric Savoy.

I would like to show my gratitude to scholars that have shown interest in my work on James: Susan M. Griffin, Maria Farland, Duncan Faherty, Sandro Jung, Lynda Zwinger, Gert Buelens, Eric Haralson, and Roslyn Jolly. I am also indebted to my colleagues María Valero Redondo and Leonor Martínez Serrano for creating a friendly atmosphere of discussion that was an important stimulant during the writing of this book. I am extremely grateful to Adrian Poole and John Carlos Rowe for the very friendly and attentive manner in which they have responded to queries, offered sound advice, and given constant support to my work. Without their critical encouragement, this book would not exist.

I am very grateful to Michelle Salyga and Bryony Reece for their faith in this project and constant support through the completion of the manuscript.

And to Vaishnavi Madhavan for her invaluable help during the copy editing process. I also want to thank the two readers at Routledge for the interest, advice, and constructive criticism.

I also acknowledge the support of the Spanish Ministry of Science and Innovation. The writing of this book was facilitated by the funding the research project PID2019–104408GB-100, "Henry James in Literary Contexts" received during the years 2020–2023.

# 1 Apophrades

## The Return of the Dead: Notes on Belated Freedom

I

At the beginning was anxiety. At the beginning, and all the way through. Staring at the idle wanderers in Regent's Park, Milly wonders: "Their box, their great common anxiety, what was it, in this grim breathing-space, but the practical question of life?" (*Wings* 178) For anxiety is, we are told, that which nothing precedes, that which doesn't deceive.[1] And so is finite *life*, the object of her "practical question."[2] But anxiety is, we are also reminded, the very textual exertion (poem, novel) we often mistake for the overcoming of anxiety.[3] This—that "the suppression of anxiety was a thin idea" (*Wings* 461)—Densher by contrast realizes too late. These are, I know, grandiosely misapplied and potentially banal statements, ringing with the "superficial cleverness" Cocteau attributed to Freudianism in *The Infernal Machine*, his theatrical recreation of the myth of Oedipus.[4] But I stand programmatically by them. Not because I want to be clever, but rather because I hope to remain *superficial* in accordance with parameters of dialectical critique we associate with the deeply depth-suspecting hermeneutics of suspicion (Marx, Nietzsche, Freud). To remain dialectically superficial is to accept the profound bearing that real *holes* have on the charting of meaningful narrative *surfaces*. As (b)anal—but also vaginal—as that.

Freud dreamt once of a patient, a young woman called Irma, who complained about the failure of his treatment to mitigate her pain. During a party, in the dream, she refused to have her throat—the "grim breathing-space" of her tracheal *persona*—properly inspected by Freud, who managed however to catch a glimpse of the cavity. In a second part of the dream, Freud receives clinical assistance from a group of colleagues and friends. This is how Lacanian theorist Joan Copjec explains the oneiric episode:

> The dream space becomes fantasmatically populated with Freud's doctor friends: Dr- M., Otto, Leopold; in other words, the space becomes "Oedipalized". By this I mean, first of all, that the second part of the

DOI: 10.4324/9781003199564-1

dream is defined as a turning away from the object a that erupted in the first part. In the second part, Freud no longer wants to know; his primary desire is a desire not to know anything of the real that provoked in him so much anxiety.

(*Read* 120)

I find this transition from the confrontation of the Real—Irma, her pain, the white scabs in her throat, the unconscious—towards "the symbolic community of his fellow doctors," what Stanley Fish would call an *interpretive community*, extremely suggestive.[5] In a letter dated 25 March 1864 and sent to his friend Thomas Sergeant Perry, a twenty-year-old Henry James conveys a "spiritual, transcendental message" by way of an odd phantasmagoria. He is alone in a Newport house haunted by other presences:

> I write with a pen snatched from my angel-wing. It is very pleasant up here but rather lonely, the only other inhabitants being Shakespeare, Goethe and Charles Lamb. There are no women. Thackeray was up for a few days but was turned out for calling me a snob because I walked arm-in-arm with Shakespeare. I am rather sorry, for I am dying to hear the end of *Denis Duval*: that is an earthly expression.
>
> (*Letters I* 49)

First and foremost, this epistolary confession attests to the radical precedence of anxiety: "I write [. . .] but rather lonely [. . .] I am dying." Nonetheless, if we compare it with Freud's dream, what is here ostensibly missing is the traumatic confrontation with the Real that should precede the primal scene dominated by the symbolic community of fellow writers. Are these "other inhabitants" there to assist James in his attempt at interpreting the traumatic experience of his failure? But what traumatic experience? What failure? If he had poked something at a young woman's hole or fun at her pain (made her pregnant, led her to suicide, sent her to a convent), then Shakespeare and Goethe are understandably helpful—also Lamb, for his personal and family record of mental illness was rather unordinary. After all, as Gibbon noted, "we seem to have lived in the persons of our forefathers" (*Memoirs* 41). And also of our fathers, like Thackeray, of whose forced but providential evasion from the family house we can only say it proves he nearly always managed to remain at two removes from the Real. The traumatic experience is not specified. But we are told, significantly, that "there are no women," just like in the political "*séances*" evoked in *The Princess Casamassima*, "only the right men were present" (206), an unambiguous sentence that rules out, of course, *the wrong* men, and leaves *all* women in a limbo of un-specification.[6] We know at least, and the notation is very symptomatic, that Hyacinth "[hasn't] seen any ladies"

(*Princess* 196).[7] We also know we are bound, with James and his tutelary ghosts, to know—to assist him in the interpretation of a reverie (a fantasy) that is itself the failed interpretation of another thing—the dream-work of another dream—of which we know nothing. *Prepossessing Henry James* is, in a restricted but actual sense, an attempt to interpret James's brief epistolary phantasmagoria.

There are no ladies, but James spent his life inspecting the rifts, cracks, and lacunae of the American female consciousness with the clinical tenacity of a Chillingworth. Or the audacity of an infatuated American artist drifting across European salons:

> Roderick as usual was in the field, and, on the ladies taking the chairs which had been arranged for them, he immediately placed himself beside Christina. As most of the gentlemen were standing, his position made him as conspicuous as Hamlet at Ophelia's feet.
>
> (*Roderick Hudson* 176)

The inspection of the lady's crack is *ab initio* construed as a variation on Hamlet's bawdy scrutiny, in a climactic scene of the tragedy, of Ophelia's genitalia, the "no thing" that lies "between maids' legs" (3.2.107). *Nothing*—the only thing that *stricto sensu* precedes anxiety—is the same *no thing* that is (or is not) between the maid's legs, or inside her throat.[8] Tellingly, Nancy Armstrong locates the beginning of modern domestic fiction in the traumatic event of a gentleman—*Pamela*'s Mr B—attempting "to penetrate a servant girl's material body" (*Desire* 5–6);[9] also, the only diegetic event worth discussing in *Finnegans Wake*—the first systematically attempted swan song to the tradition of domestic fiction—was the exposure of a girl's genitalia, in a Dublin Park, to the voyeuristic gaze of her father, described in a ballad as "King of the Castle" (*Finnegans* 45).[10] From the diachronic angle afforded by the recursive resetting of such primal scene of *libido sciendi*—the scopic-analytical examination of female lacunae—Shoshana Felman's sentence "thus it is that the whole of the story is governed by the hole in a letter" (144) reads as an anagrammatic adulteration of an original, possibly repressed, formulation: "thus it is that the whole of the story is littered by the hole in a governess." And the hole in the governess—surely augmented by the turns of the screw—is the vacuum inside the young woman that features as condition for the occurrence of a flawed individual (the nothingness of subjectivity from Descartes to Lacan) who may be further vacated by the historical determinants of her native land: commenting on James's growing sensibility to America's cultural "emptiness," Robert Pippin has astutely observed that "America" in James' oeuvre names "uncertainty and new *vacancy* as well as new possibility" (*Henry James* 5, 44; emphasis added). William Gaddis mocked this promissory vacuum when he regretted the hopeless attempts "to fill in this yawning sentimental churchgoing flagwaging vacant remnant of the founding fathers" (*Frolic* 325). A gap, a hole, a lacuna, an emptiness, a vacuum, a new vacancy—inside a throat, a mind, a body, a girl, a nation. All the male doctors gathered around the onerous examination. And Hamlet, finally defeated, confiding, like the ghost-hunting sentinel at the play's opening: "I have seen nothing" (*Hamlet* 1.1.20).

Let us return to the epistolary phantasmagoria, also haunted by dubious ghosts. With brisk nonchalance, James manages to telescope some basic motifs of Gothic romance (*angel, loneliness, house, inhabitants*) into a primal *scene of instruction*. He is master of the house, not king of the castle. As Gibbon wrote in his *Memoirs*, "few works of merit and importance have been executed either in a garret or a palace" (157). The scene, at any rate, takes place in a no-place, a visionary abode that supplements the truth of James's situation, which is no other than the anxiety of an amateur writer confronted with the blank surface of *le vide papier que la blancheur defend* and not dissimilar from the anxiety of an inexpert doctor glancing at white scabs in an empty throat. As Philip Horne explains,

> James is trying to finish or "to rewrite that modern novel I spoke of to you" (LL 3)—almost certainly a short story—and, not having finished it, imagines himself in heaven. The logic is neat. Thackeray being dead, *Denis Duval* must remain unfinished; James's story being unfinished, James must therefore die—or have died.
>
> ("Henry James, Winchelsea" 220)

The logic of the reverie is indeed neat, and it confers an uncanny retrospective light on an ulterior parallel fact: James had to die (and must therefore be dead) for *The Ivory Tower* to remain unfinished. But is it? Is *unfinished* the opposite of *finished*? The overlords of *determinate negation* and *infinite judgement* (Kant, Hegel, Lacan, Žižek) would protest. Is James himself unfinished or is he still "up [there] with a pen snatched from [his] angle-wing"? Harold Bloom, Derrida, and Nicholas Royle would concede the latter.[11] Me too. In the neat logic of James's "spiritual, supernatural message," one may venture to assert, with Žižek, that "truth has the structure of a fiction" (*Organs* 148). James articulates the truth of his creative anxiety through a petty, domestic, hauntological farce, less the *divina commedia* of his ascension to heaven (I disagree with Horne) than the human, all too human *comédie* of the other writers' tarrying in the negative of clinical purgatory. James knows, with Gibbon, that at bottom, all anxiety is "domestic anxiety" (*Memoirs* 152), and wants the dead there (at home) to forestall the anxiety of their influence on his writing, there to in turn prepossess them, to take them from behind, like Plato takes Socrates in the superb *coitus a tergo* examined in Derrida's *carte postale*, through an "incredible chicane of filiation and authority," composing a "family scene without a child in which the more or less adoptive, legitimate, bastard or natural son [*bâtard ou naturel*] dictates to the father the testamentary writing which should have fallen to him" (*Postal* 61; *Carte* 67). You will hear the end of *Denis Duval*. Grab a pen and a piece of paper. Now copy. No wonder James, to secure his antecedence and mastery, should have "favoured the figure of the turned back for the artist's guardianship of a private and creative space" (Poole, "James and the Shadow" 82).

In his long essay on *Hawthorne*, James famously observed that in America there were "no palaces, no castles, no manors, nor old country-houses, no parsonages, nor thatched cottages nor ivied ruins; no cathedrals, nor abbeys, nor little Norman churches; no great universities nor public schools" (*LC I* 352). What all of these "Old World" buildings have in common is their availability to spectral haunting, and the last two submit an alternative version—the scholastic Gothic—to the traditional pattern, where the occupant is a neophyte visited upon by the sinful lessons of the dead masters. This version accommodates "bizarre attachments and dependencies, the doubles and the twins, the Masters and Slaves, dead authors and living researchers, and other such pathologies of social dependence" (Pippin, *Henry James* 58). Like the spires and domes "miraged in the peculiar atmosphere" of Christminster at dusk (Hardy, *Jude* 16), the pattern accommodates anything but the truly deserving soul, whence came James' aggravated anxiety. Admittedly, and Hardy could bear witness to this, such scene reinforces the "ghostly intimation in the belief in the justice of traditional, aristocratic ideology" that is consistent with "conservative ideology" (McKeon 344). The spectral board of fellow writers signifies the advent of a symbolic proto-meritocratic aristocracy (a *noblesse de robe*) that has left behind the material obscenities of a blood-and-sword genealogical aristocracy.

## II

Harold Bloom described the "scene of instruction" as the "imposition of the figure of belatedness" (*Map* 37) by an authority figure to a latecomer.[12] The scene of instruction is, therefore, "necessarily also a scene of authority and of priority" (38). In the Jamesian scene, the authority of the "other inhabitants" rests partly on their priority—on their being inside the house before the new dweller arrives. For, needless to say, "the ghost does not return to Elsinore, it lives there" (Zupančič 184). James doesn't mention other important precursors sojourning in what he may have symbolically taken to be the James House—writers like Hawthorne, George Eliot, or Turgenev. He alludes exclusively to authors whose books he was reading at the time he penned the letter, surely with no aim at being comprehensive regarding those he favored most. In this apt dramatization of the concessive and repressive energies informing the literary tradition, the latecomer's freedom is limited. If the resulting society *is* also "a contract [. . .] between those who are living" and "those who are dead" (Burke 194), the first are manifestly coerced into signing it. And if a *scene of instruction* "always depends upon a primal choosing and a being chosen" (Bloom, *Map* 39), it is the fatalistic outcome of James's *being chosen* by the other (earlier) occupants that speaks most to the deterministic-deconstructive reading I intend to conduct in this book. In his reading of the scene where the ghost addresses Hamlet, Derrida remarks that the balance sheet of Marxism's inheritance cannot be recorded in a static manner:

> These accounts cannot be tabulated. One makes oneself accountable (*comptable*) by an engagement that selects, interprets, and orients. In a practical and performative manner, and by a decision that begins by getting caught up, like a responsibility, in the snares of an injunction that is already multiple, heterogeneous, contradictory, divided—therefore an inheritance (*héritage*) that will always keep its secret. And the secret of a crime.
>
> (*Specters* 116; *Spectres* 153)

The undisclosed lapsus is not only, as in *Hamlet*, the Biblical crime of original fratricide. The crime is more primordial and more secret, and it also fatally concerns *Hamlet*. The morphology of the negatively prefixed term *prepossession* contains a key to our problem, to wit, the relation of deconstruction

> to what must (without debt and without duty) be rendered to the singularity of the other, to his or her absolute precedence or to his or her absolute previousness, to the heterogeneity of a pre-, which, to be sure, means what comes before me, before any present, thus before any past present.
>
> (*Specters* 33)

Because it is both a *primal fantasy* and a *fantasy of origins*, like the scene elaborated by Freud in *Totem and Tabu* (Homer, *Lacan* 66), *Hamlet* is a static, unremovable property of the *previous gift*—the literary inheritance—to which James is *willy-nilly* indebted. The other is Dickens. The rest of the goods he may select, interpret, and reorient more or less at wish. *Hamlet*, by contrast, spells an injunction—*remember me* (*Hamlet* 1.5.112)—whose mechanical, inscriptive force forestalls our power to evade it. No messianic justice, *pace* Derrida, can over-determine (and relieve of anxiety) this immanent process. One may in fact speak of an asymmetric determinism. Such off-balancing of what should be a two-way process echoes the way the civic-humanist relation of "ruling-and-being-ruled" (Pocock, *Virtue* 48) gets deranged by the anteriority of a law to whose authority the subject is inescapably *subject*. Grappling with the question of liberal origins, in a section of his book *Virtue, Commerce, and History* (1985) devoted to the problem of antinomian libertarianism, Pocock observed that "it is impossible to assert even the most radical liberty without asserting some conception of authority at the same time" (54). Twenty years earlier, Leslie Fielder argued that the freedom of the characters in *The Scarlet Letter* is ironic, "for what they must learn freely to accept is the notion that freedom is the recognition of necessity" (*Love* 232). All too evidently, any liberty obtained at the cost of a conception of authority or the recognition of necessity is but a dialectical—if not ironic—semblance of liberty, which explains why Harold Bloom could contend in 1973 that "poems arise out of the illusion of freedom" (*Anxiety* 96). So do novels: the "illusion of freedom" is after all the explicit theme of *The Ambassadors*, possibly James's most representative and perfect novel. Let me get this clear from the outset. James doesn't choose between two species, say, *Hamlet* and others. Or Dickens and others. He chooses rather between a species (*Hamlet* and Dickens) and the genus choice. In other words, James has always-already chosen *Hamlet*, and only afterwards he *hamlets* (encircles, immures, domesticates) choice. James has always-already chosen Dickens, and only afterwards he *dickens* (devils, deuces, compromises) choice. The contingent outcome of his free will (choice) is necessarily prepossessed by a *fatum* (the mnemic-psychic inscription of *Hamlet* and Dickens) that hopelessly antedates and foreordains deliberation, evaluation, and election.[13]

## III

So at the beginning is anxiety. In other words, *es spukt*: "it haunts, it ghosts, it specters, there is some phantom there, it has the feel of the living-dead—manor house, spiritualism, occult science, Gothic novel, obscurantism, atmosphere of anonymous threat or imminence" (Derrida, *Specters* 169). To Žižek's question "So where are we, today, with regard to ghosts?" (*Fragile* 9) we reply that we are in the manor house of Jamesian language, locking the garret's door from the outside. John Ashbery observed once that "the whole question of influence appears very vexed to the poet looking through the wrong end of his telescope, though not to critics, who use this instrument the way it was intended" (*Other* 4). This means that "one can't choose one's influences, they choose you" (4), an idea that is manifestly bound up with the problem, formulated by Derrida, of the effectivity of spectral presences (*Specters* 31). James was very aware of this. His expertise in novels (stories, romances, adventures, narratives) both molded his imagination and enriched him with surrogate experience. In his reading of D'Annunzio's novels, he observed that "his subject is what is given him—given him by influences, by a process, with which we have nothing to do" (*LC II* 918). As readers or critics, we may not have much to do with this *given*, with this subject (and the "influences" that bequeath it), but the implication is that D'Annunzio is totally powerless before such fatal donation. Writing about Maupassant, James points out that "he judges himself as he goes, and he can only go step by step over ground where every step is already a footprint" (*LC II* 533), and in an essay on Trollope he argues that if the author of *Barchester Towers* "derived half his inspiration from life, he derived the other half from Thackeray" (1344). James, in short, did not turn his back on the *factum brutum* of epigonality, of inheritance, footprints, derivation. Whenever he could, he attested to such necessity.

A ghost—be it King Hamlet, Shakespeare, Goethe, Lamb, or Thackeray—may well be a thing of nothing, but it has the potential of haunting, and structurally over-determining, a field of presence. Indeed, one of the writers who chose to influence Ashbery was (the ghost of) Henry James, a fact that remains insufficiently acknowledged by critics of the American poet. But he was also influenced by earlier Ashbery, the speculative persona who wondered about "Our looking through the wrong end/Of the telescope as you fall back at a speed/Faster than that of light to flatten ultimately/Among the features of the room" (*Self-Portrait* 82). In this book I will shift from the critical to the creative way of looking through the telescope, for it is always instructive to inquire why and how James decided, for example, to see Thackeray turned out of the house of his fiction, falling back at fast speed, flattening ultimately among the features of the room. Or why Shakespeare remained to walk arm in arm with James. Let us not lose sight of the regressive *mise en abime* of the critical action: we look through a telescope at an author looking, through a magnifying glass, at a girl's chasm, and seeing nothing. Maybe he hears something, but it is hard for a girl to talk with her mouth totally open and surrounded by gazing men.

The fiction by means of which the subject-author, in our case Henry James, tries to "recover authority" (Pocock, *Virtue* 54)—and thereby to increase his positive liberty in a field saturated with the necessity of alien authority—is therefore a fantasy this author must however traverse. *To traverse a fantasy* is the psychoanalytical way of naming what more traditional criticism would have called *to substantiate a dream*.[14] In a genealogical sense, the first relevant configuration of this fantasy—which I will call a *fantasy of deliberation*—in English literature can be found in the tragedy *Hamlet*, with the authority of a critical consciousness striving to assert itself in a field haunted by ciphers of authority and figures of power (God, the ghost and memory and name of his father, his "commandment," native "custom," Claudius, King Fortinbras, prince Fortinbras, the oppressor's wrong). Pippin has suggested that James's practical reason ignores "the conception of agent causality so important to Kant" and that

> being an agent for James much more involves the state of my self-understanding and insight, not a matter of casual power. (I am "freer" to the extent that I understand more and better; there is no insistence on could-have-done-otherwise causal autonomy).
>
> (*James* 50, n5)

Similarly, Hamlet is moved by a *libido sciendi*—akin to what Pippin very aptly calls, in allusion to *The Turn of the Screw*, "a kind of rage to understand" (*James* 89). This doesn't mean, however, that he succeeds as an autonomous agent, nor that he achieves understanding. The prince's initial manner of overcoming the Oedipal blockage of limited insight and therefore of *understanding more and better* is to exercise deliberation, to consider the pros and cons of suicide—"Oh that this too too solid flesh could melt" (*Hamlet* 1.2.129); "To be, or not to be; that is the question" (3.1.58)—with self-slaughter envisaged as an end to oppression (as an unburdening of, a disembedding and extrication from societal determinants) and as a gate to blissful rest (to sleep, to melt).[15] Like Strether, Hamlet is always "considering something else; something else, I mean, than the thing of the moment" (*Wings* 13).

The necessity of the existing *field* spells the social, legal, and political circumstances helping shape Hamlet's interiority. "*Hamlet* without Hamlet" is the name de Grazia has ingenuously given to this field, assuming that in the play there's more on display than the romantic swell of an *Ich*. In the case of James, the *experience* of traversing his internal fantasy—Hamlet's *fantasy of deliberation*—is what we call *narrative*. This gives him, we will see, the intellectual freedom to be pragmatically unfree, i.e. morally crippled, emotionally apathetic, socially uninvolved. Such pragmatic freedom is at bottom a romantic delusion: James argued in "The Art of Fiction" that "no one can ever have made a seriously artistic attempt without becoming conscious of an immense increase—a kind of revelation—of freedom" (*LC I* 59). Consciousness is there to block all awareness of indebtedness, since the *attempt* (from *temptare* derives the Spanish *atentado* or terrorist attack) seeks to compromise—both to compose and imperil—the already existing field that allows you to exist in the first place.

## IV

In this book I argue that the fantasy that Henry Hames ceaselessly traverses, and comments on, is *Hamlet*, from his early beginnings ("Eustace"), to the mid-period (*The Princess Casamassima*) all the way to the unfinished end (*The Ivory Tower*).[16] His narratives are not just fictions. They are also the experience of traversing—ranging across, contemplating, redirecting, evaluating, interrupting, subduing—other fictions, by him or by others. The modern novel, since Cervantes, is precisely that very thing, the experience of a critical commentary (narrative, *récit*) on an existing fantasy or fiction (plot, *histoire*). And on this score there is no difference between the apparently rival ways in which Richardson and Fielding set out to father the English variant of the genre. In both cases, a digressive, moralistic, and painfully intimate voice comments on the incidents unfolding at the level of a plot that is either that of amatory fiction (the seduction plot) or picaresque tale (the adventure plot).[17] This digressive voice—which is less overly omniscient, and therefore much more inspective, diagnostic, and detective, than Miller's Foucauldian account would have it—is still audible in James' novels.[18] On occasion it bears an uncanny resemblance with the affable ironic voice of Fielding's narrators:

> It was a place of which, unmistakeably, Chad was fond; wherefore if he, Strether, should like it too much, what on earth, with such a bond, would become of either of them? It all depended of course—which was a gleam of light—on how the "too much" was measured; though indeed our friend fairly felt, while he prolonged the meditation I describe, that for himself even already a certain measure had been reached. It will have been sufficiently seen that he was not a man to neglect any good chance for reflexion.
>
> (*Ambassadors* 63)

Whereas the first part of this passage is James's staccato modernist stammer, laden with minor fastidious specification, the second—from "though indeed" to the end—is pure Fielding (heterodiegetic) flow. Let me add that James's possibly parodic use of Fielding's detached but intrusive irony—*unmistakeably, of course, our friend, I describe, sufficiently seen*—lacks the edge to defuse the latter's power. And also that the number of fictional men who neglected no good chance for reflection became particularly large after the textual inscription of *Hamlet*. Ezra Pound, for one, pointed out in his closing remark on James' "Notes for *The Ivory Tower*" that "we note that this novel is a descriptive novel, not a novel that depicts people speaking and moving. There is *a constant dissertation going on*, and in it is our major enjoyment" (266; emphasis added). And in general the experience he tries to present his readers with is one of recurring mastery, one in which "the most radical liberty," the authorial creative freedom, is asserted. The New York Edition Prefaces are a lasting testament to the strength of a romantic-phenomenological delusion where radical beginnings, seeds, germs, and intentions are hatched and cultivated by personal intuition. But James's creative powers depended too on the arboreal tangles, rhizomatic profusions, and subtextual tensions that proliferate under the Oedipal patronage of interpersonal *tuition*—i.e. of instruction, custody, guardianship. This is what Shakespeare, Lamb, Goethe, and Thackeray are doing in a story titled *The Haunting of James House*, the contours of which is in part my intention to map: they are overseeing, supervising, guarding, and instructing Harry, orphaned auctor and foundling scribbler. Two of them, Shakespeare and Goethe, can do so because they are free from the anxiety of influence—James says in a letter that "William of Stratford (it seems to me) *had* no luggage"—or almost, for "haunting belongs to the structure of every hegemony" (Derrida, *Specters* 46).[19] Because this is, needless to say, a story of fathers and sons, absent fathers, specters and orphans (Hamlet, Tom Jones, Hyacinth, Milly, Miles, Flora). A story where the young read and see, while the less young overread, oversee, and very possibly overwrite. Discussing the boyhood appeal of *Treasure Island*, James wrote that

> what we see in it is not only the ideal fable but, as part and parcel of that, as it were, the young reader himself and his state of mind: we seem to read it over his shoulder, with an arm around his neck.
>
> (*LC I* 1251)

James, who was strongly influenced by the "ideal fable" in *Treasure Island*, never felt Stevenson's arm around his neck, his eyes reading over his shoulder. They were too pragmatically close for this eerie fantasy of suffocating intimacy to obtain. But he surely felt the custodial pressure of Shakespeare, Dickens, also Thackeray, and even their agon over his tuition: recall that Thackeray "was turned out for calling me a snob because I walked arm-in-arm with Shakespeare." The bearing that this contest of tutelage has on the structure of my book cannot be missed: I open with Shakespeare and wind up with Dickens, right after considering Thackeray. If the reader is intrigued by the fact that James doesn't mention Dickens in his Gothic reverie, let me recall that some lines before he describes the haunted house, he tells his friend that "the printer's devil was knocking at the door. You know a literary man can't call his time his own." In *The Princess Casamassima*, Hyacinth reads aloud to the dressmaker "the works of Dickens and of Scott" (153). And having someone read to you Dickens before you are able to understand is, in James's autobiographical tale, the arch-traumatic pre-possessive event, the inscriptive evacuation (nothing) that precedes—perhaps provokes—anxiety. So there you go: the hierarchy is temporarily restored. Dickens—the printer's devil is the printer's dickens—is always there, ousted from the outset, prescribing the commence and commerce of time, the grounds of narrative temporality, the possibility of subjectivation, and therefore the sheer impossibility of *personal* time, freedom, life, and the life-changing event. Like the Kafkaesque porter in *Macbeth*, Dickens is always already knocking at the door. The unconscious rationale of the slip is impeccable: the author of *Bleak House* waits at the door to reclaim what is his, at the very instant that James is anxiously trying to complete the crime, to mark the devil's writing as his own, and failing to meet the deadline that would crown him as sovereign author. Arm in arm with Shakespeare, who guides him back to the door, to come face to face before Dickens—farmer, equivocator, English tailor, devil-porter.

## V

Whether and how we may go on indefinitely calling James the Master is hard to determine, for he was decidedly not the master of his house, and it is there, in that displaced *casa paterna*, where he is the constant subject of a scene of instruction that is also a scene of tuition.[20] This is the truth that many of his narratives obliquely impart, while others, like the epistolary phantasmagoria and the twin story "The Birthplace," proffer in an exuberantly explicit manner. If "the meaning of a poem can only be a poem, but *another poem—a poem not itself*," so analogously, Bloom enjoins echoing Thomas Mann, "one cannot write a novel without remembering another novel" (*Anxiety* 55, 70). In this deconstructive sense, the meaning of James' narrative would be the *fantasy* (the fiction) his novel traverses, and this fiction is another novel supplied by the literary tradition. On this logic, there would be, of course, first-degree fantasies (stories of heroic duel, devotional pilgrimage, epic quest, palace intrigue, epic rescue, court seduction, blood feud, revenge, saintly sacrifice, pastoral rape), typically associated with the prehistory of the novel, and second- and third-degree fantasies which draw on the former but help constitute the soil of the novel proper. The first-degree fantasies are obviously ideological and serve to conceal, police, and redeem pre-modern forms of traumatic violence and non-socialized behavior. These areas of anomic convulsion, reprocessed as *sexual antagonism, gender trouble,* and *status inconsistency*, ended up becoming modal expressions of the traumatic kernel of the Real that the modern novel supposedly emerged to mediate. *Inconsistency* names the ontological rupture (a puncture) that breaks from within the symbolic order and that perpetuates itself along the fault lines that status inconsistency and sex-and-gender antagonism draw across its scripts.

John Carlos Rowe has very recently argued that "Henry James's enduring reputation has something to do with our inability to overcome the gender and sexual hierarchies, the class divisions, and the racial stereotypes of nineteenth-century America and England" ("Preface" to *Our Henry James* xiii). In my book, the racial stereotypes play no role, and the sexual-and-gender divisions and class hierarchies are seen as systemic and therefore inherently impassable splits: our inability, that is, remains James's inability, and his was surely not the visible symptom of an indolent absentee, but rather the strong novelist's persistent and voluntary failure to suture, his resistance to solve, absolve, resolve. The fact that he retro-posited, as the privileged agent of detached and uncompromised psychosocial observations, the Hamletian figure of the analytical witness is less an intentional cause than a structural effect of his realization that divisions and hierarchies irreparably rend the social field. Since the sparrow will at any rate fall (into the gaps of those divisions), and the readiness remain all, why not temporarily exit the social field, and its attendant gravitations, simply to observe how other sparrows are sucked into the very holes? *Temporarily* is a misnomer: James never quite managed to abandon the spectatorial position.

## VI

Shoshana Felman's claim that in *The Turn of the Screw* "the very act of textuality [is] triggered by the ambiguity of sexuality" (114) spells a critical theorem whose validity extends, I believe, to all Western fiction, yet one that must be supplemented with the converging formula that novelistic textuality is also simultaneously triggered by the ambiguity of social distinction. In both cases, however, the appeal to inconsistency (the sexual relation is impossible, gender difference uncertain, class and rank distinctions indeterminate) is always called into question by the irrevocable ineliminability of historical factuality: sexuality is not sex and yet *it (s)exists*; gender is constructed and yet a constructed *fact*; status is conventional, of course, but it *is right there*. James certainly held a firm and desultory belief in these three unavoidable facts—the vulgar literariness of rank, the anodyne givenness of gender division, the literal vulgarity of sex.[21] The feeling of physical (near-sexual) oppression that overcomes the reader in tales where the violation of status difference is at stake (*In the Cage, Brooksmith*) testifies to the way in which these three facts tended to converge in James's narrative unconscious. The virtual merging of sexual, gender, and social antagonisms into one single modus of inconsistency is borne out in Watt's sharp account of the impossible resolution that Richardson's *Pamela* very oddly proposes:

> In *Pamela* the courtship, if that is not too risible a euphemism for Mr. B.'s tactics, involves a *struggle*, not only between two individuals, but between two *opposed* conceptions of sex and marriage held by two *different* social classes, and between two conceptions of the masculine and

feminine roles which make their interplay in courtship even more *complex* and *problematic* than it had previously been.

(*Rise* 174; emphases added)

The second-degree fantasies are also ideological, and the scene they apparently repress is the anomic violence that, tantalizing, cyclical, intractable, is residual in the first-degree fantasies. Thackeray's refusal to depict Waterloo and James's parallel unwillingness to represent terrorist violence may betoken, for instance, an evasive response to the intractability of the historical Real[22]—such repressive concealment of the intractable the modern novel tends to rationalize as a deliberate secular operation, without fully realizing that it suppresses less supervened historical trauma than the dual (sexual and social) antagonism upon which the new secular society rests. We may speak of the systemic violence of sexual-cum-status inconsistency. The modern novel is thus blind to the ideological strategy that sets it going in the first place. The case of Fielding is instructive. By stressing the comic inadequacy of epic patterns to contemporary circumstances, he believed he delivered both the destitute present from the pathos of contingency (underdetermination) and the classical past from the burden of meaning (overdetermination).[23] This is of course a story that has been many times told, but it is not often evoked in connection with James, an artist who has been customarily placed either beyond ideological conflict or beyond the specific version of that conflict that prompted the so-called *rise of the novel* (Watt). My point is that this conflict inexorably articulates any novel produced within the controlled genealogical dissemination of the textual apparatus we call the novel. A cultural practice that introjects epic priority into a domestic tale of "being-with specters," the genre of the novel is sustained by "a politics of memory, of inheritance, and of generations" (Derrida, "Exordium" to *Spectres* XVIII), which is also, as Bloom rightly suggested, a "genealogy of imagination" (*Anxiety* 117). It is important to stress that what gets inherited, and therefore apt to be rejected, appropriated, or revised by the newcomer, is a tendentially unconscious—whether open or consolatory, indeterminate or conformist, novel or romance—*imaginative response to systemic inconsistency.*

The fantastic nature of the ideological operation yielding a generic moral-comic universalism based on order and repetition inhibited Fielding from seeing the genuine scope and reach of the contingency (the Real) of the society he lived in. The fascinating thing is that Fielding—and, later, Dickens, and, more sporadically, James, in "the habit and interest of walking" the London "streets" ("Preface" to *Princess* 33)—spent much of his adult professional life visually exploring this very inconsistent contingency. By surveying the different cross-sections of London society, including the criminal hives of Newgate, he became intimately acquainted with what Hegel derogatorily called *ineffective* or *inactual reality* ("Introduction" to *Ency-clopedia*, section 6). Eagleton's observation that Fielding's novels are "more about judgement and observation than about experience" (*Novel* 69) is only partly true. And yet, however visually exposed to such a dismal spectacle of unresolved human constraint, Fielding sought refuge in an ideological position of delegated vision (the position of the narrator-character) that was predicated on the illusion of freedom—freedom from a contingency and antagonism that knocked at his novels' doors in gentrified apparel. Like the doctors in Freud's dream, the fellow novelists examine the traumatic hole—the Real in the field, the gap in the symbolic order that sexual antagonism, gender trouble, and status inconsistency un-phenomenally formalize—and return to the room of collective consultation: each novel stages a fantasy of deliberation, the debate between the narrator and his precursors over some gash in the fabric of the symbolic order. Such fantasy of deliberation is obviously grounded on the philosophical need to keep "the radical gap" open (Žižek, *Bodies* xx). Second-degree fantasies became thus resourceful ideological devices for subsequent novelists to emulate, or simply rewrite. As a *construction*, the fantasy is not open to symptomal *inter-pretation*, but only to reconstruction, to compulsive retelling (Žižek, *Plague* 48–49). Otherwise put, novels don't provide truth, only *knowledge* (Badiou, "Formulas of 'L'Étourdit'" 49–55). For James, to write a novel is to experience the rewriting of a prior novel. In this book, I will argue that *The Princes Casamassima* rewrites the novel that is only virtual in *Hamlet*, *The Wings of the Dove* rewrites the narratives of sacrifice in Gibbon's *Decline and Fall*, *The Turn of the Screw* rewrites *Amelia*, which in turn is a revision of *Pamela*, *The Ivory Tower* rewrites *Our Mutual Friend* and *The Ambassa-dors* rewrites—and further un-finishes—*Denis Duval*. In the act of travelling over a prior fiction, his narrative draws on the latter's resources to obtain an illusion of freedom by joining, with the prior author, on the attestation of nothing. The Slovenian philosopher Slavoj Žižek has argued that "the function of fantasy is to fill the opening in the Other, to conceal its inconsistency—as for instance the fascinating presence of some sexual scenario serving as a screen to mask the impossibility of the sexual relationship" (*Sublime* 138). Fantasy would conceal the fact that the symbolic order (the Other) "is structured around some traumatic impossibility" that defies symbolization. We may call that, following Lacan, "the real of jouissance." Through fantasy, Žižek argues, "jouissance is domesticated, 'gentrified'" (139). Jouissance, in James's tales, emerges as an instance of sexual-cum-social inadequacy that is symptomally qualified as *awkward*. Unsurprisingly, perhaps, *Shawkwespeare* and *Thawckweray* constitute, for James, two major symptoms. Thus, after we "traverse" the fantasy, desire peters out into the death drive: "beyond fantasy" there is no yearning or any kindred sublime phenomenon, "beyond fantasy" we find only drive, its pulsation around the *sinthome*. " 'Going-through-the-fantasy' is therefore strictly correlative to identification with a *sinthome*" (*Sublime* 138–139). Fantasy, in short,

> is basically a scenario filling out the empty space of a fundamental impossibility, a screen masking a void. "There is no sexual relationship", and this impossibility is filled out by the fascinating fantasy-scenario—that is why fantasy is, in the last resort, always a fantasy of the sexual relationship, a staging of it. As such, fantasy is not to be interpreted, only "traversed": all we have to do is experience how there is nothing "behind" it, and how fantasy masks precisely this "nothing". (But there is a lot behind a symptom, a whole network of symbolic overdetermination, which is why the symptom involves its interpretation).
>
> (141)

So *es spukt*. There is *sinthome* because there is anxiety, and there is, to crown it all, our yearning for interpretation—a pull of epistemic desire placed before the blankness of a depthless "nothing." But this is our experience of the dead end or deadlock. For James this ordeal takes rather the (re)form of the compulsive death-drive quickening the writing of a new novel. *Dead end, deadline, deadlock, death-drive*, too many deaths for so unheroic a life. To be sure, James was not only a compulsive writer of what reads, in each case, approximately, as one and the same novel, but also a compulsive reader, and in this capacity, he reveled, especially in his younger years, in exposing the theatrical shallowness of the screen other novelists drew in order to mask their void. This he did, more crudely than cruelly, in his infamous review of Dickens' *Our Mutual Friend*, which I will examine in my final chapter. Neither then, when he penned the review, nor later, when he sought to rewrite Dickens' extraordinary novel, was James particularly willing to confront the fact that all novels stage a bidimensional fantasy intended to conceal a void, the void (in the division) of the impossible sexual-cum-social relationship. In other words, if, as James contends, *Our Mutual Friend* is superficial, then the narrative elaboration of this contention titled *The Ivory Tower* is also without depth. What goes for one goes for the other. But *Our Mutual Friend* is not only a tale that proclaims the unlikelihood of the sexual relationship by constructing it as a sentimental fantasy—the *fantastico modo* whose banal telos is the marriages of Bella and Lizzie. It is also a tale of unlikely social rapports prompted by an inconsistent ground (*Grund, Boden*), by accidents—falls, drownings—taking place along, above, and under the river. And we can use, Žižek insists, "this notion of fantasy in the domain of ideology proper: here also 'there is no class relationship', society is always traversed by an antagonistic split which cannot be integrated into symbolic order" (*Sublime* 141). Although it is quite true that late Dickens was prone to make the same melodramatic mistakes he made in some of his early narratives, it is also indisputable that the awkward rashness that goes into the fabrication of his shoddy novelistic resolutions can be read as a measure (a sign, a *sinthome*) of his imperfect—but real, ineliminably real—recognition that the impossible lurks inside the real, or is the Real. The impossible, that is, the sexually and social impossible that works as cue and motive of the sham sexual relation (the married couple) and of the fake social relation (the organic society). The fact that James could give up neither *donnée*—the heterosexual pair and the hierarchical society—proves that he was not writing, never writing, in *The Ivory Tower* or elsewhere, beyond, under, or behind the screens set up by Dickens. He was rather refracting those very mirrors.

## VI

Let us consider more closely the second Lacanian formula, "There is no class relationship," which can be radically translated as "Society doesn't exist." Society here names the organic or saturated conception of the community as *Gemeinschaft* (as opposed to *Gesellschaft*) that is at the core of conservative (neo-medieval, Tory) ideology.[24] Jean-Luc Nancy would talk of a worked (*ouvrée*) community. Žižek has lucidly delineated the dialectical logic that makes the organic social whole depend upon an abject supplement:

> In the domain of ideology proper [. . .] "there is no class relationship", society is always traversed by an antagonistic split which cannot be integrated into symbolic order. And the stake of social-ideological fantasy is to construct a vision of society which does exist, a society which is not split by an antagonistic division, a society in which the relation between its parts is organic, complementary. [. . .] We may say that "Society as a corporate Body" is the fundamental ideological fantasy. How then do we take account of the distance between this corporatist vision and the factual society split by antagonistic struggles? The answer is, of course, the Jew: an external element, a foreign body introducing corruption into the sound social fabric. In short, "Jew" is a fetish which simultaneously denies and embodies the structural impossibility of "Society": it is as if in the figure of the Jew this impossibility had acquired a positive, palpable existence [. . .] fantasy is precisely the way the antagonistic fissure is masked.
>
> (*Sublime* 141–142)

Žižek goes on to say that going through the social fantasy is correlative to the identification with a symptom. The Jew—actually, the "conceptual Jew"—is a social symptom, "the point at which the immanent social antagonism assumes a positive form, erupts on to the social surface, the point at which it becomes obvious that society 'doesn't work', that the social mechanism 'creaks' " (143). I have quoted this speculative elaboration in full because what Žižek has to say about this "conceptual Jew" is readily transferable to James' repeated narrative construal of what we could call the "conceptual heiress." For the innocent girl—the rich, saintly, virtuous, American heiress—is also a social symptom, possibly not different from the Jew. Both are two faces of the same coin: money. The sacrificial victim, rejected girl, reclusive sister, martyr, and potential saint are all fetishes that simultaneously deny and embody the structural impossibility of society. They embody it because their infinite surplus of ethical and financial value cannot be accommodated within the bourgeois *mediocritas* around which the new commercial society revolves. They deny it by prompting novel, if exorbitant, spiritual communitarian configurations around their memory. The James of the New York Edition "Prefaces" claims very often to adopt—with respect to his heroines and heroes—the Horatio-position of the witness who commemorates them by *telling their story*.

In *The Ambassadors*, Maria Gostrey sees herself as a symbolic embodiment of her country:

> I bear on my back the huge load of our national consciousness, or, in other words—for it comes to that—of our nation itself. Of what is our nation composed but of the men and women individually on my shoulders? I don't do it, you know, for any particular advantage. I don't do it, for instance—some people do, you know—for money.
>
> (12)

Like the religious counterpart of her implicit analogy (Christ), the sacrificial role of her fusional trope—an ideologeme of in-separation—is executed disinterestedly, without personal gain. By contrast, the conceptual Jew and the conceptual heiress perform their task of communal representativeness not solely *for* some particular advancement but rather *from* a specific vantage point. Not only, perhaps, *for* money, but signally, *from* money. "To 'identify with a symptom' means to recognize in the 'excesses', in the disruptions of the 'normal' way of things, the key offering us access to its true functioning" (*Sublime* 144). It may not be totally inaccurate to conjecture that James identifies with Milly and Rosanna—not to mention Isabel Archer. Maybe these rich heiresses, and some immaculate heirs (Gray and perhaps too the master in *The Turn of the Screw*), stand for the complementary reversal of the Jew, and as such, they remain symptoms of antagonism erupting through the surface.[25] They are the photographic negative of the archetypal conceptual Jew: figures of accumulation, emblems of superfluity, tropes of excess. While the stereotypical Jew stands for *usury*—the exorbitant rate of interest—the rich heiress stands directly for incalculable *interest*.[26]

A conservative liberal with what appears to have been a limited sexual desire, James is invariably doomed to examine the truthfulness of the two statements of impossibility chosen by Slavoj Žižek to prove his Lacanian conception of ideology in terms of the symbolic order, the imaginary, floating, and residual signifiers and the traversing of the fantasy. These two statements are: "Society doesn't exist" (140–142) and "There is no sexual relationship" (xviii, 78, 141). The function of fantasy, for James, is to conceal that, though society exists, it inconsists (is not), and that there are sexual relationships that also antagonistically inconsist (are not)—to screen the fact, that is, that both inconsistencies subtend the horizon of what James, with characteristic indefinition, calls human *life*. If traversing a fantasy is, as I am going to argue, a mode of ideological resolution germane to narrative interpretation, then the settlement that is reached (the death drive repeating itself compulsively before the evidence of nothing) can hardly be regarded as consolatory in any positive sense. Anxiety, that is, remains. The angst of irresolution, in James as in other writers, takes the form of compulsive repetition, visible not solely in the revisiting of the original fantasy, but also in the rewriting of the first traversal: think of how *The Princess Casamassima* paraphrases *Hamlet*; on how *The Wings of the Dove* is James's final correction of *Daisy Miller*, but also on how it rewrites the primal (repeated) scopophilic narrative of martyrdom and sacrifice lodged in Edward Gibbon's *Decline and Fall of the Roman Empire*; on how *The Turn of the Screw* revisits *Pamela* through *Amelia* (it should have been titled *Pamelia*, or *Lamella*, to honor Lacan); on how *The Ivory Tower* deficiently plays over Dickens' *Our Mutual Friend*; on how *The Ambassadors* amplifies *The American* and diffusely (in)completes Thackeray's *Denis Duval*. The defense against repetition leads strong writers to an "adventure of discontinuity" (Bloom, *Anxiety* 87) and this adventure is of course a crossing or passage—the traversal of a fantasy—which in turn involves the reinstatement of repetition, for "something truly knew can only emerge *through* repetition" (Žižek, *Organs* 11; emphasis added).

To sum up, James' phantasmagoria, his epistolary fantasy-scenario, accommodates some of the names of the authors whose novels, fictions, and fantasy-scenarios James would carefully traverse in the course of his long career as an author. Two names stand out in particular, Shakespeare and Dickens, placed at the two extremes of the chronological span covered in this book, ranging from *Hamlet* (1601) to *Our Mutual Friend* (1865), and including *Pamela* (1740), *Joseph Andrews* (1742), *Amelia* (1751), *The Decline and Fall of the Roman Empire* (1776–1789), and *Denis Duval* (1863). If we look at the chronology closely, we notice that my attention will be drawn to the node spanning 1748–1751, the *anni mirabiles* of English fiction, when three massive responses to *Pamela* got published—*Clarissa* (1748), *Tom Jones* (1749), and *Amelia* (1751). I guess a different book could be written focusing on the other miraculous span that arose exactly a century later—the tight arc of three years that witnessed the publication of *Dombey and Son* (1846–1848), *Wuthering Heights* (1847), *Jane Eyre* (1847), *Mary Barton* (1848), and *Vanity Fair* (1847–1848). James is of course also somehow reacting to the aftershocks of this second imaginative concentration (his silence over the Brontës is telling), but my less predictable choice is grounded on the persuasion that, although "*Hamlet* and Dickens" is the formula that sets the necessary limits to James's narrative imagination, the matheme *Hamela* (*Hamlet* + *Pamela*) also retains a fatal inscriptive force, furnishing his imagination with a cracked girl, a local habitation, and a curious male. The inscription had lasting effects in the tradition, as Faulkner's *Sanctuary* (1931) rather ghastly demonstrates. The narratives I have selected are broadly taken to constitute a set of variations on the original master narrative, *Hamlet*, a fantasy of consciousness beyond society, placed above and against the fray of social classes, gender castes, and sexual cases. *Hamlet* is a play that informs at various levels the two most important novels written in England in the eighteenth century: *Tom Jones* and *Clarissa*. *Tom Jones*, where we find the first fictional-narrative meditation on *Hamlet* before Goethe (Book 16, chapter 5), intermingles the trauma of bastardy and the problem of an expanded consciousness in a way that will prove particularly productive to James in *The Princess Casamassima*. And *Clarissa* is the first sustained narrative dramatization of the Jamesian motif of tragic female sacrifice in English literature. The impact of *Hamlet* on Richardson's work is more noticeable in *Clarissa*—described by the author as a "tragedy": while the titular heroine actualizes and depletes most of Ophelia's characterological possibilities, the male hero, Lovelace, comes off as a new Hamlet, "an intellectual—*philosophe* and libertine" (Fiedler, *Love* 72). There is an interesting sense, moreover, in which *Love and Death in the American Novel* (1960) could be read as suggesting that *Clarissa* is the first American novel (*Love* 62–72, 217–290). Much would be gained in Jamesian studies, I believe, if this conjecture were imaginatively pursued. But before love deteriorated into death, there was *Pamela*. Note that, in my interpretation, the apperceptive consciousness that *sees* Mr. B invading Pamela's room, closet, and body, is Fielding's narrative voice. In a sense, Fielding's masterly decision was to ask Hamlet to serve as witness and commentator of the trials of the "virtuous" maid. The *Hamela* master-narrative is here presupposed—it is the precondition of the creative game—and James stakes his freedom on the romantic-idealist make-believe that he himself posits his own presuppositions: that he chooses them rather than being chosen by them. This make-believe is his fiction, some salient instances of which will become the objects of my close reading.

## VII

Let us consider in some detail the essential features of this master-narrative. Its protagonist is a sex-and-property-disinterested—and therefore free and potentially Bohemian—male. He is indifferent to sexual intercourse because he is immature, scared of intimate emotional entanglement, or a closet homosexual—maybe all three things at once. This indifference may also be the outcome of a continued habit of exploitative sexual practice, in the way the libertine is indifferent to the sexual. This doesn't mean that he is immune to the rare truth of love. He is disinterested in wealth and property either because he nurses egalitarian yearnings or because he is so rich that he can spare both the conceptual Jew (usury) and the conceptual heiress (interest) in ways that, respectively, Antonio and Bassanio for instance could not. James's mystified grasp of the latter position is best instanced in his laudatory portrait of Turgenev, the champion of "noble disinterestedness" (*LC II* 1034). The disinterest of the standard James male is radical and absolute, meaning that he is interested in either *nothing* or *everything*, which amounts to the same (no)thing.[27] If you are *one of those on whom nothing is lost* it is very likely that you lose exactly *everything*: this Hyacinth, Densher, Strether, and very probably Gray Fielder know well. In principle, the James male cannot be interested in *one* person or *one* thing, for such circumstance spells the fatal contingency of a plot. Think of Mr. B in *Pamela*, who, of all women, takes a fancy to the *one* "foolish Hussy" (*Pamela* 23). Plots—the conventional plots of romance and romantic stories, amatory fictions, adventure tales making up the prehistory of the novel—often take the form of quest narratives that revolve around the search of the Holy Grail (heroic narratives), personal salvation (lives of saints), social status (picaresque tales), or the body of the maiden (seduction plots). To enter a plot is to force a resting place somewhere along the disseminative drift of signifiers—to pretend to fulfill, with transcending meaning (content, signified), what is formally and transcendentally empty. But empty—this is important—doesn't mean disfigured or unformatted. To fall into a plot implies, for the disinterested male, to tumble in a realm of pragmatic decisions and moral deliberations over the various courses of action that turn up on his more or less reluctant way toward the one object. To enter a plot is to begin to plot, and therefore to barter your freedom for unfreedom, your old liberty for a new deliberation. In *The Elements of Law, Natural and Politic*, Thomas Hobbes described *deliberation* as the "alternate succession of appetite and fear during all the time" a certain object-motivated "action is in our power to do." *Deliberation*, on this etymo-logic, is "the taking away of our own liberty" (*Human Nature* 71). To act is to free yourself from your deliberation. To be sure, the characters drawn into a quest-plot are markedly unfree in that they pursue an

*interest*—they are (*esse*) strategically placed in between (*inter*) an assort-
ment of actors and objects—but they are also radically free insofar as they
are given the chance to act, to put, that is, an end to their deliberation and
perform explicit actions of personal will. As Hobbes says in *De Cive*, anticipating an idea he will develop in *Leviathan* (I.VI), "the will is the final act
of deliberation" (*On the Citizen* 38). Thus, the fantasy of deliberation that
the disinterested narrator enacts is bracketed or suspended between two
points of maximal freedom—the freedom to be completely disinterested,
even from plots, and the freedom to be actively drawn into the pragmatic
intensities of the plot, the most important of which is volitional decision:
think of Fielding (or Hamlet) staring at Mr. B. who in turn spies, "through
the Key-hole" the figure of Pamela lying "all along upon the floor, stretch'd
out at my Length" (*Pamela* 32).[28] The fact that the will of James' heroes
and heroines is very often hemmed in by an external written Will (a letter, a testament) is not a negligible paradox in this regard. The narrator
or mouthpiece character holds a middle position of deliberative disbelief,
"which is flattered as superior discernment," encouraging the reader "to
anticipate problems, make suppositional predictions, and see possible outcomes and alternative interpretations" (Gallagher 346). This doesn't mean
that the narrator-character disbelieves the fantasy he traverses. His relevant
fiction is truth itself, and he calls it "history."

But just as there is a pragmatic way to put an end to deliberation—Milly's
death, for instance, or Hyacinth's suicide—there is also a speculative way
to put an end to what Sartre interpreted as our condemnation to be free.[29]
In this case, the paradigm is again Hamlet, whose avoidance of heroic,
political, and sexual action should be read as an out-and-out—yet more
dialectical than phenomenological—*abstention from the plot*.[30] By abstain-
ing from pragmatic externals—"I know not 'seems'" (*Hamlet* 1.2.76)—
Hamlet pledges himself to a deliberative interiority recursively condemned
to expressive failure. As Isabel Archer sublimely remonstrates, "I don't
know whether I succeed in expressing myself but I know that nothing else
expresses me" (*Portrait* 253). Hamlet becomes the *historian*—in the old
sense of contemporary witness—of his defective, defected, and deflected
self, the critical chronicler of the inactions of himself as unlikely hero. In his
deliberation, he pretends decision hinges upon free will, as if his choices—
to be or not to be, to reject Ophelia or not, to take revenge or not—were
not exclusively formal, thetic options in a rigged game. He indulges his
fantasy of freedom to temporarily transform a necessary outcome—his
agony, the rejection of Ophelia, killing his uncle, and dying—into a matter
of free choice, only to return, once the fantasy is traversed, to the death-
drive of an implacable necessity (*Plague* 40): "O, I die, Horatio!" (*Hamlet*
5.2.294). The Hamlet narrative of traversed fantasy offers however some
deviations from the standard pattern: in his case, "the explicit symbolic

gesture which guarantees the choice" is precisely the phantasm (the father as Law), while the "phantasmic kernel of his being," his obscene excess, is the "noble mind" that others, and the Other, desire. This becomes very clear in *The Princess Casamassima*, where Christina desires an intellectual-moral excess (Hyacinth's noble spirit, his enlightened merit, his virtue), which is placed out of the range of the archaic aristocratic "cycle of generation and corruption" (Žižek, *Plague* 42). Likewise, Hamlet's "noble mind" (*Hamlet* 3.1.149) became the object of desire for generations of Puritan educators, proto-feminist activists, and Victorian intellectuals, who sought to stabilize a female subjectivity around some of the coordinates (ultra-sensible interiority, spiritual merit) laid out by such mind. This constructed subjectivity was later used to determine, in turn, the feminization of the homosocial male continuum. The upshot of this loop is that what we call the feminization of the homosocial bourgeoise intellectual is at bottom a residual vicissitude of *Hamletization*.

Hamlet is the philosophical historian—the critical-moral commentator—of the revenge tragedy and seduction drama to which he has been condemned and in which he fails to perform satisfactorily. In this capacity he prefigures many an aloof, discriminating spectator in the standard James narrative, who very often coincides with the narrator but in some cases is also a central character. This abstinent, garrulous, detached, and super-critical Hamlet persona is also the narrator in novels by Fielding, Gibbon, Dickens, and Thackeray. More often than not, the narrator has a foot in both camps, the outside realm of critical observation and judgement (deliberation), and the inside realm of the pragmatic plot (action), and this bifocal position is secured through delegation—through the presence of a character that stands for the narrator inside the plot. At any rate, the defining feature of the Hamlet persona is passive exteriority. I take this passive exteriority to be however inflected by the active powers of criticism, and to embody the subversive force of a *conservative ideology* that reacts both against the aristocratic ideology and against the progressive ideology that (wrongly) claimed to have superseded the latter. Hamlet the sensitive and critical observer (Hamlet 3) *sublates* both the royal prince (Hamlet 1) and the radical democrat (Hamlet 2) who supposedly rose to debunk the prince. It is through the speculative freedom of Hamlet 3 that the novel proper gets started. When, in her account of the rise of the modern novel, Armstrong argues that "against genealogy the [didactic, female-oriented] treatises posited domesticity" (18) she overlooks the fact that the (aristocratic) functions of "generation and genealogy" (11) could also be waived in favor of the converse function of detached para-domestic voyeurism, the *Wakefield* function at work in *Our Mutual Friend* and whose first distinguished operator is the effeminate defector called Hamlet.[31] Did the treatises contemplate too the possibility of a (reactive) abstention from domesticity?

## VIII

Let us reconsider the merging of the two male parts, those of worldly, cynical observer and the libertine, voluptuary rake. The former character, a literary precursor of Husserl's uninterested and nonparticipant witness— the *uninteresierter Zuschauer* or *unbeteligter Zuschauer* (*Cartesianische* 73)—is often sexually inactive, perhaps a repressed homosexual. The latter is erotically charged and ready to discharge. Neither manages to fine-tune his libidinal energy to the poise of middle-class marriage. They are confronted with a standard courtship plot, quite often invited to engage, but they always refuse. Their disinclination takes two forms: a circumspect banishment from the scene of courtship, in order to become a witness, or a violent irruption, causing both the dissolution of the scene and the sacrifice of the heroine. The singularity of Hamlet is that he realizes both operations, becoming simultaneously the reckless abuser and cynical witness. The net result of these operations is the ejection of the girl from the social scene of courtship. My impression is that this result is also the purpose of the operations carried out by a male who saw himself, from the outset, as alien to the scene. The hero's exteriority has various causes: sexual disinterest, excessive sexual interest, a sense of social superiority. The scene is bourgeois, and the hero is either literally an aristocrat (a member of the *noblesse d'épée*) or metaphorically a member of the intellectual aristocracy, the *noblesse de robe* (moral observer, judicious narrator, philosophical historian). Hamlet was the former, Fielding's male narrator—an intellectual function of his pragmatic heroes, Joseph Andrews, Tom Jones, and William Booth—the latter.

In the dynamic economy of the novelistic plot, if a character exits the playground, another character must leave it in order to secure dramatic balance. Thus if the male hero defects, the female heroine must also necessarily go. In other words, Hamlet wants to exit the game board. He wants to become an external observer of the lives of characters involved in the game, the free critical analyst, interested in entanglement (plot, knot) of the sexual (erotic) and financial (patrimonial) situation created by others. He wishes to waive the dramatic or lyrical enunciation and adopt a third-person voice where his critical pneuma can more amply resonate. His is the external voice of the epic storyteller, which will reappear with the eighteenth-century narrator: ironic, detached, curious to the point of sadistic cruelty (think of Laclos or Lewis). For this position to be granted, however, a young woman must also withdraw from the board. It is a simple law of dynamic compensation: if I renounce my role (Hamlet) then you (Ophelia) must renounce yours. If I fail to become a stage avenger, then you must forgo your hope of becoming a stately bride—you must *get thee to a nunnery*. If I become an observer, then the first thing I wish to observe is your *Entsagung* (renunciation) of social duties, your withdrawal from the community, your sacrifice. In other words, for the James-position to exist, a young woman must be sacrificed—she must either die into social shame or physically into the grave. Her sacrificial banishment is often decreed from the outset: she is either very sick (Rose Muniment), post-alive (Daisy), or pre-dead (Milly). It is important to stress that her expulsion is both a function of the male's prior decision to forego the heroic-erotic play-field and very often the tragic outcome of seduction. Since 1520 at least, to *seduce* is to persuade a vassal to desert his allegiance or service (from Latin *seducere* "lead away, lead aside or astray," from *se-* "aside, away" + *ducere* "to lead"). To lead Ophelia aside to a secluded place, and rape her outside of the nomic sphere, is exactly what Hamlet does in the sources (Saxo Grammaticus, Belleforest). The logic is not only "If I decamp, you quit" ("To a nunnery, go," *Hamlet* 3.1.148) but also "Because I force you to desert, I seduce you into decamping and you procure no apparent jouissance, I quit too" ("What should such fellows as I do crawling between earth and heaven?" *Hamlet* 3.1.3.1.127). Perfect casuistry for castration-anxious scions and sexual cowards.

Still, what looks like a structural reaction may well be informed by an unconscious drive to prevent the girl from remaining in the plot to tell her version of the story.[32] Maybe James had, like Strether, "the sense that she knew things he didn't" (*Ambassadors* 7), apart from the suspicion that examining her cavities would not reveal a core of knowledge. Despite his somewhat condescending admiration for Sand, and his conflictual appreciation of Eliot, James was never at ease with the prospect of the girl—let alone a low-class girl like Pamela—telling the story. On that score, he sided with Fielding to maintain, by all conceivable means, the impassable divisions of the *Stiltrennung*.[33] His paternalistic scoffs at Jane Austen are symptomatic—even if her narrative voice tended to adopt the neoclassical male bass inherited from Fielding. And so is the scorn he indirectly lavishes at the governess. In many senses, and this Miles was too young to foresee, freedom for James depended on not "being in woman's 'hands' " (*Ambassadors* 111).[34]

Tony Tanner gave a sharp account of the moment in *Daisy Miller* in which the effete, unamusing, and distanced Winterbourne—the infantile malcontent who, like Hamlet, neither drinks nor dances—takes the definite step of relinquishing the American girl:

She is with Giovanelli, and Winterbourne, out walking, sees them together. From that point on he thinks "the riddle had become easy to read. She was a young lady whom a gentleman need no longer be at pains to respect." Effectively *he drops her*, and there is a hint that, in response, she simply abandons herself to the Roman fever which she subsequently contracts after her evening stroll through the polluted space of the old center of European civilization, and quickly dies.

(*James* 31–32)

*He drops her*: this is an ingenious way of naming a complex move that, in my interpretation, is exclusively structural, and only tendentially ideological: the unaffiliated male (narrator) derives rank (intellectual honor, moral virtue) *through* the female conduit (the sacrificial exclusion of the girl), but *from* the male reservoir (the author's ideology).[35] This renunciation—the sacrificial exclusion of the girl—is of course a fantasy, not only because no real choice is involved—the choice is a formal and empty gesture: he *must* drop her—but also because the refusal of *jouissance*, and the simultaneous emergence of the symbolic Law, is the very primordial loss that fantasies implicitly narrate (Žižek, *Plague* 42–43). Also structurally necessary is, of course, in Eliot's *Daniel Deronda*, the relinquishment of the Jew.[36] Although the dropping of the girl could be historicized in social-political terms, or motivationally and volitionally justified along broadly mythical, anthropological, or psychosexual lines, the structural elucidation is the one that best preserves the radically *disjunctive* nature of the experience of love. Lacan's infamous axiom that there is no sexual relationship comes down to the fact, duly reported by a Bellow narrator, that "men and women are determined to get out of one another (or tear out) what is simply not there to be gotten by any means" (*More* 161). Because, let me clarify, the peeping Tom *loves* the girl. He loves her in a mirror, darkly, but loves her. And this love can be philosophically construed as the nominal commitment to the event of an encounter between mutually incommensurable beings:

> *There are two positions of the experience of love.* "Experience" is construed in its broadest sense as the presentation as such of the situation. And there are two presentative positions. We can agree that these two positions are sexuated, and to call one woman, and the other man. The approach thus far is strictly nominalist: no empirical, biological or social distribution is acceptable here.
>
> (Badiou, *Conditions* 183)

We may question the convenience, for the James case, of eschewing a "social distribution" that at the turn of the century was ready to accommodate the homosexual experience, but Badiou's striking formulation has the advantage of unburdening the love "situation" of the " 'superstructural' or 'illusory' conceptions"—regularly obtained from pre-novelistic sources—that quite often obscure it. Chief among these conceptions is the conventional "magic of sexual desire" (Armstrong, *Desire* 24), already unfashionable for the "new sexual ideology" that redefined, during the English eighteenth century, the "relations between men and women" (Watt 180). According to Watt, "the conception of sex we find in Richardson embodies a more complete and comprehensive *separation* between the male and female roles than had previously existed" (183; my emphasis), and this historical-cultural separation *expresses*—in a Spinozian sense—the persistence of a deep structural division. The fact that, as Badiou avers, *the two positions are totally disjunct*, helps explain both the erotic situation of man-woman separation and, more decisively, their enforced symmetrical exteriority from what used to be their evental stage. *Separation,* one of the key concerns in Jamesian fiction, is a philosophical trope—a *philosopheme*—handed down by the narrative tradition. Sedgwick once stipulated the "self-evident fact" that "people are different from each other" (*Epistemology* 22), and no semblance of erotic fusion or social incorporation can eliminate this "residuum of difference" (*Ambassadors* 6).[37] Her liberal axiom unwittingly underpins the "fundamental entitlement to a free life of an individual" (Pippin, *James* 54), and foreshadows his strong conception of Isabel Archer's exigence: "she must be free, and freedom means first of all independence, not being attached or committed anywhere, not being identified with a role or function, not, indeed, 'being' anything" (132–133). For such differential residuum forever lingers, activated by a principle of survival we may compare to a Hobbesian-Spinozist *conatus.* Humans are different and separate: this persuasion both enlivens and shadows Strether's inaugural hours of consciousness in England. Central to the novel's opening paragraph is the notation of Strether's "separation" from his comrade Waymarsh and of things perspectivized "on Strether's part" (*Ambassadors* 1). We later see his fellow countrywoman Maria Gostrey described as "the other party" of an unexpected "appointment" (5), and even her later allusion to Chad's mother as "a great *parti*" (50). Strether's most elemental *part* is the *part* of his separation from other *parties,* a position of critical (Hamletian) detachment he gloats in at first. But he will end up burdened, the narrator points out, with "the oddity of a double consciousness": there was, we are told, "detachment in his zeal and curiosity in his indifference" (2). Strether, we gradually learn, is a separate part drawn to orbit around more momentous parties. He will presently construe this orbitation as the breakdown of separation, or, more specifically, as a loss of limits: "He had believed he had a limit, but the limit had been transcended within thirty-six hours" (8). And so, after this loss, this blurring, this transgression, Strether becomes in-separate with the others, and therein *incipit* plot—the novel is on track. *Separation, part, party, parti*—the etymology is stubborn. The second ambassador (Chad is the first) cherishes the prospect of spending his first hours at Chester without being "met" (the inverted commas are James's), "independently, unsociably, alone" (*Ambassadors* 2). Like Hamlet in England, or in the islands of his mind. While onstage and inside the plot, they may have been moved by narcissistic drives of subject-object desire that betray a yearning of the One (erotic fusion, the sexual relation), but the event of love occurs beyond this scenario of union:

> Furthermore, it is only in love that bodies have the purpose of marking the Two. The body of desire is the corpus delicti, the delicti of the self. It secures the One in the guise of the object. Only love marks the Two by a sort of letting-go (*dé-prise*) of the object, a letting-go that proceeds only because there was a hold exercised over it in the first place.
>
> (Badiou, *Conditions* 191)[38]

We have just evoked the moment when Winterbourne lets Daisy go. We could also recall the occasion in which Densher realizes he must let Milly, who is already gone, definitely go for him—the moment when he gives her (as object, as money) up, and himself and Kate away. Or the case of Strether, at the novel's close, turning down Maria Gostrey's extraordinary offer, giving her up, letting her go, asserting his escapist drive: "I must go." Through this relinquishment, desire—sexual, material, monetary desire— is transmuted into love. When Hamlet "sends" Ophelia to a nunnery, to a brook, and eventually to the grave, he is unconsciously consigning her to the adjourned rendezvous of co-positional and therefore incommensurable love. (Hamlet, incidentally, would have been shocked to see the popularity that his solution—to a nunnery, go—would enjoy among seventeenth- and eighteenth-century intellectuals and writers).[39] It comes as no surprise that he should nominally admit to loving her—"I loved Ophelia" (*Hamlet* 5.1.254)—only when he sees her in the grave. To be sure, James would never go that far—such extreme of Gothic morbidity was the province of unpolished Yankees, like Poe, or border Britons, like Emily Brontë—but his early creative persona certainly flirted with the pattern, as "The Romance of Old Clothes" demonstrates.

## IX

The story, for James, must be told by the defecting Hamlet male, the "innocent voyeur," an intellectualized and "impotent Peeping Tom" equipped with the life experience of a child. Leslie Fiedler buttressed his remarks on *What Maisie Knew* with a heuristic schema that retains extraordinary interpretive force. Since it has, moreover, the axiomatic condensation of a wisdom riddle, I have decided to break it into lines and transcribe it poetically. It reads like a Lewis Carroll parody of *Songs of Experience*:

> In the Jamesian version of the Fall of Man,
> at any rate, there are four actors, not three:

the man, the woman, the serpent, and the child,
presumably watching from behind the tree.

(344)

In my reconstruction of this tendentially pre-ontological (hauntological) *primal scene*, the woman is forced to quit the prelapsarian stage because the boy has gone behind the tree. At a deeper level, we will see, the boy hides because the girl is *always already* gone. At any rate, what is left is the man (the second man, a most common figure in James's fiction) fighting with the serpent, which is either the Dark Lady, the witch, the white maiden gilded by fortune, or simply the allegorical embodiment of a commercial, philistine, mercenary, capitalistic, unresponsive Society—the symbolic Big Other that James calls Britannia in *The Wings of the Dove*.

In the *Hamlet* original, the boy Hamlet goes behind the arras, Ophelia underwater, and the surviving men (Horatio, Fortinbras) are not given the chance to grapple with the nominal serpent (Claudius) or the figural serpent (Gertrude), who are also dead. Two snakes have been extirpated, but the garden of evil, the "unweeded garden/That grows to seed" (*Hamlet* 1.2.135–136), remains. New things rank and gross in nature—and new melancholy boys and flower girls—will emerge to reinitiate the plot. If the flower girl expires, it is due either to her radical innocence or to a hidden guilt that infrastructurally connects her to the serpent. Or to both, like Daisy and Milly, virginal yet diffusely blighted by plutocracy and capital. Fiedler's riddle has the additional advantage of providing us with the missing scene—the first traumatic stage—in James's phantasmagoria. Now we know why James rushed first behind the tree and next into the house to receive the counsel of the *symbolic community of his fellow doctors-writers*. He has witnessed *trouble in paradise*, has been *surprised by sin*, and has decided to remain existentially stranded in the position of the critical-analytical witness.[40] This part offers him the resources of detached cognition involved in what Pippin has called "the Strether Problem," and lucidly described as

the problem of those characters whom some ironic self-consciousness, or illness, or aesthetic distance and awareness, or moral scruple, or unconscious self-loathing or just bad luck have removed from the partiality and violence and great flow of life itself and who must sit in the sidelines and either observe or wait.

(*James* 94)

Hamlet's histrionic self-presentation, during his first conversation with Ophelia, as a sinful creature "crawling between earth and heaven" (*Hamlet* 3.1.128) is a measure of his distaste before the girl's dark interiority—the gap, the throat, the nothing—which her *second face* (3.1.142) has placed beyond detection. Recall that such detection is the apparent goal of his earlier mime show in her chamber, where he fell "to such perusal of my face/As he would draw it. Long stay'd he so" (2.1.77–101). Just like Freud:

> I take her to the window in order to look into her throat. She resists a little, like a woman who has false teeth. I think to myself, she does not need them. I had never had occasion to inspect Irma's oral cavity. The incident in the dream reminds me of an examination, made some time before, of a governess who at first produced an impression of youthful beauty, but who, upon opening her mouth, took certain measures to conceal her denture. Other memories of medical examinations, and of petty secrets revealed by them, to the embarrassment of both physician and patient, associate themselves with this case. [. . .] What I see in the throat: a white spot and scabby turbinal bones.

This "white spot" is arguably the paradoxical uncanny object that is real and "cannot be subjectivized," the "absolute non-subject," the "hole in the positivity of the real," the "stain which 'is' the subject" (Žižek, *Metastases* 33). In due time, James will send an inside-hiding governess to a *nunnery* of sorts. In due time, too, we will discuss her "petty secrets," white spots, holes. For now, let me simply register Hamlet's parallel obsession first with Ophelia's "nothing" (the blankness behind her painted face and her vagina) and second with her mother's diseased womb or "ulcerous place" (*Hamlet* 3.4.138).[41]

# X

Thackeray's being in the house before James arrives or his turning out of the house disappointed are not facts the latecomer has any control over. They connote an irrevocable necessity. They are as much a part of his fate as member of the league of the *Spätgekommenen* or latecomers (Nietzsche, *Unzeitgemässe* 122) blessed with *ironic self-consciousness* as is the irrepressible circumstance that he is "dying to hear the end of *Denis Duval.*" There is nothing he can do against this state of literary possession, which is also one of domestic haunting. James is literally *prepossessed* by the tutelary deities or ghosts of Shakespeare, Goethe, Lamb, and Thackeray. Like Milly in *The Wings of the Dove*, he "sinks into possession" (311) of a house not his own. And the fact of its being prepossessed by other writers spells the mark of unfreedom. Gert Buelens wrote a book titled *Henry James and the Aliens in Possession of the American Scene*: mine could have been titled *Henry James and the Ghosts in Possession of the English Novel.*

James discusses the relation between personal freedom and tradition in his "Preface" to *The Wings of the Dove*:

> There goes with it, for the heroine of *The Wings of the Dove*, a strong and special implication of liberty, liberty of action, of choice, of appreciation, of contact—proceeding from sources that provide better for large independence, I think, than any other conditions in the world. [. . .] I had from far back mentally projected a certain sort of young American as more the "heir of all the ages" than any other young person whatever [. . .] so that here was a chance to confer on some such figure a supremely touching value. To be the heir of all the ages only to know yourself, as that consciousness should deepen, balked of your inheritance.
>
> (xxxiv–xxxv)[42]

Milly, we know, will die in a semi-empty palace in Venice. The narrator will labor indefeasibly to demonstrate that her immense "liberty of action, of choice, of appreciation, of contact" is a (paradoxical) function of her freedom *from* the wealthy New York that attaches to her like an invisible, but ever presumed, value—the "imaginary value" (McKeon, *Origins* 170), James's "supremely touching value." She is, James specifies, "balked of [her] inheritance," prevented from enjoying it because she is doomed. This is all based, of course, on a fantastic moral mystification, for, try as he might, the *object* of desire (Milly) cannot be deprived of its *cause* (surplus-value).[43] A parallel fantasy of radical and unlimited freedom is rehearsed in *The Ivory Tower*, the story of another young American who, confronted "with bright immensities," is momentarily licensed to enjoy "an uplifting, a fantastic freedom" (83).

The fantasy of the young man dwelling in a haunted house is the skeleton of another unfinished novel by James, *The Sense of the Past*:

> If he had an underhand dream that his house might prove "haunted" [. . .] the thing might after all have been forgiven to his so belated freedom. Experience had lagged with him behind interpretation, and the worst that could have been said was that his gift for the latter might do well to pause awhile till an increase of the former could catch up.
>
> (52–53)[44]

In this variation of the theme, James introduces the contrast between *experience* and *interpretation* and thus momentarily reopens the old battle of books, the *querelle des anciens et des modernes*: can a modern author, with more experience than learning, add something to the literary tradition? Can James do something more than deny that he is a snob and beg Thackeray to stay? Can he *narrate* such denial or *novelize* his yearning to walk arm in arm with the author of *Henry Esmond*? *The Sense of the Past* was published two years before T.S. Eliot argued in "Tradition and the Individual Talent" (1919) that what makes a writer "traditional" is the "historical sense, which is a sense of the timeless as well as of the temporal and of the timeless and of the temporal together" (*Prose* 38). In James's 1909 allusive formulation, it is the *sense of the past* or *historical sense* that makes the writer aware of his being "the heir of all the ages."[45] Allusive because the phrase is drawn from a line Tennyson's poem, "Locksley Hall" (line 178)— "I the heir of all the ages, in the foremost files of time" (*Works* 109)—a poem that, incidentally, evokes a boy's crushed infatuation with his cousin, possibly the *experience* behind the composition of *The Wings of the Dove*. The Milly-Minny imaginative conflation is probably true, but even the most personal memories of a writer tend to become (textually) mediated in the echo chamber of a consciousness that is always-already the consciousness of a precocious and premature reader. As Denis Duval confesses in his narrative, "I was so young that I could not understand all I read" (446), which means he was already reading, and always-already being mediated by symbolic configurations, before he could understand—them or anything else. We will return often, in the course of this book, to this extraordinary sentence, not least because it offers a precise formulation both of James's brutal prepossession—his *awkward* being *taken from behind*—by Dickens, and of his attempt to retaliate from behind, very much like "le Platon instituteur en érection derrière l'élève Socrate" (Derrida, *Carte* 28).[46] Placed in tandem with his comment on the role of the adult reader confronted with the challenge of reading (or rereading) a novel like *Treasure Island*—"what we see in it is not only the ideal fable but, as part and parcel of that, as it were, the young reader himself and his state of mind: we seem to read it over his shoulder, with an arm around his neck" (*LC I* 1251)—Duval's sentence speaks to a poetics of *perverse custodial prepossession*. The narrative tradition clusters around an Id "*qua* blind force dominating the subject behind his back" (Žižek, *Metastases* 25). The avuncular act described by James has none of the casual, harmless innocence we see delineated in Maria's corporal approximation to Strether—"to make him pass his hand into her arm in the manner of a benign dependent paternal old person who wishes to be 'nice' to a younger one" (*Ambassadors* 14). For one, there are other ways of hugging from behind. For another, we are all very aware that the cause of Miles' death is an awkwardly protective embrace.

It goes without saying that the author who knows himself, however faintly, however darkly, to be prepossessed, will react by trying in turn to take his or her spectral precursor from behind. This is no Burkean contract with the dead, let alone a prospective design to foster the production of the unborn. In a book significantly titled *Tales from the Mighty Dead*, philosopher Robert Brandom argued that "traditions are lived forward but understood backward" (45). He was partly wrong, for *traditions of understanding* are largely lived backward: their participants turn back in despair, preemptively, before they feel the precursor's hand on their shoulder, and more. But short of managing to perform such demonic feats of self-arrogation (*the coitus a tergo* of *prepossession*)—a positing of one's own presuppositions that is like the son's own spilling of parental seed (James is neither Milton nor Blake)—the ephebe or latecomer may content himself with exercising an alternative mode of clandestine posteriority, the mode of retral voyeurism described by Fiedler as "watching from *behind* the tree." Everything meaningful is, in short, conceived or reaped late and from behind. I mean a narrator character (the chronicler) or a central character (the center of consciousness) watching other characters going down the ways of the world, sowing their wild oats, falling in love, out of love, in wedlock or disgrace, becoming, in short, irreparably drawn into a contingent plot where finite beings make mistakes—mischiefs, mismatches, misalliances. What is relevant about such perverse gazing into *das Leben des Anderes* is that this life, the accidental life of others, is for James, or any other strong novelist, already scripted by the narrative tradition; it is, that is, less an observed than a read experience. Put otherwise, in *The Ambassadors* James places Strether in the position of a critical observer-reader of a melodramatic tale by, say, Balzac. The result is in turn perspectivized through the lenses of a "chronicler" (35) who observes Strether, the protagonist of a second-degree narrative that is tendentially Thackeray's. While Strether seeks to neutralize the flush literality of a Balzacian tale of transgressive triangular infatuation, the narrator seeks to further deepen the indeterminacies of the resulting Thackerayan tale of avuncular perversion, vicarious curation, and libidinal supervision. The fact that Balzac is one of Thackeray's strongest precursors should come as no surprise. James retro-reads Thackeray retro-reading Balzac. There are, in short, three novels in *The Ambassadors*, and the diplomatic tasks delivered across its prose are primarily errands of intertextual dissemination and control, dispersal, and concentration. James's vicarious jouissance *comes* from the kenotic traversing of a Thackerayan fantasy. This is less reaction-formation than complaisant retaliation—or "transumption of a literary predecessor" (Rowe, *Theoretical* 79)—for having been so pleasurably retro-possessed—by him: "I am dying to hear the end of *Denis Duval*." Dying: ah *la petite mort* through Devil Do-in-ass.

If, to defer to a James metaphor, experience is "a kind of huge spider-web, of the finest silken threads, suspended in the chamber of consciousness and catching every air-borne particle in its tissue" ("The Art of Fiction," *LC I* 52), we would do well to reconcile ourselves with the notion that these particles, in the case of a writer, are words, and that they are less air-borne than tissue-borne. Considering, moreover, that *tissue* and *text* are terms that share their etymology (Barthes, *Plaisir* 100–101), we may also want to recall that words are text-borne as well as text-born. The reader may object that no James scholar is unaware of this commonplace—that his writing is allusive, rich in literary evocation, mediated by the writings of others, responsive, agonistic, reconciliatory, antagonistic. True, but this awareness has not prevented his work from being quite often source-wise under-edited. Let me offer four examples. First, as I will show in the second chapter, the editors of James' early letters fail to mention numerous instances of Hamletian resonance in them. Second, the frequent references in *The Tragic Muse* to Yolande were not, until recently, identified as pointing to Henrik Hertz's play *King René's Daughter* (1845). Third, no existing edition of *Daisy Miller* annotates the Coleridgean echo in "Have you been all alone?" And fourth, no existing edition of *The Wings of the Dove* annotates the Tennyson allusion ("Locksley Hall") latent in the phrase "the heir of all ages" in James' New York Edition "Preface" to the novel. Shakespeare, Coleridge, Tennyson: James read them, internalized them, rewrote them. Since it is no small part of the critic's task to record and report this intertextual transaction, failure to do so is less to be attributed to scholarly neglect than to a horizon of expectations where these intertextual attestations are probably regarded as banal. Indeed, influence-studies and source-hunting are not exactly—have never been—prominent in the agenda of James studies. Various reasons may be adduced for this: 1) the sacrality of his masterly authorial singularity, which would render all collations negligible (James is the Master, leave him alone); 2) the converse density of his authorial-critical erudition, which would make any attempt at allusion-identification simply impractical (he read so much, leave me alone); 3) the generic classification of his work inside a tradition, that of the novel, that is seldom regarded as amenable to the calculus of influence (he is not a poet, what is the fuss?). Indeed, the *angst* of oppressive connections is an ailment of egomaniacal poets, unsuited for the circumspect students of life and avid explorers of the air of reality we call romancers, story-tellers, or novelists. To be sure, trapped in Romantic prejudice, James paid little attention to questions of narrative influence in his many essays on novelists, but the simple fact that his critical work played such an important part of his literary professionalization may be taken as a symptom of his need to take stock of, to tabulate, to make himself accountable in relation to his sources.

Tennyson's "Locksley Hall" begins with a young man left alone in a semi-haunted house around and over which the "curlews call" and "dreary gleams about the moorland" flie (*Works* 102). As in James's epistolary phantasmagoria, the description of the setting is addressed to male "comrades." In Sedgwick's exact terms, the clinical elaboration of dream-work always takes place *between men*, although I tend to read this *between* as a differential relation or non-relation (Deleuze, *Différence* 236–237). The Gothic psychomachia of a youthful imagination wrestling with the ghosts of precursors is an out-and-out masculine affair. The young James was adamant: "There are no women." But there were, of course, some important women. And not only his cousin, but also some decisive writers masking behind the name of George (Sand and Eliot). However, I will not consider them in the present book. And not because they have been rejected, but rather because other names, "other inhabitants" in the traditional house of narrative, have prevailed more forcefully. They are the names that, in Bloomian logic, account for James's "being chosen." The names, in short, are William Shakespeare, Samuel Richardson, Henry Fielding, Edward Gibbon, William Thackeray, and Charles Dickens.

I am interested in Henry James the writer because (not despite the fact that) my real concern is Henry James the reader. And yet, where does compulsive and purportedly absolute and independent writing (and reading) place one within a democratic world marked by the massive collapse of *Stiltrennung* brought about by social freedoms—the "strange freedom" that shocks the prude governess in *The Turn of the Screw* (16) and the old bachelor in *The American Scene*—and class indifference, a literary field where insolent readers turn up at the door of the writer to ask about his cracked meanings, interrogate the holes in his sentences, and peruse the blots in his papers? It places James in the awkward position of someone impatient to renounce his freedom, begging for an alternative, elite society whose members (Shakespeare, Goethe, Lamb, Thackeray) may literally prepossess him. It places him in the attic, staring at the madwoman.

## XI

According to American philosopher Robert Pippin, the central theme of James' fiction is freedom—"just what one must do in order to achieve 'having one's life,' or presumably not having it be someone else's" (*Henry James* 159). To prevent one's life from becoming someone else's is literally to prevent *prepossession*, which coincides with the "unavoidable aspiration to a historically different life, a free life, a freedom inevitably and necessarily cooperative and therefore damaged" (58). Pippin brandishes the formula "trying to live" (59–60)—immortalized by Valéry in *Le cimetière marin* (1922): "Il faut tenter de vivre"—in order to capture the dialectical sense of damage and failure involved in the process of individuation or free subjectivation. The problem, as we will see, is that Pippin takes life to mean something like an experiential field of dialogue, recognition, mutuality, and reciprocity, and there is no evidence that James held this commonplace "Hegelian" view. James, I think, never quite gave up the romantic faith in life as the anticipation (prolepsis) or memory (analepsis) of *the* climactic private event, what Pippin parodically dismisses as "a rev-elation, a fact, or a ghost" (*James* 108). More specifically, James would want us to see "what other gears in a complex life that particular wheel turns," that wheel being "one's entitlement to treatment as a free subject, to a life of one's own" (*James* 3). This view confirms McKeon's claim that, "after the origins," the novel went to a place where "the autonomy of the self consists in its capacity to enter into larger negative relations with the society it vainly conceives itself to have created" (419). More recently still, Nancy Armstrong reads such dialectical relations as sponsoring a construal of individual freedom premised on the subject's overcoming of "the limits of his or her social position" (*Novels* 55). But it must be stressed that the overcoming never fully takes place, because to be *subjectivated* is per defi-nition to be barred, to be negatively self-related, to be haunted and prede-termined by the boundary of internalized exteriority before conventional exteriority actually responds to the subject-to-be as a historical and objec-tive *Nicht-Ich*.[47] In Jamesian fiction, having (owning, possessing) one's life is sometimes imaginatively premised on possessing a house of one's own. But this condition never fully obtains. His central characters are, at best, transient tenants, temporary occupants of someone else's house: this spells a mode of makeshift possession, like the married lady's occupancy (think of Christina) of her husband's household, or the dubious ownership of Bly that the uncle and master enjoys (Rowe, *Theoretical* 131–133). In *The Ambassadors*, little Bilham proclaims he is "for the time in possession" (72) of the *troisième* where Chad resides in Paris. Thus possessing a house of one's own, being in full legal possession of it, is more a desire than an actuality. The resulting predicament—the precariousness of a tenant who is prepossessed by the original owners of house he wrongly believes to be in possession of—is explored by James in "The Jolly Corner" and *A Sense of the Past*, narratives where a male protagonist agonizes inside a house visited by ghosts, a situation which rehearses our primal scene of spectral house prepossession.

My aim is to examine the way James' vision of freedom is compromised—both informed and inhibited—by narrative *prepossession*, by the work of strong imaginative precursors like Shakespeare, Richardson, Fielding, Gibbon, Thackeray, and Dickens. I will also try to explain why, of all people, Thackeray's ghost stays longer. Drawing on recent research on the spectral dynamics and indirections of literary influence by scholars like Adrian Poole, Philip Horne, Nicola Bradbury, Tamara Follini, and Peter Rawlings, but also on earlier deconstructive work by John Carlos Rowe, who examined the Hawthorne-James relation as a major case of literary influence, I aim to offer a speculative-dialectical account of the way James is simultaneously resourced and restrained by his sources—the way, that is, in which the prepossessing Master's "chamber of consciousness" is literally prepossessed—at times, preempted—by other (earlier) residents. In her essay on *The Turn of the Screw*, Shoshana Felman glosses Robert Heilman's dissatisfaction with the abuses of psychoanalytical readings of the tale and quotes him to the effect that "the scientific prepossession may seriously impede the imaginative insight." Intrigued by the trope, Felman adds:

> Another critic [Mark Spilka], repeating and emphasizing the term "prepossession," agrees: "We must agree, I think, that Freudian critics of the tale are *strongly prepossessed*." But what precisely is a "prepossessed" critic if not one whose mind is in advance in the *possession* of some demon, one who, like James's children, is himself *possessed*? Possessed—should we say—by the ghost of Freud?
>
> (101)

As I will try to show in the third chapter of this book, Felman overlooks the importance of James's originary prepossession, of his being visited by the ghosts of previous novelists—and preyed upon by a printer's devil knocking at the door (the relevant forerunners, in the case of *The Turn of the Screw*, are Richardson and Fielding). The same objection can be raised apropos Pippin's emphasis on the continuous space of mutual dialogic recognition between Jamesian characters, for this focus obscures the relevance of a more primordial realm: the discontinuous intertextual field where the character James defectively engages with—perversely co-opts, affably misrecognizes—the specters of his precursors. Harold Bloom charts this kind of field as a map of relentless misreading, and Žižek confirms: "precisely when one philosopher exerted a key influence upon another, this influence was without exception grounded in a productive misreading" (*Bodies* xix). It is, I believe, preposterous to think that novelists misread less than their fellow philosophers and poets.

*Narrative* is here an inclusive category that permits the reinforcing contiguity of texts by Shakespeare, Gibbon, or Dickens. I take narrative to depend on *narrativization*, "the mode in which the contingency of past events becomes transposed into a homogeneous symbolic structure" (Žižek, *Metastases* 36). Narrative tropes, in sum, pop out at us not only "as tigers and as Romans, but as Shakespeareans, astronomers and navigators" (James, *Turn* 37). At bottom lies the concern whether personal freedom is compatible with some central tropes of bourgeois-narrative emplotment (professional career, matrimony, patrimony, sacrifice)—if freedom can indeed bear the strain of being no more than "the contingency of necessity" (Žižek, *Metastases* 36)—and whether a "liberal" morality of self-reliance (Emerson) is indeed moral in any discernible sense. The choice of strong precursors is not casual: they all stand out for their conscientious and imaginative treatment of the problem of freedom, described by Hegel as "the highest destiny of the spirit" (*Lectures on Aesthetics* 97). Nor is it, of course, restrictive. Other forerunners could have been chosen, other ghosts detected, other (sub)texts presumed. But I would have written a different book. I understand the act of literary criticism as a blind bet: the contingency of the initial choices—which is a function of the transferential necessity of extant (in our case, Jamesian textual) accidental hints and symptoms—will dictate a specific hermeneutic necessity. And, as always, the proof of the pudding is in the eating.

## XII

Doubtlessly, some scholarly attention has been paid to the literary sources of Henry James, but this interest has been pursued in local ways, without concern for larger patterns. Largely due to the ill repute that source-hunting and influence-studies enjoy amongst literary scholars, who see it as a passé scholastic exercise unlikely to yield significant interpretation, there has been no systematic attempt to provide a unified vision of James' indebtedness to his strong precursors—let alone the critical need to accredit that such strong precursors exist—particularly to his forerunners in the Anglo-American tradition. Two important exceptions are John Carlos Rowe's *The Theoretical Dimension of Henry James* (1985) and Richard Brodhead's *The School of Hawthorne* (1986). This is odd, for James is commonly regarded as the last exponent of a contested *great tradition*, as the writer who indeed *consummates*—at once perfects, absolves, and terminates—the totality of the contingent conventions of realist fiction. This places him in a privileged position for critical examination, since reading James in intertextual dialogue with his ancestors in the tradition—what Gibbon calls "the parents of the mind" (*Memoirs* 76)—amounts to understanding better the always-already haunted (or prepossessed) nature of that very tradition. The question is therefore not "How did we become possessed of our tradition?" (Brodhead, *School* 3) but rather "How could James have always-already lost such possession, if he was to become the Master?" Thus, mine is both a study on James' productive unfreedom vis-à-vis his English sources and an inquiry into the resourcefulness of English narratives to reimagine freedom.

Matthiessen wrote once that "James dwelt very little in the past. His impressions and his reading were preponderantly, almost oppressively, contemporary" (*Major* 40). This is only partly true, as the novelist dwelt copiously in the writings of dead and older authors. Actually Matthiessen's claim that "a rewarding book could be written about James in terms of his relation to the evolution of the nineteenth-century novel" ("Preface" to *Stories of Writers and Artists* xii) testifies to a parallel awareness of James' role as heritor of a textual legacy he did much to develop. The prospective book would be more rewarding still if the relation could extend back to the eighteenth century. My book will not yield that ideal, but it may contribute to it. Needless to say, Matthiessen was very possibly thinking of James' relation to novelists like Balzac, Hawthorne, George Eliot, Flaubert, Zola, and Turgenev when he mentioned "the evolution of the nineteenth-century novel." The scope, richness, and complexity of James' devoted critical response to these novelists turns their influence on him into a predictable object of study. My suffocatingly English and familiar choice—Dickens and Thackeray—is less predictable and less in keeping with the standards of Jamesian cosmopolitan worldliness that have oriented his liberal and post-structuralist academic reception. And yet, one may choose where to travel, even where to become a permanent resident, but not where to be born.

Four figurations of freedom impinge on James' narrative unconscious: social freedom (democratic), civic liberty (republican), individual private freedom (liberal), individual creative freedom (romantic). All four are thematically operative in his stories and novels, but only the last openly folds back on the problematic at hand, providing it with a dimension of meta-literary reflexivity. Still, the other three figurations must also be factored in as fundamental ideological instigations of narratives of freedom. Broadly speaking, I expose the claims of Jamesian liberal-romantic freedom—presumably derived from "the parlor liberalism of the New England transcendentalists" (Rowe, *Theoretical* 51)—to the evidence both of his subjection to literary precursors *and* of his dependence on an expansively democratic literary field. Though his romantic notion of freedom, ranging from Emersonian self-reliance to Hegel's potency of "unconditioned [. . .] absoluteness" (*Phenomenology of Spirit* 80) may find support in liberal and republican figurations of liberty, it is seriously compromised by the publicity exigencies of middle-class professionalism. In his late essay on *The Tempest*, James foregrounded the play's "free elegance" (*LC I* 1206) as evidence of its sovereign author's "endowment for Expression, expression as primary force, an independent passion" (1211). His belief in the "independent, absolute value of Style" reads like an autumnal reprise of the sovereignty of artistic romantic freedom championed by Hegel in his *Lectures on Aesthetics*. Curiously, striving to establish his own creative-critical independence, James abstains from quoting a single line from the play. But *The Wings of the Dove*, for instance, is "suffused with echoes of *The Tempest* and its marine magic" (Poole, *Shakespeare* 232). James, however, always opposed the realization that no style is absolute, no passion independent, no expression primary, no elegance free. Just as the meaning of a poem may be another poem (Bloom), the meanings of a novel may well lie in a subtextual elsewhere made of other novels, other essays, other poems. One may qualify the reading protocols of the deconstructive model (de Man, Hartman, Bloom) by reaching out to recent hermeneutic responses

to the problem of influence in James and Victorian studies more generally. Adrian Poole asks us "to think for example (in no particular order)
of borrowing, stealing, appropriating, inheriting, assimilating; of being
influenced, inspired, dependent, indebted, haunted, possessed; of homage,
mimicry, travesty, echo, allusion and intertextuality" (*Shakespeare* 2). I am
interested in the "ghost effect" (Felman, "Turning" 98) at work in terms
like "haunted, possessed," for they hint at a Hamletian-Gothic mode of
intelligibility—conceivably, a *hantologie* (Derrida, *Sprectres* 31)—that is
typically Jamesian. Lustig has observed that "the ghostly, far from being a
terror, had for James begun to represent the pinnacle of extended, enlarged
experience" (*Ghostly* 4).[48] Similarly, Poole proposes a dialectic between
total control and wholesale dispersal to explain two aspects of memory
and creativity in James, "one receding into an impenetrable interiority, an
eternal implosion; the other erupting, exploding and dispersing into multitude" ("Romance" 12). Poole examines James' conception of memory
as "at once textile and textual, something woven together or falling apart,
into shreds" (6), a trope congenial to deconstructive reading. It is thus the
critic's task to identify the "tattered webs" of earlier literary texts that lin-
ger more forcefully in James' text-haunted memory. Tamara Follini follows
Douglas-Fairhurst's suggestion that accounts of influence by nineteenth-
century writers follow a Jamesian concern with the image of the circle, as
they are "attracted to metaphors of cohesion and dispersal, proximity and
distance, orderly transmission and chaotic sprawl" ("Indirections" 92).
Thus, for instance, the scattering of Shakespearean words in James's narratives attest to the conflicting dynamics built into the "living memories of
his reading" (10). The oscillation between dispersal and concentration, dissemination and control, forces a reconsideration of the role of free immediate agency in a creative process that is always-already bound to engage in
the spectral mediation of material *écriture*.

The problem with the parallel notions of *influence* of *dispersal* is that they
rely excessively on the poststructuralist logic of slipperiness, dissemination,
and the "plurality of the signifying process" (Žižek, *Sublime* 139). To be
sure, Bloom brought the floating signifiers back to earth in his Oedipal reading of the poetic tradition, where *influence* is a relatively controlled process.
There are rivers, of course, and rivulets, and affluents, but also stagnant
waters like those of the Venice canals or the lake in *The Turn of the Screw*.
Žižek asks us to reconsider the dimension that in ideology lies "beyond
interpellation," namely "the square of desire, fantasy, lack in the Other and
drive pulsating around some unbearable surplus-enjoyment" (139).

## XIII

The narrator of Henry Fielding's *Amelia* notes at one point that the titular
heroine of his story is wanting in scholarship. "Her Reading," he avers,

"was confined to *English* Plays, and Poetry" (272). This seemingly minor remark throws into relief the gap separating Fielding from his heroine. The former, we know, peppers his major narratives with abundant citations of classical authors, including some English "classics" like Shakespeare or Milton. But his literary memory is also besprinkled with lines and phrases lifted from "lesser" poets and playwrights whose names—Dryden, Dennis, Suckling, Addison, Congreve—make up, to be sure, the diminished pantheon Amelia is familiar with. We may thus risk the tentative formulation that just as there was a Quijano inside Cervantes—or, by his own admission, a Madame Bovary inside Flaubert—there was also an Amelia inside Fielding. The historical and generic awkwardness caused by such coexistence, the brisk retrieval of classical lore (Virgil, Horace, Thucydides), and its factitious translation to emerging urban-bourgeois conditions of social existence led Fielding to frame the definition of the "new province of writing" he was both mapping and claiming to create—the novel—with the insanely consistent phrase *comic Epic-Poem in Prose* (Preface to *Joseph Andrews* 3). Thus, for instance, whereas the author enthuses in the moral liabilities of the epic poem, *Amelia* is all for the sentimental thrill of comic (erotic, domestic) prose. The result of such heteroglossic combination is of course a novel, one indeed among a selected group (*Moll Flanders, Pamela, Tom Jones*) that set a new textual tradition afoot, transforming forever the map of what Henry James was to call, in his essay on *Thackerayana: Notes and Anecdotes* (1875), "English literature" (*LC I* 1289). The moral of this story is speciously simple, for it affords an additional twist. Henry James, the author held to crown the *great tradition* of the English novel as it developed mainstream in the geography of nineteenth-century *English literature*, was fluent in neither of the two traditions that went into the making of the modern novel. Unversed in classical culture and only familiarized with early modern English literature, he could pride himself of a literary education that was closer both in matter and *manner* to Amelia's than to Fielding's—or, to stretch a bit the contrast with familiar references, closer to Richardson's or Clarissa's than to Swift's or Johnson's. Standing by the old arches of the Odéon, Strether lingered "before the charming open-air array of literature classic and casual" (Ambassadors 66). If the final conjunction portends any significance, then one may risk the claim that James favored *literature casual*. Pound famously observed that "if James *had* read his classics, the better Latins especially, he would not have so excessively cobwebbed, fussed, blathered, worried about minor mundanities." Pound was too, let me note in passing, one of the few contemporary "critics" who bothered to place James in the wake of what Richardson and Fielding had attempted.[49] In fact, the only field in which James could boast of scholarly erudition and critical sagacity was that of the novel whose tradition *Amelia* contributed to consolidate. And his work remains part of the answer to the question, memorably raised by Armstrong, of "why, at the inception of modern culture, the literate classes in England suddenly developed an unprecedented taste for the writing for, about, and by women" (*Desire* 7). To be sure, James was a formidable intellectual, gifted with very uncommon powers of critical discrimination, but his mind was also a product of a bourgeois literary field saturated by, in George Eliot's ultra-critical formulation, "Silly Novels by Lady Novelists." The fact that the constitution of this field was ab initio—from Fielding's reaction against *Pamela*—animated by a recusation of silver spoon coziness, romance-sentimental cant, the mean heroisms of private honesty and individualistic sensationalism, doesn't lessen the degree of James's absorption in the maze of these womanish banalities.[50] It surely didn't allay "James's own personal fears he would become nothing but one of the scribbling tribe of woman romancers" (Rowe, *Theoretical* 82). Although his arguments concern an exclusively "Victorian anxiety of influence," Rowe's florid phrasing captures the eighteenth-century conditions (professional tribalism, scribblers versus authors, the romance-novel dialectic) constituting the field to which James's fears would later react. This feminization of the role he was to inherit—the semiprofessional scribbler of intellectualized romances figuring vacant heroines—allows us to broaden and historicize further the coordinates of the conventional set of gendered oppositions that are often employed to grasp the complexity of the James persona, not least the fascinating question of his homosexuality, the only proof of which existence is our determination to keep raising it. His disinclination, moreover, to consider the immense relevance of *strong* woman novelists (not romancers) like Jane Austen, Elizabeth Gaskell, Emily Brontë, and Charlotte Brontë renders this feminization all the more complex.

The apparently irrelevant question of James' textual effeminacy is bound up with problems of genealogy. Hereditary conventions of gender and genre are inextricably related. There are also, to be sure, alternative claims to origin—to the origin, that is, of the English novel—in Spanish picaresque fiction, in prose satire, in Defoe, but the contention that *Pamela* and *Clarissa* inaugurate a textual tradition of realistic sentimental bourgeois prose fiction, circumstanced by domestic confinement, and informed by an unyielding drive to emotional-moral examination, is too convincing to be pushed aside. *Pamela* and *Clarissa* share the rare privilege of being the two narratives that F.R. Leavis leaves unexamined in what should have been the opening chapter of *The Great Tradition*. True enough, he bothers to acknowledge Richardson's importance, but he limits it, consciously following a critical convention, to his "strength in the analysis of emotional and moral states" (4), and he suggests a name linkage—"Richardson-Fanny Burney-Jane Austen" (49)—that grants the author of *Pamela* the impromptu role of adumbral and semi-furtive grandfather of his genealogy. But no condescension can occlude the fact that if Leavis' tradition matters, it is precisely because the novelists included show "strength in the analysis of emotional and moral states." That is their *forte*. Only this strength brings together Richardson, Austen, Eliot, James, and Conrad, to the exclusion of Defoe, Scott, most of Dickens, Thackeray, Stevenson, and others. This implicit realization devolves original preeminence to Richardson and renders negligible Leavis' clumsy footwork around Fielding in the opening sections of his book. If he appeared uncertain as to whether and why Richardson mattered, his comments on Fielding's relevance as the writer who "[opened] the central tradition of English fiction" (3) show a very weak and derivative grasp of the subject. He has little to say of Fielding besides contending that he led to and "made Jane Austen possible" (3)—a fair observation that should stretch back to include Richardson— and observing that he learnt the "art of presenting characters and *moeurs*" in the school of journalism or that his "concern with human nature [was] simple." In the remainder of his meagre paragraph he expresses bewilderment at the fact that some people (most notably, Scott and Coleridge) appear *really* to have enjoyed *Tom Jones*. This hardly explains why, how, and whether Fielding indeed opened so central a tradition.

I guess this deficit in appreciation can be imputed to an ingrained habit among critics of the English novel to split the field into two neatly divided bands, that of the rise of the novel, featuring Defoe, Richardson and Fielding, and that of its consolidation and culmination in the great tradition, from Austen to James, what came after (Joyce to, say, Morrison) being the province (modernism, postmodernism) of a new critical industry—the post-structuralist. The fact that the hermeneutic manners and routines of interrogation engaged in this new industry have proved particularly illuminating when retrospectively applied to the excluded names in both lists (Swift, Sterne, Smollett, Dickens, Hawthorne, Melville, Emily Brontë) is, I believe, a matter to ponder. But this need not detain us here. What matters is that James's culminating function in the second series and his liminal position between it and that of a full-fledged modernity has determined a scenario of reception that is unremittingly blind to questions of deep indebtedness and enlarged tradition. If the implicit rules of a certain game of domestic and sentimental narrative realism were originally laid, as Leavis indolently concedes, by Richardson, then it seems justifiable to initiate a discussion of James' oeuvre with a consideration, however exiguous, of the dialogue this oeuvre may have established with *Pamela* and *Clarissa*. There is no real need to explain the grounds of Richardson's precedence over Fielding, as it was Richardson who made Fielding the novelist possible, and it was Fielding who inaugurated a tradition of *responses to Pamela* that constitutes no small proportion of the novels published in the late eighteenth and nineteenth century. What remains profoundly surprising is that this all too evident fact—that we can explain *Mansfield Park*, *Bleak House*, *Villette*,

*Daniel Deronda*, and *The Tragic Muse* without recourse to *Moll Flanders* but not without reconsidering *Pamela*—should escape notice or be deemed altogether irrelevant from a critical standpoint. Also important to our purposes is that, as Ian Watt observed, "*Amelia* is much closer to Richardson's close study of domestic life than Fielding's previous works" (*Rise* 292).

## XIV

Harold Bloom considers that, while *Clarissa* inaugurates the tradition inside which *Emma*, *Middlemarch*, and *The Portrait of a Lady* successively make (their) sense, "*Tom Jones* founds another line, the rival tradition that includes Dickens and Joyce, novelists as exuberant as Fielding, and metaphysically and psychologically more problematic" (*Novels* 28). If Bloom is right, then James is a colossus that bestrides both worlds. Let me give another example of the hermeneutic loss that may follow from an excessively narrow or mechanistic application of historicist period-categories. The designations *modern moral life* and *modernity* used by Robert Pippin in his reading of James are meaningless if they are not sharply defined—both historically and conceptually. Taking them for granted leads quite often to the neglect of a broad picture brimming with instances, cases, and particularities that controvert and potentially undo the claim to exceptionality that underpins the specification "*modern* moral life" (emphasis added). According to Pippin, "James's major preoccupation in his account of the modern world is just this figure of loss, loss of the forms of social hierarchy, predictability, and expectation that made interpretation, meaning, and some psychological stability and determinacy possible" (*James* 28). A cursory glance to the critical work of Ian Watt, Michael McKeon, Terry Castle, Leo Damrosch, Nancy Armstrong, John Richetti, Tom Keymer, and others would serve to confirm that the loss of the forms social hierarchy, predictability, and expectation making interpretation, meaning, and determinacy possible was not only well underway in the eighteenth century, as the novels of Swift, Defoe, Richardson, and Fielding prove, but that this loss was precisely the genetic cause of the network of ideological responses informing those novels in the first place. There is also a sense, in fact, in which this loss can be retrieved as the ultimate cause motivating whatever "modern moral lives" we may feel scholarly tempted to identify: one may speak of uncertainty, doubt, emerging social forms, and altered moral states in the work of Chaucer, Marlowe, Bunyan, etc. The idea that a significant author lived in an age of significant social change and that her work may therefore read as a significant (whether speculative-critical or ideological-conforming) response to it is just a critical commonplace. Why should James' world be more altered, indeterminate, and disjunctive than the worlds of prose writers like Dickens,

Austen, Lewis, Walpole, Haywood, Behn, or Nashe?[51] If a truly pivotal crisis is to be suggested, then we may say that 1688 marks the turning point in British social life to which most of the alterations chronicled by James and detected by Pippin can be reasonably traced back.[52] Two names would fall from my extempore list of writers (Nashe and Behn), and Eliza Haywood would come in to occupy the provisional place of the *originatrix*. It is not casual that Richetti opens his magisterial study of eighteenth-century fiction with her work, and it would be very propitious if the book could stretch further to include that of Henry James. For if *Clarissa* can be conceived as the first American novel, then *The Turn of the Screw* should be read as the last English eighteenth-century narrative.

But then, of course, what role do we assign in this impromptu gene-alogies of the imagination to the Danish bachelor? To his credit, Pippin shrewdly observes that

> at least since Shakespeare's *Hamlet*, modern tragedies of uncertainty, indeterminacy, and self-doubt, all in contrast with classical depictions of very determinate moral dilemmas, could be cited to undercut any such claim, on James's behalf or independently, for such an epochal self-consciousness

and he quotes from Hillis Miller's *Ethics of Reading* (1987) to make room for the deconstructionist claim that the "inevitable failure of 'reading'" may be seen more "as a matter of the structure of language itself" than as the outcome of historical conditions. The resulting dialectical constel-lation of motifs permits the articulation of an argument—*Hamlet* is the contingent-historical source of a narrative tradition informed by a non-historical, structural, and therefore necessary core of subjective uncertainty, doubt, and indeterminacy—that subtends the totality of the claims I shall be putting forward in this book. If Shakespeare is the "allusive medium" (Rawlings, "Henry James" 96) of James's writing, then *Hamlet* is both the regressive script grounding the medium and the distant object of most of its allusions. *Hamlet* is not exactly part of our story, but rather the text that constitutes its transcendental conditions of possibility. Hastened by the repression of *jouissance* and by the angst of facing up to the gaps of reality, *Hamlet* maps out the expiative and expirative possibilities of the modern tale:

Absent thee from felicity awhile,
And in this harsh world draw thy breath in pain,
To tell my story.

(5.2.289–291)

## Notes

1 I follow Copjec's Lacanian line of reasoning in *Read My Desire*, 118–126. This excellent book was originally published in 1994 by the MIT Press. See also Badiou, "Formulas of L'Étourdit'" 60.

2 For a discussion of *chronolibinal anxiety* in the context of mortal life, see Hägglund, *Dying for Time*, 1–19, and 106. For the Derridean question of thinking being (*l'être*) before life (*la vie*), see Naas, *Plato and the Invention of Life*.

3 Bloom argued that "A poem is not an overcoming of anxiety, but is that anxiety" (*Anxiety* 94).

4 The cited phrase is from Halpern, *Shakespeare*, 248.

5 An *interpretive community* is "made up of those who share interpretive strategies not for reading (in the conventional sense) but for writing texts, for constituting their properties and assigning their intentions" (Fish 483).

6 Dietrich Hoffendahl "doesn't trust women" (*Princess* 331).

7 Of course, the term *séance* is used often in *The Bostonians*.

8 For the implications of the pun nothing-vagina, especially in the Sonnets, see Belsey, *Shakespeare*, 73–93.

9 In Fielding's *Joseph Andrews*, Fanny unwittingly places herself in a reverse postural predicament, "reclining her Head on [Joseph's] Bosom" (*Joseph* 167).

10 Deane, "Introduction" to *Finnegans Wake*, xxviii.

11 For Nicholas Royle's notion of the spectral *outlife* of life, see *In Memory of Jacques Derrida*, 144–147; but also *How to Read Shakespeare*, where we read: "What is a ghost? What does it mean to 'follow' the dead?" (59)

12 Although scholars like Nicola Bradbury have questioned the validity of "the Bloomian model" ("Temporality" 225) when applied to James, I believe it still holds hermeneutic potential. I obviously follow in the footsteps of John Carlos Rowe's very original application of Bloomian ratios to the understanding of the way James's narrative textuality is informed by his permanently threatened "bid for authority" (*Theoretical* 87).

13 Žižek: "freedom is *stricto sensu* the contingency of necessity—that is, it is contained in the initial 'if . . .' in the (contingent) choice of the modality by means of which we symbolize the contingent real or impose some *narrative necessity* upon it" (*Metastases* 36; emphasis added).

14 See, for instance, Battesin, "The Problem of *Amelia*," 615.

15 Pippin alludes to "the Oedipal echoes of the primeval independence-dependence struggle [. . .] with Americans and Europeans enacting the problem of the founding of a new civilization in these Oedipal terms" (*James* 61), but he refuses to acknowledge the hermeneutic suitability of the psychoanalytic appropriation of Oedipus, especially in its structuralist direction. Obviously, Pippin must keep Lacan at bay if he wishes to sustain his belief that "we understand what others are doing by understanding their motives and reasons, their desires and beliefs, by understanding what they take themselves to be after and why. This all obviously implies that they can somehow identify what they desire and believe, and either disclose it or not, to others or even to themselves" (72). Lacanian is the attempt to sabotage this (naïvely Hegelian) social ecology of mutually transparent *Lesbarkeit*.

16 I agree with Tintner's suggestion about James's successive re-workings of *Hamlet* (168).

17 Richetti may not sufficiently alert to the extent to which Fielding's novels are letters to the reader, and therefore are not unlike Richardson's epistolary novels.

18 See Miller, *The Novel and the Police*, 21–27. Copjec has accused Miller's thesis of insensitivity to the ineliminable difference—the "not-identical-to-itself"—that

lies at the core of all processes of subjectivation and signifying deficiency (lack and excess). The conception of the nineteenth-century realist-novel narrator as "nobody in particular, nobody but a generalized consciousness" (Copjec, *Read* 160) is blind to the role of the particular narratorial perspective of an inquisitive gaze that is epistemically interested because oedipalized, and therefore traumatically entrapped in the *Familienroman*.

19  The letter to Violet Hunt is dated 11 August 1903: *Letters*, Vol. IV, 281. The allusion, here interpreted *pro domo mea*, is cryptic and demands attention to the figurative context, carefully analyzed by Tanner in "Henry James and Shakespeare" (*American Mystery* 143–146). See especially Rawlings: *Henry James and the Abuse*, 119–121. Bloom insists that Goethe, Milton, and Hugo were the strongest post-Enlightenment poets because they were "the most triumphant of the modern wrestlers with the dead" (*Anxiety* 72). Goethe receives sustained attention in 51–56. The exceptionality of Shakespeare is examined in *The Western Canon* (45–75) and *Shakespeare* (1–20).

20  In his review on D'Annunzio's novels, James mentions twice the *casa paterna* (*LC II* 929).

21  Rowe argued that although Trollope and James "are eminently critical of the divisions and distinctions of classed societies, both refuse the anarchy of any complete rejection of such order." James proposed, rather, the exercise of fine "discriminations" (*Theoretical* 64).

22  For Fredric Jameson's view of historical non-representability, see *The Narrative Unconscious*, 102. For Waterloo, see my article "Lying Epitaphs: *Vanity Fair*, Waterloo, and the Cult of the Dead." For James's resistance to the depiction of terrorist action, see Poole, "Introduction" to *The Princess Casamassima*, xlvii.

23  See Richetti. Pippin has also stressed the bearing for the constitution of a "modern" novel like James's of the opposition between "the necessities, regularities, deadly conformism" of an old society and the new uncertainties and ambivalence of the modern world (*James* 16).

24  The classical essay is Ferdinand Tönnies' *Community and Civil Society*. For an application of his ideas, and Jean-Luc Nancy's on community, to the field of the novel, see my essay "Togetherness and Its Discontents."

25  Although there is a potential distortion in the governess's perspective, he may have inherited handsomely: "She *conceived* him as rich, but as fearfully extravagant—*saw* him all in a glow of high fashion, of good looks, of expensive habits, of charming ways with women. He had for his own town residence a big house filled with the spoils of travel and the trophies of the chase" (*Turn* 4).

26  For the association between usury and excessive *jouissance*, see Batsaki.

27  Douglas-Fairhurst recalls Chesterton's comments on Dickens's "democratic optimism," underlying that which "was the conviction that everything is potentially interesting" (*Becoming* 129).

28  For the voyeuristic compulsion of characters around Pamela's concentric spaces (room, cabinet, body), see McKeon, *Secret*, 651–658. For the masturbatory use of book sex, including that of the novel *Pamela*, see *Secret*, 298–299.

29  Two important admirers of James have written about the Sartrean conception of freedom: Murdoch, *Sartre*, 52–63; Jameson, *Sartre: The Origins of a Style*, 48–53; *Valences of the Dialectic*, 223–256. Murdoch's book was originally published in 1953, but she added an interesting "Introduction" in 1987.

30  Husserl's near-dialectical understanding of abstention (*Enthaltung*) implies that the world is not completely lost in the *epoché*, but retained (*behalten*) by those of course on whom nothing or nearly nothing is lost, least of all the lady in the

group portrait (*Gruppenbild mit Dame* is the title of a brilliant Heinrich Boll novel).

31 I allude to Hawthorne's short story "Wakefield" (*Twice-Told Tales*, 1837), in which a man absents himself from his house without explanation, to live "in the next street to his own," and spends decades examining the way in which his wife and home are "affected by his removal."

32 For James's "condescending view of women," see Habbegger, 4–15.

33 For Richardson's revolutionary attempt to bridge the stylistic divide, see Watt, *Rise*, 187–189.

34 For James's attitude towards Austen, see Duckworth.

35 I am here playing a variation on a dialectical scheme proposed by McKeon (*Origins* 157).

36 I make this controversial claim in an essay on Eliot's novel published in *Representations.*

37 For Isabel's inviolable sense of selfhood, autonomy, and "individual distinction," see Gorra, *Portrait*, 52–63, 115. Rowe pits Isabel's "pretension to free and autonomous identity" against the determinism of the American anxiety of influence: *Theoretical*, 33. For the indictment of nineteenth-century individualism, see also 65.

38 See also Badiou, *L'immanence des vérités*, 611–624.

39 For the concern for the maintenance of women and the connected proposals, by Mary Astell, Daniel Defoe, and Richardson, to accommodate them in religious institutions or convents, see Watt, *The Rise of the Novel*, 164–165.

40 Katherine Snyder significantly uses the phrase "Trouble in Paradise" in the title of the first chapter of her study *Bachelors, Manhood, and the Novel, 1850– 1925*. For a biographical reconstruction of Henry James and his sister Alice as Adam and Eve "on the edge of the event," see Coulson, 33–34.

41 In her discussion of this obsession, De Grazia alludes to scholarly comparisons of Hamlet's words to Gertrude to a surgeon knife, and to engravings that reference "Nero's notorious desire to see his mother Agrippina's womb" (*Hamlet without Hamlet* 102–103).

42 She is referred to as "the potential heiress of all the ages" (*Wings* 78).

43 For this paradox, see Žižek, "The Specter of Capital" in *The Fragile Absolute*, 9–17.

44 See J. Hillis Miller's Derridean (hauntological) reading of this unfinished novel in the last chapter of *Literature as Conduct*.

45 This added awareness generates an apperceptive "sense of the sense" of the past: see Rowe, *Theoretical*, 38.

46 For Kant, "we act pathologically when there is something driving our actions— serving either to propel us forward or to impel us from behind" (Zupančič 7).

47 For *internalized exteriority*, any sensible reconciliation of dialectical materialism and psychoanalysis would do. See, for example, Žižek, *The Metastases of Enjoyment*, 19–20.

48 See Colin Davis's essay on "Hauntology, spectres and phantoms" and the book on *Spectres of Marx* edited by Michael Sprinker.

49 In Pound's essay on James's "Notes for *The Ivory Tower*," he measures James's critical originality in urging "the comprehension of the novel as a 'form'" against the achievement of "Fielding and Richardson" (265).

50 In Sabor's terms, applied to some male characters in Fielding's *Amelia*, which includes "Doctors," James behaves often like the soldier who defends "English manhood from the threat posed by an over-educated woman" (102).

51 In his essay on *The Golden Bowl*, Pippin argues defensively that "there have been complex psychological novels before and after James, full of self-deceit, confusion, shaky interpretations, and uncertainty, and none of that seems to have had much to do with any historical sensibility or any great vortex in world history" (32). Laclos, he points out, "seems not have had any large views about the ever dwindling cultural resources of mass society" (32).

52 For a very persuasive periodization of modernity that reaches back to the Glorious Revolution, the "Introduction" to Pincus, *1688*.

# 2  Askesis

## The Imaginary Value: Parables of the Bastard Son From *Hamlet* to *The Princess Casamassima*

I

The immediate source of *Hamlet* is the so-called *Ur-Hamlet*. This critical conjecture has variously assisted scholars trying to account for the abnormal psychological excess displayed by the protagonist in Shakespeare's most mature versions of his tragedy (Q2 and Folio). This excess is a negative abyss of verbal nothingness (the *hole thing*) that the prince carries inside him (Lukacher, *Daemonic* 140) and that thinkers since the Romantic period have gravitated around.[1] Like a clique of doctors, say, around a girl's open mouth. Because the critical tradition is compelled to postulate desperate solutions to the mystery of Hamlet's singularity, this particular shortcut takes the radical form of the claim that *Hamlet* is the source of *Hamlet*. I mention this as a function of the abnormality of a text that appears to have realized the dream of Milton's Satan—that of being influenced only by itself.

Let us therefore concede for the sake of argument that in the beginning there was much anxiety—"Oh yes, I daresay I can find the child" (*Princess* 53)—but there was no influence: "I have seen nothing" (*Hamlet* 1.1.20). The ensuing operation is predictable enough [anxiety – influence = *Hamlet*] and turns Shakespeare's tragedy into a convenient starting place—for Henry James, anyway. A place to get *freely* started, of course, if needing a locus to begin is at all compatible with freedom. Dover Wilson suggested that *Hamlet* is a *tragedy of freedom*—"the tragedy of a genius caught fast in the toils of circumstance and unable to fling free" (*Happens* 39). In an extended sense, this freedom—the unlikely, restricted freedom of orphans, maids, upstarts, geniuses, bastards, and second sons—is the stuff that novelistic dreams are made of, from Defoe to Balzac, from Richardson to James, from Marivaux to Joyce. Hyacinth, described by the narrator of *The Princess Casamassima* as "one of the disinherited, one of the expropriated, one of the exceptionally interesting" (120), is admittedly a genius of sorts caught in the toils of circumstance.[2] I am consciously reporting

DOI: 10.4324/9781003199564-2

the Romantic, escapist, interpretation of the play centered on "the tender, delicate, sensitive prince, unequal to the sacred duty of revenge, endlessly inventing excuses to escape the harsh reality of action" (Belsey, *Shakespeare* 140). If I thus favor an interpretation that misreads *conscience* for *consciousness* it is because both the Romantic tradition and the narrative tradition that presumably sought to sublate its "expressive individualism" (Armstrong, *How Novels* 8) productively shared this misreading. Admittedly, the toils of circumstance coming at the modern novel are not dissimilar from those Hamlet and Hyacinth were bound to confront—*disinheritance* and *dispossession*. The mechanisms of reaction-formation to a legacy of disinheritance are in both cases (*Hamlet* and the modern novel) also consonant: the active internalization of providence—"We defy augury" (*Hamlet* 5.2.157)—and the passive reprocessing of desire—"the readiness is all" (5.2.160). According to Michael McKeon, the aristocratic ideology "names the impulse [. . .] to conceal the perennial alterations in ruling elites by naturalizing those elites as a static unity of status and virtue, the ongoing 'rule of the best' " (169). In the modern age, this ideology became the target of a two-stage attack, first launched by a *progressive ideology*, and second by a *conservative ideology* that was also reacting against the latter. Whereas the progressive ideology rejected, on essentialist grounds, the necessary link between birth (status) and honor (virtue), the conservative ideology put forward a more pragmatic-instrumental critique, suggesting that although worth could not be genealogically secured, it was nonetheless *de facto* advanced by "the distinction of birth" (Gibbon, *Memoirs* 42). Thus, "the defense of a noble lineage not for its intrinsic value but for what Swift calls its 'imaginary value' is suggestively comparable to the rationale by which extreme skepticism returns to the notional veracity of romance" (McKeon 170). This suggestion is confirmed by the Hamletian linkage between conservative ideology and extreme skepticism (171). We are thus left with a paradoxical configuration where the satirical radicalness of extreme skepticism meets the pragmatic convenience of the imaginary values that sustain *romance*. Needless to say, no attempt can be made to understand what Henry James was up to without coming to terms with his dialectical outmaneuvering of melodrama and sensation— the disappearance, the nostalgia, the very *possibility of romance*. And remember that *The Princess Casamassima* fails because romance, for James, was not an impossible fallout. The novel begins, let me recall, with a boy staring at tough toffy and hard lollipops at a shop-window across the street, but also at the half-glimpsed treasures—songbooks, pictorial sheets, romances—offered by the periodical literature at display in the establishment (*Princess* 54). What McKeon calls "the notional veracity of romance" is not a self-evident concept. Implicit in his formulation is the idea that the mode in which extreme skepticism reappropriates "romance" is dialectical, overcoming its major deficiency (the tendency to falsification) and yet retaining a visible, but often overlooked, advantage, i.e. the capacity to posit—in fact, retroposit—an "imaginary value" that produces rather than reflects the social-cultural advantages of aristocratic standing.[3]

The economy of this *imaginary value*, at bottom a convenient *fiction* or *fantasy*, is the object of this chapter. In the logic of this libidinal-soteriological economy, the conservative ideology can be seen as inviting the skeptical and reactive subject *to traverse a fantasy*, whether inherited or of his own making. And this is the fantasy, of course, of personal worth. For if what Jonathan Swift—the archconservative ideologue in McKeon's magisterial precis—suggests is that "elevated birth affords opportunities for education, travel, and companionship which are otherwise not available, and that this will give the edge to the noble youth" (*Origins* 170), then what happens to the *common*—non-noble or not fully noble—youth to whom these apparent privileges become *de facto* available? In his *Memoirs*, Edward Gibbon argues that in his enlightened time, "attainments" like "the arts of reading, writing and vulgar arithmetic" are "so generally diffused that they no longer constitute the liberal distinctions of scholars and gentlemen" (62). Other procurements like travel contribute to the displaced (or replaced) aristocracy of the spirit. Think of James's compulsive rehearsing of the international version of *moral luck*—or lucky morality: [American youth + money = European experience].[4] One such common youth is, for instance, Henry James Jr, but also many of his novelistic personae: Daisy, Isabel, Chad, Milly, Gray. Also, *mutatis mutandis*, Hyacinth. In an important conversation, Christina tells Hyacinth that "natural tact and taste"—formerly the endowments of blood aristocracy—were not easily found "in any Anglos-Saxon in whom it hadn't been cultivated at a vast expense; unless, indeed, in certain little American women" (337). This confirms that Hyacinth, perhaps also James, is at bottom—at the bottom of the romantic ideology that identifies naturalness, social-cultural eccentricity, and Bohemianism—a *little American woman*, or, more precisely, Daisy *redux*. In fact, what do you need to set the international novel in motion if not education, travel, companionship, and a room with a view? Both these characters and their narrator are subjects interpellated by a conservative ideology, called up to traverse the fantasy of their own aristocratic worth, subjects invited to indulge a dream of status elevation. Only in the case of Hyacinth is this formula beset by the sentimental-romantic banality of discovered parentage and reappropriated noble birth. And this is so because *The Princess Casamassima* is the James novel that most ostensibly betrays not only its reliance on shallow Dickensian romance, but also its indebtedness to *Hamlet*, the literary work where such *conservative fantasy* arguably originates.

## II

Let me explain. Obviously, there is no status elevation, whether real or imaginary, in the case of the Danish prince, but this doesn't mean that his story doesn't occur under the conditions of *status inconsistency* where both elevation and demotion may occur. Indeed it is this very inconsistency—visible, for instance, in the indecisive and unstated terms of the elective monarchy, in the misgivings surrounding the relation between the prince and the court lord's daughter, in Claudius' frightened stance towards "the people muddied" (*Hamlet* 4.5.77) or "rabble" (4.5.98), and in Rosencrantz's and Hamlet's scornful remarks on "common stages" (2.2.329) and "common players" (2.2.334)—that facilitates his elusive downgrading, his conversion from noble prince to "whore" ready to "unpack [his] heart with words" (*Hamlet* 2.2.563). This conversion, I submit, helped prompt the transit from heroic parameters (tragedy, epic poem) to the postclassical literary conditions that framed the so-called *rise of the novel*: what was Pamela—to many of Richardson's contemporaries, anyway—if not a whore who unpacked her heart with words? And what the governess of *The Turn of the Screw*, to many readers, if not a sexually repressed and hysterical woman who unpacked her heart with words? But let me not anticipate: this parallelism is the topic of the third chapter. The choice child of an "upstart Crow"—Robert Greene's description of Shakespeare (Honan 158–162)—Hamlet is a *downstart*, an effete and slightly effeminate hero whose first important resolution is—like the hero in Thackeray's *Henry Esmond*—to speed up his own *status demotion* and back out from his domestic tragedy. His retreat resembles Lady Aurora's volunteer egression from the aristocratic *domus*:

> But I've got out of it; I do as I like, though it has been rather a struggle. I have my liberty, and that is the greatest blessing in life, except the reputation of being queer, and even a little mad, which is a greater advantage still.
>
> (*Princess* 221)

*My liberty [ . . . ] the reputation of being queer, and even a little mad*: these phrases brilliantly synthesize Hamlet's confidential disclosures to Horatio and Gertrude. The rest, for the prince, is silence; for Pynchon, foreplay (*Rainbow* 99); for James, the madness of art ("The Middle Years", *Selected* 254). Structurally, therefore, Lady Aurora embodies the social displacement performed by Hamlet. And structurally, too, Hyacinth reverses her gesture by capitalizing on the imaginary value of Christina's aristocratic worth. His symbolic investment in this formal—and therefore potentially *empty*—"imaginary value" is ironically counterposed by the gash in the fabric of Lady Aurora's symbolic real.[5] On first meeting her, Hyacinth notes "a certain disrepair in her apparel [. . .] given by a hole in one of her black gloves, through which a white finger gleamed" (136). Hegel once argued that "a mended stocking is better than a torn stocking: not so self-consciousness" (*Aphorismen* 558). Let us recapitulate: one of the two declassed aristocrats in the novel has a hole in a glove, the other (Hyacinth) will perforate his head with a bullet. But then Robert Pippin, taking a dig at Žižek's magnus opus on Hegel, holds that he doesn't "fully understand the claims about holes in the fabric of being" ("Back to Hegel?" 12), and Pippin is an honorable man.[6]

The American philosopher, in his book on James, described the "vast historical alteration" that gave rise to modernity as "a change in basic mores and sensibilities" that was "especially visible in the privileged [. . .] classes" (*James* 11). So far so good. But his characterization of these classes as "reflective, intensely self-conscious, freed-from-the-necessity-of-labor" is probably biased by Jamesian elevations. The privileged classes were freed from the necessity of labor, but not necessarily reflective and intensely self-conscious: England had no shortage of "mere fox-hunting, horse-dealing squires" (*Denis Duval* 498). Tanner rightly observed that at the time he was writing *The Princess Casamassima*, James had "little illusions about the injustices and degradations of the English class system." In a letter to a friend, he described its upper classes in the following manner:

> The condition of that body seems to me in many ways to be the same rotten and collapsible one as that of the French aristocracy before the revolution minus cleverness and conversation; or perhaps it is more like the heavy, congested and depraved Roman world upon which the barbarians came down. In England the Huns and Vandals will have to come up from the black depths of the (in the people) enormous misery, though I don't think the Attila is quite yet found—in the person of Mr. Hyndman. At all events, much of English life is grossly materialistic and wants blood-letting.
>
> (*HJL* 3:146)[7]

The reversal of the telos of Enlightened narrative that James here apocalyptically foresees will be the topic of my fourth chapter. For now, I am interested in the second part of the suggested subtraction—"minus cleverness and conversation"—because it portends a rank of lesser gentility depreciated further by its utter deprivation of an "imaginary value" (education, travel, companionship) that has been presumably stolen by the accultured middle-class. That James was not exaggerating, any attentive reader of Austen, Edgeworth, Charlotte Brontë, Dickens, and Thackeray stands witness to. Pippin's "privileged classes" were *reflective* only in a mirror-stage manner, and alone *self-conscious* if aware of the type (rank, class) they believed to embody. The speculative reflexivity that promoted the states of negative, abyssal self-consciousness that we associate with Hamlet—and with Nicholas Nickleby, Jane Eyre, Henry Esmond, Daniel Deronda, or Jude—was not something they could easily afford.

Gifted with a "noble mind" (*Hamlet* 3.1.149), obsessed with his inner-most worth, proud to assert that he has "that within which passes show" (1.2.85), and outraged by "the spurns/That patient merit of th'unworthy takes" (3.1.75–76), Hamlet has severed virtue (his noble *mind*, his *within*, his *merit*) from its genealogical, blood-and-sex connection and internalized it, thus prompting the constitution of the psychological-moral domain of experience that Nancy Armstrong wrongly sees as an exclusively female invention (*Desire* 28–59). The fact that the eighteenth-century female con-sciousness moved on to colonize that particular domain shouldn't eclipse the very conspicuous fact that what she rightly calls "domestic fiction" (23) was discovered by the genus *man of feeling* whose first important specimen is Hamlet: in this light, Sterne's sentimental man and Joseph Andrews are not, as she believes, anomalies (4). The fact that, in Shakespeare's trag-edy, what De Grazia calls "the generational upset" (*Hamlet* 91, 100) is beholden to Hamlet's enforced dispossession should not stop us from real-izing the audacity of his compensatory "generational inversions" (107), of which fathering his own identity is perhaps the most impressive.

By protesting, very early in the play, "I know not 'seems'" (*Hamlet* 1.2.76), the prince enforces a distinction between *being* and *seeming* that crystallizes as the major objection to the aristocratic ideology, dominant in the play, that sought to naturalize (to deformalize) the *static unity of status and virtue* through the deployment of court rituals—exhibitions of deference, order, and hierarchy—which demanded of him an appropriate external behavior. Hamlet, we know, turns a deaf ear to that particular demand. His sarcastic advice to Polonius—"Use [men] after your own hon-our and dignity: the less they deserve, the more merit is in your bounty" (2.2.509–511)—speaks the arrogant truth of unbounded merit, invisible honor, and inexpressible dignity. But the existential authenticity on which he claims to fall back is of course no primeval ground. If he turns back, he meets soldiers, sentinels, "the baker's daughter" and the gravedigger. No urban bourgeoisie stands of course between his rank and that of the rustic commons. Only the "scholar" Horatio portends the emergence of a middle ground. Under these conditions, Hamlet must invent the mid-dle class.[8] As Schopenhauer pointed out, and Benjamin repeated, "bour-geois characters lack the height from which to fall" (*Origin* 111): what they did not say is that Hamlet's semi-voluntary fall makes middle-class characterization possible, "inventing the bourgeois subject as the proper telos of drama" (Reinhard and Lupton, *Oedipus* 122).[9] To that end, he clears out ground from the existing aristocratic space, and builds a DIY proto-bourgeoisie profile whose defining formal features are those of the *imaginary value*, namely "education, travel, and companionship". The primal horde is thus domesticated to "the boudoir culture of modern Denmark" (Reinhard and Lupton, *Oedipus* 76), and this way psychoanalysis gets started. Hamlet—the primordial analysand—enjoys high education (Elsinore, Wittenberg), extensive travel (Wittenberg, the city, England), and select companionship (Horatio).[10] He can walk, we are told, presumably with a book in his hand, for "four hours together" in "the lobby" (*Hamlet* 2.2.161–162). As a devoted playgoer (2.2.315–320), he can boast of an aesthetic education. It is no accident that the late-eighteenth-century theoretical formulation of this education should single him out as the earliest exemplar of the inchoate *aesthetic consciousness*.[11] For all his "extreme skepticism," conservative Hamlet indulges his own imaginary value, and sets out to traverse an *aesthetic fantasy of worth* that is largely a formal masterpiece of his own making: I didn't take revenge on my father's death, I failed to remember his manliness, my erotic affairs have miscarried, but you, he instructs Horatio, will remember me—you will "tell my story" (*Hamlet* 5.2.291). What story? We know of the centrality of storytelling in tragedies, of which Desdemona falling in love with Othello's life-narrative (*Othello* 1.3.127–169) is the grandest instance, but not of the in-built narrative destiny of evanescent tragedies. This is new. The transformation of *tragedy* into *story* takes of course a great deal of domestication, a turning away from the heroic towards the familial (Welsh 12–13). But there was world enough and time for Hamlet's story to become *the story*, the first bourgeois fantasy, competing in England with *The Pilgrim's Progress*, and translations of the *Odyssey*, *Don Quijote*, and *Guzman de Alfarache*, to represent the genetic matrix from which the new genre—the first modern English novel—sprang.[12] *Clarissa* and *Tom Jones*, let me recall, are two turgid rectifications of *Pamela* that look back extensively to *Hamlet*. The prince's fantasy of worth discounts the essentialist and substantialist prerogatives of the aristocratic ethos, disowns the birth strictures of genealogical nobility, and turns them into an *imaginary value*, retro-positing them as formal conditions of his own making—my words, my plays, my travels, my friends.[13] By yearning to posit his own necessary presuppositions—the cultural and social effects of his accidental status—he internalizes and aestheticizes the *fantasy of virtue* that is his story, turning worth (value) into a formal rather than a substantial thing. But this introjection of earliness (the internalization of his own self-created worth) can only be accomplished by forgetting his father—the genealogical cause of all his merit. This he cannot do, the commandment is too strong—"Remember me" (1.5.91)—but he can at least de-substantialize this particular memory and re-formalize it at wish: Hegel used to say that we remember best what we don't understand, perhaps refuse to understand, and Žižek tirelessly urges that "Law is grounded only in its own act of enunciation" (*Plague* 100). Hamlet needs and yearns to become *causa sui*, and this metaphysical feat is necessarily predicated—at the level of unconscious ideological mystification, of course—upon the radical abrogation of sexual procreation. Hamlet's relentless "sexual revulsion" (Freud 204) is not solely a symptom of the sexual inconsistency that signally erodes the play, nor a mere index of Puritanism: it reveals rather his deep-seated repudiation of substantial, blood-and-sex, genealogical identification.

Hamlet's dispossessed, disentitled, and disinherited condition has been eloquently highlighted by Margreta de Grazia:

> At his father's death, just at the point when an only son in a patrilineal system stands to inherit, Hamlet is dispossessed—and, as far as the court is concerned, legitimately. The promise of the patronymic is broken: Prince Hamlet does not become King Hamlet; Hamlet II does not step into the place of Hamlet I. The kingdom does not pass to the (adult and capable) only son of the dead king.
>
> (1)[14]

But Hamlet turns dispossession into an opportunity for repossession. Young Fortinbras is up for a similar transformation, but *value*, in his case, has nothing *imaginary* about it: he wants to repossess lost land (*Hamlet* 1.1.79–106). Hamlet's story begins in a crisis of disinheritance and dispossession. Everything substantial (power, command, possessions, offices) is lost, and so is the *Blut und Boden* ideology of semen, blood, and soil that sustains the ruling apparatus. But only that. For the imaginary value is not—is never lost, that is, on those on whom nothing is lost. And although Hamlet may not want to remember the content of his father's "commandment," he cannot forget the *value* and *idea* of his father: "He was a man. Take him for all in all,/I shall not look upon his like again" (*Hamlet* 1.2.186–187); "So excellent a king that was to this/Hyperion to a satyr" (1.2.139–40); "A combination and a form indeed/Where every god did seem to set his seal" (3.4.59–60). By clinging to the *idea*—the terms *look, excellence,* and *form* all confirm a Platonic ontology of forms—of the father rather than to the actual commanding father—the obscene, excessive, super-egoic embodiment of the Law—he brings about a further emptying out and *anestheticization* of the superego. Hamlet's conservative gesture is moreover reactive in that it purports to formally reduce the substantive contribution of a revolutionary present, represented in the play by the political energies of Laertes and Fortinbras. As Badiou has noted, the conservative mentality refuses to incorporate itself to the new present that springs as an evental horizon, but "it is caught up in a subjective formalism that is not, and cannot be, the pure permanence of the old" (*Logics* 54).

## III

In this chapter I want to argue that Henry James—along with some of his major characters, including Hyacinth—is prepossessed by Hamlet, who is dispossessed. Hamlet haunts, biases, and influences James, predisposing him to take the path of resurgence and prepossessing reappropriation— "This is I,/Hamlet the Dane" (*Hamlet* 5.1.241–242)—to follow the course that goes from dispossession to repossession. Much in Hamlet's sense of dispossession appears to us a consequence of his active, though melancholy-induced, misanthropy. But to postulate Hamlet's demotion as a matter of strict personal choice is misleading. For two basic reasons. First, because he is a first son obliged by reasons of state to adopt the deflationary role of second son: the fact that Denmark is an elective monarchy deprives him of the one paternal prerogative (kingship) he could have aspired to claim, and this spells a condition of disinheritance that is further aggravated by his uncle's usurpation of the nuclear family position.[15] Second, because the revelation of his mother's emotional-sexual attachment to his uncle could prompt speculation about potential adultery, and inevitably cast a shadow of uncertainty over the legitimacy of his own birth: is Hamlet the son of his own uncle and therefore a *bastard*? Does he smell that particular fault? Is he disgusted? This is unclear, but we do know that he is resentful with the way his prospects of promotion—coming into his inheritance—have been thwarted. "I lack advancement," he tells Rosencrantz at 3.2.311, in what reads as a premonitory formulation of the modern theme, dear to James, of the *missed life* (Pippin, *James* 95). To a certain extent, therefore, the inactive Hamlet performs a shocking, compensatory overreaction: he remodels his restraining conditions into enabling circumstances and turns the *revenge tragedy* on which he has landed into a standard *story of second son*, or a *novel of bastardy*. Just like James and Dickens were second sons, Hamlet is also a second son—not only because the first one (the heroic scion of legitimate patrilineal descent) is missing, but also because Shakespeare's first son Hamnet went missing. In dialectical terms, this belated and determined subject introjects (constructs) his own earliness and posits his own presuppositions. Like Machiavelli's prince, Hamlet seeks to *maîtriser son commencement* (Althusser, *Machiavel*, 127)—to begin, that is, where he wishes to begin, a place we may symbolically identify with a hole in the ground, Ophelia's grave. As Dover Wilson sharply observed, since Hamlet's antic disposition predates his decision to fake it, we may infer that "Shakespeare wishes us to feel that Hamlet assumes madness before he cannot help it" (92). Thus before he confesses "I lack advancement," Hamlet has already chosen a more essential *lack*. Is bourgeois *conservative ideology* the *imaginative madness* resulting from a lack? How much of Hamlet's free but gaping consciousness made it into Swift's? And into James's?

Let me try to respond succinctly to the second question. The story "The Birthplace" and the "Introduction" to *The Tempest* make up the most unambiguous intersections between the names of Shakespeare and James, and they have received much critical attention. But James' prepossession by Shakespeare is far from restricted to these two texts. Recall that the English poet is given pride of place in a list of inhabitants in James' house of fiction—"Shakespeare, Goethe and Charles Lamb"—and that, although this may obey a strictly chronological logic, the fact is that he "walked arm-in-arm with Shakespeare". If, furthermore, we factor in the related facts that Lamb's presence in the house is inseparable from that of the first distinguished resident, and that the esteem of Goethe in England owes part of its force to the Hamlet excursus in *Wilhelm Meister*, then the precedence of Shakespeare's name takes on a distinction not solely imputable to chronological anteriority. Nonetheless, though pride of place is not only due to pride of time, Shakespeare's antecedence is of course the material precondition of his work's determining force over the novelistic writing of his extended progeny (Swift, Richardson, Fielding, Austen, Dickens, James, Joyce . . .). Moreover, to the genealogical narrative of the history of the English novel, *Hamlet* somewhat represents a furtive root inscription, his narrative figures (demotion, wandering, speculation, critique, sacrifice, renunciation) working as masterless *tropes instituteurs* (Derrida, *Marges* 261). Furtive and masterless because the narrative cannot fully account for (symbolize) its enabling condition, one that is however on par with the rest: as a structural cause, the play-text *Hamlet* remains immanent to the field of its novelistic effects. *Hamlet*, we know, is not a novel, but it is presupposed and implied in the reading experience of many a novel, and not only of the Anglo-American tradition: think of *Fathers and Sons* and *The Idiot*, to mention only another major tradition. Alexander Welsh has recently pointed out that Hamlet is "the first great story in Europe of a young man growing up" (14), an inaccurate statement (Spanish picaresque fiction dates back to the mid-1500s) that could be correctly rephrased as "the first great story in Europe of a young educated, cultivated, and refined man growing up."[16] De Grazia has rightly noted that "existing independently of the play in which he appears, [Hamlet] glides freely into other texts, both fictional and theoretical" (4), but she omits that it is precisely the prince's dispossession—his incapacity to reclaim his inheritance of land and title—that *entitles* him to become the first modern hero. "Hamlet's disengagement from the land-driven plot is," she observes, "the very precondition of the modernity ascribed to him after 1800. Adrift from the plot, he assumes the self-determining autonomy that opens him to later projections" (4).

This is only partly accurate: first, because Hamlet's disengagement is more radical, including his unmooring from the heroic plot; and second, because seen from this more inclusive angle, the self-determining autonomy the prince assumes in his literary afterlives can be traced back to the mid-1700s, with *Tom Jones* and *Clarissa*. Fielding's novel houses the first long novelistic *excursus* on *Hamlet*, and Richardson's masterpiece unwittingly coronates one of the tragedy's inevitable projections, the aristocratic rake Robert Lovelace.

Admittedly, therefore, the cross-textual gliding of the Hamlet persona is a necessary precondition for the constitution of the modern novelistic space: Goethe's *Wilhelm Meister* and Lamb's narrative "Hamlet" provide *ex post facto* evidence of this plausibility. Indeed, its reputation as *abortive* (T.S. Eliot) or *problem play* (Tylliard) evinces a generic lack of definition that may well have worked as a tacit compositional premise in Shakespeare's non-normative and anticlassical imagination. Following Lamb's powerful cue, some scholars like Burton Raffel have suggested that in his plays, and especially in *Hamlet*, Shakespeare was looking past the stage, reaching behind the plays to something (an imaginary value?) that these only defectively put forward. He might have been hinting at a "poem unlimited" (*Hamlet* 2.2.382) or at a "dramatic essay in mystery" (Dover Wilson 19); a definition has the rare virtue of looking forward to James' best tales. Tragedy, poem, essay, tale, perhaps novel. To conceive of *Hamlet*, genetically and generically, as the cause of a twofold narrative effect—the story (narrative 1) of the English novel (narrative 2)—serves also to confirm the standard wisdom that novels are *ex definitione* riddled by thoroughgoing *Oedipalization* (genealogical effects, father-son rivalry, sexual jealousy, parricide, incest). Thus the English novel occurs when the dispersive and de-oedipalizing forces that constitute the textual field at large—think of picaresque fiction, Defoe, Scott, Cooper, Thackeray, Melville, Stevenson, Pynchon—lose part of their hold and a story (a mythos, a plot) begins to thicken around the magnet of a core family conflict, the kind of thing that happens, say, in *Pierre; or, the Ambiguities* and *Vineland*. It happens, in brief, when characters reenter the house to become repossessed by their tutelary ghosts and disciplined by a domestic plot. This occurs, for instance, in "Master Eustace," "Guest's Confession," and "Owen Wingrave," three tales by James whose Hamletian quality has been duly detected by critics.[17]

During the years following the writing and publication of "Master Eustace" in 1871, James crammed his letters to siblings and friends with echoes of *Hamlet*. A propensity for this particular tragedy ran in the family. William, in letter to his sister (Berlin, 17 October 1867), described a dinner at a professor's home in which a "discussion" broke out "about the madness of Hamlet—G. being convinced that Shakespeare *meant* to mystify the reader, and intentionally constructed a riddle." On his way home, William visited his sister. He had "exhausted Europe in a few weeks, finding it stale, flat and unprofitable" (*Letters of William James* 289). Henry's later letters of 1872–1873 are particularly drenched in overt or implicit allusion. He describes a ball at the opera as "stale, flat & unprofitable" (*Complete Letters 1872–1876 I* 158), tells Grace Norton that "sweet bells jangled" (*Hamlet* 3.1.120–149) (188), alludes to the "Danish envoy" (203), tells his sister Alice that "John is to Edmund as a Satyr to Hyperion" (264), alludes to Ernesto Rossi's Amleto (286), whimpers he has "been feeling of late rather heavy headed & seedy & absurdly incapable of dealing with book or pen" (287), tells his brother William (19 May 1873) that "my conscience gnaws me" (291) and Elizabeth Boot that "there is a somebody who shapes our ends" (315) and "I could have flung myself into the lake for desperate melancholy" (316). Much later, in August 1881, he will complain of his "too, too solid serial," referring to *The Portrait of a Lady* (*Life in Letters* 131). While most of these echoes are literal, others are keenly evocative of themes and motifs in the play, notably inaction, misanthropy, melancholy, and remorse. Most of these literal echoes remain undetected, under-glossed, and unannotated in critical editions of the letters. I take this neglect of attention to an indubitable fact of literary influence—perhaps *affluence* is the right term—as a foil for the relevance of the *Hamletian subjectivation of James's authorial persona* that is here my intention to highlight.[18] What emerges from the letters is the composite figure of a lonely young man morbidly and prematurely shrouded in skeptical spectatorial resignation; a young man who assumes the madness of his lack before he cannot help it. Disinterested and distanced from practical life, this man travels however towards a *position of intellectual freedom*. The liberty to fall into proto-Bohemian stagnancies of detached contemplation and melancholy indecision—the liberty, in short, to deliberate—that the young James exhibits in these epistles will be transferred to many of his young heroes—from Roderick Hudson to Gray in *The Ivory Tower*. Their effort at securing a site of distant spectatorial emancipation—from societal conventions and domestic-plot gravitations—is invariably bolstered by the adoption of the Hamlet role. Of course, they don't always succeed. Hamlet summoned by the ghost toward a cliff and Hamlet jumping into Ophelia's grave are incidental configurations that remind us of the necessary limits to the hero's free existential compass, of the curtailment of his liberty. It is hard to become a disinterested Bohemian flaneur when your father returns from death and your girlfriend commits suicide. Things are no easier if your mother dies in prison, while serving a sentence for murdering your father, and you are forced to restore your *standard* (your identity, your merit, your worth) from a very low social position.

## IV

*The Princess Casamassima* is full of Hamlet resonances, running from implicit echoes to explicit allusions: the "ulcers and sores of London" (91), the "bodkin" (105), the "fishmongers" (106), "the insolence of office" (282), the "little band of malcontents" (282), "the rotten fabric of the actual social order" (288), the "old societies that have run to seed, corrupt, exhausted civilisations" (352). The proverbial notion that "a cat may look at a king" (545) echoes the warning that "a man may fish with the worm that hath eat of a king" (*Hamlet* 4.3.26). When Poupin tells Hyacinth that "the conscience of the individual is absolute," he repeats Hamlet's warning to Rosencrantz: "Call me what instrument you will, though you can fret me, yet you cannot play upon me" (3.2.341). And Hyacinth "hanging about" Christina (485) reminds us of Gertrude hanging on her former husband (1.2.143). In his edition of the novel, Adrian Poole annotates other echoic phrases like "the 'Sun and Moon'" (511, n152), "a play within the play" (512, n157), and "more sorrow than anger" (531, n310). All of these may appear random and disconnected figurative echoes, but their addition produces a very uncanny effect. Surprisingly, very little critical attention has been devoted to it.[19] How alive was James when writing this novel in the mid-1880s to the fact that he was somehow rewriting *Hamlet* is hard to say. But by the time he wrote the "Preface" in 1907 he seemed rather confident:

> The agents in any drama are interesting only in proportion as they feel their respective situations, since the consciousness, on their part, of the complication exhibited forms for us their link of connection with it. But there are degrees of feeling—the muffled, the faint, the just sufficient, the barely intelligent, as we may say; and the acute, the intense, the complete, in a word—the power to be finely aware and richly responsible. It is those move in this latter fashion who "get most" out of all that happens to them and who in so doing enable us, as readers of their record, as participators by a fond attention, algo to get most. Their being finely aware—as Hamlet and Lear, say, are finely aware—makes absolutely the intensity of their adventure, gives the maximum sense to what befalls them. We care, our curiosity and our sympathy care, comparatively little for what happens to the stupid, the coarse and the blind; care for it, and for the effects of it, at the most as helping to precipitate what happens to the more deeply wondering, to the really sentient. Hamlet and Lear are surrounded, amid their complications, by the stupid and the blind, who minister in all sorts of ways to their recorded fate.
>
> (35–36)

Similarly, he goes on to argue, the career of his "tormented youth" (Hyacinth) is conditioned by persons of more limited sense. But his "intelligent creature," signally described as "all beset and all perceptive," manages to "adventurously [. . .] dream and hazard and attempt" (35–36). Two things stand out: 1) like Hamlet, Hyacinth is a figure of deep sentience and compendious consciousness; In the "Preface" to *The Tragic Muse*, James had already invoked "the prodigious consciousness of Hamlet, the most capacious and most crowded" (1113), the consciousness of *the man of feeling*; and 2) James internalizes the notion of the "adventure" and the "adventurous"—just as there is a "complication" of the dramatic situation, there is also a "complication" of the consciousness that responds to it "feelingly" (*King Lear* 4.6.145) in order to grasp it. Hamlet's and Hyacinth's parallel adventure is one of knowledge. Theirs is a story of consciousness—a hermeneutic *plot* (*récit*) that endeavors to process the incidents of a *story* (*histoire*). But since the latter complication (the *proairetic* knot) is always-already dialectically mediated by a formalizing-cum-teleological drive of interpretation (the hermeneutic tangle), then we can conclude that the kind of narrative adventure sponsored by *Hamlet* is to give up a story (a revenge tragedy) in favor of another (a domestic-psychological novel), and therefore to exchange a vexing role (avenger) for a better part (sensitive witness). This is done by the novelistic hero as much as by his framing voice, that of the narrator. The latter is for James, the supreme intelligence:

> The teller of a story is primarily [. . .] the listener to it, the reader of it, too; and having needed thus to make it out, distinctly, on the crabbed page of life, to disengage from the rude human character and the more or less gothic text in which it has been packed away, the essence of his affair has been the imputing of intelligence. The basis of his attention has been that such and such an imbroglio has got started—on the page of life—because of something that some one has felt and more or less understood.
>
> ("Preface" 36)

In brief, Shakespeare imputes intelligence to Hamlet so that he may distinctly *make out* a story—"my story" (*Hamlet* 5.2.291)—on the crabbed page of life, and thus to freely disengage from the rude human character (a noble heroic avenger) and the more or less Gothic text (the revenge tragedy) in which this story had been presumably packed away. Thus the new tragedy titled *Hamlet* narrates the *cognitive adventure* of an intelligence that makes his story out of the debris of an old medieval legend of brutal revenge. James's allusions in the "Preface" to the ancient conflict between "flurried humans" and "bored Olympians," and to personal "bewilderment" before "the mysterious decrees of Providence" serve to reinforce further the tragic, at bottom Hamletian, backdrop of a story featuring Hyperion, Jove, Mars, Mercury, cursed spites, strange spirits, defied auguries, and fallen sparrows. *Making out* takes, for James, the analytical form of a separation, a disengaging, a *disembedding*.[20] This cross-generic, metaleptic disembedding makes the genre of the novel possible. A novel worthy of the name is not the chronicle of actions or sentiments—that is the province of the *adventure* and the *romance*, respectively, albeit often conjointly—but rather the intelligent interpretation of actions and sentiments that the author imputes to the narrator, and the narrator not seldom to the novel's central consciousness. I have already noted that no other major Shakespeare tragedy construes its events retrospectively, at its close, as the incidents of a *story* open to retelling.[21] Only *The Tragedy of Hamlet, Prince of Denmark* finalizes with its presumptive transmutation into a novel, and implicitly with the invitation—sent out to us, who still "look pale and tremble at this chance" (5.2.276)—to mutely listen to it or read it. It is no accident then that, in accordance with the genealogical narrative of the novel that James tacitly endorses, he should illustrate this novelistic principle of controlling intelligence with the case—of all novels—of *the* novel, *Tom Jones*. In the "Preface," James describes the protagonist of Fielding's novel as a finely and intimately bewildered young man that is devoid of imagination. But this lack, he explains, doesn't disqualify him as the protagonist of a modern novel, for he can compensate for it with a number of riches—his bonhomie and excess of "life," for instance, which amounts "almost to his having a mind, that is to his having reactions and a full consciousness" ("Preface" 41). In addition, there is always the narrating voice of Fielding, who is "handsomely possessed of a mind" with "such an amplitude of reflexion for him and round him that we see [Jones] through the mellow air of Fielding's fine old moralism, fine old humour and fine old style" (41). In other words, the fact that *Tom Jones* incorporates the composite consciousness of its author and its protagonist, adding intellectual reflection to life experience, turns it—we may infer—into an essential link connecting *Hamlet* with nineteenth-century fiction. Thus the tradition of the novel presupposes a lineage of *enlarged consciousnesses*, and it is to this family of "intense perceivers" (42) that Hyacinth, gifted with a "passion of intelligence" (43), belongs. There is also a structural symmetry in the way Mr Vetch and Poupin repeat John Blifil and Roger Thwackum: the four are surrogate fathers and unlikely tutors, a function awkwardly anticipated, in *Hamlet*, by Claudius and Polonius.

Interestingly, as if recoiling from the evoked Hamlet case, James warns against the dangers of an excessive intelligence and sensitivity: "If he knows more than is likely or natural," this will make him "false and impossible." It is important to stress that this falsity, this impossibility, is the very deadlock that both *Hamlet* and *The Princess Casamassima* seek to dramatize. Hence, perhaps, their implosive—suicidal—closure. In fact, the tradition of the novel could only get underway through such impossibility: the tragedy *Hamlet* liberates, via the sacrifice of its reflective protagonist, the broad mental space—the gap, the infinite critical distance—requisite for the ideological fiction of reality (realism) to materialize, in the novel, and be thrown into relief. For James, to know is to know a monadic fraction of the totality that is society, and this amounts to grasping the logic of its dual antagonism. On the one hand, the antagonism of sexual inconsistency, the crude, cyclical, irreparable fact of sexual origins and ends, the fact that sex is (*Das Sein*), that sexual being is moreover behind human being—and that we ignore what it is (*Was Sein*): in Lacanian terms "there is no sexual relationship." On the other hand, the antagonism of status inconsistency, the volatile, recursive, inexorable fiction of social categorization, the fact that rank and class *are not*, that social being is nothing—even if we know what they *are*, that they are, in fact, all there is, as Maria and Streher will confirm in their Continental scanning of "types": in Lacanese, "there is no society." Quite often, both inconsistencies jointly expose a fissure in the Real. Christina's request to Hyacinth—"I expect you to take me into the slums—into very bad places" (253)—is not only a mislaid invitation to dirty sex.[22] It is rather dirty sex in the making, an imaginary appeal to confront the locus where the Real rends the fabric of the symbolic. Paul and Hyacinth are once described as homosocially uniting in "a subterranean crusade against the existing order of things" (152), just like Hamlet associates under oath with his own set of confederates (Horatio and Marcellus), in a scene dominated by the underground labor of the fellow in the cellarage, the obscene, paternal mole (*Hamlet* 1.5.115–191). As Derrida brilliantly suggested (*Spectres of Marx* 154), this mole and the porpentine (or porcupine) are both figurative materializations both of the ghost and of whatever the ghost is trying to conjure away, and nothing suits better a mislaid invitation to (dirty sex in) the slums than being lured, like Aeneas, underground by a mole. Only walking "arm-in-arm with Shakespeare" can, I guess, compete with that. But then, of course, Pippin doesn't "fully understand the claims about holes in the fabric of being," and Pippin is an honorable man.

Similarly, Hamlet's impossible relationship with Ophelia is riddled from the outset both from revulsion at the rank and gross fact of sexual inconsistency—Hamlet cannot dissociate pure and honest Ophelia from lusty and dishonest Gertrude, and therefore from "the disgusting substance of life" (Žižek, *Plague* 83)—and from the vexing internalization of status inconsistency (by being told by her ruling males that the rake prince is socially out of her league, Ophelia learns more than Nanda).[23] In *Hamlet*, the "contemplation of foul things" (401) and of "reality of the horrors" (401) that Christina dreams with and Hyacinth courts is still turned toward an interiority plagued by morbidity and sinfulness: the prince breaks into Ophelia's chamber "As if he had been loosed out of hell/ To speak of horrors,—he comes before me" (*Hamlet* 2.1.84–85) and later tells her: "I could accuse me of such things that it were better my mother had not borne me" (*Hamlet* 3.1.127). The horror, the horror.

## V

However integral to *Hamlet* and *The Princess Casamassima*, the problem of sexual discordance—the unlikelihood of the sexual relationship—is subordinated to the more central impossibility of society. In a novel where those standing above are concerned "about the lower orders, the rising democracy, the spread of nihilism, and all that" (188), it stands to reason that rank antagonism should become a central issue. Indeed, the *question of status inconsistency* becomes itself tendentially thematized in the novel as "the social question" (122, 345) and described as "the impending change of the relations of class with class" (245). This inconsistency is therefore best ascertained as the central characters' tendency to put their received social identity (rank, status, social class) under unbearable pressure. The victim of blood-aristocratic degeneration, the prince Casamassima is an effete endowed with "aristocratic slimness" (234).[24] His wife's social class remains shrouded in mystery. When Hyacinth tells Paul that it is appropriate for "a woman of that class" to want "to know what is going on among the like of us," Paul replies: "It depends upon what class you mean" (208). Christina claims to have "no possessions" (411), "nothing in the world" (412). We learn that she has given up a lot to retain a status warranted through a marriage whose legal securities she is unwilling to forgo. She doesn't contemplate the possibility of waiving "her right" and accepting the legal solution of a "separate maintenance." She would rather return to the prince than dare "to face the loss of luxury" (323). Hyacinth doesn't understand. Nor do we; this major flaw in her moral constitution is at odds with her yearning to join the revolutionary cause. Verging on revelation, Hyacinth wonders whether he would not find her "rather vulgar" (267). Christina is alert to the fact that "in the darkest hour of her life she sold herself for a title and a fortune" (259), but this awareness doesn't place her above ideological mystification.[25] She is far from invulnerable to bad faith and specious rationalization. She poses as "a person for whom the aristocracy was a collection of bores" (312), claims to "have very little respect for distinctions of class" (247) and judges it "convenient" to "[overstep] them" (247). In conversation with Hyacinth, she professes to endeavor to "fill up the inconvenient gulf that yawns between my position and yours? You know what I think of 'positions'" (324). This gulf is the hole in the fabric of society. But then, alas, Pippin doesn't "fully understand the claims about holes in the fabric of being," and Pippin is an honorable man.

The filling up of that generic gulf commands the efforts of other characters, like Lady Aurora, who claims not to know anything about her "position" (*Princess* 223). Reluctance to accept a socially received position places Christina and Lady Aurora in parallel but antithetical roles—beggar playing princess and princess playing beggar, respectively. Both profit from a time-out-of-joint in order to reprocess *position* as *posture*, if not *posing*. The social latitude of Captain Sholto and Millicent raises a different kind of problem. Sholto is vulgar but "unmistakably a gentleman" (223), and Millicent is "plebeian but brilliant" (231), "another London type" (231), whose father worked in the pit of a mine when Rosy was ten:

> Yes, in the mines, where the filthy coal is dug out. That's where my father came from—he was working in the pit when he was a child of ten. He never had a day's schooling in his life; but he climbed up out of his black hole into daylight.
>
> (146)

Hamlet the Dane also came from a black hole—Ophelia's grave and nothing—into daylight, and perhaps into himself. But then, of course, Robert Pippin doesn't "fully understand the claims about holes in the fabric of being," and Pippin is an honorable man.

But Hyacinth, tormented from birth by "the mysteries of his lineage" (219), is by far the most socially displaced person in the novel. Mr. Vetch's question to Christina reveals his contradiction: "I don't understand you very well. If you like him because he's one of the lower orders, how can you like him because he's a swell?" (466) But also Christina's, obviously. Although he knows to be "out" of society, he is determined to become, "among the disinherited," the one who will "keep up the standard" (164). What standard? The fact that there is "blood in [his] veins that is not the blood of the people" (219) lends a grotesque ratification to entitlement to his being called, by Christina, a "tremendous aristocrat" (463), and by Mr. Vetch "a little aristocrat" (465). The ironic tenderness of this converging designation is overpowered by the *bruta facta* of a personal history marked by status inconsistency. This generates a constant *anxiety of affiliation*. When introduced to the Marchant family at Medley Hall, a place where butlers stand behind your chair, "insidious distinctions" are "made" and "shades of importance illustrated" (300), he is pleased to confirm that his "station" has not been discovered.

The distinction of rank is the most basic. Later, when Hyacinth suggests to Madame Grandoni that they are different because she doesn't "have her living to get, every day," she pauses in the doorway and replies,

" 'I believe I am nearly as poor as you. And I have not, like you, the appearance of nobility. Yet I am noble,' said the old lady, shaking her wig. 'And I am not!' Hyacinth rejoined, smiling" (305). James's *social reality*—a pleonastic phrase if there ever was one—is inconceivable without the *Traumarbeit* of "insidious distinctions." For Hyacinth, achieving such distinction amounts to cashing the imaginary value (opportunities for education, travel, and companionship) his personal circumstances (*milieu, race, lieu*) have supposedly deprived him from. James's father wrote that

> a true society would guarantee to every man woman and child, for the whole term of his natural life, food, clothing, shelter, and the opportunities of an education adapted to his tastes; leaving all the *distinction* he might achieve to himself, to his own genius freely influencing the homage of his fellow men.
>
> (qtd. by Matthiessen, *James family* 12)

To achieve distinction is therefore to *formalize* your interiority in *conformity* to *formative* experiences and this formalization amounts to the separationist constitution of an inside nothing—spirit, soul, mind—one may boastfully redescribe as everything. It is not casual that Hyacinth's singularity is described through Platonic tropes of empty paradigmatic interiority: "a fine example," "greatness of soul" (289). The operation of constructing oneself a consciousness (and conscience) is, Poupin reminds Hyacinth, therefore contingent on social determinants: "You owe me no explanations; the conscience of the individual is absolute, except, of course, in those classes in which, from the very nature of the infamies on which they are founded, no conscience can exist" (*Princess* 405). *Absolute* means unrestricted: *absolvere* is to make separate, from *ab* "off, away from" + *solvere* "to loosen, untie, release, detach." Conscience is absolute because detached, and is therefore also distinct—like individual people, for liberal conservatives like James, and liberal radicals like Derrida or Sedgwick. The spiritual *nothing* separates you from others (the aristocratic brutes, the bourgeois philistines, the people) but also—alas—from yourself. *Distinction* derives from *distinguere* "to separate between, keep separate, mark off, distinguish," perhaps literally "separate by pricking," which in turn comes from the assimilated form of *dis-* "apart" + *-stinguere* "to prick." To *prick*, in turn, is to make a mark or shallow hole with a pointed instrument. The prick is both the hole and the projecting member, weapon, or instrument that brings it into being. To *distinguish* is thus to aggravate the gash (the nothing) of an inconsistency (a difference, a separation) by means of a patriarchal, and potentially analytical, weapon. I *mean* indeed *country matters*. Call it, say, *phallogocentrism*. According to McGinn, Hamlet "has looked within, as Hume did later, and found not a coherent, substantial self but a mysterious chasm, a gap where the simple self ought to be, a kind of throbbing nothingness" (43). What McGinn doesn't say is that Hamlet looked within because something outside badly in-consisted (was out of joint) and the gap he discovered was the speculative effect—the delay or interval—inserted by his own looking: it is unsafe to look at a mirror when one is past the imaginary and the symbolic phases. But then, of course, Robert Pippin doesn't "fully understand the claims about holes in the fabric of being," and Pippin is an honorable man.

Miss Pynsent, for instance, is terrified with the contingency of Hyacinth marrying "beneath his station" (105): "His station!—poor Hyacinth had often asked himself, and Miss Pysent, what it could possibly be" (105). Although he fancies Millicent, Hyacinth can tell Miss Pynsent that "the kind of girl that would look at me is the kind of girl I wouldn't look at" (156). This reminds us of Laertes' warning Ophelia to keep "out of the shoot and danger" of Hamlet's "desire" (1.3.35) because he is "subject to his birth" (1.3.17). Laertes is right, for Hamlet's social arrogance at 3.1.91–160 can hardly be dissimulated. Actually, his remark to Polonius about the way his "daughter may conceive" (2.2.186) is anything but socially unbiased.

## V

The constitution of Bohemia proved convenient for the reallocation of dis-affiliated subjects in situations of fin-de-siècle social-ideological crisis and transition.[26] Mr. Vetch and Christina are described as having been Bohemi-ans, but the label could also be loosely attached to Captain Sholto and Lady Aurora. What about Hyacinth? When Mr. Vetch tells him that he is neither aristocrat nor bourgeois, but a Bohemian, "Hyacinth was only half satis-fied with this, for it was by no means definite to him that Bohemians were also to be saved; if he could be sure, perhaps he would become one him-self" (124). In another place, Sholto tells Madame Grandoni that Hyacinth "looks much more like a poet, or a pianist, or a painter" (350), and it was uncertain whether the revolution could spare these superfluous members of society. And yet, with historicist hindsight, we realize that the category could have saved him, that as a near-perfect Bohemian (semi-aristocratic, disinherited, bookish, sensible), he could have entered an emerging homo-social fraternity of artists, dodged the political temptation, perhaps sur-vived as a dark Hardy underdog. But he didn't. Neither did Hamlet, whose artistic subjectivation was thwarted, from the outset, not only by the inher-ited complexity of his political position, but also by the traumatic weight of a domestic tragedy. His famous lament—"The time is out of joint. O cursed spite,/That ever I was born to set it right!" (1.5.189–190)—conjures both the magnitude of the domestic violation (fratricide, incest) and the proto-existentialist desolation at the crude fact of birth.

Hyacinth enjoys the Hamletian freedom of perambulation and specu-lation. He seeks to steer clear from the Oedipal gravitations of a family plot or domestic tragedy. His interest in revolutionary politics looks like a preemptive way of eluding the hardship of domestic entrapment. As we saw in the "Introduction," this abstention prompts the parallel banish-ment of a woman from the plot—towards the figurative exile of a nunnery, or the literal locale of death. In *The Princess Casamassima*, Ophelia is dismembered into several women: first, the childhood friend and sweet-heart Millicent, "forsaken maiden" (158) and "magnificently plebeian" (160); second, the aristocratic saint (Lady Aurora); and third, the deprived bedridden proletarian (Rose). None of the three becomes the conspicuous object of Hyacinth's like or dislike—he more or less gives them up for the equivocal charms (the "standard" or "imaginary value") of the Princess. Still, Rose is the most adept repetition of Ophelia, not only because she and Hyacinth are both named after flowers, but also because she is also the sister of Paul, who conceivably stands for Laertes—caring brother (147) but chiefly man of action, pragmatic and determined, inside courtier and revolutionary initiate.[27]

The boy Hyacinth is "shrinking and sensitive" (61), and already "ironi-cal" at the age of ten (56). His powers of internalization are remarkable. "The child," we are told, "would take everything in and keep it" (63). His entitlement to become a second Hamlet—the unripe man of "mind impatient" and "unmanly grief" (1.2.94–96) on whom nothing is lost— is therefore safely warranted. Also propitious, in this connection, is his contradictory social characterization: whereas some see him as a "little gentleman" (56), the fiddler describes him as "a prostitute's bastard" (71). The boy grows into a man subject to spells of chronic infantility. Milli-cent, for instance, notes "his incurable verdancy" (159), and everyone per-ceives his "morbid vanity" (165). These apparent psychological symptoms are expressions of a deeper ideological impasse, informed by sexual and status antagonism. Hamlet is of course no *gentleman*, but his voluntary demotion lays the groundwork for his becoming one, and although he is nowhere described as a *bastard*, the inference is written large across the play's unconscious script. In *The Poetics of Melancholy in Early Modern England*, Douglas Trevor argues that

> Hamlet clearly views his mother's coupling with her second husband as a betrayal of her first, ushering into the semantics of his self-construction the unsettling insinuation that he is perhaps an illegitimate son, since a single betrayal of the husband renders the wife vulnerable to endless speculation about her fidelity.
>
> (82)

Considering the prince's extraordinary imaginative powers, especially when it comes to the visualization of his mother's lust, this "insinuation" becomes indeed highly probable. This conjectural line of thought is further reinforced by the fact that in both relevant sources, Belleforest and Saxo Grammaticus, Gertrude had "coupled" with Claudius before her husband's death. As de Grazia has explained, "Denmark's electoral constitution [. . .] allows for a situation impossible in a primogenitary monarchy: the Prince remains at court in company of the King who was preferred over him" (88–89). King Hamlet, moreover, "made no provision to secure the succession of his son against the contending claims that might legitimately arise in an elective monarchy" (91). This oversight can be accounted for by adducing the revulsion of bastardy as motivation. In fact, de Grazia later recalls Laertes' explicit warning (4.5.117–120) to the effect that "revenge puts the legitimacy of a son to the test. Any reluctance to avenge a father's murder disgraces the entire family triangle, proving the son a bastard, the mother an adulteress, the father a cuckold" (93). Trevor speaks, confidently, of "Hamlet's existence as a bastard" (82), and bastardy, we know, is the embodiment of social trauma—a combination of sexual antagonism and status inconsistency.[28] Finally, let me recall that in James's first reworking of *Hamlet*, the boy (Eustace-Hamlet) is the bastard son of Mrs. Garnyer (Gertrude) and Mr. Cope (Claudius).

## VI

Like *Hamlet*, then, *The Princess Casamassima* enacts a hardship of status inconsistency. Tony Tanner has written that "while [Hyacinth] can never be at home in his own class, he can never hope to gain lasting access to one above him. He has no one. He was nowhere to go—indeed nowhere to *be*" (*James* 63). Nowhere to *be* or *not to be*. His tragic family history explains, of course, a great deal. Constant reference is made to "the anecdote of his origin, of his mother's disaster" (282), to "the dim, dreadful, confused legend of his mother's history" (166). As he grows up, he begins to flesh out "the horror of his mother's history" (169): "he reconstructed his antecedents, took the measure, so far as was possible, of his heredity" (167). On reading old issues of *The Times*, he discovers that "the reflection that he was a bastard involved in a remarkable manner the reflection that he was a gentleman" (168). Such reasoning is inverted in *Hamlet*, for the prince's decision to *become* a gentleman—launched towards a future story—involved most remarkably the suspicion that he *was* a bastard—hanging from an archaic tragedy. Still, the structural symmetry remains behind the chiasmus, and so does the plot's moral core: both stories revolve around the mother's sexual fault—incest with a brother-in-law (Gertrude), extramarital sex with an aristocratic lover (Florentine). The difference is that Hamlet awakens to his mother's mischief more suddenly, during the conversation with the ghost—although he already harbored a profound distaste for the alacrity of his mother's second marriage. Nonetheless, the "moral shock" (Dover Wilson 43) is the same. Both are being asked to reconcile with the criminal evidence of their mothers' lust: Hamlet is requested not to harm his mother, and speaks daggers to her during a bedroom and bed-ridden conversation, and the child Hyacinth (in a scene parallel to Oliver's closing visit to Faggin) is forced to accompany his stepmother to the prison room where his mother lies dying.[29] Both, in short, respond to this interpellation from the meshes and convolutions of a *bastard course* (Derrida, *Glas* 6)—a surreptitious track that confounds the continuities of pure genealogy.[30] Miss Pynsent realizes that Hyacinth's mother "couldn't call him after a man she had murdered" (168). When Hamlet salutes Horatio for the first time, a brief exchange follows: "HAMLET. Horatio—or I do forget myself. HORATIO. The same, my lord, and your poor servant ever. HAMLET. Sir, my good friend; I'll change that name with you" (*Hamlet* 1.2.162–163). Not only is the prince revealing his eagerness to declass. He is also signifying alertness to the impropriety of his carrying *le Nom-du-père*. In both cases, virtual bastardy stands for the structural event of genealogical discontinuity, and Oedipus makes the structure work, for "French mothers are usually so much to their sons" (202). Their being so much, their excessive sexual attention to family males, is the cause of discontinuity. At bottom, the mother's fault turns into an impossible bottom, a receding hole, a persistent fracture in the (symbolic) fabric of her being, open to inspection by anyone but herself:

> O Hamlet, speak no more!
> Thou turn'st mine eyes into my very soul,
> And there I see such black and grained spots
> As will not leave their tinct.
>                    (*Hamlet* 3.4.78–81)

Freud saw in Irma's throat "a white spot and scabby turbinal bones." The difference between the soul and the throat was already questioned in the Renaissance, and it became meaningless after Valéry argued that "ce qu'il y a de plus profonde en l'homme, c'est la peau." As to the difference in shades of evil between black or white—it obviously became irrelevant after *Moby Dick*. So at the beginning is anxiety, and at bottom, or "about her waist, or in the middle of her favour" (*Hamlet* 2.2.227), lies the female nothing that sets narrative interpretation in motion. But then of course Robert Pippin doesn't "fully understand the claims about holes in the fabric of being," and Pippin is an honorable man.

Whenever Miss Pynsent tried to console Hyacinth "for the horror of his mother's history by [. . .] reminding him that he was related," through the Purvises, "to half the aristocracy of England, he felt that she was turning the tragedy of his life into a monstrous farce; and yet he none the less continued to cherish the belief that he was a gentleman born" (169). The phrasing—"to cherish the belief"—is of the essence, for it is belief in "the imaginary idea," and the acting on that belief, that matter. James naturalized the belief and sustained the delusion by securing a conventional plot of discovered genealogy whose circularity rendered the novel all the more insipid: in *Oliver Twist*, by contrast, the disclosure of the boy's "gentility" comes almost as a surprise. In James' novel, the revelation comes so early that it looks as if he were trying to rewrite *Hamlet* from scratch, forcing the protagonist to discover the means of assuming his congenital demotion, and of pretending that his sordid fate was the outcome of his own decision. But the truth is that Hyacinth doesn't want to declass—to withdraw, to extravagate, to suspect, to wander, to misgive—and this is James's major deviation from his source. I am not suggesting that Hamlet *wants*: it is rather the playtext's unconscious—its deeply antiheroic strain, compelling the aristocratic prince to mock territorial disputes—that decides for him. Very seldom, or never, does Hamlet boast about his honor or adduce it to settle a dispute. In fact, he only flags the concept to emphasize his difference from people who readily engage in action "when honour's at the stake":

> Rightly to be great
> Is not to stir without great argument,
> But greatly to find quarrel in a straw
> When honour's at the stake.
> (4.4.9.43–46)

James remodels the play's ascetic drive (its political quietism) into a reactionary reaction-formation—the defeated mock-revolutionary fever of activists, also perhaps moved by "a fantasy and trick of fame" to "fight for a plot" (4.4.9.51–53). The overall effect is, as Tanner pointed out, a rather messy affair, solely accountable in terms of biological determinism (it is worth recalling that Eliot, in *Daniel Deronda*, invoked too the prestige of descent and the rights of the blood to account for the singularity of a hero that is Hyacinth's immediate precursor):

> As his hero or central figure, James chose not a robust child of the working people but an anomaly. Hyacinth Robinson (one can hardly imagine someone called "Hyacinth" working passionately alongside a Lenin!) is the illegitimate son of a decadent English lord who was murdered by a working-class French prostitute. Thus, perhaps rather too obviously, there is a clear genetic reason for the duality in his nature.
>
> (*James* 60)

But there are, as I am trying to show, other ways of explaining away the *duality* of resentment and admiration. I construe it as in-built affordance of the Hamlet-based novelistic dispositive, a structural resource that permits to reconcile the position of the resentful social malcontent who stakes it all on "patient merit" (*Hamlet* 3.1.73–76) and the role of the recessive critic and ascetic aesthete whose drive—whose "inassuageable appetite" (Tanner, *James* 60)—is all for an "imaginary value" (the art of theatre) paradoxically nurtured by the oppressors, the insolent and the generally unworthy. Hyacinth is not a player. He follows the trade of bookbinding (97). But he becomes a player of sorts both when he steps into the rented salons of the Princess and when he impersonates the revolutionary in the London underground. De Grazia takes the "antic disposition" to be for Hamlet a descending ladder granting him access to conventional theatrical types like the Fool or the Devil. It is symptomatic that Hyacinth fears, on meeting the Princess, that she should "take him for a clown, for an idiot" (191).[31] This histrionic tendency obfuscates further the discrimination of Hamlet's social-professional identity. And who or what is Hyacinth? "He was not what he seemed, but even with Pinnie's valuable assistance he had not succeeded in representing to himself, very definitely, what he was" (156). If he was not what he seemed, it is because, like Hamlet, nominally at least, he straddled rank divides and professed to know "not 'seems'" (1.2.76), but also because a systemic chasm confounded all attempts at social categorization.

To be sure, his supervened demotion turns him into a pariah, an indiscernible outcast, apparently placed outside the hierarchical grid of social ranks and classes. In a sense, his very exclusion signals the inconsistency of this symbolic hierarchy. This is the very argument Žižek employs to explain the recursive historical stigmatizations of the "conceptual Jew," and it is no accident that Hyacinth's immediate precursor should be an Anglicized Jew (Deronda), and even less so that Hamlet should have become, in psychoanalysis, the textual ground where speculation on the super-egoic Law and the name of the Father should thrive—and stipulate that those excluded from identification with the symbolic Order are bound to relapse into psychosis. Anxiety, neurosis, psychosis, dream-work, these are all expressive configurations of mental work, and, as Kierkegaard once said, and Harold Bloom repeated, "he who will not work must take note of what is written about the maidens of Israel, for he gives birth to wind, but he who is willing to work gives birth to his own father" (qtd. Bloom, *Anxiety* 73). Hamlet, we know, refuses to have his pipe played by others, the heart of his mystery plucked out, his wind thereby recovered (*Hamlet* 3.2.342–364). And we are also aware that his attempt to work by giving birth to his own father prompts a major generic (genre) and genetic (genesis) catastrophe in literary continuity—the transformation of a late tragedy into an early novel. But more on Hamlet's ascetic work at the end of this chapter. In sum, I am not arguing that Hamlet is on that count or otherwise a Jew. I am suggesting that his readiness to be labeled a conceptual Jew—and therefore a social pariah—is directly proportional to his ability to sabotage the big Other—a symbolic, normative nexus comprising big (m)Other and the Mother-Fuckers (King Hamlet and Claudius)—*without* renouncing Oedipus, without disowning, that is, the memory of his sovereign father: "He was a man. Take him for all in all,/I shall not look upon his like again" (*Hamlet* 1.2.186–187).[32] This was sometime a paradox, but now the time, and Žižek, give it proof.

## VII

Hyacinth enjoys walking through London, watching people who have not received their wages and "wandered about, disinterestedly, vaguely, with their hands in empty pockets, watching others make their bargains and fill their satchels" (*Princess* 106). Sympathy for them will promote his own turn away from the contingencies of a *weary life* towards contemplative, even artistic, disinterestedness. In this particular direction, Bohemia remains for him an open possibility. But also terrorist political activism, the disinterested (indifferent) outcome of an excessive, infinite, interest in empty—and therefore absolute and potentially explosive—social signifiers. What the aesthete and the revolutionary share is disinterest in the scripts and settings of bourgeois domestic life: their exaggerated—James calls it "unnatural"—interest in the *ideas* (Kant) of beauty or justice is a measure of their disinterest in everything else.[33]

So "the imaginative, irresponsible little bookbinder" (163) never loses the "boyish habit" of strolling about the streets (157), his "relish of vague perambulation" (162). Hamlet, we know, was once in "the City"—which editors identify as London—haunted the playhouses, and back in Elsinore, "you know, sometimes he walks four hours together/Here in the lobby" (2.2.157–158). We see him walking with a book in his hands along this outdoors corridor. Like the prince, moreover, Hyacinth has "sudden inconsistencies of temper" (155), and his "passionate idealism" (156) often degenerates into pathological melancholy:

> He was liable to moods in which the sense of exclusion from all that he would have liked most to enjoy in life settled upon him like a pall. They had a bitterness, but they were not invidious—they were not moods of vengeance, of imaginary spoliation: they were simply states of paralysing melancholy, of infinite sad reflection, in which he felt that in this world of effort and suffering life was endurable, the spirit able to expand, only in the best conditions, and that a sordid struggle, in which

one should go down to the grave without having tasted them, was not worth the misery it would cost, the dull demoralisation it would entail.

(163)

This central meditation conflates two soliloquies—"O that this too too solid flesh would melt" (*Hamlet* 1.2.129–159) and "To be, or not to be; that is the question" (3.1.58–90)—and Hamlet's digression about the futility of the world and human existence, which begins "I have of late, but wherefore I know not, lost all my mirth" (2.2.287). But Hyacinth's meditation deviates from the source because it makes the expansion of the spirit depend upon "the best conditions," a naturalist phrase that can only mean "the best social conditions." On this logic, Hamlet has been decidedly blessed with the best infrastructural conditions, and has turned away from them (court, rank, family) in his pursuit of a superstructural figment—an imaginary value. Short of any precise actualization, this value remains latent throughout the play: the defector from a heroic tragedy retains the formal capabilities obtained through first-class *Bildung* and reorients them in whatever pragmatic direction (social observation, art, knowledge, homosocial bonhomie) he decides to cultivate. This entails a relapse from the realm of the Symbolic back to the Imaginary—and the destination of such reversion is of course part of Hamlet's secret, which is also Hyacinth's. This recalcitrance even Christina vaguely realizes: "He is a strange mixture of contradictory impulses. [. . .] How can I enter into his affairs with you? How can I tell you his secrets? In the first place, I don't know them, and if I did—fancy me!" (465)

Hamlet likes theatre and reads. That much we know. And his readings may have induced his extremely satirical disposition, the likeliest outcome of a skeptical-cum-Stoic self-education. Hyacinth is exposed to similar attitudes. Mr. Vetch, his tutor and representative in the novel of art, literature, and philosophy, was "a revolutionist, or even a critic of life" (67) who indulges in "diatribes against the British middle-class, its Philistinism, its snobbery" (68) and complains of "this sodden, stolid, stupid race of ours" (76). He has a penchant to "go off into [. . .] dreadful wild theories" (76) and shows "disinterested sympathy" (115) towards the art of bookbinding. In this characterization, we recognize the traits of Morris's archaizing aestheticism, roused by radical social theory. Under such influence, Hyacinth receives as a present the essays of Lord Bacon (114) and fosters "a dream of literary distinction" (112). The likeliest result of the implicit operation (Lord Bacon + literary distinction) is of course Shakespeare. In short, Hyacinth undergoes a "kind of education of taste" through the influence of Mr. Vetch. He attends plays and operas, but shuns the sensorial excesses of the fashionable world. Much is made in the novel, for instance, of Hyacinth's rejection of liquor (157), which is reminiscent of Hamlet's

Puritan revulsion at the Danish vice of drinking (1.4.10–38). Although other factors may be at play—in Lacanese, "the campaign against the primal father is visible in the increasing abhorrence of the pleasure of others" (Copjec 157)—such repugnance is obviously the outcome of an extreme sensitivity: "For this unfortunate but remarkably organised youth, every displeasure or gratification of the visual sense coloured his whole mind" (157). He has, the narrator observes in anticipation of a classic Jamesian locus, "the sentient faculty of a youth on whom nothing is lost" (164). And nothing means nothing, not even "things rank and gross in nature" (*Hamlet* 1.2.136). The powers of social discrimination are no doubt bolstered by such keen receptiveness, and Hyacinth finds in Christina a prodigious accomplice, not only as an interlocutor in discussions about art, but also as a guide in tasks of sordid urban observation:

> On the Sundays that she had gone with him into the darkest places, the most fetid holes, in London, she had always taken money with her, in considerable quantities, and always left it behind. She said, very naturally, that one couldn't go and stare at people, for an impression, without paying them, and she gave alms right and left, indiscriminately, without inquiry or judgment, as simply as the abbess of some beggar-haunted convent, or a lady-bountiful of the superstitious, unscientific ages who should have hoped to be assisted to heaven by her doles.
>
> (476)

In this impressive passage, James's irony loses some of its control. Is he really reviling acts of philanthropy sustained by a combination of pathological social curiosity and *mauvaise foi*? How would such implicit judgement qualify the enthronement of Christina elsewhere? Who knows? What is indisputable is that the image of the Princess as "the abbess of some beggar-haunted convent" drifting along dirty streets "to stare at people, for an impression" is profoundly reminiscent of legendary facts in the life of Byzantine empress Theodora, upon which James may have modeled traits of the character of Milly in *The Wings of the Dove* (see chapter 4), but also that *staring at fetid holes* is the central action in the primal scene informing the intertextual rapports my book examines. But then, of course, Robert Pippin doesn't "fully understand the claims about holes in the fabric of being", and Pippin is an honorable man.

## VIII

Let us reconsider the question of Hyacinth's *imaginary value*. His life can be split into two periods, before and after meeting Christina. This explains why reference can be made to a time "when he was not letting his imagination wander among the haunts of the aristocracy" (160). A connection is clearly established between *aristocracy* and *imagination*. *Faute de mieux*, degraded to protracted probation, ousted from the substantial wards of genealogical aristocracy, Hyacinth seeks relief in ideology-and-form aristocracy—what Swift calls the "imaginary value." During his first conversation with Christina, Hyacinth states that he is "one of many thousands of young men of my class—you know, I suppose, what that is—in whose brains certain ideas are fermenting" (196). Two kinds of *ideas* are fermenting—*moral-political ideas* about social change, revolution and justice, and *aesthetic ideas* about spiritual nobility. The Princess, who will accelerate the growth of the latter, is drawn to him because he has "general ideas" (198). An odd circularity of mimetic desire ensues. General ideas were, let me recall, what James, according to T.S. Eliot, congenitally avoided. It is customary, and perhaps correct, to think of conservative liberals—Locke to Burke—as recoiling from *general ideas*, abstract theoretical notions that are crudely enforced on reality. These became the food for extravagant, cosmopolitan, and potentially Bohemian thought. Madame Grandoni mentions that Christina "lived with artists, archaeologists, ingenious strangers, people who abounded in good talk, threw out ideas and played with them" (256). By contrast, ignorance—of ideas, not of practices—characterizes the terminal aristocracy represented by the Prince, "as ignorant as a fish, and as narrow as his hat-band" (257), but also many revolutionaries at the Sun and Moon, whose "most insistent ignorance" (280) is scenically brought to the fore. Nevertheless, James's ideology didn't stop him from indulging aesthetic ideas that could determine, and compromise, the moral-political field. His conservative liberalism was not far from Ruskin's conservative socialism. It is also worth recalling that chapter eight of Ruskin's autobiography is titled "The State of Denmark," a telltale fact that goes some way towards demonstrating the central role that Hamlet had in fashioning Ruskin's *imaginary value* of a vanished nobility.

Ruskin's musings over Gothic art in *The Stones of Venice* provide a perfect backdrop to some of James's critical excursions in his "Preface" to *The Princess Casamassima*. Take, for instance, the following, where the novel connects with *Hamlet* through Scott's most "Gothic" narrative:

> Edgar of Ravenswood for instance, visited by the tragic tempest of *The Bride of Lammermoor*, has a black cloak and hat and feathers more than he has a mind; just as Hamlet, while equally sabled and draped and plumed, while at least equally romantic, has yet a mind more still than he has a costume.

(40)

At stake, once again, is the dialectical (mediation-related) question of the "imaginary value" transacted in conservative ideology. The problem with the previous comparison is that James overlooks the ideological force of the material externals—the black cloak, the hat, the feathers. Any of these has the potential to become a symbolic cover for the *objet petit a*: "the object of fantasy, [. . .] that 'something in me more than myself on account of which I perceive myself' as 'worthy of the Other's desire'" (Žižek, *Plague* 9). Recall that Hamlet is first addressed by Claudius and Gertrude as an excessive mourner dressed in "suits of solemn black" and "inky cloak" (*Hamlet* 1.2.78–79) and that Ophelia measures his mental distraction by his wearing "no hat upon his head" (2.1.80). And also that Hamlet fails to recognize his innermost self in those very externals ("forms, moods, shows"), which, he complains, don't "denote me truly" (2.1.83). Yet, for all his protestations to the contrary, Hamlet is, according to Ophelia's summary description, "the glass of fashion and the mold of form" (3.1.152). He is also a "noble mind," of course, but the aristocratic ideology that Ophelia expresses finds no fault in making the external man and the Lutheran *innere Menschen* coincide. Its sustaining aesthetic ideal furnishes the prince with "a minimum of phantasmic identity": "it is the Other's desire itself which serves as the mediator between the 'barred' subject $ and the lost object that the subject 'is'" (*Plague* 10). In Jamesian terms, Hamlet may have a "mind" apart from a "costume," but it is his having a costume that entitles him to engage in *la traverse du fantasme*, "in an acceptance of the fact that *there is no secret treasure in me*, that the support of me [the subject] is purely phantasmic" (10). Hamlet, of course, doesn't appear to condone this extreme, and he claims that he does have that within which passes show. Still, he will also cling to his *name* in a parodic manner, with a force of utterance—"This is I,/Hamlet the Dane" (5.1.241–242)—that reveals dependence on the contingency of fetishism. For the psychoanalytic extreme proclaims that it is his external show (his cloak, hat, feathers, and name) that mediates him—his barred self—and his (objective) self, making "him" symbolically possible. The dialectical alternative opened by this defective constitution is crucial: whereas Hamlet's demotion consists in trying to give up his *objet petit a*, his objectal excess—what Lear calls "addition"—and to naturalize himself as exclusively a noble mind—an innermost site of merit, virtue, worth, and intelligence—Hyacinth's promotion depends upon the sacrifice of intelligence made by a noble mind in exchange for an aesthetic idea (fashion, form) that is uncannily close to the Victorian (Tennysonian, Ruskinian) fantasy of a cloaked and feathered prince.[34] While Hamlet defects by trying to become Hyacinth's aesthetic excess (internal spiritual virtue), Hyacinth exceeds himself by aspiring to become Hamlet's excreted objectal excess (external objectal virtue). The first is a triumph, the second a failure.

Sure enough, Hamlet gives up a great deal—some forms, mores, additions, and externals of aristocratic ideology—but his extreme skepticism doesn't fully discount the imaginative convenience of other presumably superfluous superstructural trappings: "There are more things in heaven and earth" (1.5.168), he tells Horatio, thinking about the ghost and the eschatological hierarchy it mediates. Hyacinth is probably skeptical enough to scoff the Prince's claim to trace "his descent from the fifth century" (249), but he is not free from antiquarian nostalgia. It was Ruskin who praised "the conservative influences of that upper-class British home which our young man had always supposed to be the highest fruit of civilization" (*Princess* 222). According to McKeon, "this ghostly intimations of belief in the justice of a traditional, aristocratic stratification is entirely consistent [. . .] with conservative ideology." He calls it "a socially useful fiction, a cautiously instrumental faith that germinates in the soil left by the flowers of progressive belief once conservative critique has [. . .] quite deracinated them" (*Origins* 344).

Our *flowers of progressive belief* are Rose and Hyacinth, also the herbs that Ophelia hands out before drowning in the brook. Conservative ideology can dispense with them: Hyacinth and Ophelia die, and Rose will follow before long. I am interested in the way in which *ghostly intimations* and *phantasmic supports* supply the possibility of an *imaginary value* to which Hamlet himself desperately clings while he declasses and loses himself as object. Like Rose, Hamlet and Hyacinth refuse to "see the aristocracy lowered an inch" (149). They merely want to evacuate belief (and value) from its metaphysical cargo of genealogy, semen, blood, honor, sword, tooth, and claw and to restore it to the imaginative proportions of simulacra. Tell my story, he begs Horatio, tell my socially useful and beautiful fiction, in what appears to be an early step towards "the instrumentalization of belief" (McKeon 382–409).

## IX

Drawn into aristocratic premises, Hyacinth's aesthetic imagination is assailed by touches of a "romantic world" of "effortless majesty," "extraordinary light nobleness," and "radiance of grace" (191). The vocabulary that chronicles this sensorial assault mingles neoclassical commonplaces about beauty, the telos of the developmental narrative of civilization, and romantic notions of sublimity.[35] Christina, for Hyacinth, is "a woman with a lot of jewels and the manners of an angel" (208). Although prompted by a passion of "resentment and contempt" against the Italian aristocracy, she is "a creature compounded of the finest elements; brilliant, delicate, complicated, but complicated with something divine" (251). She is, in a word, the embodiment of beauty: "I have been in a beautiful house, with a beautiful woman" (361), Hyacinth tells Mr Vetch. "I have come because only because a lady who seems to me very beautiful and very kind has done me the honour to send for me" (242). Whereas he shows no interest in what Lear would call her nominal *superflux*—"I suppose all titles are great rot" (361)—he is mesmerized by other, more formalized, additions: "You should see the place—you should see what she wears, what she eats and drinks" (363). Lady Aurora also considers her "extraordinarily beautiful—the most beautiful person she had ever seen" (429). The cumulative effect of these platitudes weakens rather than invigorates James's clumsy attempts at fleshing out her singularity. Repeating in a late Victorian novel that a woman is (like) a beautiful angel—let alone an ethereal dove— is the best way of having the reader lose interest in her potential rarity. But James had other, much subtler, ways of restoring the reader's absorption in his novel. Consider the following description, which stands somewhere between Thackeray's *Henry Esmond* and Woolf's *Orlando*:

> She showed Hyacinth everything: the queer transmogrified corner that had once been a chapel; the secret stairway which had served in the persecutions of the Catholics (the owners of Medley were, like the Princess herself, of the old persuasion); the musicians' gallery, over the hall; the tapestried room, which people came from a distance to see; and the haunted chamber (the two were sometimes confounded, but they were quite distinct), where a dreadful individual at certain times made his appearance—a dwarfish ghost, with an enormous head, a dispossessed brother, of long ago (the eldest), who had passed for an idiot, which he wasn't, and had somehow been made away with.
>
> (308)

In accordance with the logic of cultural transmogrification that this extraordinary fragment invokes, the apparition is the obscene super-egoic supplement of Law, a monstrous and grotesque transfiguration of King Hamlet's ghost, complemented with the son's histrionic idiocy.

To pass for an idiot without being an idiot is Hamlet's signature achievement, which he inherits from the legendary figures of Brutus and Amleth. This takes an ability to distance (to bar) yourself from yourself, which in turn depends on the possession of a nothing (a gash, a hole) we call conscience or simply the mind. Yet for imitation, or mimicry, to flourish, a phantasmatic transference is in order, and the logic that makes it possible is the *economy of the imaginary value*. Both Hamlet and Hyacinth travel, like theatre, and talk with friends (and players) about theatre inside the playhouse that is society. Both Hamlet and Hyacinth are, in short, apperceptive existential players, that is to say, actors who know themselves to be actors. It is a knowledge that gives them a distinction, a knowledge that constitutes and widens the nothing of their consciousness. And only as actors who pretend to be whom they are not can they actually move on to real (ascetic) action—revenge versus death (Hamlet), terrorist act versus suicide (Hyacinth).[36] Still, since they are at one remove—at an inch distance, separated by an interim, distanced by the distinction of their nothing—from the action they feign to perform, this performance (revenge, terrorist act) is less a straightforward exploit than a temporary passion of nobility, "the perfume and suppliance of a minute" (*Hamlet* 1.3.9).

Not casually, therefore, the closest parallel between *Hamlet* and *The Princess Casamassima* concerns the treatment of the question of heroic action, what the novel calls the "economy of heroism" (288). Millicent's perception of Hyacinth as an actor sets the tone for the novel's configuration of his histrionic personality. He holds, however, no monopoly on the farcical, for Christina is already repeatedly described in *Roderick Hudson* as "an actress" (174, 239, 312). Although he had "the hand, as she said to herself, of a gentleman," and in spite of the fact that Millicent was "not acquainted with any member of the dramatic profession [. . .] she supposed, vaguely, that that was the way an actor would look in private life" (104). "He looked," in short, as "ingenious and slightly wasted" (105) as the Danish prince. Millicent suggests he should have become an actor. He replies he doesn't care for fancy costumes, and suddenly reconsiders:

> He wished to go through life in his own character; but he checked himself, with the reflection that this was exactly what, apparently, he was destined not to do. His own character? He was to cover that up as carefully as possible: he was to go through life in a mask, in a borrowed mantle; he was to be, every day and every hour, an actor.
>
> (109)

These are the mask and borrowed mantle of the "antic disposition" (*Hamlet* 1.5.173). The theatre-box conversation about foreign and British schools of acting (184) echoes the long discussion in *Hamlet* about theatrical innovations, dramatic genres, and styles of acting at 2.2.280–484. Central to the economy of heroism is therefore *acting* and the *antic*. Hyacinth's partial awareness that "all is not well" (*Hamlet* 1.2.254) and the notion that the revolution was aimed at a "general rectification" (124, 363) are very possibly inspired in two memorable *Hamlet* lines, "The time is out of joint. O cursed spite/That ever I was born to set it right!" (*Hamlet* 1.5.189–190), which bring to the fore his reluctance to sincere, heroic action. Lady Aurora's despondent apprehension of the impossibility of rectification—"if things were right" (217)—confirms too the intensity of a debate about ontological rectitude upon which depends Hyacinth's turn to either action or antics. He perceives the waste of social energy that occurs in "secret societies" (171) and "political clubs" (181), the cradle of "sterile heroisms and abortive isolated movements" (200). These homosocial revolutionary venues and fraternities emerge as compensatory spaces, purgatorial ranks, replacement stations for the evicted aristocrat, and for other strayed members of the intervening classes, and Hyacinth senses their spurious, simulacral, roots turned up in the air, catching humidity and minerals from the superstructure. The underground political meetings are tellingly described as a séance, devoid of women and haunted by "leading spirits" (196–197). And the discussions progress through éclats of bombastic oratory and coups of moral intimidation. Pace Pippin, no (Hegelian) ethical mutuality, recognition, or reciprocity—and therefore no Hegelian "freedom"—obtains in this milieu.[37] Calls to action are urged through "blind obedience" (333), with the mechanical and obscene emptiness of Kantian morality: "The act was yet indefinite. [. . .] The only thing settled was that it was to be done instantly and absolutely, without question" (333).[38] Hyacinth's occasional resolution to action (294) is as histrionic and motivationally hollow as the ghost's calls to memory and Hamlet's self-calls to heroic revenge. This is his response to an accusation that nobody in the room is ready to risk his precious bones:

> I can't help it. I'm not afraid; I'm very sure I'm not. I'm ready to do anything that will do any good; anything, anything—I don't care a rap. In such a cause I should like the idea of danger. I don't consider my bones precious in the least, compared with some other things. If one is sure one isn't afraid, and one is accused, why shouldn't one say so?
>
> (294)

This speech collapses several moments in the tragedy where Hamlet hopelessly seeks to persuade himself of his own temerity and intrepidity (3.2.358–62; 4.4.9.20–56) into a crest of sham purporsiveness but it also resonates with his fearless display of Stoic resignation (5.2.175–202). For Hyacinth, described as "a detached, irresponsible witness of the evolution of his fate" (547), will also enter "a phase of his destiny where responsibilities were suspended" (318). The perfect moment to "defy augury" (*Hamlet* 5.2.157).

## X

Lukacher has shrewdly observed that one of the play's most incisive holes—"Pyrrhus' ear" (*Hamlet* 2.2.457)—"is Hamlet's daemonic figure of conscience because deep within the silent voice of conscience Shakespeare discerns not the moral law, not a realm of values, but the silent play of the letter" (135) and yet Žižek and Zupančič would discern in such graphological caesura—Lacan's "hole without faith"—the very mechanical reason of

Kant's moral law.[39] A theatrical dimension of empty mimicry controls the whole process. Hyacinth knows he doesn't really believe—he "pretends to believe," as Paul tells him at Greenwich. He doesn't really care in the way the revolutionaries, and even the Princess, appear to care—"That I shall have ceased to care for what you care about" (336)—although, as I have already noted, he will also turn that particular stone and discover a major hole. Like Hamlet, he feels "unpregnant of [. . .] his cause" (*Hamlet* 2.2.545), "the beastly cause" (336). But maybe most of the revolutionaries are: this is a lesson James may have passed to other skeptical liberals like Naipaul. According to Stefanie Markovits

> while (as he indicates in the Preface by comparing Hyacinth's situation to that of the Prince of Denmark) we are indeed once more in the world of the nineteenth-century *Hamlet*, where intelligence threatens to close off the possibility for action, James seems to be just as concerned that action could close off the possibility for consciousness.
>
> (146)

To close off the possibility for consciousness amounts to filling out and therefore saturating the gap—the *hole thing*—of consciousness. Hyacinth fears such an outcome. By the time Paul, who "disapproved of delay" (292), summons him to recommit and reengage—"Haven't you been out at grass long enough for one while, didn't you lark enough in the country there with the noble lady, and hadn't you better take up your tools again before you forget how to handle them?" (392)—Hyacinth is already engrossed with other tools, although we confirm at the end that he knows how to use a weapon. Similarly, in the final act of the tragedy Horatio also asks Hamlet to shake off indolence and take up his tools (sword) in order to prepare for the imminent duel with Laertes. Hamlet regally replies: "I have been in continual practice." The whole conversation at 5.2.175–202 deserves close attention. In spite of his apparent resolve to take action, Hamlet acknowledges some internal concern: "Thou wouldst not think how ill all's here about my heart" (190). Horatio insists:

HORATIO: If your mind dislike any thing, obey it: I will forestall their repair hither, and say you are not fit.
HAMLET: Not a whit. We defy augury. There is a special providence in the fall of a sparrow. If it be, 'tis not to come. If it be not to come, it will be now. If it be not now, yet it will come. The readiness is all, since no man of aught he leaves knows what is't to leave betimes. Let be.

James redrafts this exchange in the conversation between Paul and Hyacinth at Greenwich that covers most of chapter 35, perhaps the best in

the book. Hyacinth admits to being "strung up on the gallows," referring to "Hoffendahl's job" (442), and adds that he has "thought of it a
good deal." Paul remonstrates that he "never spoke of it. You don't like
it; you would rather throw it up" (442), and the bookbinder protests that
he doesn't "want in the least to throw the business up" and asks: "but did
you suppose I liked it?" Then, after some remarks about Paul's paradoxical
quietism, Paul warns his friend:

> "There's one thing you ought to remember—that it's quite on the cards
> it may never come off." "I don't desire that reminder," Hyacinth said;
> "and, moreover, you must let me say that, somehow, I don't easily
> fancy *you* mixed up with things that don't come off. Anything you have
> to do with will come off, I think."
>
> (443)

The parallelism with the *Hamlet* passage is striking. Both exchanges follow after—and succinctly terminate—speculation over one of the characters' resolve and disposition to act. Both culminate in a meditation on
the inevitability of a future outcome prompted by the consideration of the
role that chance (fortune, providence, luck) plays in the course of human
events. The *augury* that Hamlet defies is transformed into the probabilis-
tic *cards* that Hyacinth discounts. The suggestion is rejected with similar hard-
ness: "Not a whit. We defy augury" and "I don't desire that reminder."
In addition, both Hamlet and Hyacinth express their faith in *readiness*
through an iterative weighing of what comes (*not to come, not to come,
will come*) or comes off (*never come off, don't come off, will come off*).
Hamlet's earlier "leaping" into Ophelia's grave finds an echo in Hyacinth's
later corroboration:

> " 'I did jump at it [the job] upon my word I did; and it was just what
> I was looking for. That's all correct!" said Hyacinth, cheerfully, as they
> went forward. There was a strain of heroism in these words—of hero-
> ism of which the sense was not conveyed to Muniment by a vibration in
> their interlocked arms."
>
> (447)

## XI

Christina reconstructs her expulsion from the aristocracy as a voluntary
defection into lower ranks to chase the *imaginary value* of revolutionary
socialism. Hyacinth refashions his banishment from the aristocracy as a
matter of fate, and his promotion upwards from the lower ranks as an
occasion to pursue and discover the *imaginary value* of spiritual nobility. From a conservative-liberal viewpoint, both are deluded by ideological

fictions. At any rate, each mediates the other's ideological conflict, and the site of mediation is no longer the blood-and-sword of aristocratic heroism and popular revolution, but rather *language*—the literacy that a *noblesse de robe* unwittingly vouchsafed to the middle classes, and eventually the popular classes, as the modern instrument of social promotion. Recall that Christina wants to *talk* with Hyacinth: "She has a tremendous desire to talk with someone who looks at the whole business from your standpoint" (185). And *talking*—conferring with sentinels, players, gravediggers—is the only thing Hamlet seems willing to do of his own accord. The reciprocal mediation of language furnishes a dialectical space enabling the replacement of a *logic of filiation*, based on parentage, nurture, ancestry, and blood, by a *logic of affiliation*, based on friendship, culture, experience, and language. Hyacinth's *foris-familiation*—the interruption of his genealogical filiation—prompts his underground affiliation to an ideal of social justice as well as his superstructural affiliation to an imaginary idea of aristocratic superiority. Hyacinth's mother's morganatic marriage—"by the left hand" (58)—is somehow paralleled by the Princess' expulsion.[40]

In his epistolary phantasmagoria about the haunted house, James said that "There are no women." This is only partly true. In the "Preface" to *The Princess Casamassima*, he explained how he employed in his novel the inherited technique (Balzac, Thackeray) of "going on with a character" from an earlier fiction and asking her to deliver a new service. Echoing Thackeray's allusion to the puppets Amelia and Becky, James construes this redeployment in terms of a puppet emerging from a doll's box. Still, the image of resuscitation prompts a more intriguing analogy:

> Nothing would doubtless beckon us on further, with a large leisure, than such a chance to study the obscure law under which certain of a novelist's characters, more or less honourably buried, revive for him by a force or a whim of their own and "walk" round his house of art like haunting ghosts, feeling for the old doors they knew, fumbling at still latches and pressing their pale faces, in the outer dark, to lighted windows. I mistrust them, I confess, in general.
>
> (44–45)

The Thackerayan context is bound up with Gothic echoes from *Wuthering Heights*, from the scene where Mr. Lockwood spends the night in Catherine's room. The fact that Christina, of all women, is willing to come in, is extremely revealing. Of all of James's heroines, she is the closest to Hamlet—dispossessed, worldly and "world-weary" (45). She and Hyacinth complement one another. James the narrator needs to take "full possession of [his] matter" (47), to rise to the standard of imputed intelligence that the novel demands. The matter is social-sexual antagonism, the consistent inconsistency of social reality. Their relation is one of mutual scrutiny: Hyacinth (his noble mind) wants to understand Christina while Christina (her noble mind) wants to understand Hyacinth. But both are misrecognizing their object: whereas Hyacinth sees the imaginary value—an affair of libidinal-aesthetic attachment and desire—of a declining but *beautiful* aristocracy, Christina is drawn by the imaginary value—a function of ideological curiosity—of revolutionary socialism. Both, of course, aristocracy and socialism are screens to ulterior realities—the crude facts, respectively, of genealogical sex and class volatility. The crude fact is that the truth of aristocracy is just a matter of material sexual continuity, and that the truth of socialism is the unthinkability of the social, the unreality of society. Both facts are, for James, embodied in the (conceptual) woman, the representative of the collective "women" that is not welcome in the haunted house of his art. Or is she? The woman whose cavities are there to be penetrated and observed, scrutinized, scanned, inspected, whose mouths and legs and minds must be opened, in order to confront their absorbing nothing. James acknowledges, with astounding honesty, the limitation of his "knowledge" (48) with respect to political agitation and underground subversion. And he enlists Hyacinth and Christina to his cause, as "intense perceivers" who are "only guessing and suspecting and trying to ignore, what 'goes on' irreconcileably, subversively, beneath the vast smug surface" (48). The adverbial "irreconcileably" bears witness to James's pointed awareness of the persistence of social inconsistency and antagonism. But then, of course, Robert Pippin doesn't "fully understand the claims about holes in the fabric of being", and Pippin is an honorable man. Hyacinth's and Christina's ignorance, James argues, is a kind of "wisdom" (48). It is the outcome of a "tragic" human effort at understanding—the effort of "the social ear as on occasion applied to the ground," the social nose "[catching] some gust of the hot breath that I had at many an hour seemed to see escape and hover" (48). Visualize Henry James with his ear applied to the ground, sounding the surface for the subversive tremor, with his nose inhaling the air of reality, sensing the sexualized heat of the social. The image is unlikely. That is why he chose Hyacinth and Christina to perform this task for him. They carried it out like Doctor Freud and his peers examining Irma's throat. When they were done, Hyacinth reentered the house, with James and the rest. The ghost of Christina was left out, like Catherine Earnshaw, fingering the doors and windows.

Hyacinth misrecognizes Christina and she misrecognizes him. The same happens with Hamlet and Ophelia. They want that something (excess, *objet petit a*, autonomous organ) in the other that *is* not the other but nonetheless unwittingly supplements it as an existent. As David Halperin sharply formulated: "I want you but you are not what I want" (qtd. in Hillman, "Philosophical Sex" 81). She singles him out because he is one of the people that has the surplus qualification of having "general ideas" about the "social question." He singles her out because she represents the beauty—the refined, civilizational luxury—of leisure classes. But each wants to be admired and desired for another reason—Hyacinth on account of his having read German philosophy—"you never wondered at anything after you discovered I had read Schopenhauer" (394)—and Christina because she is privy to the secrets of underground conspiracy. Each offers the other this *objet petit à*, but neither is interested. The copy of Tennyson's poems Hyacinth unsuccessfully planned to give Christina at the close of chapter 17 serves a double function. On the one hand testimonial, for it contains a particular poem, "Locksley Hall"—a "dramatic monologue by a kind of modern Hamlet" (Horne, "James among the Poets" 72)—which James loved and asked Tennyson to read aloud. And on the other symptomal, for the volume is the *agalma* (the surplus detachable ornament) in an episode of libidinal transference that resembles a Freud dream. The phrase used often by Madame Grandoni in conversation with Hyacinth—"Che vuole?" (What do you expect?)—a question he will reappropriate ironically, expresses part of the misunderstanding that inheres in the libidinal misrecognition that Lacan identified with the question *Che vuoi?* As Honer explains, "Fantasy is the way in which subjects structure and organize their desire. [. . .] 'What am I in the Other's desire? Fantasy is a response to that question" (86). It is anything but casual that Ophelia misrecognizes Hamlet both as a "noble mind" and a "mould of form."

## Askesis

When the genealogy of blood fails, or is diverted and irreparably sidetracked (through incest, bastardy . . .) then it can only be replaced by what Harold Bloom rightly calls a "genealogy of imagination" (117). Members of this lineage believe, of course, in the *imaginary value* and are prone, like Hyacinth, to sublimation or *askesis*, "a way of purgation intending a state of solitude as its proximate goal" (*Anxiety* 116). Sublimation is the vanishing of an original impulse "because its energy is withdrawn in favor of the cathexis of its substitute" (Fenichel, qtd. in Bloom, *Anxiety* 119). Cathexis is concentration of emotional energy, and it translates the German *Besetzung*, which Freud himself, in a letter to Ernst Jones, translated with the Jamesian term "interest" (Jones 69). Although the involved processes may appear to us entirely mechanic or passive, Bloom insists on the act of "elaboration" involved in ascetic sublimation, on the ephebe's "making [of] his culture" (119)—and on his "raptly contemplating his own central place in it." In short, "creation-by-evasion [. . .] depends upon sacrifice" (119). Hyacinth's concentrated sacrifice, his purgation of solitude, finds temporary expression in the social cause, but his sublimation fails, and the state of solitude, the condition of his separation—of "his withdrawal from participation in life" (Zizek, *Parallax* 128)—returns with a vengeance in the final scene of the novel, when he commits suicide in a London room. James tells us his story. Hamlet's sacrifice is of course his adumbrated death (the fall of *the* sparrow), but the creation-by-evasion he achieves at the end of his prolonged ascetic sublimation is nothing less than his *story*, the task of whose composition and telling falls upon the scholar—the oratorical Horatio. To be sure, Hamlet doesn't fail to contemplate his own central place in the (proto-bourgeois, novelistic) culture his own defections and death have given rise to:

> O God, Horatio, what a wounded name,
> Things standing thus unknown, shall live behind me!
> If thou didst ever hold me in thy heart
> Absent thee from felicity awhile,
> And in this harsh world draw thy breath in pain,
> To tell my story.
>
> (*Hamlet* 5.2.286–291)

## Notes

1 See "Conscience Makes Cowards: The Disintegration and Reintegration of Shakespeare" in Zachary Lesser's *Hamlet After Q1*, 157–206.

2 All quotations from *The Princess Casamassima* are drawn from Derek Brewer's edition (London: Penguin, 1987).

3 This point is elucidated by McKeon in an earlier chapter: "Romance, Antiromance, True History," *Origins*, 52–64.

4 For the concept of moral luck, see Nussbaum, *Fragility*, 1–21.

5 For the politically strategic *emptiness* of social forms, values, and signifiers, see Laclau, *Emancipations*, 36–46.

6 For Pippin's recent view of Hegel as a "social rationality pragmatist" and the deflationary implications of this view vis-à-vis Žižek's ontological take, see Johnston's article. Pippin's view is developed in *Hegel's Practical Philosophy*. Derrida resisted in several places—*Positions* (110–121) and *La carte postale* (468–472, 501, 505)—Lacan's topological conception of castration and the hole (*trou*), but his transcendental take on the same problem is perfectly compatible with the figurative phenomenalization of inconsistency (as *différance*) that is always underway in literature as a privileged mode ideology and/or reality. Alan Bass calls attention to this dispute in page 6, note 5 of his edition of *Margins of Philosophy*, and Julie Rivkin astutely reminds us of the relevance of this problematic to Jamesian studies in *False Positions*, 211.

7 Adrian Poole has also called attention to this important passage in his Introduction to *The Princess Casamassima*, XLVIIII.

8 For the modernist treatment of Hamlet's "bourgeois heart," see Halpern, *Shakespeare*, 232. Also, more generally on Shakespeare's contribution to the vicissitudes of the public sphere, see 69–92.

9   Franco Moretti's influential interpretation of the "fully realized tragedy [as] the parable of the degeneration of a sovereign in a context that *can no longer understand it*" (*Signs* 55) lends additional support to my sociological argument.

10  Julia Lupton believes that Hamlet deploys "promissory language of friendship in order to hollow out an inward space of pure expectancy": *Thinking with Shakespeare*, 83.

11  Indeed, openly or implicitly discussing *Hamlet*, Schiller and Goethe furthered the nascent *ideology of the aesthetic*.

12  Depending on the scholar, this list of stories may vary, but only within limits. See Doody, *The True Story of the Novel*, 1–2.

13  Hamlet's "words, words, words" (2.2.192) evoke Lenin's "learn, learn, learn," the kind of exhortation that places the subject outside the domain of desire and before the abyss of the (death) drive. See Žižek, *Plague*, 54.

14  De Grazia's complaint at critical inattention to Hamlet's "disappointed hopes for succession" is partly overblown: Dover Wilson's famous book on *Hamlet*, from which the quoted phrase is drawn (*What Happens in Hamlet* 32), devotes much energy to substantiating the claim that a central cause of "Hamlet's bitterness was his exclusion from the throne" (Carver, qtd. in Dover Wilson, 339).

15  De Grazia: "Elevated to the throne by the electorate and fastened to it by his marriage to the Queen, Claudius has preempted the heir-presumptive" (86); "While it is common for sons to suffer the death of fathers, it is decidedly uncommon for an only son to inherit nothing of his deceased father's estate" (87).

16  De Grazia reminds us that "From 1800 on, after Goethe had prominently featured *Hamlet* in his widely influential *Wilhelm Meister*, the question of Hamlet's age tends to be seen in the context of 'coming-of-age' narratives. Even in the late twentieth century, Hamlet has been associated with the *Bildungsroman* or novel of development: indeed it has been considered the precursor of the German romantic form" (83). Barbara Everett comments on the importance of Hamlet for the constitution of Goethe's *Bildungsroman*, but insists on the specificity of the English novel's return to the Shakespeare play, using *Great Expectations* as an example. And Everett, *Young Hamlet*, 28–29. See also Höfele, *No Hamlets*, 4–7.

17  For these and other related tales written in the span of years 1872–1873, see Rawlings, "Henry James," 99; Everett, *Young Hamlet*, 29.

18  Eustace's subjective figure, reminiscent of Hamlet, foreshadows Alan Badiou's characterization of the *sujet réactif*, unable to remain faithful to a past truth or to produce a present (*Logics* 54–58). An exception to the neglect I denounce is the extraordinary sensitivity to Hamletian allusion that Bradbury shows in her edition of *The Ambassadors*: see note 18, 401–402.

19  Adrian Poole ("Introduction" lxxxix) is an exception, and he acknowledges the work of Oscar Cargill and Adeline R. Tintner. Cargill places his comparison between Hamlet and Hyacinth under the influence of Turgenev's appropriations of the Shakespeare play. The bearing of the "fatal Hamletism" on the novel would be visible in his moralistic rejection of women and also in his resignation to fate (116–117). Tintner pays attention to the parallels between the play-within-the-play scene in *Hamlet* and the performance of *The Pearl of Paraguay* in James's novel (175–178).

20  In *Modern Social Imaginaries*, Charles Taylor discusses the "great disembedding" marking the transit to modernity, characterized by reform, disenchantment, and the individual emancipation from organic communities and institutional corporations: "This involved the growth and entrenchment of a

new self-understanding of our social existence, one that gave an unprecedented primacy to the individual" (50).

21 Othello's life "story" is an important ingredient in the tragicomic plot of his tragedy, partly described as "story" by Othello when he alludes to Iago's scheme. Still, the tragedy closes with a meta-theatrical allusion to "this act."

22 Consider also: "He had ceased, himself, to care for the slums, and had reasons for not wishing to spend his remnant in the contemplation of foul things; but he would go through with his part of the engagement" (Princess 401); and Christina's outburst: "I want so much to know London—the real London. It seems so difficult!" (411) The adjective *real* is here used with Lacanian prescience.

23 See Žižek's astute comments on the Hamlet-Ophelia relationship apropos of the threat of the *Frau-Welt* (the woman who stands for terrestrial life): *Plague*, 82–84. He obviously draws here on Lacan's reading of the Hamlet-Ophelia relationship, where the girl features as a "symbol signifying life." For a brilliant discussion of Lacan's take on Hamlet, see Reinhardt and Lupton, *After Oedipus*, 74–82. See also, Belsey, *Shakespeare*, 15–33.

24 "He had much of the aspect which, in late-coming members of long-descended races, we qualify to-day as effete; but his speech might have been the speech of some deep-chested fighting ancestor" (234). He is referred to as a member of the "ignorant and superstitious Italian race" (239). James will later confront, with ambivalence, a Nietzschean celebration of this race in D'Annunzio's novels.

25 Neither does Hyacinth's allegedly capacious consciousness. Zacharias is right to stress his "limited perception and consciousness of himself and of his circumstances" (89), with which he establishes, therefore, an *imaginary relationship* whose representation we call, following Althusser, *ideology*.

26 See Sedgwick, *Epistemology*, 193. And my essay on Bohemia in James, where I track the more or less explicit affiliation to Bohemianism made by several characters of the novel (Mr Vetch, Captain Soho, Cristina Casamassima, Lady Aurora), personages who *perform* all sorts of peripheral circlings around society.

27 Rose tells Hyacinth that their names represent flowers (135).

28 In Belleforest's version of the story, there is an explicit allusion to his being taken as a "bastard" (289).

29 In Shakespeare's play, the Ghost assures Hamlet of his mother's innocence, but a residual suspicion instills the violent manner in which both magnify her "crime"—marrying and having sex with his uncle.

30 For the Derridean concept of bastard course, see Critchley, *Ethics*, 1–29, 48.

31 De Grazia further argues that "Irregularities—of speech, behavior, comportment—which modern readings take as symptoms of psychic disorder were once the signature stunts and riffs of the Clown, madman, Vice, and devil: all stock figures of privation and therefore suitable role models for the dispossessed prince" (5).

32 See Santner, *The Royal Remains*, 142–187; Benjamin, *Working with Walter Benjamin*, 22–244. For an interesting Lacanian- Žižekian reading of Hamlet as early noir, see Charnes, *Hamlet's Heirs*, 26–42.

33 Although, for instance, Hyacinth is told by the Captain that he has a precious faculty "of inspiring women with an interest—but with an interest!" (203) he believes that Christina is moved by "disinterested feelings" (210), specifically (and paradoxically) by an "unnatural interest in politics" (210).

34 The fact that James was very fond of the Hamlet allusion "My father, in his habit as he lived!" (3.4.130) may reveal something about his unconscious association between rank and genealogical propriety and dress. See Herford's essay on this allusion.

35 This is particularly evident in his considerations of "the sense of the wonderful, precious things [Parisian civilization] had produced, of the brilliant, impressive fabric it had raised" (382–383), and his praise in Venice of "the monuments and treasures of art, the great palaces and properties, the conquests of learning and taste, the general fabric of civilisation as we know it" (396). For his celebration of "the conquests of civilization," see also 464.

36 For Schopenhauer's discussion of Hamlet's refusal to suicide, see Stern, 68–70.

37 According to Pippin, freedom for Hegel "consists in being in a certain reflective and deliberative relation (which he describes as being able to give my inclinations and incentives a certain 'rational form'), which itself is possible [. . .] only if one is also already in certain relations (ultimately institutional, norm-governed) to others, if one is a participant in certain practices" (*Hegel's Practical* 4).

38 For the compulsive and unfree nature of the moral act in Kant, see Zupančič, 31–35.

39 See Žižek, *Plague*, 104–106, 178 and Zupančič, *Ethics of the Real*, 220–225. For Shakespeare's general skepticism about the abstract moral law, see Greenblatt, *Shakespeare's Freedom*, 74–94. Žižek discusses *Hamlet* as a drama of failed interpellation in *Sublime*, with the prince recognizing himself as "the addressee of the imposed mandate or mission" (*Plague* 135). Halpern develops this idea, arguing that Hamlet "never fully internalizes" or "*fulfills*" the Father's commandment, "rather, he blindly and automatically *repeats* it" (249–250).

40 See Korey Garibaldi's essay on morganatic marriage.

# 3 Daemonization

## The Strange Freedom: *The Turn of the Screw* and the *Pamela* Controversy

The only referable ghost that appears in *The Turn of the Screw* is that of Richardson's character Pamela:

> Seated at my own table in clear noonday light I saw a person whom [. . .] I should have taken at the first blush for some housemaid who might have stayed at home to look after the place and who, availing herself of rare relief from observation and of the schoolroom table and my pens, ink, and paper, had applied herself to the considerable effort of a letter to her sweetheart [. . .] in spite of my entrance, her attitude strangely persisted.
>
> (57)[1]

Then follows a long descriptive passage of the aspect of the person the governess believes to be her "vile predecessor"—dressed in black, haggardly beautiful, dishonored, tragic, melancholy, detached, indifferent. I invite the reader to compare this scene with the Joseph Highmore painting "Mr B finds Pamela writing," now in the Tate Collection. The governess strives Hamlet-wise to "fix" and to "secure"—to *screw*—in her memory the "image" of the apparition. The person she sees uncannily resembles the waiting-maid in Richardson's narrative, a young woman surrounded by pens, ink, and paper, who is also a writer. Unlike the immediate "vile predecessor" in James's tale, the governess may not be the *lady* she believes she is. In point of fact, under conditions of status inconsistency, she becomes the less-than-lady scribe that pens the inset narrative. She becomes, like Pamela, an *author*. And the secrecy around the clandestinity of writing (private papers, letters, journals) is similar in both narratives. James inherited this contested *scène de l'écriture* (Derrida, *L'écriture* 293) from his English eighteenth-century predecessor.[2] In both tales we confront a story of miss-writing—"Have you written, Miss?" (63)—and misappropriated words, misused words, offensive phrases, stolen letters, and repeated stories.

DOI: 10.4324/9781003199564-3

Michael McKeon suggested decades ago that the rise of the English novel was informed by a complex dialectic where questions of truth and questions of virtue were inextricably interwoven. *The Turn of the Screw* has been recursively received by the critical tradition as an obscure allegory of truth, and therefore as an epistemological tale. Much has been said, for instance, about the salience of the acts of *seeing* in a tale where some see more than others, and about the bearing that these acts have on its cognitive makeup. *The Turn of the Screw*, Shoshana Felman has pointed out, "in every sense of the word, is a *reflection* of, and on, the act of *seeing*" (132), an observation confirmed by the governess in the following admission: "What it was most impossible to get rid of was the cruel idea that, whatever I had seen, Miles and Flora saw *more*—things terrible and unguessable and that sprang from dreadful passages of intercourse in the past" (51). This reading is, I believe, correct. But by foregrounding the action of seeing—something we may impute to the governess as much as to scholars— we overlook the comparative importance of both the *passion* of seeing (to suffer to be shown something) and the related actions of talking about, saying, and giving names to what you don't actually see but are visually offered. I am of course using the verb *see* in an extended sense, implying to grasp and understand. Being invited to *see* what you still don't *understand* is of course what happens to Maisie (Pippin, "On Maisie's Knowing" 129) and to Denis Duval in Thackeray's unfinished novel—"I was so young that I could not understand all I read" (*Denis* 446)—a sentence that echoes Gibbon's "I was too young to feel the importance of my loss" (*Memoirs* 66), in reference to the death of his mother when he was only ten years old. The limitation of *being too young*, as much as—along with—the excess of *seeing too much*, is what James's tale explores. As a rule, we tend to talk (*doxa*) about we do not see (*episteme*), and if we talk long and wrong enough, we end up believing (*pistis*) it. I am not trying to say that *The Turn of the Screw* doesn't lodge an epistemic predicament about the transparency of sight: the tale effectively presupposes a naive epistemic realism— recall Fielding's irony behind Joseph Andrews's claim, "I believe I might aver, that I have writ little more than I have seen" (*Joseph* 164)—qualified by the relativist principle that Paul imparts to Hyacinth: "It all depends on what you see" (*Princess* 445). I am implying, rather, that the story takes for granted such predicament—"we work in the dark" ("The Middle Years," *Tales* 227): nobody can see what the governess claims to see beyond herself or what she holds inside her mind, her soul, her throat—and that the weight of the story lies in the layered clinical debate the girl manages to orchestrate around her invisible contents. And that this involves a degree of voluntary self-exposure—look at my open throat, listen to my words, read my tale—that calls for moral arguments about virtue as much as for epistemic arguments about truth.

But before we move ahead in this direction, let me recall that a rehearsal of our master plot has already taken place—the man, Peter Quint, goes behind the tree, slips, and dies *because* the woman, Miss Jessel, has already exited the narrative space towards her own mysterious death. It is the impenetrability of this incomplete story that sets the second governess's analytical imagination on fire. She joins a medical board, "the most splendid assembly or politest circle" (*Tom Jones* 153)—comprising Mrs. Grose and the participants in the opening fireside conversation—whose assigned task is to *examine* Miss Jessel, but she becomes in turn the ejected miss in her own seduction plot, sent to a nunnery of sorts by her absentee master, and therefore a potential object of clinical excavation. It is important to recall that the governess describes herself as a "sister of charity" (*Turn* 61) inside a Protestant country house that is in a sense a secularization of the Catholic nunnery.[3] Marvell adverted that the country house "scarce endures the Master great" ("Upon Appleton House," *Poems* 77), a fact that Maria Edgeworth in *The Absentee* and James in *The Turn of the Screw* dramatized to different effect.[4]

There is, in short, a discreet omnipresence, in the tale, of questions of virtue, vaguely denoted by McKeon as "ethical and social concerns" (384). By paying attention to these neglected concerns, I want to suggest that the dramatization of cognitive predicaments is subservient to the unstable logic of its social and ideological anxieties.[5] The phrase of the title occurs twice in the body of the tale. First, when Douglas remarks that "if the child gives the effect another turn of the screw, what do you say to *two* children—?" (*Turn* 1). Second, when the distressed governess asserts her right to demand, "after all, for a fair front, only another turn of the screw of ordinary human virtue" (77). The screw is turned in order to test the resilience of two related moral variables: *childish innocence* and *young female virtue*. Both are central to the story, and the latter is arguably the ideologeme whose unpacking cues the inception of the modern English novel with a text, *Pamela*, significantly subtitled *Virtue Rewarded*. Lukacher has argued that *The Turn of the Screw* "is really a pathetic tragedy of a woman caught in the machinations of a decadent patriarchy" (127), a description that befits *Clarissa* better than *Pamela*: in the latter, the comedic resolution betrays a moral blemish (feigned virtue) that is also central to James's tale. Its title idiom was originally coined in the context of torture, which explains what the governess, acting as "executioner" (84), does at the tale's close—"I caught him, yes, I held him—it may be imagined with what a passion" (85). But how can the *virtue* of a young woman who *corrupts* childish *innocence* be at all *rewarded*?[6] Because such unspeakable act of corruption permits both an *aleatory-materialist* and a *liberal policy* to unfold: the first stipulates we should not "forget ontology," that the governess is not deluded in her compulsive search for the trace of a ghostly *real* (Lukacher 120–122) that at bottom inconsists—when she says that the children were "adorable" (*Turn* 52) she obviously means "adwhore-able," a Fielding pun that suggests their access to the ad-horrible reality of the primal scene;[7] the second policy prescribes that no Puritan censure can stop anyone, including children, from *seeing what is there to be seen*—i.e. the enhanced mischief of class-cross sexual transgression. Who rewards her? First, the Master: Henry James. Second, her master and employer: "when, for a moment, disburdened, delighted, he held her hand, thanking her for the sacrifice, she already felt *rewarded*" (6; emphasis added). The governess is—yes, the Freudianized liberal critics were right—a hysterical young Puritan woman, but she unwittingly performs a breakthrough act. In addition, she is guilty, "for if he *were* innocent what then on earth was I?" (83) The tale is ironic because James uses the woman. It is unironic in that his usage permits a liberal achievement—let the children read and see and know—congenial to the author of *What Maisie Knew* and *The Awkward Age*. And it is, finally, meta-ironic by virtue of the threat this liberation poses to James's own sense of literary propriety: what the governess accomplishes James may admire, but he ultimately cannot do, refuses to do, never does. Radical innocence (that romantic rebus) fascinated James, simultaneously seduced him and irritated him, but never to the point of procuring its downright elimination. *The Turn of the Screw* is not the joke James tried to fool others into believing it was.

James observed once that Thackeray had arrived, "in *The Roundabout Papers* and elsewhere [. . .] at writing excellent reconstructed eighteenth" (*LC I* 1294). I want to argue that *The Turn of the Screw* is also written in *reconstructed eighteenth*, that it is a masterful exercise in parodic imitation of a narrative style and an attendant domestic reality—the country house, the allegorical garden, the menacing pond, the community of dependents, the education of children—that we commonly associate with Richardson, Fielding, and Goldsmith. The parody, however, was achieved through a turn that was more romantic than the imitated style allowed.

## II

By far the most examined sources for *The Turn of the Screw* have been Charlotte Brontë's *Jane Eyre*, and Ann Radcliffe's *The Mysteries of Udolpho*.[8] Both narratives are alluded to in James's tale, one (*Udolpho*) openly, the other (*Eyre*) indirectly. But Henry Fielding's last novel, *Amelia*, is also mentioned, and the very explicit allusion occurs at a crucial point: the governess is reading a copy of it right before her third encounter with Quint. This has not escaped critical notice, but the attention devoted to it is comparatively irrelevant. The acknowledgement of the presence and pressure of *Amelia* in James's story regularly takes the form of a casual bow.

More often, however, it fails to occur. The first to examine the Fielding allusion were Valerie Purton in 1975 and May L. Ryburn in 1979. Notwithstanding their indisputable merit, both articles are restricted to vague parallelisms of characterization and plot, and their authors have failed to explain the structural function of *Amelia* in *The Turn of the Screw*, let alone to suggest the necessity of a more thorough collation. The same can be said of Lustig's rather perfunctory attempt to establish a one-to-one correlation between characters in both narratives (*Henry James* 144–146).

In her reading of the story, Shoshana Felman devotes a footnote to clarify the allusions to *Jane Eyre* and *The Mysteries of Udolpho*, with no reference to Fielding's last novel. This is very odd, for she quotes extensively, on page 152 of her brilliant essay, from the passage where *Amelia* is mentioned. This is what she quotes, reads, and asks us to read:

> I sat reading by a couple of candles (. . .) I remember that the book I had in my hand was Fielding's *Amelia*; also that I was wholly awake. I recall further both a general conviction that it was horribly late and a particular objection to looking at my watch. (. . .) I recollect (. . .) that, though I was deeply interested in the author, I found myself, at the turn of a page and with his spell all scattered, looking straight up from him and hard at the door of my room. (. . .). -I went straight along the lobby (. . .) till I came within sight of the tall window that presided over the great turn of the staircase. (. . .) My candle (. . .) went out. (. . .) Without it, the next instant, I knew that there was a figure on the stair. I speak of sequences, but I require no lapse of seconds to stiffen myself for a third encounter with Quint.
>
> (ch. 9, pp. 40–41)[9]

Is *Amelia*—the novel, the title, the name, the graph, the italicized word that is left hanging in the paragraph's opening—the very purloined letter Felman fails to *see* in her otherwise orthodox Lacanian reading? The name is right there, bulking askance in the very first sentence, and yet it is also not there, for it appears to slip away into one of those parenthetical gaps (. . .) with which the scholar has interspersed the fragment. It is very likely that Felman's lack of familiarity with this most unfamiliar (unread and neglected) novel prompted her to disown it as a hermeneutic option. It is paradoxical that the most sophisticated hermeneutic piece on the tale to date, an essay which works its way through circuitous attestations of non-presence, can be said to revolve (turn) around the absence of the tale's subtext. Consider what goes down the drain in Felman's selective quotation:

> I had not gone to bed; I sat reading by a couple of candles. There was a roomful of old books at Bly—last-century fiction, some of it, which,

to the extent of a distinctly deprecated renown, but never to so much as
that of a stray specimen, had reached the sequestered home and appealed
to the unavowed curiosity of my youth. I remember that the book I had
in my hand was Fielding's "Amelia"; also that I was wholly awake.

(38)

The governess later confesses to being "deeply interested in my author"
(39). A combination of repression and secrecy (*deprecated, sequestered,
stray, unavowed*) seems to control the logic of this comment, endowing it
with an aura of bashful confession. But what is there to be ashamed about?
The governess has at least accomplished what very few of her readers can
pride themselves of: she has read or is reading *Amelia*. It looks as if the
character were apologizing, before the tribunal of her prospective readers, for an interest (*curiosity* is her word) in a *stray* narrative *specimen*
of *distinctly deprecated renown* that she knows in advance those readers
will not share. It is quite symptomatic that Felman has decided to erase
the girl's convoluted justification. She should have known better: what
could be more convenient for the interpretation of a putative allegory of
equivocal vision than to *see* (read, understand) what the governess has
*seen* (read) when she was "wholly awake"? The narrator of James's story
tells us that, on first meeting her "prospective patron," he "proved a gentleman, a bachelor in the prime of life, such a figure as had never risen,
save in a dream or an old novel, before a fluttered, anxious girl out of a
Hampshire vicarage" (4). The disjunction inside the exception—"save in a
dream or an old novel"—signifies that if, in this pre-visionary episode, she
was wholly awake, she was not in a dream—ergo she must have been *in an
old novel*. *Amelia* is indeed *an old novel*, but no older than *Pamela*. Both
are intimately related, the former being the last in a sequence of responses
to the latter that Fielding spent much of his life spinning: *Shamela, Joseph
Andrews, Tom Jones,* and *Amelia* all look back to *Pamela* as to its contested origin, contentious parent, and disputed *raison d'être*. In fact, *Amelia* moves more resolvedly, and respectfully, "into territory associated with
Richardson," the territory of "distressed heroines" (Sabor 95). The very
choice of titular name involves an ostentatious display of genealogical
dependence (Pamela > Pamelia > Amelia) to which James's tale bows in
deference through his sardonic investment in the children's (and the governess's) presumed bl*amele*ssness (*Turn* 37).

## III

Let us concede, for the sake of speculative argument, that the governess's
*old novel*—the one that is two (*Pamela* + *Amelia*) and keeps her wholly
awake—is actually *Pamela*.[10] Nota bene: my speculation is not completely

unfounded. In Shirley Jackson's *The Haunting of Hill House*, constant reference is made to the doctor reading—and falling asleep while reading—*Pamela* (*Haunting* 304, 306, 310, 331) and later *Grandison* (34), and there is also mention of *Clarissa* and Fielding's novels (304, 347). Jackson, moreover, uses *The Turn of the Screw* as a determining subtext for her narrative, which incorporates an inset horror tale complete with children, a governess, ghosts, a brook, and a garden. The combination of both strategies—the explicit allusion to eighteenth-century narratives and the implicit recourse to the James subtext—yields what I take to be the most eloquent appraisal to date of the way *The Turn of the Screw* is indebted to the Richardson-Fielding intertextual mesh woven around *Pamela*. It is difficult to improve on what someone as talented as Jackson did, but we can try other, more arid, roads to reach the same intersection.

Pamela and the governess are not only similar in that, holding a subaltern social position in a country-house, they are both apprehensively in love with their masters, and secretly yearn for interclass transgression, but also in that their troubled subjectivation is marked by an *affected profession of virtue*.[11] There is a sense—an ambivalence built into both tales—in which the country maid or governess, a paragon of integrity and example of ladies, is also a "hypocritical, crafty girl" (Keymer and Sabor, *Controversy I* xviii). Sexual frustration gets bound up with fantasies of social mobility and interclass marriage. The plot of both tales turns on "seduction, abandonment, and imprisonment" and involves an "intoxicating fantasy of rags-to-riches advancement and providential reward" (Keymer and Sabor, *Controversy I* xv). The complaints, in *Shamela, Joseph Andrews*, and *Amelia*, against scheming maidservants, the upsetting of subaltern hierarchy, and marital *misalliance* are a clear function of the power of Richardson's transgression in *Pamela*. Never was *status inconsistency* more brutally in display than in the limpid confessional prose of this introspective maid. James, in *The Turn of the Screw*, follows Fielding's lead in excoriating the collusion of moral deception and social freedom that lies at the core of Richardson's first masterpiece. Against the radically *strange freedom* (*Turn* 16) implied in "the erotic transgression of class" (Robbins, *The Servant's Hand* 201), James joins Fielding's celebration of the liberal exemptions of a free conversation—or contemplation—premised on the protection of specific adult secrets, but also on his rejection of a Puritan education that prevents children from having free access to the open adult world. The first condition is represented by the detached master in James' story, an emblem of recalcitrant liberal privacy: his absolute condition is, remember, that the governess "should never trouble him—but never, never: neither appeal nor complain nor write about anything" (*Turn* 6). Note the bottom line: employees do not write to their employers, servants do not write to their masters, or, if you wish, to reveal the patrician prejudice organizing the violent reaction against the publication of *Pamela*, maids do not write, *tout court*. The second is enforced, parodically, by the governess's sadistic impulse to *have the children see what they should never see*—first, that the social hierarchies can be upset, and second, that a "base menial," promoted to valet, can socially and sexually approach a governess.

My aim in this chapter is to reconsider the rationale of the Richardson-Fielding-James connection from an ideological standpoint, open to questions of rank, class, and virtue. I claim that James's story belongs in a tradition of literary texts that respond ironically to the "irrepressible creative nerviness" (Lockwood 548) that prompted and followed the revolutionary publication of Richardson's *Pamela* (1740). In two crucial studies, Tom Keymer and Peter Sabor have mapped out "The Pamela Controversy" as the "deluge of print" (*Controversy I* xvii) that accompanied the publication of Richardson's narrative—a media event described by Fielding as an "epidemical Frenzy" (qtd. Lockwood 550)—in the form of "piracies, criticisms, cavils, panegyrics, supplements, [and] imitations," and to the "struggle of interpretation" (*Marketplace* 1) that these diverse appropriations, transformations and misreadings contributed to. Some of the earlier responses, like Fielding's *Shamela* and *Joseph Andrews* or Haywood's *Anti-Pamela*, were overly parodic in their capacity to unpack subversively self-defeating hermeneutic possibilities that lied dormant in Richardson's text. These canonical responses, and other minor texts titled *Pamela, or the Fair Impostor* and *Mock-Pamela*, also testified to the original text's capacity to put forward a brutal ideological inconsistency that could only be neutralized through sarcasm, parody, or satire. But could it really? Was it ever properly neutralized? I have already mentioned Leslie Fiedler's provocative suggestion that *Clarissa* is the first American novel. Let me add the apparent fact that *Pamela* became "the first novel printed in America" (Keymer and Sabor, *Marketplace* 2). My surmise is that James is still responding to it, still trying to contain and stabilize the ideological inconsistency of Richardson's American classic through the writing of a tale that parodically mobilizes its ideological structure and rehearses some of its enabling (scenic, dramatic) conditions. It is worth observing that the battle of divided allegiances that broke out after the publication of *Daisy Miller*, splitting the field between Daisy Millerites and anti-Daisy Millerites, was foreshadowed by a parallel episode of conflicted reception in the previous century, marked by the emergence of two bands, Pamelists and anti-Pamelists.[12]

James was probably aware of the complex hermeneutic dialogue that emerged from this epoch-making intertextual clash. Fielding's narrative response to *Pamela* proved that, as F. Schlegel pointed out, the best theory of the novel is another novel. In addition, James's sarcastic allusion at the

prudery of Richardson and Fielding, who turned away from social frankness about sex, and went "under the mahogany" in order to avoid eye
contact with "the great relation between men and women, the constant
world-renewal" (James, *LC I* 107), proves that he was aware of the moral
implications lurking behind the self-conscious emergence of the modern
novel. The constitutive ambiguity of the character of Pamela springs from
her multiple inconsistencies, all of which were detected by early reviewers: *stylistic*, because she wrote above her station (in neoclassical terms,
the language of the maid is improperly or indecorously elevated); *moral*,
because she feigned a virtue (the subtitle of Haywood's response, *Feigned
Innocence Detected*, is a formidable reversal of the original subtitle, *Virtue
Rewarded*) that she failed to put into practice when she became rewarded
and socially assimilated;[13] *social*, because she violates rank distinction by
accepting the marriage proposal of a country squire. In fact, this realization was the triggering factor in Fielding's splenetic response. The governess' moral ambiguity is also a frequent consideration made by critics of
James's ghost story. The maid and the governess are not only similar in
that, holding a subaltern social position in a country house, they are both
apprehensively in love with their masters, but also in that their troubled
subjectivation is marked by an *affected profession of virtue*. Both indulge
in proclamations of personal moral integrity and notoriously excel in the
art of decoying (Keymer and Sabor, *Marketplace* 83–90). The problem
of sexual frustration, I have already observed, gets bound up with fantasies of cross-class marital bonding. The complaints, in *Joseph Andrews*,
against scheming maidservants and hyper-marriage are a clear function
of the power of Richardson's transgression—the social liberty or *strange
freedom*—in *Pamela*. True enough, the role "the erotic transgression of
class" plays in James' tale has been noted by some scholars, like Bruce
Robbins, who in a brilliant study titled *The Servant's Hand: English Fiction
from Below* (201) makes his analysis of *The Turn of the Screw* genealogically depend on his reading of *Pamela*, and highlights the freedom for indiscretion and impertinence of its protagonist with no apparent realization of
the striking resemblance between both tales and no interest in pursuing the
comparison. This *strange freedom* is the overall theme that organizes my
approach, in fact my whole book. It is a liberty to inconsist further what
is already inconsistent—to stop wearing a hat when you already overdress
as a gentleman and master of the house—to authorize yourself in the act
of digressing around antagonism, the liberty cherished by a higher-born
heroine in her own set of letters—"My talent is scribbling, and I the readier
fell into this freedom, as I find delight in writing" (*Clarissa* 408)—and the
liberty Fielding wrongly believed was a privilege of enlightened, spectatorial and speculative males.[14]

## IV

Keymer and Sabor have described *Pamela* as a "site of ideological contestation" that dramatizes the "relationship between virtue and class" (*Controversy I* xix). They implicitly follow McKeon's suggestion that Richardson's novel subserves a plot of typically progressive ideology (*Origins* 359), even if, in the last instance, it serves the ends of continuity, not change (391). Although the clash between Pamela's progressive strain and Mr. B's aristocratic ideology closes with a rather unrevolutionary solution (assimilation), "the message that inherited social status is strictly 'accidental' and strictly uncorrelated with the 'natural' gifts of virtue and merit is central enough to the ideology of *Pamela*" (365).[15] The semantic reduction of the notion of virtue to its crass sexual connotation is part of the moral violence exerted by Richardson in his novel. "Pamela's essential power," writes McKeon, "is the passive and negative one of being virtuous, of resisting the sexual and social power of others" (364). In *The Turn of the Screw*, power gets erratically reallocated among menials engaged in a contest of mastery, and virtue is dwarfed to the exiguous dimensions of domestic decency: the governess displays her sham-virtue by advertising her readiness and ability to protect the children from forbidden knowledge, and the children, especially Flora, stand for the virtuous chastity or virginity; in his preface to the tale, James described it as "a full-blown *flower* of high fancy" ("Preface," *Turn* 123; emphasis added).

But the sexual concern masks deeper ideological trouble. *Pamela* is not simply the story of a girl repelling the sexual advances of a man. It is the story of a maid that crosses the rank divide and triumphs socially by manipulating the master who mishandles her. And Pamela, McKeon observes, is not "the only case of social mobility" in the novel. Mrs. Jervis is "a Gentlewoman born, tho' she has had Misfortunes" (*Pamela* 17), and Pamela's father has not always been obliged to engage in "hard Labour" (313). "It is a world," the critic concludes, "already primed for status inconsistency" (365). And yet the novel also contributed greatly to encourage the visibility of the antagonism it presupposes. Social historians have detected that, in the wake of its publication, there was a surge of intermarrying between the serving class and the gentry (Lockwood 551). To be sure, our governess fails to marry her diffident and reclusive master, and James's adoption of the realistic solution to the problem of cross-class marriage evinces perhaps his willingness to contribute to the ongoing sequence of dissenting appropriations of *Pamela*. This of course involved, in part, adopting Fielding's voice, a move no doubt facilitated by the presence, in Richardson's near-heteroglossic novel, of a conservative perspective likely to ridicule the moral pretense of its protagonist, and, by extension, the progressive ideology she purports to embody. Nancy Armstrong rightly called attention to the naturalness with which Mr. B's housekeeper assumes her master's right to sexually assault the maid (*Desire* 5): "Are not the two Sexes made for one another? And is it not natural for a Gentleman to love a pretty Woman? And suppose he can obtain his Desires, is that so bad as cutting her Throat?" (*Pamela* 110) The choice between raping her and killing her is both brutal and false. Brutal because it's in keeping with the unsentimental realism that sustains the conservative ideology, and yet false because at variance with the set of promotion tools available to it. One such tool is not exactly the knife used to cut the girl's throat, but almost: it is the cotton forceps and laryngeal mirror used by the Freudian doctor and his clique of colleagues to examine that very throat. Let me recall, in passing, that in Tennyson's "Lady Clara Vere de Vere," the rebuked lover reminds the cold Lady who "[pines] among your halls and towers" of the death of a previous admirer, and reproaches her that "there was that across his throat/Which you had hardly cared to see." The consequences of her indifference are plain enough, and foreshadow the events at Bly:

> Lady Clara Vere de Vere,
> There stands a spectre in your hall:
> The guilt of blood is at your door.
>         (*Complete Works* 25)

But let us return to *Pamela*. The housekeeper actually responds to Pamela's assertion that "to rob a person of her Virtue is worse than cutting her Throat" (110). When the inspecting male sees nothing (no content, no master-signifier, no soul, no phallus, no nodal organ of thought or *jouissance*), the possibility of castration is attenuated, and stealing gets ruled out as a viable option. The male strives to obtain solely a temporary alienation of her meaning. Examining the throat stands here figuratively for, say, reading the girl's letters, which is exactly what Mr. B (and Fielding, behind him, taking Richardson from behind) aspires most to do, short of possessing her body. His voice is another prefiguration, in the novel, of what the conservative voice will become: an aristocratic tone (Lovelace's in *Clarissa*) filtered through the progressive mud, clinging in despair and panic to the *imaginary value* (politeness, manners) that the low-class maid offers him in exchange for her body. Fielding's voice—and James's too—is therefore bound to connive with the vocal-ideological perspective intimated by the housekeeper and qualified by Mr. B: we will neither kill nor rape the girl, we will not even (at this point) expel her from the novel towards death or a convent: like Clarissa, later, she is always already inside an *adwhoreable nunnery*. We will simply observe her, open her mouth, and inspect, simply listen to her, set the fire, lean on the armchair, peruse her letters, read aloud a tale or two. We will try to expose her gaps, identify the places where her voice cracks, her story inconsists, and digress cavalierly around that void. What is the framing para-text around the governess's tale if not a genteel, fireside actualization of precisely this clinical scene?

Fielding's novels, especially *Joseph Andrews*, *Tom Jones*, and *Amelia*, are performatively organized like a talk, a scene of verbal intercourse where the narrator presents the incidents and judges them, digressing and expatiating on the moral values involved. The novels are not only a "record of corruption, oppression, and disorder in society at large and in the private sphere" (Battestin 614), but also the enmeshed digression conceived with the reader in mind, whom the narrator constantly and jocularly addresses. This is the opposite of what we find in Richardson, whose narratives are presented as private epistolary exchanges between explosive subjectivities that the reader can only read—as we and the fireside interlocutors read the governess's tale in *The Turn of the Screw*—with a liberal sense of improper violation. Fielding's attempt to bring the correct secrets correctly to the fore, and to allow the young, including the female young, to engage in polite talk, is a landmark achievement. It is fascinating to confirm how eagerly Jane Austen and some of her heroines saw themselves interpellated and willing to respond.[16] Fielding's voice is the embodiment of an ideology that is in turn "the issue of a double critique, first of aristocratic ideology by progressive, then of progressive ideology by conservative" (*Origins* 385). McKeon's argument that Richardson's rendition of social mobility "could resonate for Fielding with the culturally fraught effrontery of the rise of the undeserving" (396) could also extend to the democracy-affronted James. Fielding's technical reaction deserves some attention. In conservative logic, he clings—like Hamlet—to the "imaginary value" of the aristocratic ideology, but by the time he writes, these values have become socially institutionalized in the collective *forms* (not substances) of social deference, custom, and the law. Unlike right-winged Hegelians, who will end up worshipping these configurations of objectified Geist, Fielding recognizes their *fictionality*. McKeon lucidly foregrounded this aspect of Fielding's conservative mentality and spoke of an *instrumentalization of belief*. Thus "instrumental belief in institutions whose authority may be fictional— social deference, custom, the law" (392), implies the acceptance of these institutions as arbitrary social forms (imaginary values) that the contingencies of historical development have rendered necessarily convenient— an argument that looks ahead to Edmund Burke. Fielding respects, instrumentally, "customary *noblesse oblige* and the hallowed system of the English law," but this doesn't mean, warns McKeon, "that they are able to counter the endemic condition of 'status inconsistency'—perhaps the more precise term for Fielding would be 'status indeterminacy'" (403). And the expression of this respect takes the form of a "reclamation of fictionality" (394) that defuses the *existential veracity* Richardson endowed his heroines with. In *Shamela*, particularly, this reclamation is premised upon principles of rationality deployed to contain the excess of a Puritan (Methodist) emphasis on justification by grace, which tended to legitimate self-proclaimed—not performed and socially justified—professions of self-righteousness and virtue. The ironic handling of narratorial intrusion and commentary subserves such reclamation, and so do the framing devices of documentary historicity (the dance of telescoped narrators around a hidden manuscript). I believe this multimodal ironic reclamation of fictionality energizes the construction of *The Turn of the Screw*. Nothing undermines more the governess's constant profession of righteousness than the way she is drawn, by the ironic echoes of the para-textual debate, to question the first governess's respectability: her explosion—" 'Miss Jessel indeed—she!' Ah, she's 'respectable,' the chit!"—reverberates with the brutal question around which turns the framing fireside conversation: "And what did the former governess die of? Or so much respectability?" (5)

Fielding, in short, allows the undeserving girl to talk and, like Irma in Freud's tale, to complain about pain in her throat. This is his progressive concession. His conservative maneuver is to confer with his readers, mundanely and ironically, about the clinical case, and to reach, by way of conclusion, "the conservative truth that status inconsistency yet reigns in the modern world of progressive 'social justice' as surely as it did in ancient, aristocratic, culture" (385): you, the, assimilationist parvenu, have finally married and yet still feel the pain, you feel that things still fall apart, are out of joint, and inconsist, well, you should have known better. James's handling of the dialogic-narrative is, however, different from Fielding's—he neither takes for granted his precursor's universalist premises nor shares the (Hegelian) ethical-communitarian longings that Pippin, for instance, identifies in James. The American philosopher censures the critical attempt to place the governess's "moral distortion in her relationship with everyone else" (120) within a hermeneutic framework—combining "the Gothic reaction" and its "post-structuralist response"—that is supposedly caught in a meaningless pursuit of determinate meaning (mystery, riddle, revelation, secret, ghost) (123). Thus, Sedgwick's readings of homosexual panic and

> Freudian readings, of *The Turn of the Screw* in particular, would have to count as equally defensive, reactive, Gothic readings. They assume precisely what James is trying to problematize or ironicize: that there must be a real, determinate "beast" or "ghost" lurking behind or underneath and that it must just be properly, finally named by our sharp-eyed, excavating critic.
>
> (*Henry James* 123–124)

This is wrong. James is not ironicizing in advance the post-structuralist pursuit of hidden meaning. On the contrary. The fact that he renders such pursuit more complex and indeterminate—that he "problematizes" it, in Pippin's correct terms—doesn't imply that he renounces the romantic search of a beast or a ghost. There is no dialogic stage of mutuality, reciprocity, and recognition in the James social world: characters do not speak to reconfigure novel modes of ethical recognition or to fall back on shared doxa. They speak to disambiguate the deictics (*he, she, they, it, all, everything, nothing*) whose maddening indeterminacy stands in their way towards a social or moral success that is uncompromisingly individual. Not even marriage stands for a locus of semiotic repose: when desired by the individual, marriage in James's world works solely as a formal condition for individual achievement, not as the compromise telos of a communal aspiration. That marriage is no solution to any conflict, no resolution to antagonism, no fulfillment to vacuity, no redemption to fault, no reward to sacrifice is one of the conservative lessons Fielding handed down to Thackeray, who in turn passed it on to James.[17] Pamela's and the governess's overexertion of "industrious virtue" are no compensation for an inside gap that resonates with the void of the society in which we believe to exist.[18] *Amelia* is the novel where this lesson obtains its most effective narrative illustration.

But the road to *Amelia* offered Fielding other resting places—*Shamela* and *Joseph Andrews*, especially—more immediately gratifying in their parodic echo of *Pamela*. The new novelist sharpens and perfects his conservative weapons in each station of the way. In *Shamela*, for instance, he convokes a board of male sages (Parson Oliver, Parson Tickletext, Parson Williams) to confer around "the Mouth of a Sinner" (*Shamela* 328), "the Mouth of a Woman" (*Pamela* 134). One of the doctors cynically voices out his conservative concerns:

> The Instruction which it conveys to Servant-Maids, is, I think, very plainly this, To look out for their Masters as sharp as they can. The Consequences of which will be, besides Neglect of their Business, and the using all manner of Means to come at Ornaments of their Persons, that if the Master is not a Fool, they will be debauched by him; and if he is a Fool, they will marry him. Neither of which, I apprehend, my good Friend, we desire should be the Case of our Sons.
>
> (313)

Interestingly, our governess is deprived of the luxury of *looking out for* her master, who has placed himself in a position of invulnerable detachment. And yet, her tale is proof that she has been somehow *debauched by him*— originally, to *debauch* meant to lead astray, and more specifically, to lure someone off the job. The governess, we will see, is somewhat improperly displaced from her job to the position of mock lady of the house. Also conservative is Fielding's liberal conception of social reality, open to all classes and human specimens, and not only to those among the lower classes who are likely to become delusively softened by the siren calls of sentimental progressivism. This results in a broadness and harshness of social reference that many critics considered indecorous. George Cheyne, for instance,

> told Richardson that *Joseph Andrews* "will entertain none but Porters and Watermen", and six years later Fielding was scorned anonymously for writing, in *Joseph Andrews* and *Jonathan Wild*, "the adventures of Footmen, and the Lives of Thief-Catchers": Low Humour, like his own, he once exprest,/In Footman, Country Wench, and Country Priest.
>
> (417)

Let me recall that the governess is almost a country wench, and Peter Quint almost a footman.

When Richardson attacked the "lowness" of *Amelia* arguing that he "found the characters and situations so wretchedly low and dirty" (qtd. in Bree, Introduction to *Amelia* 28), he resorted to a notion of experience that was in principle visual: "His brawls, his jarrs, his gaols, his spunging-houses, are all drawn from what he has *seen* and *known*" (qtd. in Sabor 100; emphasis added). But the addition of the participle *known* makes room for the verbal experience that is one of the staples of Fielding's comic realism, and it is solely through that *verbal experience* that Richardson can infer that Fielding has *seen* too much. Do we *see* what we *hear* when we *read*? Or do we rather, like the governess (and Quixote, and Catherine, and Bovary) read when we see? I will leave these questions hanging.

*Amelia*, Fielding's last novel, centers around a most Thackerayan topic—postnuptial experience, or, the trials of marital life. In the exordium, the narrator states that his "history" deals with the "various accidents"—distresses and incidents—that a very worthy couple are subject to "after their uniting in the state of matrimony." These accidents, he adds, "seemed to require not only the utmost malice, but the utmost invention, which superstition hath ever attributed to Fortune." The importance of *moral responsibility*, announced in the Shakespearean coda on the foppery of the superstition about fortune (*King Lear* 1.2.118–133), has led a scholar like Linde Bree to stress reconciliation, in the novel, of unprecedented levels of verisimilitude and the "eighteenth-century desire to see morality in action" ("Introduction" 15), a desire that had been inflamed by the publication of *Pamela*. Morality, in *Amelia*, hinges upon the difference between the fatalism of the passions and the necessary liberty of moral agents (Battestin 625–230). Booth is incarcerated at the novel's opening and much action and conversation takes place inside a prison. For Denmark's not the only prison. Upon revisiting Lincolnshire Estate, where she had been "imprisoned," Pamela exclaims: "What a different Aspect every thing in and about this House bears now, to my thinking, to what it once had! The Garden, the Pond, the Alcove, the Elm-walk. But, oh! my Prison is become my Palace" (*Pamela* 349)[19] When, in James's tale, the strangely free Peter Quint comes into view "like a sentinel before a prison," we feel the diachronic trope has reached a maximum of ideological crystallization. Fielding's idea that "Life may as properly be called an Art as any other" and his claim that

> by observing minutely the several Incidents which tend to the Catastrophe or Completion of the Whole, and the minute Causes whence those Incidents are produced, we shall best be instructed in this most useful of all Arts, which I call the Art of Life.
>
> (*Amelia* 58–59)

resonates with James's regular aestheticization of moral concerns in his fiction, with his conviction, that is, that fiction is an *imaginary value* because it procures a morally valuable form of the imagination. In a letter to Wells he asserted that "it is art that *makes* life, makes interest, makes importance, and I know of no substitute for the force and beauty of its process" (*Letters IV* 770). Informing, forming, and reforming the lives of others, especially children, takes therefore a great deal of moral courage. Bildung hinges upon the liberal courage to leave the prison's doors open. This the governess is keenly aware of: "To watch, teach, 'form' little Flora would too evidently be the making of a happy and useful life" (*Turn* 8). The fact that she regards her "life with Miles and Flora" as her "charming work," while they happen to be "leading a life of their own," to the point where Miles begs "to see more life" (18), produces a critical strain. The boy was right. Life may be an art, open to formation and reformation, but Bly's a prison.

## V

Let me raise a question: why would the governess want to hold, turn, and eventually kill Miles? Very simple: she wants Bly to become a definitely blighted place. Like the protagonist of *The Haunting of Hill House*, she kills to curse the house that is already half-damned and inexplicably haunted. The death—of herself in one case, of the child in the other—provides a solacing retrospective explanation to the case. But why would she want to damn the house? Arguably, to prevent a future governess from arriving to it. The governess knows she is a latecomer, one of a series, that without being a lady proper she is bound to remain "the same lady" (53), she knows that there was a predecessor, also in love with the master, and that she left the house and died; she knows that, in accordance with this logic deferral and succession, she will herself leave the house and die, unable like Pamela to regress in marital bliss. Everything in *The Turn of the Screw* occurs "with recurrence—for recurrence we took for granted" (33), and Mrs. Grose translates this precept into terms that the governess cannot withstand: "Well, Miss, you 're not the first—and you won't be the last" (8). Her evasive reply—" 'Oh, I've no pretensions,' I could laugh, 'to be the only one' " (9)—is the most important sentence in the tale. She wants not only to remain what she is—a living human animal (a congregation of more or less aleatory metaphysicians, like Machiavelli, Hobbes, Spinoza, Leibniz, Nietzsche, Freud, Deleuze, and Bloom is constituted around the worship of such *vis*, such *conatus*, such *Trieb*)—but also to remain unique and singular, *to be the only one*. This appeal to exclusive singularity is predicated upon the avoidance of prepossession. To be possessed is to renounce your uniqueness, to accept your epigonality, to bow in deference to a supervising precursor—"the lady who had prepared them for my discipline" (*Turn* 49). As a latecomer in a horizon of *ewige Wiederkehr* she is confronted with the horror of finding herself to be only a replica.[20] To be prepossessed is to be possessed in advance, to know, before you actually fall under the spell of your precursor, that "you're not the first." Before the dead returned, this hauntological tale of *fiction* and *repetition* (Hillis Miller) was already marked by "the return of the dead" (*Turn* 49). The method she devises to preclude prepossession by another—to cancel the necessity of her secondariness—is sophisticatedly simple: by imaginatively staging a case of ghostly apparition, she gains preemptive and preventive control over the risk of prepossession. By orchestrating a controlled and supervised play of ghosts she averts the risk of being accidentally played on by her spectral precursor—of being taken by the dead mistress from behind. This is, after all, a strategy of legitimate palliating spiritualization of crudely material interests, no more deviant than those deployed by perverse ladies in medieval courtly poetry.[21] The governess turns her possession into something (a chimera) of her own conscious making: we may call this fantasy poetry, romance, or simply misprision. It is, at any rate, a fabulous instance of "disciplined perverseness" (Bloom, *Anxiety* 95). And she succeeds. By deploying a refined " 'romance' adventure of service"—McKeon's description of *Pamela* (371)—she interrupts the series, discontinues the chain, and inscribes her singularity. The master will never forget her. Douglas will never forget her. The narrator will never forget her. Neither will we. And, as Rowe and Lukacher have suggested, her fantasy is more Real than reality itself.

One beautiful spring day an already married Pamela discovers she is also a replica (476–477). The incident involves a farmhouse, a governess, and four misses, only one of whom embodies the real mistake, the real mischief, the miss. This whole scene of the visit to the farmhouse reads like a dreamlike pre-creation, a visionary adumbration, of the awkwardly genteel country atmosphere that permeates *The Turn of the Screw*. Mr. B and Pamela go on an excursion for breakfast at a Farmhouse. The housewife regularly receives the visit of the ladies that live at the nearby Boarding School. Years earlier, Mr. B had seduced a girl called Sally Godfrey. One of the misses boarded at the school, Miss Goodwin, is his daughter, although he reluctantly introduces her to his new wife as his niece. When Pamela approaches her with affection, taking her in her arms, she rebukes her, arguing that she is not even allowed to address Mr. B as her uncle. Once the desperate ruse is exposed, Mr. B is forced to explain the reach of his "past liberties" (487):

> When I was at College, I was well received by a Widow Lady, who had several Daughters, and but small Fortunes to give them; and the old Lady set one of them; a deserving good Girl she was; to draw me into Marriage with her, for the sake of the Fortune I was Heir to; and contrived many Opportunities to bring us and leave us together. I was not then of Age; and the young Lady, not half so artful as her Mother, yielded to my Addresses before the Mother's Plot could be ripened, and so utterly disappointed it. This, my *Pamela*, is the *Sally Godfrey*, this malicious Woman, with the worst Intentions, has informed you of.
>
> (432)

This daughter of a widowed lady of small fortunes called Sally Godfrey becomes, suddenly, Pamela's precursor, a ghost that will haunt her new blissful marital state, openly proclaiming the one *inconsistency* that Pamela herself had brought into her marriage. She becomes a permanent reminder of the gap of impropriety she has inserted in a legitimate flow of genealogical continuity. Sally is a Pamela before Pamela. Or, better, Pamela is Sally *rediviva*, as Mr. B maliciously suggests: "that I doubted not to make my Pamela change her name, without either act of parliament, or wedlock, and be Sally Godfrey the second" (486). The fate of her "vile precursor" becomes a source of concern—"I wonder whether poor Miss Sally Godfrey be living or dead!" (448)—but the question is irrelevant, for, dead or alive, Sally has already turned into her accompanying ghost. The previous exclamation is inserted between article 6 and 7 of the memorandum Pamela drafts in her Journal as "rules for my future behavior." Interestingly, the seventh suggests the possibility of her own perverseness, and the eight subsequent rules concern the education of children. All critical editions of *The Turn of the Screw* should include them in an appendix. The emphases are all mine:

8. That the Education of *Young People of Condition* is generally *wrong*. Memorandum, That if any part of children's education fall to my

lot, I never indulge and humour them in things that they *ought to be restrained* in.

9. That I accustom them to bear Disappointments and *Control.*
10. That I suffer them not to be *too much indulged* in their Infancy.
11. Nor at *School.*
12. Nor spoil them *when they come home.*
13. For that *Children generally extend their Perverseness from the Nurse to the Schoolmaster: from the Schoolmaster to the Parents*:
14. And, in their next Step, as a proper Punishment for all, make their own Selves unhappy.
15. That undutiful and *perverse Children* make bad Husbands and Wives: And, collaterally, *bad Masters and Mistresses.* (448)

By calling attention to these rules I am not implying that we should impute moral perversion to Flora and Miles. What I am suggesting is that the governess profits from the (conservative) expectation of the children's predictable perverseness to orchestrate her fantasy. It is not enough that they should hint at certain things; they should be forced to see them.

## VII

Edmund Wilson was right: the tale is "study of morbid psychology," namely female hysteria; it is a "variation on one of James's familiar themes, the thwarted Anglo-Saxon spinster" (94–95); it offers, in fact, a "solid and unmistakable picture of the poor country parson's daughter, with her English middle-class consciousness, her inability to admit to herself her sexual impulses" (95). This, I think, is basically true, and it corresponds to James's conscious intention. Psychology and ideology are woven together in this complex diagnosis, for her "hysteria" is inseparable from her "English middle-class consciousness." Psychological morbidity is socially induced. The governess' consciousness is, we are told, limited. She represses the following: 1) her awareness of her sexual impulses; 2) her complete realization that she is in love with the master; 3) her consciousness of the fact that she wants to be unique. She is by contrast fully conscious of the plan she has designed, even if her narrative conceals the intensity of this awareness. She knows that she wants the children fully to see what they may have only imperfectly grasped: the improper cross-class sexual relation that existed between the master's former valet, Peter Quint, and the previous governess, Miss Jessel. As Bruce Robbins has pointed out,

> love between the classes is of course precisely what the governess discovers in the earthly paradise at Bly. The corruption she perceives

has to do with the children's knowledge of sexual relations between the former governess and one of the servants, who was "dreadfully below."
(200)[22]

But this is the very corruption she herself longs for, since, Robbins rightly adds, the governess is in love with the master and what she "herself desires is of course nothing but the erotic transgression of class" (201). What she aspires to is, in short, "to repeat the ghost's transgression and indulge a love that is prohibited by the social hierarchy" (202). She desires the *jouissance* of the Other—or, to be more precise, *the others*. Her imaginary relation with the master repeats both the former governess' conjectural relation with him and the surrogate relation that ostensibly stands (or appears) for it: her relation with the master's man dressed up in his clothes. Peter Quint is openly described as a grotesque, vulgar, and highly sexualized replacement of the master, capable of displaying an authority (avuncular, domestic-political, sexual) that the latter fails or refuses to exercise.[23] But she doesn't want her transgression to come through as a repetition. She wants her "romance"—this is the term Robbins correctly borrows from Fredric Jameson—to be unique. She is of course at the service of her master, but also self-employed to imagine—like the protagonist of *Northanger Abbey*—more than she is conceivably, empirically, pragmatically cued to believe.[24] This is probably the reason why she is so meticulous in the reconstruction of the wickedness and awkwardness (the horror, the horror) of a relationship that mesmerizes her: she may triumph over the former governess in seducing the actual master (that is her hope) but she will never reach the peak of libidinal transgression—the forbidden *jouissance*—that her predecessor has probably enjoyed (that is her fear). The thought of it would lead her to the forbidden quick-sands of French erotic fiction, including Sade: *La philosophie dans le boudoir* offers some gruesome instances of interclass sexual transgression. The governess knows the relation between Quint and Miss Jessel took place, because she is told by Mrs. Grose, and she is imaginative enough to presume an inchoate imaginative apprehension, on the children's part, of this misalliance. Her plan is to complete what the children have only imperfectly hinted at. For Flora and Miles it probably sufficed to see these characters leave Bly to know that something was amiss in the way of their being there, a mode of closeness they knew something about because of the inappropriate intimacy they (high-class children) enjoyed with them (adult household employees), especially with the subaltern Peter. The governess' insistence on their re-apparition was sufficient motive to upset them in a profoundly disturbing manner. Sufficient motive, in sum, to bring the situation to a breaking point, and force the visit of the master. She probably didn't intend to break the boy, but the boy had no other choice than breaking.

There is one important fact about the story that has in part escaped scholarly attention. From the moment the governess begins to claim having seen the ghosts, the object of her and of Mrs. Grose's concern is less the occurrence of the apparitions than the proximity, first, between Peter Quint and Miss Jessel, and second, between these persons and the children, configuring a sort of perverse *party quarrée* (Fielding, *Amelia* III.IX, 156). The governess is adamant: "The four, depend upon it, perpetually meet" (46). And the past occurrence of such dismal conclave—the meeting of the ghosts of "the others, the outsiders" (51), who "*were* rascals" (47), and the children—is likely to recur. What bothers her is an interpersonal closeness—an attachment, the violation of detachment—consequent on "a servant exceeding his or her station" (238).[25] Why doesn't the governess ask the housekeeper if she has ever seen the apparitions as apparitions and not as real people? That the governess doesn't seem to care about the fact that the house is haunted is perfectly understandable: she knows it is not. What is remarkable is that within the coordinates of probability (verisimilitude) that she has stipulated for a game the housekeeper is willing to play, neither woman finds it incumbent upon herself to discuss the one issue that academic readers of the story have battled over for decades: are the ghosts real or not? They speculate about the motive of the apparitions (the *why*), about their configuration (the *how*), not about their reality (the *what*). In *Hamlet*, by contrast, debate is raised about three problematic issues: first, the *whether of the ghost*—the possibility and reality of the apparition, seriously questioned by Horatio at first (*Hamlet* 1.1.27); second, the *what of the ghost*—its identity, which oscillates between the spirit of the deceased king and a devil taking its form (1.4.40–45); finally, and subservient to the other two questions, the *why of the ghost*—why is the spirit here, what does it want to warn us against, inform us about (1.4.47–57)? In *The Turn of the Screw*, the first question (the reality of the apparition) is never seriously considered.

The governess pretends to be solely concerned about the renewed meetings of these four characters. Never was property or possession so distinctly defined in terms of proximity: " 'They're not mine—they're not ours. They're his and they're hers!' 'Quint's and that woman's?' 'Quint's and that woman's. She wants to get to them.' " But the collapse of rank distinction revealing status inconsistency is more dramatically rendered in the following account:

> They don't know, as yet, quite how—but they're trying hard. They're seen only across, as it were, and beyond—in strange places and on high places, the top of towers, the roof of houses, the outside of windows, the further edge of pools; but there's a deep design, on either side, to *shorten the distance* and overcome the obstacle.
>
> (47; emphasis added)

I noted previously that the governess' task is to fabricate an exceptional case, which may interrupt the series that makes her unexceptional. And she does so by mobilizing the imaginative resources and conventions of Gothic romance she may be acquainted with as a potential reader of *The Mysteries of Udolpho* and *Jane Eyre*: "I had the view of a castle inhabited by a rosy sprite" (9). But it is *Amelia*, I suggested, that provides the narrator with the imaginative horizon that makes the tale possible in the first place. We have, therefore, two narrative consciousnesses, one inside the other. The first is the literary (Bovarian) consciousness of the governess as inside narrator, awash in romance conventions and yet learning to remain wholly awake to the realist "art of life." The second, and more capacious, is the literary (Flaubertian) consciousness of the external narrator, teeming with the negative irony of realism. Fielding furnishes James with narrative irony in order to set his "sinister romance" ("Preface" 124), his "little firm fantasy" (126), in motion. The reciprocal interpenetration of both modes (romance and ironic realism) is something the late James acknowledged. In his 1865 review of M. E. Braddon's *Aurora Floyd*, he distinguishes between Ann Radcliffe's "mysteries," described as "romances pure and simple," and those of Wilkie Collins, which are "stern reality" (98). Interestingly, James contends that *The Woman in White*, "with its diaries and letters and its general ponderosity, was a kind of nineteenth century version of *Clarissa Harlowe*" (98). This genealogical aperçu reinforces the eighteenth-century atmosphere of *The Turn of the Screw*, and the appropriateness of our reading it as a kind of *nineteenth century version* of *Pamela*.

If I place such an emphasis on the *literary education* of the governess, it is because this particular feature of her personality has been either passively neglected or actively denied by critics. Take, for instance, Robert Pippin's description of the girl, and compare it, say, with his appreciation of Isabel Archer as a woman who, according to her chronicler, had "a reputation of reading a great deal" and was immersed in the world of "the music of Gounod, the poetry of Browning, the prose of George Eliot" (*Portrait* 88–89). The governess, by contrast, is just

> a young, unworldly girl from a religious background, a vicarage, we are led to believe, so remote (so pre-modern perhaps) that it might be on another planet, a girl with no experience even of novels, plays, who has never even seen herself in a full-length mirror.
>
> (Pippin, *James* 114)

But who is *this* girl? If you detract from, say, Emily Brontë the massive bulk of her intense readings (of plays, poems, the Bible, newspapers, and novels) you are left with a rustic ingénue that approximates Pippin's idea of the girl. But this diminished creature, the result of a mathematical operation, is absent from the pages of *The Turn of the Screw*. Nobody freshly landed from Immanuel's Land or another planet can fantasize as lusciously as the governess. Recall that such capacity for fantasy reveals, paradoxically, according to genteel standards, a socially induced lack of manners and imagination: "To have frequent recourse to narrative, betrays great want of imagination" (Chesterfield, qtd. in Womersley, *Transformation* 100). This outmoded charge obviously places the loquacious governess on a par with Fielding and James, eminent narrators, and all three more than an inch below the Elysium of polite gentility. To imagine and mystify—*to fill out*, to use a recursive verb in *The Ambassadors*—so effectively, you need some deviant symbolic mediation or literary prepossession. You need, at least, to have been imaginatively taken from behind—if not to nurse the hope of impregnating (introjecting the earliness of, preempting the mastery of, fathering yourself through) your precursor. Had she had, as Pippin suggests, "no experience even of novels," she wouldn't have chosen *Amelia*—a voluminous, three-volume, novel—to kill her hours at Bly. The psalms, *The Imitation of Christ*, *The Pilgrim's Progress*, or even *The Vicar of Wakefield* would have been more reasonable choices for an "unworldly girl from a religious background."

Or she could have chosen *Pamela*, written prima facie by another romancier and plotter. Mr. B accuses the maid of "horrid romancing" (*Pamela* 179) and traces her literary talents to a family habit of excessive and superfluous reading: "the Girl's Head's turned by Romances" (93). The reading of Richardson's novel would have turned further her romance-infested mind, encouraging a romantic aspiration to transgress social norms of status separation. Perrault's version of the Bluebeard folktale, which James significantly mentions in his Preface to the tale, could have also been a suitable choice. Thackeray was compulsively drawn to this particular folktale of "a woman's transgression against an express prohibition" (McMaster 200), and he rewrote and refashioned it in gruesome drawings featuring scenes of female beheading, and lonely ladies waving handkerchiefs in castle battlements, which remind us both of Mrs. Grose's resolve that she and the governess should keep their heads—"we must keep our heads" (*Turn* 30); "we were to keep our heads" (32)—in their haunted, masterless "castle" and the vision of Quint standing in the battlements (16–17). In *The Adventures of Philip*, Thackeray also included several references to the motif of the skeleton in the closet, as well as a chapter-opening illustration (chapter 3) where the huge initial "S" covers the door of a "skeleton closet" (*Philip* 119) that is being furtively opened by a boy and a girl.[26] This ungainly drawing works as a perfect pictorial-allegorical anticipation of the referential concretion that James's tale works so admirably to avoid. If the governess had chosen Thackeray's novel, and eyed the picture, her fantasy would have taken a not very different turn—of the key.

## VIII

But she chose *Amelia,* and in the course of her wakeful reading she drew along significant strips and shreds of the textual net Fielding's last novel was woven into. Let us now examine the fabric more closely. Douglas explains that the story is written, and that he doesn't have the manuscript with him. "It's in a locked drawer—it has not been out for years. I could write to my man and enclose the key; he could send down the packet as he finds it" (2). *The Turn of the Screw* is premised, tellingly, upon *the turn of a key.* The possibility of the story—its physical availability as document, its arrival to the community of listeners, its aural presentation as tale— depends upon access to a locked drawer that is granted to a servant. The difference between—to put it in Coetzee's memorable terms—*he and his man* inscribes the primal scene to which the story is inexorably indebted. The servant (his man) receives a letter with a key to a drawer, and privileged access to private papers: this temporary incident of subaltern mastery pre-figures the contained (dialogized) disclosure of liberal secrets that organize the entire text. The servant, the manuscript, the drawer, the letter, the key: these are, to be sure, basic ingredients of English eighteenth-century fiction, in particular of that inaugural textual *dispositif* that Richardson unforget-tably modulated in *Pamela.*[27]

We next discover that the author of this story was Douglas' sister's governess. As Henry Sussman has pointed out, this places Douglas in the curious position of a surrogate Miles. It is a position of secondariness. Everything in this tale turns around the uncanny logic of *difference and repetition* (Deleuze), of difference between social positions (master, govern-ess, housekeeper, valet, servant, maid) that keep reemerging in vicarious scenes—of difference. There is a story, let me add, not so much because these divergent roles are always further recast in derivational scenes but rather because the difference that organizes their repetition is temporarily violated in one of them. When the *distance of difference*—what we call *distinction*—collapses, we get the *proximity of equality* (fusion, intimacy, intercourse) that the story encodes in terms of demonic sublimity. The hor-ror of propinquity is initially evoked through the "impropriety" of Doug-las' "love" for his sister's governess, and next in the related *awkwardness* of her love for her first master. Through the indirection of the surrogate narrator's love for the governess, we reach the story's most important vio-lation of social decorum. If I italicize the very awkward noun *awkward-ness* it is because James uses it three times in the tale, exactly as often as he uses the adjective: there is reference to the "great awkwardness" (*Turn* 5) of the first governess's death, to the "awkwardness" often brought off by the children's and the governess's insane prospect of writing to the master (52), to the "mere alien awkwardness" the governess has basely created for a "being so exquisite" and so full of "possibilities of beautiful inter-course" as Miles (81). The frictions caused by the intercourse between the master and the first governess, the master and the second governess, and the second governess and Miles invariably lead to an awkward outcome. Etymologically, *awkward* is what is *turned* the wrong way, the perverse, the untoward, the backward. We may want to recall that Douglas first discloses the news about a "horrible" tale while presenting "his back" (1) to the fire, a position that reminds us of the underground-cave prisoners in Plato's *Republic*, or that the governess sees Quint's figure

> turn as I might have seen the low wretch to which it had once belonged turn on receipt of an order, and pass, with my eyes on the villainous back that no hunch could have more disfigured, straight down the stair-case and into the darkness in which the next bend was lost.
>
> (40)

She later looks down from the top of the stairs to recognize "the pres-ence of a woman seated on one of the lower steps with her back presented to me, her body half-bowed and her head, in an attitude of woe, in her hands" (42). But more on awkwardness later.

## IX

The governess is described as "the youngest of several daughters of a poor country parson" (4)—a depiction that inevitably evokes the Brontë sisters—and the master or "patron" comes through as "a gentleman, a bachelor in the prime of life, such a figure as had never risen, save in a dream or an old novel, before a fluttered anxious girl out of a Hampshire vicarage" (4). The term *gentleman* marks here all the difference, for this particular governess is not yet described as a *lady*. Indeed, as Peter Laslett pointed out in a memorable study, "the term gentleman marked the boundary at which the traditional social system divided up the population into two extremely unequal sections." And yet, during the sixteenth and seventeenth century a "marked inconsistency" set in, proving "most pronounced at the bound-ary between [. . .] the gentry and the rest of society," and giving rise to "a considerable intermediate area of uncertain status between the élite and the mass" (*World* 27–29). Needless to say, the horror of James's tale unfolds in the twilight of this intermediate area. The élite in *The Turn* is of course the master, a terminal version of "the independent country gentleman" that republican ideologies identified with "the leading repository of moral dig-nity and worth in modern societies" (Skinner, *Liberty before Liberalism* 95). He is separate, not dependent—independent, not obnoxious. He is what Isabel Archer fails to be, because she has fallen "into a condition of

avoidable dependence on the goodwill of others" (*Liberty* 119). And this
is, let me recall, pace Pippin, a Hegelian condition. But whereas the *incom-
municado* master is a gentleman, the governess is an unlikely *lady*.[28] She is
thus first alluded to indirectly, when Douglas, before "reading" the story
to the group, mentions "the young lady who should go down as governess"
(5). The second time she is conferred the distinction of this title is in the
story proper penned by the governess herself, but the word is put in Miles'
mouth, who resents being "with a lady always [. . .] and always with the
same lady. [. . .] Ah, of course, she's a jolly, 'perfect' lady; but, after all, I'm
a fellow, don't you see?" (53). The ironic innuendo—the distance of free
direct speech, the notation of added reported speech when registering her
own "perfect" *ladiness*—is rather strong and is further compounded with
Mrs. Grose's dry rebuttal at the governess' claim to see Miss Jessel across
the lake: "She isn't there, little lady, and nobody's there—and you never
see nothing, my sweet!" (70). *Little lady, perfect lady*: these demeaning
locutions contrast with Flora's unassuming right to be called "little lady"
(11, 25, 35) and "young lady" (74), and, more crucially, with the respect-
ful allusions to Miss Jessel as a real lady—the "young lady" mentioned
by Douglas (5), by the new governess (12, 49), and by the housekeeper
(12). The genuine standing of the first governess as lady is the focus of
an immensely relevant exchange between the second governess and the
housekeeper:

> "I must have it now. Of what did she die? Come, there was something
>    between them."
> "There was everything."
> "In spite of the difference—?"
> "Oh, of their rank, their condition"—she brought it woefully out. "*She*
>    was a lady."
> I turned it over; I again saw. "Yes—she was a lady."
> "And he so dreadfully below," said Mrs. Grose.
>
> (31–32)

What is it that the governess *sees* when she concedes, after turning it over,
"I again saw"? Conceivably, she is less interested in the scandalous nature
of the relation between the two former workers, "in spite of their difference," than with the fact that the former governess was indeed—alas—a
lady. She is later described as having gone "off" at some point—possibly
pregnant, to her home, and eventually to die—but this is the same turn of
phrase that marks, in his first letter, the liberal distinction of the master—"
I'm off!" (10)—which is of course the distinction to be indifferent about
distinction: only those *dreadfully below* care about the contingency and

virtual inconsistency of a difference that those above simply take for granted. The first governess dies, yes, but she is not "sacrificed" (55) like the second: whereas the former chooses her destiny—she could decide, with aloofness, "to go home, as she said, for a short holiday" (12)—the latter is trapped in a gruesome plot. But gruesome for whom? A woman who feels "lifted aloft in a wave of infatuation and pity" (14) by the ruinous task of fathering (preserving, feeding, clothing, instructing, and defending) the unlikely Bly "commonwealth" (Filmer, *Patriarcha* 12); a woman who, under such circumstances and already beset by discipline trouble, considers that it "was the first time, in a manner, that I had known space and air and freedom" (14) is not the kind of person likely to invest terms like "home" and "holiday" with the positive connotation other people often attach to them: this fate she shares with the unforgettable protagonist of *The Haunting of Hill House*. What the governess dismally realizes is that the pronominal emphasis—"*She* was a lady"—doesn't so much set Miss Jessel apart from a non-gentleman as distinguish her from a woman (herself) who is perhaps less than a lady. "*She* was a lady" also implies "*You* are not a lady": this is what she "again saw." To be sure, a profound ideological incongruence caused such categorical ambivalence:

> The structure of the [Victorian] household pointed to the governess's anomalous position. She was a lady, and therefore not a servant, but she was an employee, and therefore not of equal status with the wife and daughters of the house. The purposes of her employment contributed further to the incongruence of her position.
>
> (Peterson 11)

But the fact is that the former governess had it both ways: she was seigneurial enough to be rightfully in love with a gentleman like the master, and liberal enough to demean herself to the lowness of interclass sex with servants. She had her cake and ate it too. In *Amelia*, Mr Booth narrates how he was once taken ill in a cart to a country house and "left in the care of one maid-servant." The girl came into the hall "with the footman who had driven the cart," and "a scene of the highest fondness" follows:

> the Fellow proposed, and the Maid consented, to open the Hamper and drink a Bottle together, which, they agreed, their Mistress would hardly miss in such a Quantity. They presently began to execute their Purpose. They opened the Hamper, and, to their great Surprise, discovered the Contents. I took an immediate Advantage of the Consternation which appeared in the Countenances of both the Servants, and had sufficient Presence of Mind to improve the Knowledge of those Secrets to which

I was privy. I told them that it entirely depended on their Behaviour to me whether their Mistress should ever be acquainted, either with what they had done or with what they had intended to do.

(II.V. 112)

The secret intercourse between the maid and the footman doesn't violate in principle the strictures of rank separation, but by drinking the wine of their betters, these "two Delinquents" (112) transgress, like the subalterns at Bly, strict rules of property and propriety. Likewise, the former governess ate and drank: she reached the jouissance the higher classes believed was more opulently accessible to the Molls, Mollies, Fannies, and Nancies of "the alley and the gutter" (*Oliver Twist* 267). *Noblesse oblige.* Too much for a "poor country parson's daughter" to handle mundanely. And any reader of Charlotte Brontë's *Villette* knows that when the upright *bonne* is about to break under the strain of class consciousness, she begins to see ghosts. In *The Princess Casamassima*, Captain Sholto also stresses the way cross-class democratic *freedom* is irremediably attended by a *strange* ghostliness.[29] Noblesse, indeed, oblige. Foucault elaborated this maxim in his discussion of the way in which the aristocratic blood-caste distinction was developed into a bourgeois sex-class distinction. This discussion throws light on the anxiously repressive and hygienic soteriology—the "biological, medical [. . .] precepts" (Foucault, *History* 124)—the governess wishes to deploy at Bly: when she imaginatively transfigures the unclean Miles into a hospital patient, she muses "I would have given, as the resemblance came to me, all I possessed on earth really to be the nurse or the sister of charity who might have helped to cure him" (61). *The Turn of the Screw* enacts the problematic and ever-imperfect transition "from a *symbolics of blood* to an *analytics of sex*" (148). What Foucault calls here blood is plain animal sex, and what he calls sex is *sex observed and scrutinized.* In fact, the spectral omnipresence of the monstrous *lady-male servant intercourse* turns the tale into a defective sublimation of the standard Sade vignette, with the "exhaustive analysis of sex [carried] over into the mechanisms of the old power of sovereignty and endowed [. . .] with the ancient but fully maintained prestige of blood" (*History of Sexuality I* 148). The governess, in short, is wrongly trying to (analytically) sexualize a site of blood. "According to the Foucaldian hypothesis," writes Armstrong,

> our thinking is most completely inscribed within middle-class sexuality when we indulge in this fantasy, for the repressive hypothesis ensures that we imagine freedom in terms of repression, without questioning the truth or necessity of what we become with the lifting of bans.

(*Desire* 13)

If I say that the governess tries wrongly, it is because liberal James is never conservative enough to instrumentally lift the bans and fully give up the blood-based "caste distinction" (Foucault, *History* 124).

## X

Domestic trouble begins when the master, in the role of "guardian" of his nephew and niece, sends the children to his "other house" in the country. So far, this sounds perfectly apropos. But he decides to keep "them there with the best people he could find to look after them, parting even with his own servants to wait on them" (5). The narrator deems it "awkward" that the children should have had no other relatives and that the uncle should have been so absorbed in his "affairs" that he failed to visit them. A faint echo of Prospero's prehistory can be sensed in this reproach. But more awkward still is that she should decide to give up *his* servants. The anomalous reallocation of the subalterns is a first symptom. The second is that they are allowed to become masters of the house: "He put them in *possession* of Bly" (*Turn* 5; emphasis added). His mother's former maid, Mrs. Grose, is "placed at the head of their little establishment—but below-stairs only" (5). This involves rash promotion: "She was now housekeeper and was also acting for the time as superintendent to the little girl" (5). Maid, housekeeper, superintendent: this is a plain case of overemployment. But these maladjusted and expedient rearrangements had started earlier, when the first governess went "off" and "a young woman—a nursemaid who had stayed on and who was a good girl and clever [. . .] *she* took the children altogether for the interval" (12). The housekeeper's emphasis on the pronoun (*she*) foreshadows the occurrence analyzed previously, thus reinvesting the sentence with the implication that this clever nursemaid was *not* a lady either. Considering these domestic disturbances, it is no surprise the master should find it expedient to look for a shortcut: the absolute *potestas* of the new governess. But the solution is hopeless: "There were plenty of people to help, but of course the young lady who should go down as governess would be in supreme authority" (5). A dystopian polity of servants—"there were, further, a cook, a housemaid, a dairywoman, an old pony, an old groom and an old gardener, all likewise thoroughly respectable" (5)—is thus constituted, with the unnamed governess as Lady Queen, flanked by Mrs. Grose in the role of garrulous "counsellor" (10). One may speak of the culmination of "the decay of 'housekeeping'" (Watt, *Rise* 158) and the collapse of the patriarchal family, whose beginning Watt traced back to the Jacobean period. There is something Swiftian about the circumspect outline of this makeshift commonwealth, structurally split into two distinct groups, "the part of the servants" and "the part of the children" (43). The title is *The Lady of the Blies*, and it alludes to the delusional daughter of the country parson who struggles to obtain "an odd recognition of my superiority—my accomplishments and my function—in [the housekeeper's] patience under my pain" (44). The question is: will they all survive?

The power given to the governess at Bly is not dissimilar from the domestic power Pamela gains at Lincolnshire. Both are perfect embodiments of status inconsistency. The maid, who enjoys the benefits of an ideology of feudal paternalism projected on domestic service, is however described by the impatient Mr B. as a "strange Medley of Inconsistence" (*Pamela* 75). McKeon has spoken of the squire's "total discomposure at the status inconsistency of this half-girl half-lady, half-servant half-mistress" (371), and explained the larger context in terms of the "volatile modernization of feudal conceptions of institutional service," which turned "domestic service within the last bastion of feudal patrimonialism, the family." As a result of it, "in eighteenth century England, the theory of domestic service continued to be dominated by a 'medieval' model of personal discretion and submission that was increasingly at odds with the practicalities of wage employment" (369). The heated debate, in Book IV, chapter 2 of Fielding's *Joseph Andrews*, over "the Terms *Master* and *Service*" (246–247) is proof of the ongoing relevance of this disputed issue, all the way up to James, whose plots force tendentially free protagonists to gravitate around that "last bastion of feudal patrimonialism, the family." In *Pamela*, the girl is not just a commoner confronting a member of the gentry; she is also a servant placed below a master. In *The Turn of the Screw*, written at a time when class orientation has smoothed and *almost* overrun the edginess of status inconsistency (McKeon 419), the governess undecidedly wavers between an enlightened-liberal respectable lady and a submitted medieval servant. I have already pointed out that the governess has a literary education which she tries to project on the children. This obviously betokens her professional faculty as a governess. What about Pamela? McKeon aptly summarizes that "from Mr. B's mother Pamela learns the more delicate labor of needlework and the gentle arts of singing, dancing, and drawing; and from her she receives the cast-off clothing B. so liberally and alarmingly supplements after his mother's death" (370). This transmission of labors, arts, and clothing makes up the educational program she benefits from at the Bedfordshire estate. Labors, arts, and clothing are part of the "imaginary value" that will gentrify her. McKeon had observed that "elevated birth affords opportunities for education, travel, and companionship which are otherwise not available, and that this will give the edge to the noble youth" (*Origins* 170), but the *imaginary value* lodged in those opportunities (education, travel, companionship) was also, in a progressive sense, accessible to maids. "I have been," Pamela realizes, "brought up wrong, as Matters stand" (371).

## XI

Literary descriptions of awkward arrangements of domestic power were not difficult to come by. In Fielding's *Amelia*, for instance, we come upon similarly allegorical dramatizations of unvirtuous domestic misemployment:

> Figure to yourself then a Family, the Master of which should dispose of the several economical Offices in the following manner; *viz.* should put his Butler in the Coachbox, his steward behind his Coach, his Coachman in the Butlery, and his Footman in the Stewardship, and in the same ridiculous manner should misemploy the Talents of every other Servant; it is easy to see what a Figure such a Family must make in the World.
>
> (59)

Like this family, the community of menials in *The Turn of the Screw* makes indeed *una brutta figura*. Domestic chaos becomes morally unbearable when the hierarchies of education are at stake. In Gibbon's *Memoirs*, James could have encountered allusions to orthodox relations between the "domestic tutor" and the "pupil" (63–64), but also some piquant cases of uncanny domestic disarrangement. The English historian evokes the incident of children abandoned in the "house," "family," and "private academy" of the Reverend Mr Philip Francis. Gibbon, who was a temporary resident of the place, is shocked to discover that "Mr Francis's spirit was too lively for his profession; and while he indulged himself in the pleasures of London, his pupils were left idle at Esher in the custody of a Dutch usher, of low manners and contemptible learning" (*Memoirs* 70–71). Idle master, abandoned pupils, misplaced custody, low manners: on these conditions, things are likely to take a bad *turn*.

The arrival of a governess involved no automatic alleviation of social anxieties. Although the governess's labor's restriction to domestic duties placed her in "the cast of respectable women," conduct-books upholding ideals of domestic femaleness found women who worked for their living to be "morally bankrupt." The governess, therefore, "was commonly represented as a threat to the well-being of the household" (Armstrong, *Desire* 78–79). The arrival of James's governess to Bly is shrouded in a vague sensation of "mistake" (6). This psychological feeling carries deeper ideological confusion. Watching "its open windows and fresh curtains and the pair of maids looking out," the lawn, the gravel, the tree-tops, and a "civil person" at the door "who dropped me as decent a curtsey," she feels she was "the mistress of a distinguished visitor" (7). She is surprised at the "liberality with which I was treated" (7)—like a mistress. This bodes further trouble. Whatever she really takes herself to be—poor country lady, governess, mistress—the fact is that she aspires to gain immediate recognition: "I reflected that my first duty was, by the gentlest art I could contrive, to win the child into the sense of knowing me" (9). Knowledge, commonly reduced by readers of the tale to denote the grasp of the unfathomable or sexual intercourse, is primarily *knowledge of social standing.* Her professional authority is always called into question: her "employer" assigns her tasks—dealing, for instance, with the headmaster at Miles' school—that she is unfit to carry out. Her "colleague," Mrs. Grose, former maid, temporary head of the establishment, current housekeeper, and private "counsellor" to the Mistress, Queen, and Lady of the House, is also unable to execute the task.

Peter Quint's first apparition is marked by the social impropriety of failed etiquette and excessive visual intimacy: "there was a touch of the strange freedom, as I remember, in the sign of familiarity of his wearing no hat [. . .] our straight mutual stare [. . .] he never took his eyes from me" (16). The idea is later reiterated in reference to Miss Jessel, when the housekeeper and the governess are looking for Flora:

> "No; she's at a distance." I had made up my mind. "She has gone out."
> Mrs. Grose stared. "Without a hat?"
> I naturally also looked volumes. "Isn't that woman always without one?"
> "She's with *her?*"
> "She's with *her!*" I declared. "We must find them."
>
> (64)

A sense of violation is suggested. This "queer affair" is retrospectively construed as one of *excessive nearness*—"the visitor with whom I had been so inexplicably and yet, as it seemed to me, so intimately concerned" (17–18)—and sets the governess on the track of "any domestic complication" (18). Like Hamlet, she suspects foul play and holds fast to the "inference" that "some one had taken a liberty rather monstrous" (18). *Strange freedom, monstrous liberty*: these spell, we will see, the discontents of the *liberal imagination.* Like Trilling—and, genealogically, like Eliot Norton, the James brothers, Wilson, and Matthiessen—the governess did not study with her pupils "only fiction and verse" (18), which means of course that she overtreated them to exactly this liberal diet. As Felman has rightly demonstrated, the governess' imagination is now fully at work, even if the housekeeper calls her to task: "How can I if *you* don't imagine?" (21) Her imaginative limitation doesn't prevent her, however, from realizing the dreadfulness of the scene. As in *Hamlet*, the opening concern is about the identity of the apparition witnessed in the castle's battlements. In the final apparition, I have already noted, Peter Quint comes into view "like a sentinel before a prison" (81). This resonates too with Dickensian echoes: it reminds us of the passage, at the end of chapter 34 of *Oliver Twist*, where Monks and Fagin watch through the window how Oliver sleeps over a desk with books. The scene was immortalized by Cruikshank in his engraving "Reappearance of Monks and the Jew," and James mentioned these "vividly terrible" illustrations of "the low and the awkward" in his autobiography as producing an indelible inscription in his childhood memory.[30] Monks and Fagin, we know, were no men of the genteel world, but what about Quint? "Was he a gentleman?" (22) The negative answer is repeated: " 'No.' She gazed in deeper wonder. 'No' " (22). Then follows this relevant exchange:

"But if he is n't a gentleman—
"What is he? He's a horror."
"A horror?"
"He's—God help me if I know *what* he is!"
(22)

The metaphysical impenetrability of his (or its) identity, further confirmed by the estimate that "he's like nobody" (23), is less relevant than the question of social unreadability he strikingly poses: "He has no hat" (23). The governess and the housekeeper gropingly concur that he is not a gentleman—" 'but never—no, never!—a gentleman.' [. . .] 'A gentleman?' she gasped, confounded, stupefied: 'a gentleman *he*?' " (23) And yet he is "remarkably handsome" and "dressed," the governess believes, "in somebody's clothes." Mrs. Grose confirms: "They're the master's!" Correctly or not, the governess will later refer to him as "that gentleman" (42). Such categorial volatility is alarming. The episode of social-domestic usurpation that this observation entails both foreshadows the uncanny arrogations of the talented—and positively Jamesian—Mr. Ripley and harks back to the symbolism of "ill-fitting garments" (Spurgeon 325) informing Macbeth's anticipation of magnicide. The use of the trope of "strange garments" (*Macbeth* 1.4.143) and "borrowed robes" (1.3.107) "to express status inconsistency" is also a signature symbolic strategy in *Pamela*: Mr. B insists on giving the maid his mother's clothing as a present, and the locked portmanteau containing it haunts the girl as a reminder of her transgression. In *The Turn*, the remaining intermittent exchange between the two women construes an alternative scene of domestic usurpation:[31]

I caught it up. "You *do* know him?"
She faltered but a second. "Quint!" she cried.
"Quint?"
"Peter Quint—his own man, his valet, when he was here!"
"When the master was?"

Gaping still, but meeting me, she pieced it all together. "He never wore
his hat, but he did wear—well, there were waistcoats missed.
They were both here—last year. Then the master went, and Quint
was alone."
I followed, but halting a little. "Alone?"
"Alone with *us*." Then, as from a deeper depth, "In charge," she
added.

(23)

## XII

The case of the hysteric governess has been persuasively argued by the critical tradition. But what about the master? What about the gentleman who
"went," leaving his entire household "in charge" of a *valet de chambre*, a
male household servant of the meaner sort who takes his master's waistcoats? This very much argues for the case—notably, a Sadean fantasy—of
a perverse impotent master who draws surrogate pleasure from having his
man display the absolute domestic (political and sexual) power he can no
longer exercise.[32] The governesses fall in love with him, and he returns
their love with the gift of a sexual doppelgänger, a stand-in better qualified to stand—and stay in. The episode of semiotic replacement implied in
this transaction can only be explained in terms of an ideological transition
whose liberal boundaries make room for the aberrant indeterminacies of
what James, in the tale, calls *the strange freedom*:

> The vestigial but resilient ties of eighteenth-century domestic service to
> the cultural ethos of feudal service made it a particular unstable social
> institution, balanced uncertainly between status and class orientations.
> This can be seen in what happens to the conventions of servants' wear-
> ing apparel. Livery remained customary for lower menservants, but a
> system of signification that once conferred the honor of service was now
> as likely to suggest a demeaning slavery. "Body servants" received a
> more subtle "livery", the cast-off clothing of their masters or mistresses.
> Although such a custom might aim to advertise the elevation of the
> employer, it could equally serve a contrary end by blurring the sumptu-
> ary distinctions between ranks, so that the servant appeared not as the
> signifier of his betters but as the self-sufficient signified.

(McKeon 370)

Peter Quint's extended duties also include the education of the children.
This obviously runs against the sense of propriety Parson Adams upholds:
"the first care I always take, is of a Boy's Morals" (*Joseph* 200). "I prefer,"

he adds, "a private School, where Boys may be kept in Innocence and Ignorance" (201). But Flora and Miles are stuck with a man of very questionable manners. The governess stresses the "particular fact that for a period of several months Quint and the boy had been perpetually together" (34), that they "had been about together quite as if Quint were his tutor" (35). The governess is intrigued by the housekeeper's courage "to criticize the propriety, to hint at the incongruity, of so close an alliance" (34). To her mind, Quint is gradually turning into a "phantom of inconsistency" (Badiou, *Being* 53). When the latter reminded the first governess of this incongruity, Miss Jessel asked her to mind her own business. But the housekeeper lets Miles know that "young gentlemen [should] not forget their station" (34). Fascinated with this account, the governess demands a more specific confirmation: "You reminded him that Quint was only a base menial?" (34) She did, but Miles replied that the housekeeper she was "another" (36). The account of the menial's final fate tested the limits of James's genteel imagination.

> On the dawn of a winter's morning, Peter Quint was found, by a laborer going to early work, stone dead on the road from the village: a catastrophe explained—superficially at least—by a visible wound to his head; such a wound as might have been produced—and as, on the final evidence, *had* been—by a fatal slip, in the dark and after leaving the public house, on the steepish icy slope, a wrong path altogether, at the bottom of which he lay. The icy slope, the turn mistaken at night and in liquor, accounted for much—practically, in the end and after the inquest and boundless chatter, for everything; but there had been matters in his life—strange passages and perils, secret disorders, vices more than suspected—that would have accounted for a good deal more.
>
> (27)

This mode of realism, more at home in a Hardy novel, can be traced back to Fielding. Some elements of the description—notably, nighttime, liquor, loneliness, the head wound, the slope, the ditch—are actually present in the account of an accident that befell Pamela's brother. Joseph drinks wine with a friend in an inn, and continues his journey on foot, when he is "met by two Fellows in a narrow Lane and ordered to stand and deliver." A fight follows where Joseph receives

> a Blow from behind, with the Butt-end of a Pistol, from the other Villain, which felled him to the Ground, and totally deprived him of his Senses. The Thief who had been knocked down had now recovered himself; and both together fell to be-labouring poor Joseph with their Sticks, till they were convinced they had put an end to his miserable Being. They then

stripped him entirely naked, threw him into a Ditch, and departed with their Booty.

*(Joseph Andrews* 44–45)

Interestingly, the clothing they strip him of were *borrowed robes*, the "coat and breeches of a friend." Quint's "fatal slip" is obviously more fatal, but Joseph's is not devoid of moral meaning. He is not, however, the only character in his novel to make slips. Mrs. Tow-wouse's husband, for instance, goes to bed with Betty, the "beggarly saucy dirty Servant-Maid" (72). More importantly, Lady Booby's waiting-gentlewoman, significantly called Mrs. Slipslop, is "the Daughter of a Curate" (21) who "made a small Slip in her Youth and continued a good Maid ever since" (27). The suggestion is that "an occasional slip in the dark" may not kill you, but take one single step down the ladder and life will become more sinister, or more ridiculous. Joseph works as stable boy and footman to Thomas Booby. Unlike Peter Quint—who simply "went"—he is discharged from a household that includes Peter Pounce as a steward. Like the first governess, Lady Booby—who "can't remember all the inferior Servants in [her] Family" (138)—has exposed herself to "the Refusal of [her] Footman" (36). Unlike Miss Jessel, she ends up rejected. Although she has a rather liberal grasp of her moral compass—"No woman could ever safely say, *so far only will I go*" (36)—she censures her waiting-gentlewoman "for that extraordinary degree of Freedom in which she thought proper to indulge her Tongue. 'Freedom!' says Slipslop, 'I don't know what you call Freedom, Madam; Servants have Tongues as well as their Mistresses'" (37). Later, Slipslop protests that "it is not the business of an upper Servant to *hintorfear* on those occasions" (243). When her lady accuses her of being jealous, she replies: "I assure you I look upon myself as his Betters; I am not Meat for a Footman I hope" (244). And on mentioning "Mr. Joseph," the lady replies: "Pray don't Mister such Fellows to me" (246). The anticipated moral Lady Booby draws from this set of connected social reversals is an apt description of the problem at Bly: "dear Reputation was in the power of her Servants" (38).

In Book II, chapter XIII of *Joseph Andrews*, Fielding introduces his *allegory of the ladder* to illustrate the division of the human species "into two sorts of People, to wit, high people and low People." The meaning of these categories is not taken for granted, but ironically scrutinized to conclude that "high People signify no other than People of Fashion, and low People those of no Fashion," with the proviso that "this word *Fashion* hath by long use lost its original meaning." Originally, he argues, a "Person of Fashion" was "a Person who drest himself in the Fashion of the Times," and "the Word really and truly signifies no more at this day": think of the implications this has for Quint's appropriation of his master's clothes. "Really and truly," argues Fielding, because some take the word today to imply something different, to wit, a "Conception of Birth and Accomplishments superior to the Herd of Mankind." With ironic pragmatism, Fielding is cutting down the category to fit a merely ornamental sense—an *imaginary value*—shorn of genealogical implications of gentility and aristocracy. Then follows the allegory of the *ladder of dependance*—perhaps inspired in a passage of Filmer's *Patriarcha*—and the intimacy-promoting breaches of propriety—the correspondence in private, the condescension, the degradation—that punctuate the moral landscape of *The Turn of the Screw*:

> Now, the World being thus divided into People of Fashion and people of no Fashion, a fierce Contention arose between them; nor would those of one Party, to avoid Suspicion, be seen publicly to speak to those of the other, though they often held a very good Correspondence in private. [. . .] This Distinction I have never met with any one able to account for: it is sufficient that, so far from looking on each other as Brethren in the Christian language, they seem scarce to regard each other as of the same Species. This, the Terms *strange Persons, People one does not know, the Creature, Wretches, Beasts, Brutes,* and many other Appellations evidently demonstrate [. . .] for these two Parties, especially those bordering nearly on each other, to wit, the lowest of the high, and the highest of the low, often change their Parties according to Place and Time; for those who are People of Fashion in one place are often People of no Fashion in another. And with regard to Time, it may not be unpleasant to survey the Picture of Dependance like a kind of Ladder; as, for instance; early in the Morning arises the Postillion, or some other Boy, which great Families, no more than great Ships, are without, and falls to brushing the Clothes and cleaning the Shoes of *John* the Footman; who, being drest himself, applies his Hands to the same Labours for Mr. *Second-hand*, the Squire's Gentleman; the Gentleman in the like manner, a little later in the Day, attends the Squire; the Squire is no sooner equipped than he attends the Levee of my Lord; which is no sooner over than my Lord himself is seen at the Levee of the Favourite, who, after the Hour of Homage is at an end, appears himself to pay Homage to the Levee of his Sovereign. Nor is there, perhaps, in this whole Ladder of Dependance, any one Step at a greater Distance from the other than the first from the second; so that to a Philosopher the Question might only seem, whether you would chuse to be a great Man at six in the morning, or at two in the Afternoon. And yet there are scarce two of these who do not think the least Familiarity with the Persons below them a Condescension, and, if they were to go one Step farther, a Degradation.
> (136–137)[33]

## XIII

Let us consider a crucial scene of improper "Familiarity" and potential "Degradation" in James's tale, the scene when the governess and Flora are confronted from "the other side of the lake" by her "predecessor," "a figure [. . .] of horror and evil, a woman in black, pale and dreadful" (30) who "only fixed the child" (31). This encounter, the governess suspects, may not be the first and is likely to be repeated in the future (30). She assumes it has in fact occurred again when Flora escapes alone to the lake for a small boating "adventure" of her own, only to be found later by the governess and Mrs. Grose standing on the grass by a bank, stooping down "to pluck—quite as if it were all she was there for—a big ugly spray of withered fern" (67). The overlap, on both occasions, of dubious childish innocence and potential adult perversion generates a suffocating atmosphere of anti-pastoral transgression. The clearest precedent for this scene is a crucial incident in chapter XIX, "The Child at the Brook-Side," of *The Scarlet Letter*, where Pearl gazes "silently at Hester and the clergyman" while she stands at the farther side of a brook, right at the curve where it "chanced to form a pool,"

> so smooth and quiet that it reflected a perfect image of her little figure, with all the brilliant picturesqueness of her beauty, in its adornment of flowers and wreathed foliage, but more refined and spiritualized than the reality. This image, so nearly identical with the living Pearl, seemed to communicate somewhat of its own shadowy and intangible quality to the child herself. It was strange, the way in which Pearl stood, looking so steadfastly at them through the dim medium of the forest-gloom; herself, meanwhile, all glorified with a ray of sunshine, that was attracted thitherward as by a certain sympathy. In the brook beneath stood another child,—another and the same,—with likewise its ray of golden light. Hester felt herself, in some indistinct and tantalizing manner, estranged from Pearl; as if the child, in her lonely ramble through the forest, had strayed out of the sphere in which she and her mother dwelt together, and was now vainly seeking to return to it.
>
> (*Scarlet* 224–225)

The girl stubbornly refuses to cross the brook because her mother is no longer carrying the scarlet letter.[34] The mother picks it up, fastens it again in her bosom, and the girl is finally persuaded. But she remains apart, "silently watching Hester and the clergyman" (229). If this is not material for a ghost story, what is it? James was intrigued by the scene, although he found fault with the rhetorical strategy:

> Hawthorne is perpetually looking for images which shall place themselves in picturesque correspondence with the spiritual facts with which

he is concerned, and of course the search is of the very essence of poetry. But in such a process discretion is everything, and when the image becomes importunate it is in danger of seeming to stand for nothing more serious than itself. When Hester meets the minister by appointment in the forest, and sits talking with him while little Pearl wanders away and plays by the edge of the brook, the child is represented as at last making her way over to the other side of the woodland stream, and disporting herself there in a manner which makes her mother feel herself, "in some indistinct and tantalising manner, estranged from Pearl; as if the child, in her lonely ramble through the forest, had strayed out of the sphere in which she and her mother dwelt together, and was now vainly seeking to return to it." And Hawthorne devotes a chapter to this idea of the child's having, by putting the brook between Hester and herself, established a kind of spiritual gulf, on the verge of which her little fantastic person innocently mocks at her mother's sense of bereavement. This conception belongs, one would say, quite to the lighter order of a story-teller's devices, and the reader hardly goes with Hawthorne in the large development he gives to it.

(*LC I* 408–409)

Is the image of Flora wandering away across the ladder of dependance to a further bank of the lake also "importunate"? Or is it rather in picturesque correspondence with a spiritual fact? And what about her holding a bouquet of withered fern? Isn't there a correspondence between that emblem and Pearl's Ophelia-like "image, crowned and girdled with flowers" (Hawthorne, *Scarlet* 226)? And a further correlation between both and the "lovely Flora," as she appears in *Tom Jones*, rising "from her chamber, perfumed with pearly dews," to follow the fragrant winds (134)? In the same essay on Hawthorne, James alludes to a description of what could be a Hugue Merle painting of "an elfish-looking little girl, fantastically dressed and crowned with flowers [who] glances strangely out of the picture" (402) which is a distinct prefiguration of Flora. But there are others. Take the following anti-pastoral in *Amelia*:

The next evening *Booth* and *Amelia* went to walk in the Park with their Children. They were now on the Verge of the Parade, and *Booth* was describing to his Wife the several Buildings round it, when, on a sudden, Amelia, missing her little Boy, cried out, "Where's little *Billy?*" Upon which, Booth, casting his Eyes over the Grass, saw a Foot-Soldier shaking the Boy at a little Distance. At this Sight, without making any Answer to his Wife, he leapt over the Rails, and, running directly up to the Fellow, who had a Firelock with a Bayonet fixed in his Hand, he seized him by the Collar and tript up his Heels, and, at the same time, wrested his Arms from him. A Serjeant upon Duty, seeing the Affray at some Distance, ran presently up, and, being told what had happened, gave the Centinel a hearty Curse, and told him he deserved to be hanged. A By-stander gave this Information; for Booth was returned with his little Boy to meet Amelia, who staggered towards him as fast as she could, all pale and breathless, and scarce able to support her tottering Limbs. The Serjeant now came up to Booth, to make an Apology for the Behaviour of the Soldier, when, of a sudden, he turned almost as pale as Amelia herself. He stood silent whilst Booth was employed in comforting and recovering his Wife; and then, addressing himself to him, said, "Bless me! lieutenant, could I imagine it had been your honour; and was it my little Master that the Rascal used so?—I am glad I did not know it, for I should certainly have run my Halbert into him."

(*Amelia* 200)

The sergeant is Booth's "old faithful Servant Atkinson." The father greets him heartily and thanks him for his action. The child is later reprimanded. The officer in charge agrees, "for that idle Boy ought to be corrected" (202). Two violations of distance occur in this scene: first, the degradation of "the Foot-Soldier shaking the Boy at a little Distance"; second, the serjeant's familiarity with the son of a lieutenant and former master, whom he takes "by the Hand." What Fielding calls *the picture of dependance* is at risk. Serjeant Atkinson is a pin holder of status inconsistency. He is Amelia's foster brother, but becomes Booth's servant. He shows throughout an

almost unparalleled Fidelity of poor *Atkinson* (for that was my man's name), who was not only constant in the Assiduity of his Attendance, but during the Time of my Danger demonstrated a Concern for me which I can hardly account for.

(*Amelia* 142)

Not only does he make this uncanny apparition in the park scene. At one point he *crosses the window* of Mrs. Ellison's parlor (Book 5, chapter 2), like Monks, Fagin, and Quint. In another bucolic scene he plays the Esmond role of domestic usurper, playing with the children and Amelia (222).

But it is in *Pamela* that we find the most direct prefiguration of the vindictive, visionary unconscious organizing the lake scenes at Bly. The pale and dreadful woman that confronts Flora and the governess from the other side of the lake is the ghost of Pamela, a nemesis, freshly emerged from her imaginary drowning:

And then, Thought I, (and Oh! that Thought was surely of the Devil's Instigation; for it was very soothing, and powerful with me) these wicked Wretches, who now have no Remorse, no Pity on me, will then be moved to lament their Misdoings; and when they see the dead Corpse of the unhappy *Pamela* dragged out to these dewy Banks, and lying breathless at their Feet, they will find that Remorse to soften their obdurate Heart, which, now, has no Place there!—And my Master, my angry Master, will then forget his Resentments, and say, O this is the unhappy *Pamela*! that I have so causelessly persecuted and destroyed! Now do I see she preferred her Honesty to her Life, will he say, and is no Hypocrite, nor Deceiver; but really was the innocent Creature she pretended to be!

(92)

We may want to know that the innocent creature she pretended to be suffered as a child the excesses of a "rough-natured governess." Whose eyes did the ghost of Jessel fix?

## XIV

Though unnamed in the phantasmagoria with which I opened this book, Richardson and Fielding hold a place of honor in *The Haunting of James House*. As I have noted previously, in "The Future of the Novel" (1899) James mocked Fielding's and Richardson's prudery vis-à-vis "the great *relation* between men and women, the constant world-renewal" (*LC I* 107). In order to avoid *seeing* a "relation" premised upon the physical proximity of the sexual players, the two novelists went "under the mahogany" (*LCI* 107). There was, however, a major difference between the two: whereas Richardson construed sexuality in a Puritan manner, as a shameful secret liable to explosive revelation, Fielding employed a more liberal policy, accepting sexuality as a natural fact whose moral effects on human life could become the topic of polite conversation. Fielding's liberal policy, in short, shunned the embarrassments of violated secrecy by promoting the frankness of interpersonal discussion amongst "dissentients afflicted with the malady of thought" (Mill, *On Liberty* 34).[35] Fielding was, moreover, shocked by Richardson's greater moral hypocrisy in putting virtue at the service of pornography. James was surely aware of this difference, but he made no explicit effort at reminding his readers of it. In a review of Senior's *Essays in Fiction*, he observes that "Richardson is neither a romancer nor a story-teller: he is simply Richardson," only to conclude that although "the works of Fielding and Smollett are less monumental [. . .] we cannot help feeling that they too are writing for an age in which a single novel is meant to go a great way" (*LC I* 1201). Richardson's formal singularity is effaced in the same sentence it appears to be asserted. What about Fielding's difference, from Richardson and from so much that came before and after? In the preface to *The Princess Casamassima*, James commends Fielding's "fine old moralism, fine old humour and fine old style" (41). This appraisal is probably mediated by his nearly unconditional estimation of Thackeray.[36] In a review of *Thackerayana* (1875), he mentions the Victorian novelist's familiarity with the press culture of Queen Anne's time. From this erudite acquaintance with "the Spectators, Tatlers, Worlds, Ramblers, etc. Thackeray wrote 'Esmond' and the 'Humorists'" (*LC I* 1288). We know James admired *Henry Esmond*, but it is unclear whether he read *English Humorists of the Eighteenth Century*. If he did, the description of a writer with "more than ordinary opportunities for becoming acquainted with life," who tended to be "himself the hero of his books," who "liked good wine, good clothes and good company," who underwent a strict course of classical study that led him to the Continent (specifically, Leiden), who "had a paternal allowance from his father," and was gifted with "an admirable natural love of truth, the keenest instinctive antipathy to hypocrisy," a writer who "respects female innocence and infantine tenderness," and is a "wit wonderfully wise and detective" (*Humorists* 576–578) must have caught his eye. If, in addition, James happened to be reading it any time after 1895, the year of his theatrical fiasco, then the information that this writer began at one point in his career, when the paternal allowance proved insufficient to meet his mounting debts, to "write theatrical pieces" that were hissed at by audiences because they were irreparably bad, and the proviso that "he did not prepare the novels in this way, and with a very different care and interest laid the foundations and built up the edifices of his future fame," must have brought a shiver of recognition. This writer was another Henry: Henry Fielding. In the same chapter, James could have read that "human nature is always pleased with the spectacle of innocence rescued by fidelity, purity and courage" (579), a statement whose ironic underdoing paves the way to Bly. Fielding, adds Thackeray,

> no doubt, began to write [*Joseph Andrews*] in ridicule of "Pamela", for which work one can understand the hearty contempt and antipathy which such an athletic and boisterous genius as Fielding must have entertained. He couldn't do otherwise than laugh at the puny cockney bookseller, pouring out endless volumes of sentimental twaddle.
>
> (580)

It is easy enough to nod at this, to be drawn into the current of Thackeray's scorn, and it is no doubt likely that James was in no small measure pleased with the sting. To suggest that the governess of Miles and Flora is inclined too to pour out endless volumes of sentimental twaddle—"like a whore, unpack [her] heart with words" (*Hamlet* 2.2.563)—that she comes through as Pamela *rediviva*, and that she is therefore the target of James' anti-Puritan scorn, may not be totally inaccurate. Still, this exercise of culturally protracted derision can hardly account for the undeniable strength

of Richardson's original textual inscription, which earned him the immediate admiration of intellectuals like Diderot or Goethe. Why is Richardson's
name repeatedly silenced in scholarly readings of novels by Henry James,
admittedly the consummator of the tradition the author of *Pamela* allegedly founded? I discussed this problem briefly in the first chapter, but let
me recall here Virginia Woolf's opinion that "Henry James achieved what
Richardson attempted" (qtd. in Leyburn 167). What Woolf doesn't say is
that this achievement would have been inconceivable without the dialectical mediation of Fielding, the only one of the two who came out from
under the mahogany in order to *see* the transgressive "relation" with fully
open eyes, to place inconsistency (the inexistence of the sexual relation
and the impossibility of social togetherness), in the contradictory form of
*female virtue*—"what the ladies are pleased to call virtue" (*Tom Jones* 38),
i.e. a *nothing* the *vir* vainly attempts to fill out—under collective medical
scrutiny, and to procure a dialogue around such a void. This dialogue is
premised on the cancellation of the "unreasoning instinct of avoidance"
(*LC I* 107), and it therefore can only take place in the open, in a public
sphere that "adopts the form of free commerce among equals like the dis-
course of adults in a private household" (Bender, "Introduction" to *Tom
Jones* xxiii). What Peter Brooks has argued apropos of *What Maisie Knew*
and *The Awkward Age*—that they "are in some large measure about the
sexual secret at the center of society" (*Henry James* 174)—applies word by
word to *The Turn of the Screw*: the argument has the additional merit of
making the sexual and the social overlap around their shared inconsistency
or void (secret, center). The Puritan governess's paradoxical achievement
is precisely to contribute to broaden the range of the liberal exposure: traversing her own fantasy of forbidden cross-class *jouissance*, she removes
the mahogany and forces the children to glance at the void and *see* (visualize) what (the relation) they had probably already *seen* (understood)—*to
be impossible, to inconsist*. Maybe Mr. B. was right when he forced Pamela
to memorize that *children generally extend their Perverseness from the
Nurse to the Schoolmaster: from the Schoolmaster to the Parents*. What
this gentleman doesn't say is that their perverseness is a function of the
inconsistency that lies at the center of the society they are being invited
to join.

To conclude, let me briefly consider James's complex position vis-à-vis the
anti-liberal, censorious, streak in Victorian education. The illiberal refusal
to discuss certain things before children or even to discuss them tout court
is a fault that James attributes mostly to Americans. In *The Ambassadors*,
the narrator ironically suggests that taking for granted the perverseness
of what is only imperfectly apprehended as improper leads to the circular
argument that if some things are assumed "too bad to be talked about,"
then we have a right to hold "a deep conception of their badness" (82).

In the crucial preface to *The Awkward Age,* James sees his story as growing out of the promise in a case that depends on "the account to be taken, in a circle of free talk, of a new and innocent, a wholly unacclimatised presence, as to which such accommodations have never had to come up." A circle of free talk is, remember, the clinical board of narrators, parsons and other cultivated spirits, that Fielding convokes around *Pamela,* and *The Turn of the Screw* opens with this very circle gathered before a fire. "One could count them on one's fingers," adds James,

> the liberal firesides beyond the wide glow of which, in a comparative dimness, female adolescence hovered and waited. The wide glow was bright, was favourable to "real" talk, to play of mind, to an explicit interest in life, a due demonstration of the interest by persons I qualified to feel it: all of which meant frankness and ease, the perfection, almost, as it were, of intercourse, and a tone as far as possible removed from that of the nursery and the schoolroom—as far as possible removed even, no doubt, in its appealing "modernity," from that of supposedly privileged scenes of conversation twenty years ago. The charm was, with a hundred other things, in the freedom—the freedom menaced by the inevitable irruption of the ingenuous mind; whereby, if the freedom should be sacrificed, what would truly *become* of the charm?
>
> (Preface to *The Awkward Age* 6)

James moves on to distinguish between three different ways in which "the awkward age is handled." In French society, the social scheme, he argues, "absolutely provides against awkwardness." This means that the French do not permit the "hovering female young" to "be present at 'good' talk:" only when youth is "corrected" by marriage are they allowed to participate in the circle of free talk. The French solution, then, favors the "liberal firesides" described in the previously cited passage. In English society, by contrast, no such arrangement is at work. The social occasion of talk is governed rather by a "compromise" that James describes as too "morally well-meant" and "intellectually helpless." Whereas the French mind, analytically and scientifically, is ultra-sensible to the propriety gradations of social difference, the English mind can only conceive of one "grand propriety," the rigorous application of which proves equivocal and is not "without a thousand departures from the grim ideal." The American theory, finally, is that "talk should never become 'better' than the female young, either actually or constructively present, are minded to allow it." This system involves "little compromise" and is "absolutely simple," like the French, "and the beauty of its success," he adds with unrepressed sarcasm, "shines out in every record of our conditions of intercourse—premising always our 'basic' assumption that the female young read the newspapers."

And then, of course, while the American young read the newspapers—or Emerson—the English adults, with the exception of Hyacinth, read *Treasure Island, Denis Duval,* and Trollope's *The Belton Estate,* described by James as "work written for children; a work prepared for minds unable to think; a work below the apprehension of the average man and woman" (*LC I* 1325).

## Daemonization

In writing *The Turn of the Screw,* James presciently conformed to the notion that "the British are more genuinely revisionists of one another, but we (or at least most of our post-Emersonian poets) tend to see our fathers as not having dared enough" (68). The governess dared. James dared. Miles died. The dominant ratio in James's tale is obviously that of *apophrades,* correctly translated by the governess as "the return of the dead" (*Turn* 49). But the trope of *daemonization* is also openly at work. Maybe the governess is a pervert who simply disavows the split condition of her subjectivity and displaces that division to the object of her desire—cross-class sex—exposing it for what it is, the Real cause of cultural-ideological distortion and fiction, and showing it divided in itself, a reality that is at once a Real traumatic kernel and a social taboo accommodated (moralized, censured, sentimentalized) for display before the Augustan and Victorian gaze. Exposing the children to such recognition kills them—kills the gaze. She forces the children to incorporate their visual apprehension into the gaze of the Other, to become, that is, complicit with the panopticon. This is more than a utilitarian fantasy of repressed desire, based "on seeing in every effect evidence of some actually existing cause" (Copjec 103). In our case, the governess *fails to see,* and this prompts her claustrophobia before a scene devoid of signs of guilt. "The guilt thus internally denied the subject comes to saturate its surroundings" (104). The crime is thus posed retroactively, and this operation renders the surroundings guilty. Her failure of sight—which is the blindness of the Victorian ideology—is compensated for by the inordinate conferral of sublime vision to the children—who see not so much the evidence of a cause, but the cause itself: the obscene charm of the bourgeoisie. Her act of perversion is to demonize the children.

*Daemonization,* according to Bloom, "attempts to expand the precursor's power to a principle larger than its own, but pragmatically makes the son more of a daemon and the precursor more of a man" (106). In daemonization, moreover, "the augmented poetic consciousness sees clear outline and it yields back to description what it had overyielded to sympathy" (101). This means that the liberal expansion and augmentation of freedom reverses the contained transaction of Burke's sublime, where the reader "yields to sympathy what he refuses to description" (101). By yielding back to description, the son's augmented consciousness is bound to *see clear outline*, forced to see it by the intermediation of the first demon—the Puritan governess. The children are thus demonized into clear sight, and supposedly made freer. The first demon in turn "falls upwards" (104–105), and this is not solely a Shelleyan trope of sublime *Verstiegenheit* or celestial extravagance—this is also a misprision of social elevation along the ladder of dependence. The governess is sublimely demonized into mock lady. This way, James appropriates, and modifies—subversively, inappropriately— the *glance of another*, of his precursor Fielding. "To appropriate the precursor's landscape for himself, the ephebe must estrange it further from himself." The ephebe, James, becomes the master of his tale—the gentleman who never came to Bly to see the *clear outline* of the ghosts.

## Notes

1　All citations from *The Turn of the Screw* are taken from Deborah Esch's and Jonathan Warren's edition of the tale (Norton, 1999).
2　In letter 5, Pamela confesses: "I love Writing" (17). McKeon has insisted on the centrality of the scene of writing (*Origins* 358), arguing that "language is her medium" (367) and that "her apparent linguistic assimilation masks a supersession of aristocratic honour" (368). See also Castle, *Clarissa's Ciphers*, 38–56.
3　One overhears echoes of *All's Well that Ends Well, Measure for Measure*, and *Hamlet*. Oscar Wilde described James's tale in a letter as a "wonderful, lurid, poisonous little tale, like an Elizabethan tragedy": qtd. in Freedman, *Professions*, 169, note.
4　See McKeon, *Origins*, 241. For the withdrawal from authority (the deconstruction of mastery) performed by the absent master, and the connection this may have with "homelessness" as a textual principle of (de)composition, see Davidson, 457–458.
5　As early as 1984, in an extraordinary reading of *The Turn of the Screw*, Rowe was denouncing the critical "exclusion of the work's wider social implications" (123).
6　The *corruption of innocence* is a central motif in *Tom Jones*. See for instance Book V, chapter 5.
7　Fielding uses this pun in *Jonathan Wild* and *Amelia*: see Sabor, "*Amelia*," 97. Two years before Lukacher, Rowe was courageously contending that there is no proper undecidability in James's tale: "it is always the effect or product of a certain forgetting of motives and drives" (*Theoretical* 145). For the *real* in *The Turn*, see also Miller, *Literature*, 299–302.
8　Max Duperray notes that in *The Turn of the Screw* James "does rely on the assumption of a romantic pretext" (147) and he examines the intertextual dialogue the story engages in with *Jane Eyre* and earlier Gothic narratives.
9　The passage can be found on pages 38–39 of the Norton edition.
10　Both Robbins and Bell mention, though only in passing, Richardson's novel in their brilliant readings of *The Turn of the Screw*.
11　The exhibition of passive virtue is also one of the causes of struggle for interpretation in Richardson's *Clarissa*: Warner, *Reading* Clarissa, 4–6.

12 The analogy is sharply suggested by Keymer and Sabor, Pamela *in the Market-place*, 8–11.

13 McKeon comments on the "social injustice" that is consequent upon the need for a reward (*Origins* 364). Her assimilation occurs within conditions of "status inconstancy" (365), greatly encouraged by her "highly equivocal possession of power" (365) at the end, when she gets married to Mr. B. This echoes the governess's mock promotion to "Lady" of the house at Bly.

14 This penchant for a freedom to transgressively observe, fantasize, scheme, meddle, and give opinion over and beyond all class boundaries foreshadows a Hegelian talent for reflective and "idle speculation" that has been associated with James's tale: see Sussman, *The Hegelian Aftermath*, 231.

15 For McKeon, the conservative reduction reaches the persuasion that "progressive 'virtue' only recapitulates the old arbitrariness of aristocratic 'honour': if inherited nobility owes its ascendancy to 'the fortunate accident of birth', the self-made upstart is similarly raised by fortunate accidents and execrable vices' " (387). For the oscillation in the meaning of categories like virtue and honour, see also *Origins*, 366–367.

16 In *Northanger Abbey*, Mr. Thorpe recommends Catherine to read *Tom Jones* and *The Monk*. Henry Austen's observation that his sister "did not rank any work of Fielding quite so high" as Richardson's *Grandison* must be taken with a grain of salt. See *Northanger Abbey*, 7, 47.

17 More generally, the lesson stipulates that that the cross-class matrimonial contract doesn't abrogate the twin notions that the sexual relation doesn't exist and that society doesn't exist, that the property contract is no defense against alienation, that the citizenship contract is no absolution to the precarious, finite body, and that the constitutional contract doesn't turn a certain convocation of politic ants into a substantial, transfinite, body. Žižek, I believe, is right, and this is the reason why his position is a bone in the throat of all progressive ideologies.

18 Pamela's post-marital plights stem largely from the lingering suspicion raised by "the more fundamental—and characteristically conservative—tendency," which is to "collapse the very distinction between positive and negative, on which progressive plots thrive, by making 'industrious virtue' itself a very suspect category" (McKeon 386).

19 There is also a lake near Mr. Allworthy's house in *Tom Jones*, 37. The motif is traditional, and it reappears, to great effect, in Iris Murdoch's *The Bell* (1958).

20 For Harold Bloom, "conceptually the central problem of the latecomer necessarily is repetition, for repetition dialectically raised to re-creation is the ephebe's road of excess, leading from the horror of finding himself to be only a copy or replica" (*The Anxiety* 80).

21 McKeon argues that medieval stories of love service concretize a "sense of disparity in status, a yearning to overcome that disparity," and exhibit the "profoundly palliating spiritualization of upwardly mobile ambitions and of the arduous material services required to fulfill them" (143).

22 In the same year of 1993, Millicent Bell put forward a similar argument: the *Turn of the Screw* "is about social classes and their relation to one another and about gender in this context" (91).

23 For Rowe's ingenious alternative interpretation, see *Theoretical*, 130–136.

24 McKeon insists on the importance of Pamela's clandestine self-employment (373) as letter writer, journal writer, romancier.

25  Perhaps even the focus on the homosocial growth of "mutual esteem" between the governess and the housekeeper, on their meeting "more intimately" (13), the fact that they "embrace like sisters" (14), deserves some attention.

26  See Juliet McMaster 208, and the article by Butterworth-McDermott. See Savoy's superb reading of the *closet* trope in his reading of *The Jolly Corner*, 6–8.

27  References to the key to her closet, to the door of her room and chamber, to the back door at Lincolnshire (check), and to the portmanteau abound in the novel.

28  Millicent Bell calls attention to the paradoxical devolution of gentility that occurs inside the Victorian household where "the girl who had once herself had a governess" and is in turn employed as a governess "might retain something of a lady's status by assuming a part of her employer's role" (92).

29  "I was looking for anything that would turn up, that might take her fancy. Don't you understand that I'm always looking? There was a time when I went in immensely for illuminated missals, and another when I collected horrible ghost-stories (she wanted to cultivate a belief in ghosts), all for her. The day I saw she was turning her attention to the rising democracy I began to collect little democrats. That's how I collected you" (*Princess* 346).

30  See *A Small Boy*, 102–113; and also his evocation of Cruikshank's illustrations during a drive through London with his family in the summer of 1858, on pages 240–241. For a lucid discussion of the impact of this visual *Oliver Twist* in James's imagination, and more particularly in the conception of *The Turn of the Screw*, see Blackall.

31  For the *usurpation* of domestic authority in James's tale, see Hadley, 62–64. Another fascinating episode of figurative role-reversal occurs when the governess visualized the maid as a waiter attending a young couple on their wedding journey, the young couple being herself and Miles, who looks at the window with his back to her. The problematic "telling" of sexuality implied in the reverie is brilliantly analyzed by Zwinger, 16–20.

32  For a sensible development of this point, see Bell, 106–107.

33  Compare to: "thus, as in a Family, where one Office is to be done by many Servants, one looks upon another, and every own leaves the Business for his Fellow, until it is quite neglected by all" (*Patriarcha* 31).

34  For James's readerly and visual fascination with the letter-mediated Hester-Pearl relation, and the "regression to childhood" this daemonic fascination entails, see Rowe, *Theoretical*, 53–55.

35  *Clarissa* may be read as a move in Fielding's direction. Castle has rightly stressed the hermeneutic violence exerted on a victim who never quite manages to tell her "Story": *Clarissa's Ciphers*, 22–25.

36  In William Golding's *Rites of Passage* we read that "we have, I believe, paid more attention to sentimental Goldsmith and Richardson than lively old Fielding and Smollett!" (1)

# 4 Tessera

## The Enthusiasm of Liberty: Martyrdom and Ascension in *The Wings of the Dove*

I

In the second book of *The Wings of the Dove*, Kate is described as "the contemporary London female, highly modern, inevitably battered, honourably free" (40). This is ironic, for we already know she is a developed specimen of the "restricted town animal [*bornierten Stadttier*]" (Marx and Engels, *German* 69), and therefore profoundly *unfree*. But Kate is not the only restrained creature in the novel. To show for Milly, as everyone seems to do, an "unlimited interest" (172), is proof of limitation, for—as Žižek and Pippin variously imply—*interest* presupposes a condition of interpersonal bondage: to be interested is to be (*esse*) placed in between (*inter*) people.[1] Aunt Maud and Kate can find themselves queens of infinite space, but they are *bounded in a nutshell*. Otherwise put, an unlimited interest is an unlimited *limit*. No important character in the novel is completely free. Most conform to the ur-liberal type of the "self-moving, appetitive, possessive individual" (Macpherson, *Political* 265). Kate is described as "the height of the disinterested" (117), and Aunt Maud as a "large [. . .] capacious receptacle" (120), but these are errors of transcultural appreciation, for the English ladies are fatally constrained to the commercial game of "give and take" (121). Others, like Milly, and perhaps Kate, pursue a sexual interest, although this the writing fails to suggest convincingly. We have to turn to James' *Notebooks* to confirm that the dove is also a carnal woman willing to "have it."

Only Densher appears to raise to a position of radical *disinterestedness*. He learns late that "the relation between Kate and freedom, between freedom and Kate, was a different one from any he could associate or cultivate" (281), but he also knows that in the meshes of interest, her liberty, and by extension his, amounts to "a small make-believe of freedom" (429). He has been passively, almost reluctantly, driven to take an erotic interest in Kate and a financial interest in their shared future, and then drawn into a dishonest scheme. The uneager and vacillating behavior he shows throughout most of the novel is tinged with Hamletian spleen and

DOI: 10.4324/9781003199564-4

evokes the Dickensian and Thackerayan figure of the *unlikely gentleman*. In point of fact, there is a sense in which the novel subjects the identity of its two central characters to the vagaries of communal accreditation: is Densher a *gentleman*? is Milly a *saint*?[2] When Densher is walking, observing, and meditating alone through the streets of London (Book II) and later along the canals of Venice (Book VIII), the reader is invited to occupy, through his register, a fresh and lively position of semi-detachment and near-disinterested exteriority. Like the drifting heroes of modernist fiction, he would like to steer free from the gravity of plots, but he is forced to sink into a Balzacian story of scheming upstarts deprived of "proposals [. . .] from rich relations" (*Wings* 9). Densher is a penniless journalist, almost a Bohemian drifting in a "world of thought" (56), and as such he qualifies for the job of the detached narrator, or his delegate. Unsurprisingly, in the "Preface" to *The Princess Casamassima*, James includes him in the list of his privileged centers of consciousness—"the most polished of possible mirrors of subject" (42). He enjoys this privilege with other "intense perceivers" (42) like Strether and "the small recording governess" in *The Turn of the Screw*.

In the two evoked scenes of urban itinerancy, the reader is invited to exit, with Densher, the elliptical trajectory of his spin around two centers (Kate and Milly), and also to breath, to scrutinize, to deliberate, and to reconsider. As a result, the reader feels thrown back into a chapter of *Nicholas Nickleby* or *Pendennis*, maybe into the opening sections of *The Princess Casamassima*. At the novel's close, a further reversion occurs, and Densher, in love with a dead woman and unscared by an uncertain future, turns into a late-Victorian fifth-act Hamlet wrestling with Laertes (Kate) for the honorable memory of Ophelia (Milly):

> I loved Ophelia. Forty thousand brothers
> Could not, with all their quantity of love,
> Make up my sum. –What wilt thou do for her?
>                    (*Hamlet* 5.1.254–256)

Forty thousand brothers or forty thousand sisters, like Kate, the "wondering pitying sister condemned wistfully to look at [Milly] from the far side of the moat she had dug round her tower" (317). This pattern of generic involutions turns the *The Wings of the Dove* into a Gothic romance of commerce, a story of unlikely reclusive sisters and very real men (and women) who try, by the walls of the convent, to make up their sum. Žižek was right to suggest that "the space of James's novels is thoroughly secular, postreligious" (*Parallax* 127), but he forgot to mention that his mapping out of such space remains, on occasion, disturbingly archaic and religious.

Adrian Poole wrote that *The Ambassadors* is a novel that "constantly looks forward to look back" ("James and the Shadow" 87). The same could be said of *The Wings of the Dove*, a novel overtly written in defiance of telic consolations.

## II

In *Tom Jones*, Henry Fielding claimed to make the readers' "interest the great rule of [his] writings" (69). In "The Art of Fiction," James confirmed that "the only obligation to which in advance we may hold a novel without incurring the accusation of being arbitrary, is that it be interesting." Indeed, his greatest challenge during the composition of *The Wings of the Dove* was to make Milly interesting. She owned, we know, an unlimited financial interest. But this was not enough. The logic of the plot demanded that Densher took an interest in her that surpassed her "sum," that is, the foreseen upshot of monetary calculus. But since James decided not to present this supervened affection in forthcoming erotic terms, the only solution was to invest in an aesthetic formula of *disinterested interest*. This of course turns Milly into a high-romantic rebus—a trope of sublime infinity or limitlessness. Like Strether in *The Ambassadors*, Milly is only interested in life, but whereas the former reclaims lost or missed life, the latter craves unfound life. She is not completely disinterested because she is in part driven to erotic passion. And not completely free because she is doomed. And yet, for all her finitude, she becomes a sign of freedom: an embodiment of the Christian "reversal of absolute necessity into freedom" (Žižek, *Metastases* 38), she is both absolute and capable of absolving others. At the novel's close she has become a Pentecostal spirit bestowing gifts upon the mortal fools she protects under her wings. How can this happen? How can a human being enmeshed in narrow societal relations become *absolute*? One way of formulating James's challenge is to suggest that he had to transmute Daisy Miller from a metaphor of thwarted liberty into a figure of boundless sublimity. It was already hard to believe that Daisy could, during her Alpine excursions, reach "a state of uplifted and unlimited possession [. . .] looking down on the kingdoms of the earth" (*Wings* 89). But the problem, for James, was not to invest the American girl with a temporary Byronic aura of unlimitedness or a transient Shelleyan halo of unpremeditation. This he could attempt without much risk of violating probability. The problem was to persuade the reader that this aura and this halo of infinite spiritual ascendancy was not a function of her New York financial *possibilities*.[3] In other words, James's "great romantic good faith" ("Preface" to *The Princess Casamassima* 40) was simply not good enough.

Or so F.R. Leavis believed. The English critic rightly found James' treatment of Milly inconsistent:

> The "Americanism" results ultimately [. . .] in a feebleness and in a perversity of valuation we may figure by Milly Theale of *The Wings of the Dove*. An American heiress, merely because she is an American heiress, is a Princess, and such a Princess as, just for being one, is to be conceived as a supreme moral value: that is what it amounts to.
>
> (143–144)

There is indeed something profoundly unexplained in the narrator's admiration toward her heroine: "the great, the disabling failure is in the presentment of the Dove, Milly Theale" (157). Leavis adds:

> A vivid, particularly realized Milly might for him stand in the midst of his indirections, but what for his reader these skirt round is too much like emptiness; she isn't there, and the fuss the other characters make about her as the "Dove" has the effect of an irritating sentimentality.
>
> (158)

Surely, a certain *indeterminacy* plagues both the appraisal of the quality of Milly's value—which despite the heavy sentimentalizing over her spiritual and moral gifts amounts basically to the possession of an obscene amount of money—and the assessment of the quality of the life she expects to enjoy before dying.[4] James is at pains to conceal the embarrassing trail of financial wealth lurking behind the blank or hole of her *imaginary value*, her indeterminate *je ne sais quoi*—in no way different from Lacan's *real thing*, the *petite objet a*, and *jouissance*. James fails to dissociate her imaginary value from her pecuniary value. The American girl thus unwittingly becomes *the sublimest object of Jamesian ideology*, and her vaguely phenomenal tropological credentials (a dove) turn her into a vacuum apt to swallow all surrounding people and objects into the whirlpool of her ascending wings—or maybe not so much swallow as expel. According to Hillis Miller,

> [Milly] can give but not take. That giving makes her a kind of black hole in reverse, not a place that absorbs everything and from which nothing ever returns, but a place from which things are emitted but into which nothing can enter.
>
> (*Literature* 224)

And yet, of course, the things emitted from a black hole amount to *nothings*. In his Preface to the novel, James elaborates, with Poesque ingenuity, the Freudian motif of the male-gaze-attracting female throat cavity:

> I have named the Rhine-maiden, but our young friend's existence would create rather, all round her, very much that whirlpool movement of the waters produced by the sinking of a big vessel or the failure of a great business; when we figure to ourselves the strong narrowing eddies, the immense force of suction, the general engulfment that, for any neighbouring object, makes immersion inevitable.
>
> (*LC II* 1291)

It is at the verge of this whirlpool that *social interest*—the standard driving force in novels configuring the "experience of intersubjectivity" (Žižek, *Parallax* 126)—degenerates into the "abysmal trap" (1291) of an *epistemic intestine*: the flows of moral recognition and credit between individuals standing in the same arena are transformed into the unidirectional gaze of males inspecting the female patient's cracked inside. The fact that Milly is very much—and this is no trope—a patient in the hands and eyes of a doctor lends an aura of consistency to my apparently wild conjecture. In more than one sense, Milly plays the same symbolic role in her novel that the golden bowl plays in the later novel:

> to all appearances, the world of the two couples is a flawless rare crystal, all of a piece, beautifully gilded with American money, but beneath this appearance there are *deep cracks*. The *cracked bowl* is thus what Lacan called the signifier of the barred Other, the embodiment of the falsity of intersubjective relations condensed in it; consequently, we should not treat it primarily as a metaphor but as an agent in and of intersubjective relations: its possession, destruction, the knowledge about its possession, and so on, structure the libidinal landscape.
>
> (Žižek, *Parallax* 141; emphases added)

The dove too transparently embodies money and is cracked. To Pippin's credit, however, this symbolic focus evinces his perhaps inchoate awareness that money is, as Marx proposed, a token of interpersonal relations that "emerges as the materialization of the symbolic institution insofar as this institution is irreducible to direct interaction between 'concrete individuals'" (Žižek, *Plague* 128–129).[5] Otherwise put, James cannot directly represent the nascent capitalist institution—what Derrida calls the *state of debt*—because its ramifying networks are inherently hostile to phenomenal reduction, but he can certainly embody its grounding inconsistency in an "underlying obscene phantasmic support" (*Plague* 94), the *synecdoche of money*, and further displace this, in a final figurative turn, to the symbol of the cracked, fleeting and self-consuming dove.[6] His refusal, at the novel's close, to cash in her value shows the extent to which he is willing to save her—to save, that is, her negative magnitude (*nihil privativum*) both from the indeterminate abyss of the Real (*nihil negativum*) and from the obscenities of determinate accountability and finite calculation. This interpretation contradicts Pippin's running claim about the transparency of interpersonal relations.

There is something to Parrington's reproach that "it was the first mistake of Henry James that he romanticized Europe, not for its fragments of the medieval picturesque, but for a fine and gracious culture that he professed to discover there" (129). As I will try to prove, James's attempt to invest Milly with the "imaginary value" of cultural fineness and grace, itself an epochal leak from the aristocratic rank-tank, is undercut by the work in the novel of barbarous forces—the primitive unenlightened force of "the medieval picturesque" and brutal post-enlightened force of capital. The narrative spiraling around her inherited *wealth* and her remaining *life* is distinctively realized through the unrealized and essentially indeterminate calibration of, respectively, the pronouns *all* and *it*. The near-Miltonic sublime *all* of her value—"all before her" (*Wings* 88); "the world all before them" (91); "with your luck all round" (186)—is at last tentatively determined through Kate's indiscrete glancing at the New York letter.[7] The *it* of her life is left hanging in the novel, but is solidly realized in the notebook entry:

> I see him as having somehow to risk something, to lose something, to sacrifice something in order to be kind to her, and to do it without a reward, for the poor girl, even if he loved her, has no life to give him in return: no life and no personal, no physical surrender, for it seems to me that one must represent her as too ill for *that* particular case. It has bothered me in thinking of the little picture—this idea of the physical possession, the brief physical, passional rapture which at first appeared essential to it; bothered me on account of the ugliness, the incongruity, the nastiness, *en somme*, of the man's "having" a sick girl: also on account of something rather pitifully obvious and vulgar in the presentation of such a remedy for her despair—and such a remedy only. "Oh, she's dying without having had it? Give it to her and let her die"—that strikes me as sufficiently second-rate.
>
> (*Notebooks* 169–170)

Note the vaporous exactitude of these undetermined phrases "physical surrender," "*that* particular case," "having had *it*." It is as if James refused, in the finished novel, to make explicit the terms of a dealing that could only be fitly described as one of male prostitution. But in the original conception he did consider an "ugly" and "vulgar" possibility. Leslie Fiedler once argued that as late as the time of Henry Adams, "the figure of a woman refined to the point where copulation with her seems blasphemous possesses the imagination of the most sophisticated American writers" (*Love* 293). But, as is often the case, *sexual antagonism* is here bound up with *status inconsistency. The Milly fantasy*, we know, is not the object of James's or Densher's desire, but rather the mise-en-scène of an unfixed desire. The setting of fantasy is, moreover, as Eagleton pointed out, "definitely connected with social privilege. A man who can mistake an ordinary woman for a high-born maiden is also someone who assumes that the world owes him a living" (*English Novel* 5). James speculated with the turn his novel could take if he were a French writer addressing a French public.

> If I were writing for a French public the whole thing would be simple—the elder, the "other," woman would simply be the mistress of the young man, and it would be a question of his taking on the dying girl for a time—having a temporary liaison with her. But one can do so little with English adultery—it is so much less inevitable, and so much more ugly in all its hiding and lying side. It is so undermined by our immemorial tradition of original freedom of choice, and by our practically universal acceptance of divorce.
>
> (170)

When the ugliness of the hiding and lying side is revealed to young English readers, when a further turn of the screw is inflicted on those of an awkward age, forcing them to become people on whom nothing is lost, then a certain English tragedy befalls, from *Paradise Lost* to *The Cement Garden*. But if Nanda could read French novels, and Flora and Miles could be invited to glance at the nasty particulars of a "temporary liaison," why didn't James proceed to complete his French novel?

Well, he was probably engrossed with the alternative challenge of fleshing out Milly's constitutive *emptiness*, of *filling out*—as Chad would say—her (w)hole. In part he believed that educated readers would join in the inspection of the cavity and replenish the gap by taking along their own richness of implication and association, mobilizing their own cultural expectations about wealth, rarity, youth, and Americanness. But he also had to do his job of scenic narrative, dialogue, and, very often, picture. This is where James' own creative limitations, his artistic unfreedom, came to the fore. He had to find a role for the girl inside a simple plot of mercenary matrimonial scheming, a role that transcended the topical significance of an heiress falling victim to a predatory couple. But how could he determine, in narrative terms, her indefinite spiritual gift? What kind of plot could accommodate that surplus? This is where he turns to the cellar of his haunted house in search for an attending ghost. And this is where we come across the name of an important precursor, and most devoted admirer of Shakespeare and Fielding: Edward Gibbon.[8] In my reading of the novel, James draws his plot of *infinite sacrifice* from Edward Gibbon's *The History of the Decline and Fall of the Roman Empire*. Along with the plot, he capitalizes both on the Enlightened narrative framing Gibbon's plot and on a related set of scenes and symbolic roles. The dominant symbolic roles are those of the medieval soldier, the Byzantine princess, and the Christian martyr. Gibbon observed that

> Commodus, from his earliest infancy, discovered an aversion to whatever was rational or liberal, and a fond attachment to the amusements of the populace; the sports of the circus and amphitheatre, the combats of gladiators, and the hunting of wild beasts.
>
> (*Decline* I.IV.117)[9]

## III

*The Wings of the Dove* is a narrative of human conflict described in the precise terms of those vulgar amusements—circus, amphitheater, gladiator combat, hunting of beasts, and we could add the persecution of Christians and naval engagements. As sacrificial object of interest and desire, Milly is figuratively implied in all of these penitential arenas, and the sympathy James asks the reader to feel for her falls foul, I submit, with "whatever [is] rational or liberal." A modern avatar of the Rhine-maiden evoked by James in his "Preface," Milly is a spiritual barbarian who has crossed the Rhine-line and infiltrated the territories of the English empire in order to play out her tragedy and elicit some pity and no fear. The chronicle of her trials rehearses the sacrificial patterns of ecclesiastical history originally designed by Eusebius of Caesarea and characterized by Pocock as "a history of combat with demons" (*Barbarism* III 72), a description which not casually befits too *The Turn of the Screw*. The correlated scenes are the soldierly fight in the battle, the maid-princess conversation in the palace room, and the beast-versus-martyr confrontation in the arena of the circus. All three scenes are theatrically configured to allow one or various spectators to contemplate, with awe and curiosity, the tragic spectacle. The first spectator is of course the deliberating narrator.

In this chapter I will consider James's relation with his eighteenth-century precursor by examining the pressure of Gibbon's figure and writing in his work, and, more particularly, the presence of his historiographic pattern in *The Wings of the Dove*. Although there has been some critical discussion about James' conception of history, the study of the influence of specific historiographical conceptions in his fiction constitutes a neglected approach.[10] In particular, the role of Edward Gibbon in fashioning James' *narrative unconscious*—one presumably informed by the "enthusiasm of liberty" (Gibbon, *Decline* I.VII.197)—remains overlooked. One exception is Adrian Poole's essay on "James and the Shadow of the Roman Empire: manners and the consenting victim," but Poole oddly covers standard Gibbonian territory without mentioning the name of the English historian. James praised Gibbon's *Memoirs* (*LC I* 1399) in a review and alluded with studied evasiveness to *The Decline and Fall of the Roman Empire* in *The Wings of the Dove* and in *Italian Hours*. If my reading is correct, his interest in Italy reaches beyond scenic Orientalism or antiquarian fascination and is energized by a historiographic agenda that sees Venice as the starting point of a Byzantine *ligne de fuite*—the place to die, no doubt, from Shakespeare to Mann, but also the lacunal urb where something (an Oriental overflowing of the measure, the spread of luxury, the melting and evacuation of Rome) began.

New work on Gibbon by Womersley and Pocock has thrown into relief the cultural relevance of Gibbon's "Enlightened narrative," the way it reshapes modern and contemporary conceptions of historical decay and primitivist revival. This narrative is described by Pocock as "the emergence of a shared civilization of manners and commerce" out of the "feudal disorders" (barbarism, religion) of the European past (*Barbarism and Religion II*, 20).[11] The subtextual grip this "Enlightened narrative" may have exerted on James' imagination is multiple, but we best sense it as a uniform mode of resistance: from inside this rational-liberal narrative he purports to undo it through reversion. James capitalized on the romantic potential of barbarous-cum-religious superstition: the portrayal of Milly as "perfect angel" (253) and "dove" (373), rushing "martyr"-like to her own "sacrifice" (52, 60, 366), as an object of "worship" (277) and "adoration" (329, 335) bequeathed to sinners to "commune with" (363) in the face of a mercenary commercial age, restores, through axiological reversal, the *romance* effectiveness of Gibbon's narrative. This reversal should be studied in unison with James's conflicted resort to Catholicism in his work. It is very surprising that Gibbon is not even mentioned in the two most important scholarly studies of James and Catholicism, by Edwin S. Fussell and Susan Griffin.

Despite James' civilizational-rationalist credentials, he nurtured a proto-modernist, conflicted adherence to pre-enlightened modes of cultural existence. By the time he wrote *The Wings of the Dove* (1902), his "sentimental allowances" for an "abandoned religious world" (Auchard, Introduction to *Italian Hours* xvi) had managed to outface his early disgust for the feudal and papal values of ecclesiastical Christianity. The seldom-noted parallelisms between James' novel and D'Annunzio's *Le vergine delle rocce* (1895) contribute to render more visible James' creative investment in a premodern tropology of heroic-erotic sanctity and Oriental monasticism, also at work in Goethe's portrayal of Ottilie in *Die Wahlverwandschafften*. By highlighting the etymological association between "decadence" and "decline," the Gibbonian approach I propose casts new light on the ideological correlation, in James' oeuvre, between the aesthetic appeal of decadence leading to bondage and the logic of historical decay—from and towards liberty. In sum, James' interest in Gibbon is twofold and potentially paradoxical: on the one hand he identified with the drifting, cosmopolitan and idle young man of the *Memoirs*, furnished with the quasi-unlimited freedom of a proto-Bohemian existence, as well as with the republican civil Liberty this same man championed in his historiographic masterpiece; on the other hand, he was morally driven towards the sacrificial figures of martyrdom and victimhood that religious persecution and systemic oppression produced in the wake of Roman-imperial decline. That this decline should have led to "the seeds of European liberty" (Pocock, *Barbarism and Religion II* 2) further compounds the paradox it is my intention to tackle. At bottom, what transpires is a consideration of the role of freedom in the decision to renounce society—the decision to immolate the daisy and sacrifice the dove—and the relationship between this—for Hegel, romantic—freedom and the ancient republican liberties of Rome. Just as there is a republican liberty—civic liberty is a positive conception, but Gibbon flirted with the negative, more Hobbesian, alliance between "liberty and law" (*Memoirs* 49)—there is also a freedom to forsake all commitments to the City and to lead a reclusive life devoted to spiritual surplus or lung-cum-intestinal excess: Milly's probable *consumption* is but a symptom of broader expenditures and deeper consummations.[12] Gibbon would call such spiritual surplus a passion, even an enthusiasm, and the freedom he recommended from it, in his digressive proto-Thackerayan assault on the shortcomings of school education, is less the positive liberty of classical and civic republicanism than the negative liberty that Hobbes blithely advocated: "Freedom is the first wish of our heart; freedom is the first blessing of our nature; and, unless we bind ourselves with the voluntary chains of interest or passion, we advance in freedom as we advance in years" (*Memoirs* 74).[13] Note that for the Enlightened historian, the Christian martyr has willingly bound herself in "the voluntary chains" of enthusiasm.

## IV

So James read Gibbon. This I take as a fact. He surely read the *Memoirs* and he very probably read passages, perhaps chapters, of *Decline and Fall*. Very unlikely the whole thing, for that is the kind of youthful feat that would have registered in a private letter. In "The Art of Fiction" James contends that Trollope's "betrayal" of the "sacred office" of the novelist as historian—to confess, as the English novelist used to do, that he was just "making believe"—shocks him "every whit as much in Trollope as it would have shocked me in Gibbon or Macaulay" (*LC I* 46). In an important essay, Peter Rawlings observes that James resorts to Gibbon because his "literary, social, and moralizing aims" differed markedly from "those of the nineteenth-century German school" (*Henry James and the Abuse* 8–9), whose scientific positivism he despised.[14] But is this rather exceptional critical aperçu enough? Do we need to read Gibbon if we wish to understand *The Wings of the Dove*? Maybe not, but I see no harm in granting the condition and attempting the connection. Gibbon's *absence*, for instance, is conspicuously *present* in the list of authors Mrs. Stringham has read in preparation for her Italian travels: the narrator mentions Pater, Marbot, Maeterlinck, and Gregorovius (*Wings* 79). Ferdinand Gregorovius is the German historian who "took up the task which Gibbon abandoned," namely, to "describe how the cross was planted on the temples of antiquity" (Münz 697). The allusion is of course to the famous account Gibbon gave of his decision to embark on his project, whose first sentence reads like a prosified Pound Canto and remains among the most memorable in the language:

> It was at Rome, on the 15th of October 1764, as I sat musing amidst the ruins of the Capitol, while the bare-footed friars were singing vespers in the temple of Jupiter, that the idea of writing the decline and fall of the city first started to my mind. But my original plan was circumscribed to the decay of the city rather than of the empire.
>
> (*Memoirs* 143)

Indeed, the original plan to cover the history of Rome during the Middle Ages was completed by Gregorovius in his book *Die Geschichte der Stadt Rom im Mittelalter* (1859–1872). James uses Mrs. Stringham's reading preferences to offer the reader a cracked pottery vessel, requesting her to complete it by finding the missing piece. This *tessera* is Gibbon, as the narrator later proclaims: "Susan had read history, had read Gibbon and Foudre and Saint-Simon" (182), only to generate a further blank of indirection, another crack in the earthen bowl, with the comment that "it would be somewhere in Gibbon" (183). This game of sinuous allusion could be furthered expanded to cover James's possible readings of Byron's *Childe Roland*, where Gibbon is extolled as *the lord of irony*, "sapping a solemn creed with solemn sneer" (III.107.998–999);[15] or his reading of *The Education of Henry Adams*, which took place after he completed *The Wings of the Dove*, but where he could have seen his own concerns about historical

decay and repetition luminously recast in apocalyptic-philosophical jargon. Adams describes Gibbon's imaginary visit to Notre Damé of Amiens,
where he "ignored the Virgin, because in 1789 religious monuments were
out of fashion" (*Education* 323).[16] And also, of course, his sitting at sunset
at the steps of Santa Maria in Ara Coeli, a biographical episode Adams
often appropriates:

> One morning, Adams happened to be chatting in the studio of Hamil-
> ton Wilde, when a middle-aged Englishman came in, evidently excited,
> and told of the shock he had just received, when riding near the Circus
> Maximus, at coming unexpectedly on the guillotine, where some crimi-
> nal had been put to death an hour or two before. The sudden surprise
> had quite overcome him; and Adams, who seldom saw the point of a
> story till time had blunted it, listened sympathetically to learn what new
> form of grim horror had for the moment wiped out the memory of two
> thousand years of Roman bloodshed, or the consolation, derived from
> history and statistics, that most citizens of Rome seemed to be the better
> for guillotining. Only by slow degrees, he grappled the conviction that
> the victim of the shock was Robert Browning; and, on the background
> of the Circus Maximus, the Christian martyrs flaming as torches, and
> the morning's murderer on the block, Browning seemed rather in place,
> as a middle-aged gentlemanly English Pippa Passes; while afterwards,
> in the light of Belgravia dinner-tables, he never made part of his back-
> ground except by effacement. Browning might have sat with Gibbon,
> among the ruins, and few Romans would have smiled.
>
> (*Education* 81–82)[17]

It is worth recalling that, in James's depiction of the Christian martyr, flam-
ing and consuming itself as a torch, he had also resorted to Carlyle's (and
Dickens') historical imagination of the French Revolution:

> Milly had held with passion to her dream of a future, and she was sepa-
> rated from it, not shrieking indeed, but grimly, awfully silent, as one
> might imagine some noble young victim of the scaffold, in the French
> Revolution, separated at the prison-door from some object clutched for
> resistance.
>
> (*Wings* 462)

In his study of James's late fiction, Matthiessen mentions that the death of
his wife led Adams "to devote his deepest intellectual energies to understanding the medieval cult of the Virgin" and that he endowed his portraits
of her "with much the same rare distinction of subtlety and refinement
that James bestowed upon his heroines" (*Major* 51). This brings us back

to the rationale of Adam's cryptic notation that Gibbon "ignored the virgin" in Notre Dame of Amiens. For what conjoins James and Adams in a common front against Gibbon is the determination to place the emblem of the Christian martyr/saint/virgin at the heart of their reactionary-romantic appropriation of decadent Rome, and thus to insert a trope of unbound (spiritual-cum-monetary) speculation in the restricted, normative syntax of civil Roman exchange. When Adams studies in Amiens the Church of the Virgin he is not merely indulging in the whims of presentism, juxtaposing contemporary political violence (the assassination of Russia's prime minister) and "ancient worship" (Tanner, "Henry James" 100). He was also commemorating the death of his lady, just like James would monumentalize her cousin in *The Wings of the Dove*:

Martyrs, murderers, Caesars, saints, and assassins—half in glass and half in telegram—chaos of time, place, morals, forces, and motive—gave him vertigo. Had one sat all one's life in the steps of Ara Coeli for this? Was assassination to be the last word of Progress?

(*Education* 393)

But *did* Gibbon ignore the virgin? Adams insists that the "fat little historian" was so determined to "dart a contemptuous look on the stately monuments of superstition" that in the end, much against his own wishes, "he brought the French revolution" (*Education* 323). For Gibbon despised the Revolution, which he saw, foreshadowing Burke, as the consequence of "the French disease, the wild theories of equal and boundless freedom" (*Memoirs* 173). But weren't the wild theories of radical equality part of the built-in revolutionary makeup of the Christian religion? And weren't the martyrs and saints the historical players who brought the impossibility of "boundless freedom" to its most hallucinatory symbolic perfection? Did Gibbon ignore those spiritual heroes and heroines? Wasn't rather his anti-Christian irony outsmarted by the irrational interest that drew him to the very figures he purported to ironize? In his *Memoirs* he speaks with studied scorn of his aunt Hester as the family "saint," and concludes: "Of the pains and pleasures of spiritual life I am ill-qualified to speak" (54). But the fact is that he sought qualification, that, at Oxford, he developed a taste for "the institution of the monastic life" and the "invocation of saints," and that he ended up at fifteen converting to Catholicism (85). Two years later he abjured this new faith, to be sure, just like James repudiated Dickens when he turned twenty-two. And yet, and yet.

So James read Gibbon. American philosopher Robert Brandom has argued that "it is silly to try to interpret Hume if one knows only his distinctively *philosophical* antecedents and context—if one has not also read Gibbon and Adam Smith and so on." And he adds that his doctoral mentor explained to him "that one could not responsively expect to understand what a thinker meant by a particular claim until and unless one had read everything that thinker had read" (*Tales* 99). The point is clear and correct. But he blunders by reversing the direction of influence: it is by reading Hume that we learn about Gibbon, and not the other way round.[18] Anyway, we get the idea. I shall not be claiming, to enforce the distinction made by Momigliano in his classical essay on Gibbon, that James's reading of the English historian *formed his mind*—this was a task reserved for *Hamlet* and Dickens—but only that Gibbon was an author that he "probably consulted in his maturity" ("Gibbon's Contribution" 451). On 27 March 1897, James published a brief review of several books in the *Harper's Weekly*. This "London Note" ended with an extravagantly contrite paragraph where he apologized for lack of space to devote to the recently published *Memoirs* of Edward Gibbon. Interestingly, the paragraph hangs from a previous appraisal of the book *The Thackerays in India*:

> If I spoke just now of the pedestal placed under Thackeray's feet, what shall I say of that furnished for Edward Gibbon by our having at last the text, delicious and incomparable, of his Autobiography and his Letters? I have been condemned to leave myself without space for a word worthy of the subject—altogether one of the richest that has lately come up. The oddity of the whole story of our perverted possession of him is only equalled by the beauty—there is no other name for it—of what relenting fate has at last restored to us. It is, doubtless, indeed, by this time common knowledge that the text of the Autobiography has been found to be no less than six separate texts, each one of a numbered and individual joy to those in whom the taste for Gibbon is strong. What has largely happened is of a nature to make it in general so much stronger than ever that I feel a double pang, at having to leave untouched one of the most rounded little romances of the literary life.
>
> (*LC I* 1399)

Three aspects stand out in this convoluted justification. First, the unlimited praise. Second, James's *perverted possession* of Gibbon. Third, the description of the *Memoirs* as a *romance of literary life*. James spares no adjective to express his enthusiasm for an autobiographical account where his earlier self probably got uncannily reflected. The story of the Protestant son of an English country gentleman who is sent to a Swiss school, converts to Catholicism, is then sent to Oxford, to read history and theology, who despairs and leaves college, and is later bound to erratically undergo, mostly in London, but also in travels to France, Switzerland, and Italy, the melancholy trials of an omnivorous literary education under the constant threat of "blind activity of idleness" (*Memoirs* 84) is obviously a narrative that could catch James's imagination. To the parallel features of premature familiarity with the Continent, academic failure, literary vocation, professional disorientation, tendency to idleness, we could add that of *status inconsistency*. Not that this was a conscious problem for a citizen of the democratic America described by Tocqueville—but it certainly was a critical issue *for* Gibbon that proved (unconsciously) meaningful *to* James. This connects with the second aspect I mentioned previously—the *perverted possession*—for we could easily redirect this trope from its original context towards the ideological conflict that underpins James's narrative efforts: where do I stand or how do I consist (socially, professionally) and why am I so interested in fated lacunar women? But also with the third aspect, for James had spent a lifetime, at least since *Roderick Hudson*, trying to fashion, out of very uncertain materials, *his* own *little romance of the literary life*.

James's *perverted possession*, his taking Gibbon from behind, entails a reversal of valences that is potentially writ large in the historian's critical program—his distrust of concentrated spiritual speculation (Platonism, Christian-Neoplatonism, Mysticism, Monasticism) may be a defensive move (a reaction formation) against an over-sweeping personal fascination: the vindication and apotheosis of the martyr-virgin saint.[19] We must bear in mind that the saint was a figure of reflective speculation that had occupied in advance the station that the defecting aristocrat (Hamlet) would have liked to settle on: get thee to a nunnery because deep down I would like to be there, because my only patrimony is Horatio's philosophy *plus* the rich unreality of "things in heaven" (*Hamlet* 1.5.168). The *imaginary value* (the spiritual excess) of the downward-moving aristocrat has been in part preempted, taken over in advance, by the Christian saint, whence comes the irresistible, necessary, structural, appeal that the latter exerts over the former. The *noblesse de robe* drops the sword, rejects genealogy, blood, semen, and land, and aims at an *aristocracy of the spirit* that the figure of the Christian martyr/saint has prematurely outlined and seized: George Eliot's nod at Saint Theresa's "spiritual grandeur" in the Prelude to *Middlemarch* bears the marks of this structural readjustment. The Christian saint has in turn displaced the Stoic sage as a model of spiritual exuberance pitted against the irrelevance of social existence. This is the transition we witness from Shakespeare to Racine, although the English poet was already significantly intrigued by the female saint: think of Jean of Arc in *1 Henry VI*. In *Hamlet* we sense the tension between the two paradigms of anti-social/domestic escapism: the suicidal Stoic republican hero and the monastic girl. At some level, the freethinking prince would like to be both. At the same level, Gibbon—officer in the English militia and reader of Gnostic tracts—too. James, by contrast, had a pain

in his back, shed his soldier skin, and became, behind the tree, the speculation of the girl.[20]

The romance of the literary life was not exempt of taxonomic tribulations. The spectre of status inconsistency haunts the emerging homme de
lettres. Gibbon knows he has been privileged, through "the distinction of
birth" (*Memoirs* 42), with the "benefits of a liberal education as a scholar
and a gentleman" (*Memoirs* 51) and with a "liberal maintenance" (51). At
Oxford, for instance, the teenager is very much aware that "no independent members were admitted, below the rank of a gentleman commoner;
and our velvet cap was the cap of liberty" (*Memoirs* 80). He also knows
he enjoys "the right of primogeniture" (57). Gibbon's father likes to style
himself a member of the "country gentleman" (*Memoirs* 52), a Tory squire
who inherited a fortune obtained through financial speculation: quite literally, Edward Gibbon is a superstructural effect of the 1688 Revolution, a
slowly unfolding historical event that helped replace landed interests with
trade interests, territorial hegemony with commercial hegemony, allowing "the merchant to make a fortune so that his heirs could live as landed
gentlemen" (Pinkus, *1688* 484).[21] The young Gibbon, treated to more
than one "domestic tutor" (*Memoirs* 63)—note the Jamesian intensity of
such category—temporarily suffers the combined agonies of a rebellious
"pupil" ready to judge his preceptors (*Memoirs* 64) and a "rebellious son"
whose father "threatened to banish and disown and disinherit" him (92).
The Hamlet echo is tenuous, but Gibbon's sly reappropriation of it leads
to the pattern of domestic usurpation that I have described earlier, with
Kierkegaard and Bloom, as that of *giving birth to his own father* (*Anxiety*
26). When he tells us that, upon his mother's death, his father "persevered
in the use of mourning much beyond the term which has been fixed by
decency and custom" (66), Gibbon out-Hamlets Hamlet and prepossesses
the *princeps* (first titleholder). James probably relished this perverse touch.
While in London, the young man finds himself lost. His father "was no
longer in the memory of the great with whom he had associated," and
he consequently found himself "as stranger in the midst of a vast and
unknown city" (110). He becomes increasingly aware of his true place in
an emerging urban middle-class world where "birth and riches are measured by the standard of personal merit" (69). To be sure, young Gibbon
grows to become a *gentleman*, a social badge that never quite shed its roots
on landed interest and the country. But he reads words, words, words, not
all of them strictly necessary for the education of a scion of the country
gentry. He turns over "many English pages of poetry and romance, of history and travels" (68). At Westminster, "reading, free desultory reading,
was the employment and comfort" of his "solitary hours" (71). He was
there allowed, he adds, "without control or advice to gratify the wander-
ings of an unripe taste" (71). The process of self-begetting, of his becoming

his own father, is reflexively afoot: "My father's friends who visited the boy were astonished at finding him surrounded with a heap of folios, of whose titles *they* were ignorant and on whose contents he could pertinently discourse" (72). Scholars like Womersley and Carnochan have rightly emphasized Gibbon's tortuous categorial wavering between *man of letters* and *country gentleman*, or between country squire and historian: "How often did I sigh," he reminisces in his *Memoirs* about his years in the militia, "for my true situation of private gentleman and man of letters" (127). One may speak of an attempt to give narrative balance and psychological consistency to what is at bottom a (shared) structural effect of plain *status inconsistency*.[22]

The fusion of the *gentleman* and the *historian* is one of the aspirations that animate Fielding's narrative project, as various digressive asides in *Tom Jones* prove.[23] Womersley sharply suggests that the "shibboleth" that distinguished the worldly authors from "interlopers" was the *genteel irony* recommended by Chesterfield and practiced by Gibbon (and Fielding): it was the mark "which defined the gentleman in terms of a comprehensive point of view and the verbal idiom which seemed naturally to accompany that expansive, even vision" (*Transformation* 111). There is no need to stress any further how much this evenness and expansiveness are fostered by the constitutive separation, disinterest, and freedom of an emerging narrative voice that James will tactically adopt. The reasons, moreover, why this technical solution suited the interests of a postromantic and post-revolutionary American historian novelist who strove to write with "principled detachment" (O'Brien 8) and "interrogative detachment" (Parker 171) are not dissimilar from the ideological grounds forcing the emergence of Gibbon's ironic persona across the surface of the history page. They sought to give vocal consistency to their status inconsistency. And nothing stabilized better their faltering voice than to appraise the vanishing figure of the woman (martyr, saint, suicidal maid, conceptual heiress) who willingly withdraws the social field. The enlightened expansiveness of the ironist cringed before the obscure pathos of the beleaguered girl.

## V

Milly becomes a cynosure first in the London social circles, enjoying "prominence as a feature of the season's end" (246), and later in her rented Venice palace. But nobody can properly determine the cause of her distinction: Lord Mark's indirect way of assessing it through a Bronzino painting is a triumphal symbolic moment in the novel. People gather to see her morph into the protagonist of the story James is at pains to conceive and unable to unfold, and the source of interest is therefore ultimately self-referential: surrounding characters and readers end up more interested in the kind of story (heroic epos, sentimental court romance, sacrificial life of saint) he may confer to his vacant character than in the character herself. *The Wings of the Dove* is the story of an indeterminate trope in search of a plot that may lend it meaning—the story, that is, of a possible symbol attempting to become a narrative.[24] Since this attempt can only succeed with the assistance of allegorical diction—allegory being the mechanic-narrative dynamization of an organic symbol—James, who shunned allegory, sought to escape the predicament by turning from story to history. But then, of course, history is also story—also a set of more or less allegorical narratives prompted by more or less static symbols.

Following a Weber insight, Adorno and Horkheimer famously argued that the "Enlightenment's program was the disenchantment of the world" (*Dialectic* 1). James's decision to open *The Wings of the Dove* with two books devoted to the careful building up of "the whole bright house of [Milly's] exposure" ("Preface" xlv) was extremely effective. *Bright house* is of course an ironic phrase. The reader is very soon asked to confront the *Entzauberung* (disenchantment) of the London world, whose first effective symbol is the house of Kate's father, a desecrated space where "she tasted the faint, flat emanations of things, the failure of fortune and honour" (1). The last phrase suggests the unavailability for literary recreation of a disenchanted world that had dispelled myths, extirpated animism, and overthrown fantasy with knowledge (Horkheimer and Adorno 1–2). This enlightened world is of course the *realm of liberty and commerce* opened by the British empire—a modern space of disembodying and disembedding, an expanse of free transactions where humans acquire "a tangible value" (6). It used to be a realm of virtue, like the prelapsarian Roman Empire, but no trace of this republican notion survives in James' portrait: commerce, with propriety understood as property, has brushed away the whole humanist memory of such world (Pocock, *Virtue* 42). The commodification of people promotes social uniformity. Kate cynically sees her father as "so particularly [. . .] the fortunate settled normal person. [. . .] 'In what perfection England produces them!'" (5) Uniformity, however, obtains within the boundaries of a given class. The American mind, we are told, unable to "understand English society" (197), must confront "all the cases" (198). English society is thus likened to a monster: "It might, the monster, Kate conceded, loom large for those born amid forms less developed" (198). The phrasing distinctly implies the stadial theory of historical development, proposed by Scottish eighteenth-century thinkers (Ferguson, Robertson, Smith), that inspires various narrative and explanatory strands in Gibbon's historiographic conception: the Americans Susan and Milly are "less developed" than the English characters in the novel. This is of course an ironic postulate, and James enjoys elaborating the resulting incongruity. Nowhere is this more visible than in his manipulation of the terms *enlightened, civilization,* and *civilized.* Kate's mean and callous father sighs, for instance, "from the depths of enlightened experience" (8). The bland stare with which English people admire her while expecting her to respond with "uplifted assurance and indifference" marks, for Milly, "civilisation at its highest" (156). She reads Kate's and Densher's apparent discretion as "a characteristic triumph of the civilised state" (210), the "effect of their all being sublimely civilised" (211). And Densher himself censures the co-optation of Milly by "the trick of fashion and the tone of society" in self-disparaging terms: "He had supposed himself civilised; but if this was civilisation—!" (247). Finally, when Densher and Kate approach the group in the galleries of St. Mark, they are described as "perfectly ready, decently patient, properly accommodating. They themselves suggested nothing worse—always by Kate's system—than a pair of the children of a supercivilised age making the best of an awkwardness" (361).

The terms *civilization, fashion,* and *society* stand here for a particular stadium of human development that, according to the Enlightened narrative, the English people shared with some European countries. This narrative of the emergence of a shared civilization of manners and commerce out of the feudal disorder of the European past (Pocock, *Barbarism and Religion* II 20) was the plot sustaining Gibbon's historiographic perspective. It is from this enlightened, disenchanted, and philosophical standpoint that the history of "the Christian millennium, covering the eleven or so centuries from Constantine to Charles V in the case of Robertson, or the nine or so centuries from Charlemagne to Louis XIV in the case of Voltaire" can be identified as an era of "barbarism and religion" (2). Gibbon, we know, didn't narrate the story of this era. He told rather "a narrative of late antiquity and the way into the Christian middle ages," ceasing in 1453, but the Enlightened narrative was the hermeneutic frame— both the vocabulary and the set of interpretive assumptions, involving various other narratives—inside which he decided to tell his story. Interestingly, the aristocratic genealogy that is obscurely presupposed in *The Princess Casamassima* stems exactly from when the history of the Christian millennium begins: the Italian prince "traces his descent from the fifth century" and his lineage innervates an "old regime" riddled with "rottenness and extravagance"—"Roman society in its decadence, gouty, apoplectic, depraved, gorged and clogged with wealth and spoils, selfishness and scepticism, and waiting for the onset of the barbarians" (*Princess* 313). Arguably, *The Wings of the Dove* is also told inside this frame, however ironically James tries to reverse the moral valences. Still, the attempt to upset the Gibbonian Enlightened teleology, and to presage the return of barbarism after civilization, informs *The Princess Casamassima,* and other earlier narratives, as an ironic undertow.[25] When Kate asks Densher to write to her from America, he replies: "Even at the risk of its really bringing down the inquisition?" (71) To be sure, James didn't need Gibbon to learn that

> a cruel, unfeeling temper has distinguished the monks of every age and country: their stern indifference, which is seldom mollified by personal friendship, is inflamed by religious hatred; and their merciless zeal has strenuously administered the holy office of the Inquisition.
>
> (*Decline* III.XXXVII.428)

But if he leafed through the volumes of *Decline and Fall*, he surely found there much evidence of the *barbarism of religion*. This may have proved instrumental for the literary *enchantment* that the telling (*récit*) of his story (*histoire*) required. Since, it turns out, James ended up aestheticizing the barbarism of religion—as Richardson had done in *Clarissa*, and Shakespeare in *Romeo and Juliet* and *Hamlet*. Indeed, Hamlet's reputation as a Gothic, barbarous, patchwork harkens back at least to Voltaire, and is a classical locus in post-structuralist criticism of the play.[26] Gertrude's near-gnostic figuration of Hamlet as "the female dove" before the dead body of Ophelia breaks the kind of antithetical aesthetic ground that some modern novels (*The Old Curiosity Shop*, *The Scarlet Letter*, *Henry Esmond*) colonized. Also *The Wings of the Dove*, where it is not the inquisition, but the dove, that ends up coming down. But in the secular philosophical logic of the Enlightened narrative, the Holy Office and the Holy Spirit amount to the same unreasonable thing, a composite of ecclesiastical despotism, Popish fraud, and theological speculation. In Womersley's succinct formulation, "Christianity undermines the empire by the uncivic tendency of its values and the unmanly pusillanimity of what it requires its adherents enthusiastically to believe" (*Transformation* 102). What (enlightened) civilization has sublated—overpassed and retained—is both barbarism and religion. And any resurgence of these two residual modes of sociocultural undevelopment necessarily brings about a re-enchantment—a *romancing*— of the desecrated empire of manners and commerce, a return to the "Barbarity and Gothicism" that, according to Shaftesbury, "were already enter'd into Arts, ere the Savages had made any Impression" on the declining Roman Empire (qtd. in Womersley, *Transformation* 103). There is, therefore, a constant promise of "adventure"—one of James's most overdetermined and undefined notions in the novel—every time barbarism and religion push at the gates of this *supercivilized* story. Just like *Tom Jones* is ironically underwritten by epic grammar and *The Princess Casamassima* is deceptively bolstered by the syntax of folktale, *The Wings of the Dove* seeks narrative ratification (telic closure, dramatic design, the sense of an ending) in the structural competency and notional veracity of romance. This allows for a constant resurgence of heroic semes that re-enchant the novel as *adventure* (267). The characters' predicaments, critical junctures, and moral impasses get encoded in a romance grammar of risk and danger, with notions like "destruction" or "catastrophe" (398) emerging, near the novel's close, in an attempt to furnish the whole with a sense of closure. This *deep romance grammar* accounts for the novel's inroads into *sea adventure* and *desert expedition*.[27] But there is more. In the preface to the novel, James speaks of "tragedy," the term Richardson reserved for his *Clarissa*, and describes the thematic liabilities of Milly's "case" (xxxv) as "tragic, pathetic, ironic." My reference to *Clarissa* is not gratuitous. Discussing Mark Twain, Fiedler spoke of "the baffled virgin-worship of the Protestant American male—remaking her, in her suffering and tragic triumph, into the image of Clarissa Harlowe, of whom to be sure, he may never have heard" (295). This also applies to James, but only in part, because James surely had heard. In addition, the novel proper contributes to this meta-literary speculation by wielding the contrastive foil of "Venetian comedy" (372). Still, for all these oscillations (adventure, tragedy, comedy), the regulatory "simple idea" that best encapsulates the narrative's aspiration to de-realize itself into the consolations—the *fantasy*, the *imaginary value*—of the literary tradition is the "the romance of [Densher's] existence" (343). For *The Wings of the Dove* is Densher's novel, the discursive space he traverses to experience the romance of his existence, which diegetically coincides with Milly's romance. He is not only assailed by the cynical calculations of self-seeking English ladies, but also by fluctuations of value in the hybrid tropological economy made up of barbarism and religion. Thus, for instance, his optimistic ruminations on the best way to perform the social role Kate has assigned him in their matrimonial-patrimonial scheme are said "to impart to failure an appearance of barbarity" (268), of which the Venetian musician's "general habit of mercy to gathered barbarians" (373) constitutes a scenic ratification.[28] The prospect of success is received with "enthusiasm," itself a variation of religious barbarity. The function of this lexical recurrence is to stress the opposition civilized-barbarian that the novel purports to question and eventually reverse.

## VI

Gibbon reserved the term "barbarian" for a variety of tribes and peoples (Goths, Huns, and others) that threatened from the outside the eastern borders of the Roman Empire. In alliance with Christian religion, this encroaching barbarism turned the Western provinces of the Empire into Latin-speaking provincial monarchies and feudal lordships, dominated by a military ideology of epic honor. This ideology, in turn, informed the vernacular literary traditions of these emerging nations: most literary productions, from epic to romance, are informed by this heroic code. It is no surprise therefore that James should inflect his story toward a version of "adventure" (178, 324) that is characteristic of the medieval-feudal romance. The drab tale of matrimonial-patrimonial scheming occurring in a cynical commercial age is suddenly redescribed in accordance with allegorical principles of medieval romance. The first effect of this formal inflection towards enchantment is the conversion of the major characters into soldiers.

I argued previously that James's most vexing challenge in the composition of *The Wings of the Dove* was to set the symbol in motion, to make the dove's wings move. This could be easily done, for instance, by arranging an allegorical procession. In *The Princess Casamassima*, the young Millicent Henning is described as a symbolic personification of the London underworlds:

> she represented its immense vulgarities and curiosities, its brutality and its knowingness, its good-nature and its impudence, and might have figured, in an allegorical procession, as a kind of glorified townswoman, a nymph of the wilderness of Middlesex, a flower of the accumulated parishes, the genius of urban civilisation, the muse of cockneyism.
>
> (93)

Millicent is not Milly, but the logic of her allegorical procession is akin to that of the American heiress. In both cases, we confront an ironic triumph—like Shelley's *The Triumph of Life*. A triumph was an ancient Roman ceremonial, conducted as a public pageant, in honor of a general after a decisive victory over a foreign enemy. I want to argue that Milly's *progress* in the novel is that of a soldier or deity carried in allegorical procession along a disenchanted world. The novel is to a large extent the set of conversations, preparations for and meditations about conversations, held by citizens gathered at critical points of the urb to see the pageant pass—something similar to what we witness in the opening scene Shakespeare's *Julius Caesar*. In James' novel, some of these commoners and tribunes of the people see themselves as soldiers confronting stronger soldiers or felines.

The first character to conceive of herself as a warrior is Kate. Her familial relations place her in a combative position, short of "supplies," at risk of "surrender" (21), knowing she will have "to burn her ships in short" (24). She is compared to a "panther" inside a "mercenary house" (201). But, for all her martial aptitude, the disproportion of her situation vis-à-vis her aunt is figured as that of a "trembling kid" thrown into a "battlefield" that is also "the cage of a lioness." James' long description of this encounter collapses the medieval duel of knights and the lion-versus-gladiator fight in the arena of the Roman circus into one single instance of combat. Through the suggestion—resonant with much barbarism (cannibalism) and some religion (communion)—of interpersonal wrestling where one fighter may "*eat*" (24) the opponent, a decisive figurative strand is woven into the fabric of the novel. While she sees herself as likely to become an unlimited asset, Kate indulges in the fantasy of her own sacrifice: the soldier at war, the sailor at sea, the girl in the lioness' cage. As soon as she begins to craft her scheme, this imaginative pattern is transferred to Milly, who becomes the true martyr. Kate's significance is in turn stabilized around a less alluring role: she is the "faultless soldier on parade" recruited by her aunt to perform in the shows she stages. These shows are unwittingly designed for Densher, the reluctant spectator, who muses: "It was as if the drama was between them" (240–241). But Densher, not unaware that he is a pawn likely to be sacrificed in the course of business transactions, is also a mercenary of sorts, apt to be thrown, like the Christian martyr, into "the cage of the lioness without his whip" (55). Figurative allusion is made to "his crucifixion" (392), a tragic outcome that fails, unlike Hyacinth's, to eventuate, although it is constantly foreshadowed. Aunt Maud tells him: "I'm not going to make you a martyr by banishing you" (60). On this figurative logic, Aunt Maud is assigned the part not only of delegated master of the show, but also of lioness, as we have seen, and pagan deity:

> "Oh, she's grand," the young man conceded; "she's on the scale, altogether, of the car of Juggernaut which was a kind of image that came to me yesterday while I waited for her at Lancaster Gate. The things in your drawing-room there were like the forms of the strange idols, the mystic excrescences, with which one may suppose the front of the car to bristle."
>
> (65)

This odd allusive eruption (Juggernaut, strange idols, mystic excrescences) is an early confirmation of the novel's diffuse penchant for a devotional-triumphal processional allegory that will ultimately stabilize itself around the emblematic representations of *The Sacrifice of the Martyr* and *The Triumph of the Virgin*: the external persecuting demons of ecclesiastical history were resisted, Pocock specifies, "by means spiritual [. . .] the sacrifice of martyrs transformed into heavenly triumph" (*Barbarism* III 72). Similarly, in *The Turn of the Screw* a Protestant virgin secures her triumph by sacrificing two martyrs and exorcising two demons.

Milly at first is just "the princess in a conventional tragedy" (86). The pressure that meta-literary reflection and figurative elaboration exert on the effects of this role assignment is simply devastating. During Lord Mark's visit to Milly in Venice, an overwhelming sense of "charm" suddenly over-takes her, full of beauty and poetry, ironically evocative of "forbidden life":

> It all rolled afresh over Milly: "Oh the impossible romance—!" The romance for her, yet once more, would be to sit there for ever, through all her time, as in a fortress; and the idea became an image of never going down, of remaining aloft in the divine dustless air, where she would hear but the plash of the water against stone.
>
> (323)

If Milly doesn't build castles in the dustless air it is because she is already inside one: for her princely romance to obtain, she only needs to change the palace into a fortress. This takes some imagination. But she is not the only character who fantasizes. "To treat Milly as a princess" is seen as "a positive need" of Densher's (182), a feeling he shares with Susan: "She's, you know, my princess, and to one's princess"—"One makes the whole sacrifice?" "Precisely. There you are!" (366). It is also James' need and irrepressible compulsion. Susan's imaginative apprehension of her and her companion's situation "as literary material" (121) is a function of the nar-rator's inability to prevent the novel from taking a delusive sentimental turn toward worn-out romance convention: "Milly was the wandering princess [. . .] waited upon at the city gate by the worthiest maiden, the chosen daughter of the burgesses" (122). This brief ornamental sketch is later fleshed out in a striking descriptive aside. Milly and Kate are alone in one of the rooms of the rented Venetian palace:

> Certain aspects of the connexion of these young women show for us, such is the twilight that gathers about them, in the likeness of some dim scene in a Maeterlinck play; we have positively the image, in the delicate dusk, of the figures so associated and yet so opposed, so mutually watch-ful: that of the angular pale princess, ostrich-plumed, black-robed, hung about with amulets, reminders, relics, mainly seated, mainly still, and that of the upright restless slow-circling lady of her court who exchanges with her, across the black water streaked with evening gleams, fitful questions and answers. The upright lady, with thick dark braids down her back, drawing over the grass a more embroidered train, makes the whole circuit, and makes it again, and the broken talk, brief and spar-ingly allusive, seems more to cover than to free their sense.
>
> (317)

The description is again deprived of its potential limpidity by the tamper-ing of a meta-literary comparison that licenses the narrator to indulge in an artful medieval reverie complete with a pale princess, ostrich-plumes, amulets, relics, and a great deal of atmospheric blackness. It is as if James, having decided to place her princess in a Venetian palace, was unable to depict her otherwise than as a princess in a Venetian palace. His similes become viciously circular. Where are we? Probably in a Near-Eastern Christian Palace. When? Probably in an age of decline, and barbarism, and religion, sometime before the Fall of the Eastern Roman Empire (1461). In his edition of the novel, Peter Brooks mentions no Maeterlinck play behind the explicit allusion, but I think we may safely venture an echo of *Princess Maleine* (1889). In Act 1, scene 4, the princess and her nurse talk in a vaulted chamber in a tower. In the second scene, the mother joins them in one of the apartments in the castle, and they sing at the spinning-wheel: "The nuns are lying sick,/Lying sick—it is their hour—/The nuns are lying sick,/Lying sick in the tower" (p. 23).[29] James could have here interwoven, in the interest of tragic irony, a variety of seemingly dispersive threads (Ophelia, the nunnery, the palace, the tower, Maleine, Milly, sickness) in a mournful canvas of barbarous religion worthy of Diderot's *La religieuse*.[30] Also relevant to this composite motif is the figure of the Rhine-maiden in Lorelei, twice mentioned by James in the "Preface" to *The Wings of the Dove*, sent to a nunnery in Brentano's poem and novel based on the legend. The Oriental setting is further confirmed by Milly's consciousness "of the enveloping flap of a protective mantle shelter with the weight of an Eastern carpet" (153–154). The gradual commodification of Milly into chastened prima donna, performing gypsy, and American ingénue, an object of wonder in display for English society to admire, for people "to have the benefit of her" (154), is nearly complete with her conversion into royal court cynosure. As noted previously, such figural temptation is too strong even for Susan to resist, and her further elaboration of it concretizes the heretofore scattered Oriental echoes in a very powerful allusion:

> The girl was conscious of how she dropped at times into inscrutable, impenetrable deferences—attitudes that, though without at all intending it, made a difference for familiarity, for the ease of intimacy. It was as if she recalled herself to manners, to the law of court-etiquette—which last note above all helped our young woman to a just appreciation. It was definite for her, even if not quite solid, that to treat her as a princess was a positive need of her companion's mind; wherefore she couldn't help it if this lady had her transcendent view of the way the class in question were treated. Susan had read history, had read Gibbon and Froude and Saint-Simon; she had high-lights as to the special allowances made for the class, and, since she saw them, when young, as effete and overtutored, inevitably ironic and infinitely refined, one must take it for amusing if she inclined to an indulgence verily Byzantine. If one *could* only be Byzantine!—wasn't *that* what she insidiously

led one on to sigh? Milly tried to oblige her—for it really placed Susan herself so handsomely to be Byzantine now. The great ladies of that race—it would be somewhere in Gibbon—weren't, apparently, questioned about their mysteries. But oh, poor Milly and hers! Susan at all events proved scarce more inquisitive than if she had been a mosaic at Ravenna. Susan was a porcelain monument to the odd moral that consideration might, like cynicism, have abysses. Besides, the Puritan finally disencumbered——! What starved generations wasn't Mrs. Stringham, in fancy, going to make up for?

(182–183)

This specific analogy finds completion in the successive image of "Milly, alone [. . .] in the great garnished void of their sitting-room [. . .] like a caged Byzantine" (183). The last image of the imprisoned lady is nowhere to be found in Gibbon. There are references to trapped Arabian royalty—Ayesha taken prisoner in "her cage or litter" (*Decline* V.L.223) or Bajazet in his "*iron cage*" (VI.LXV.843). James may have been familiar with Bajazet in his "indigne prison" through Racine's tragedy (*Bajazet* 61). And there is an interesting description of the caged fierce bears, called Innocence and Mica Aurea, kept at the bedside of Emperor Valentinian, "who frequently amused his eyes with the grateful spectacle of seeing them tear and devour the bleeding limbs of the malefactors who were abandoned to their rage" (II.XXV.978). As we have seen, *The Wings of the Dove* accommodates too this brutal imagery of sadistic captivity and mutual devouring. Still, what is remarkable in the previous passage is the explicit but elusive allusion to the author of *The History of the Decline and Fall of the Roman Empire*: the vague mention of "Gibbon and Foudre and Saint-Simon" develops into a sardonic unscholarly evasion—"somewhere in Gibbon"—whose scope of cavalier irony is lost to a modern reader that has never been, and will never be, treated to the five books of Gibbon's masterpiece. The evasive remark spells a sublime misprision, his own imprisonment in a house "with other inhabitants"—Shakespeare, Lamb, Goethe, Thackeray—which also accommodates the ghost of Edward Gibbon, grumbling, from the cellar, "Remember me."

Many Byzantine "ladies of the court" (II.XXXII.254; II.XLVII.1001) are described in Gibbon's masterpiece. It is hard to pinpoint an individual passage to which James' narrator, and Susan, the surrogate reader of the English historian, may be here referring, but the following footnote captures the sting of a derogation—of female dissimulation and secrecy—that has roots in *Hamlet* and branches in James's novel:

The females of Constantinople distinguished themselves by their enmity or their attachment to Chrysostom. Three noble and opulent widows,

Marsa, Castricia, and Eugraphia, were the leaders of the persecution (Pallad. Dialog. tom. xiii. p. 14.). It was impossible that they should forgive a preacher who reproached their affectation to conceal, by the ornaments of dress, their age and ugliness (Pallad p. 27.). Olympias, by equal zeal, displayed in a more pious cause, has obtained the title of saint.

(II.XXXII. 254, note 43)[31]

But let us pause and consider in some detail the rationale of James's analogy. Susan figuratively argues that since Milly is like a Byzantine princess, i.e. over-tutored, effete, ironic, and infinitely refined, she deserves to be indulged in a Byzantine manner. It is *indulgence*, in short, that is "verily Byzantine." In Gibbon this moral attitude of leniency and consent to unrestrained pleasure is often associated to liberality—"unbounded liberality and indulgence" (*Decline* I.VI)—and this of course links it to the *unrestricted economy*—the logic of radically disinterested giving up, of infinite abundance—that in the novel flies in the face of Britannia's *restricted economy*.[32] It comes as no surprise that the clash between both economies should be one of the central ideological conflicts in Shakespeare's *The Merchant of Venice*: a symbol of immoderate liberality, Venice stands in opposition to London as (liberal) capital of possessive individualism. In the *Notebooks*, James imagines the action of his prospective novel as taking place "at Nice or Mentone—or Cairo—or Corfu," with an Eastern-Mediterranean indefinition that suits Gibbon's orientalist inclination. In chapter 54, the English historian provides a description of Venice as the republic of the free people. He calls it "the mistress of the sea" (VI.LXI.700), anticipating the figurative investment of Milly as Rhine-maiden. The narrative of the foundation of Venice is drenched in a—free, maritime—spirit of Romantic anticipations: "In the midst of the waters, free, indigent, laborious, and inaccessible, they gradually coalesced into a republic: the first foundations of Venice were laid in the Island of Rialto." Elsewhere, Gibbon describes the "hospitable republic" (LIV) open to foreigners as a city "marked by the avarice of a trading, and the insolence of a maritime, power" (VI.LX.669). James highlights the "great mosque-like church" (353) and the adjacent square, "the drawing-room of Europe, profaned and bewildered by some reverse of fortune" (404). This Oriental-Catholic atmosphere contributes to the aesthetic elevation of some relevant scenes. Densher, for instance, enters a Catholic church, the Oratory, "on the edge of a splendid service—the flocking crowd told of it—which glittered and resounded, from distant depths, in the blaze of altar-lights and the swell of organ and choir" (477). During the Renaissance, the Venetian republic became in England a constant object of praise (Hadfield, *Shakespeare* 38–58) but it was also the site of an infamous association between historical decline, political decay, and moral corruption—cued by the inevitability, noted by Aristotle and Tacitus (56–57), of the transition from republic to the tyranny of an Oriental empire. The luxurious overflowing of the measure, consummated in the Egypt of *Antony and Cleopatra*, was already afoot in Othello's lacunar city. This is the cracked city the infinite dove chooses to die in.

Gibbon associates the decline of republican liberty and virtue to the rise of *indulgence* and *luxury*.[33] The rise of oriental indulgence—which Byron solemnized in *Sardanapalus*—dates back to the reign of Constantine, whose cultivated effeminacy poisons the supplies of republican virtue of the dying Empire:

> The Asiatic pomp, which had been adopted by the pride of Diocletian, assumed an air of softness and effeminacy in the person of Constantine. He is represented with false hair of various colors, laboriously arranged by the skilful artists to the times; a diadem of a new and more expensive fashion; a profusion of gems and pearls, of collars and bracelets, and a variegated flowing robe of silk, most curiously embroidered with flowers of gold. In such apparel, scarcely to be excused by the youth and folly of Elagabalus, we are at a loss to discover the wisdom of an aged monarch, and the simplicity of a Roman veteran. A mind thus relaxed by prosperity and indulgence, was incapable of rising to that magnanimity which disdains suspicion, and dares to forgive.
>
> (*Decline* II.XVIII.646)

Constantine is to the later Byzantine lady what Hamlet is to the whore that unpacks her heart with words—call her Moll Flanders or Pamela. Also material to Gibbon's argument is that such disease—the corruption of republican virtue—was also caused by the proliferation of religious secrecy and mystery. James's vague notation that "the great ladies of that race— it would be somewhere in Gibbon—weren't apparently questioned about their mysteries" (183) is ambivalent. On the one hand, the meaning of the term, often expressed in conjunction—"mystery and magic," "mystery and miracle," "mystery and fable," "mystery, fable and superstition"—is far from univocal. In these conjunctive locutions, the term lodges an indeterminate sense of anti-rational defiance. And this sense, in Gibbon's mindset, is always connected with esoteric Platonism and obscure metaphysics. In isolation, the mystery can be either that of the Trinity or the *mystery* of the Incarnation. In plural, it refers to the Eleusinian *mysteries*.

In the James passage, the fact that the ladies were not questioned about their mysteries can mean that they were indulged to remain secretive about their tricks of beauty and elegance, or that they were allowed to profess one of the many varieties of Christian religion that had sprung, or both. The term Byzantine, associated with devious and surreptitious operations, is also used to describe Milly's "sweetly secretive" (204) proposal that Susan receive the doctor in her place, "what was it in short but Byzantine?" (204) Religious secrecy is treated by Gibbon with characteristic malicious (proto-Nietzschean) irony:

> The precautions with which the disciples of Christ performed the offices of religion were at first dictated by fear and necessity; but they were continued from choice. By imitating the awful secrecy which reigned in the Eleusinian mysteries, the Christians had flattered themselves that they should render their sacred institutions more respectable in the eyes of the Pagan world. But the event, as it often happens to the operations of subtile policy, deceived their wishes and their expectations. It was concluded, that they only concealed what they would have blushed to disclose.[34]

And the un-disclosable, in Gibbon's detailed account, is a lurid Gothic affair of dead babies, drunk blood, and sworn secrecy—something at home in *The Jew of Malta, Macbeth*, perhaps *Hamlet*—"Swear!" (*Hamlet* 1.5.182)—yet not, prima facie, in *The Wings of the Dove*, where the "bond of blood" (23) apparently gives way to the unsubstantial, "thin blood" (211) of the feminine Holy Ghost. This is Milly's imaginary value. And yet, the "operations of subtile policy" by plotters (Kate, Densher) sworn to secrecy effectively organize a plot that gravitates around the inside vacancy of a woman whose value fluctuates between symbolic concealment and obscene disclosure—a woman whose value *is* (something materially computable) where and when she *is not* (any longer material).

## VII

Yet this is indifferent for the purposes of our interpretation, for James presently compounds both meanings in a figure of impenetrable—aesthetically sublime, spiritually esoteric—decadent feminine worth. The ladies, then, were liberally indulged to be liberal (exuberant) about their material values and furtive (frugal) about their spiritual beliefs. Perhaps the historical personage that best instantiates this figure of *liberal impenetrability* is Theodora, who rose from orphanhood and poverty to performing Wunderkind in the theatre and the circus.[35] She was sent by her mother "in the garb of suppliants, into the midst of the theatre," pursued a career as actress skilled in "pantomime arts," but her stunning physical beauty prompted, according to Gibbon, her fall into disrepute: "But this form was degraded by the facility with which it was exposed to the public eye, and prostituted to licentious desire" (*Decline* IV.XL.564). She married Justinian, and became empress, because "a glorious repentance (the words of the edict) was left open for the unhappy females who had prostituted their persons on the theatre." Gibbon loses no chance to report ironically on the transformation from "youthful harlot" into "royal mistress":

> Her private hours were devoted to the prudent as well as grateful care of her beauty, the luxury of the bath and table, and the long slumber of the evening and the morning. Her secret apartments were occupied by the favorite women and eunuchs, whose interests and passions she indulged at the expense of justice; the most illustrious personages of the state were crowded into a dark and sultry antechamber, and when at last, after tedious attendance, they were admitted to kiss the feet of Theodora, they experienced, as her humor might suggest, the silent arrogance of an empress, or the capricious levity of a comedian. Her rapacious avarice to accumulate an immense treasure, may be excused by the apprehension of her husband's death, which could leave no alternative between ruin and the throne.
>
> (V.XL.568)

This self-indulgent inclination to unbound luxury didn't prevent her from sponsoring humanitarian initiatives:

> The name of Theodora was introduced, with equal honor, in all the pious and charitable foundations of Justinian; and the most benevolent institution of his reign may be ascribed to the sympathy of the empress for her less fortunate sisters, who had been seduced or compelled to embrace the trade of prostitution. A palace, on the Asiatic side of the Bosphorus, was converted into a stately and spacious monastery, and a liberal maintenance was assigned to five hundred women, who had been collected from the streets and brothels of Constantinople. In this safe and holy retreat, they were devoted to perpetual confinement; and the despair of some, who threw themselves headlong into the sea, was lost in the gratitude of the penitents, who had been delivered from sin and misery by their generous benefactress.
>
> (V.XL.568–569)

Though not exactly a reaction-formation, Theodora's decision reveals a desire to compensate for an obscure past that was never completely a "mystery." Her biographical obscurity differs in principle from that of Milly, but little is known about the American heiress, and the resistance she poses to social knowledge and interpersonal recognition is a central concern in the novel. I am not suggesting that Milly is Maggie, a girl of the streets, but she shares with the prostitute her condition of conceptual outcast—the obscene embodiment of forbidden *jouissance*.[36] This libidinal

energy she would have stolen from her pagan persecutors, "peaceful inhabitants" of the Empire who, according to Gibbon, "enjoyed and abused the
advantages of wealth and luxury" (*Decline* I.I.31). Kate's frank confession
to her interlocutors resets the stage for the collective clinical inspection of
the dark female gap:

> You're right about her not being easy to know. One *sees* her with
> intensity—sees her more than one sees almost any one; but then one
> discovers that that isn't knowing her and that one may know better a
> person whom one doesn't "see," as I say, half so much.
>
> (246)

The Theodora intertextual precedent enriches this figure of impenetrability by proposing a moral association between the (past and mysterious)
"liberal" vices of unlimited monetary accumulation and unrestrained
harlotry, and by pointing out to the (afflicted libertine) female an escape
route in the form of a *barbarous-religious* prison: the monastery.[37] The
Hamletian under-text is again relevant. Hamlet requests Ophelia to enter
a nunnery after accusing her of sexual dishonesty: when he says "We are
arrant knaves, all. Believe none of us" (*Hamlet* 3.1.129–130), what he
really means is you "are a dreadful lot of bitches" (Joyce, *Ulysses* 728). The
solution to dispose of the *excessive girl* "among a sisterhood of holy nuns"
(*Romeo and Juliet* 5.3.157) obviously reflects on contemporary patriarchal politics, but already in Shakespeare's time the resort—in the interests
of social stability, patrimonial security, and patrilinear continuity—to this
Catholic institution was regarded as backward, as a reversion to the brutality of Papist institutions. At bottom, the notion that her palace, her castle,
her fortress, is a convent where she reigns in triumphal, and theologically
extravagant, spiritual authority gradually gains figurative traction. When
Densher suggests to Susan that Milly's life in the Venice palace "is a kind of
'court life' "— Book IV of *Decline* on Gibbon often refers to the *Byzantine
court*—she corrects and develops: "That's all I mean, if you understand
it of such a court as never was: one of the courts of heaven, the court
of a reigning seraph, a sort of a vice-queen of an angel. That will do
perfectly" (368).[38]

In the seventh book, Milly takes aesthetic possession of the rented palace, contemplates the neighboring canals from its florid rooms, looks at
"the nest of white cherubs" (312) in the concavity of the gilded ceilings.
She feels that "the rich Venetian past is here the presence revered and
served" and "this October morning, awkward novice though she might
be, Milly moved slowly to and from as the priestess of the worship" (314).
So she is a princess but also a novice in her own convent, a custodian of
mysteries. She becomes a figure of sacrificial withdrawal and retraction,

similar to Ophelia, Goethe's Ottilie, and Turgenev's Lisa.[39] Her roles are not exhausted there. Forced to defend herself, like the Byzantine empress Theodora, both from an early death and from schemes hatched against her authority, she also becomes a warrior. After a visit to her London doctor, Milly becomes "a soldier on a march" (177), hoping to be pronounced "a veritable young lioness" (179), looking "about her again, on her feet, at her scattered, melancholy comrades [. . .] their stomachs in the grass, turned away, ignoring, burrowing" (181). Aunt Maud consoles her by saying that she and Kate "could practically conquer the world" (196). Face to face with Susan after the critical luncheon with Kate and Densher, Milly "had one of those moments in which the warned, the anxious fighter of the battle of life, as if once again feeling for the sword at his side, carries his hand straight to the quarter of his courage" (287). And Densher visualizes Lord Mark's visit to Milly in Venice as "a descent, an invasion, an aggression" (407) with the princess wearing her "harness" as "a general armour" (318). Earlier in the novel, this gentleman was described as a member of the "patriciate" (108), thus deepening its ideological investiture in social-political imperial Roman conditions. Her social case, moreover, is construed as "Milly's triumph" (242) and described in processional terms, with Susan "confined to the function of inhaling the incense" (243). Gibbon describes "the numerous spectators, crowned with garlands, perfumed with incense, purified with the blood of victims, and surrounded with the altars and statues of their tutelar deities, [resigning] themselves to the enjoyment of pleasures" (I.XVI). All of which spells the return of pagan rituals:

> "Every part of the world," exclaims Libanius, with devout transport, "displayed the triumph of religion; and the grateful prospect of flaming altars, bleeding victims, the smoke of incense, and a solemn train of priests and prophets, without fear and without danger. The sound of prayer and of music was heard on the tops of the highest mountains; and the same ox afforded a sacrifice for the gods, and a supper for their joyous votaries.
> (II.XXIII.878)

The association between incense and triumphal deities is traditional, but so is the correlation between incense and bleeding victims. At bottom, the sacrifice of the military hero raised (stellified) to pagan deity is an important under-text both in *Julius Caesar* and *Othello*, two texts that in turn underwrite James' novel. For Milly is, in the last instance, fundamentally a martyr. The figuration of persecution is first presented in a brief episode that takes place in Kate's sister's house, when the narrator perspectivizes the Irish governess' unwillingness to prolong her "uncrowned martyrdom" (26) at the hands of Mrs. Condrip's children (26). In James' imagination, martyrdom is inevitably associated with compassion or pity, and bound up with the pathos of political violence. Milly's condition of patient past remedy evokes times "when pity held up its tell-tale face like a head on a pike, in a French revolution, bobbing before a window" (172). This historical evocation is reinforced by a long notation in James' notebooks, where echoes of Carlyle (*The French Revolution*) and Dickens (*A Tale of Two Cities*) can be clearly overheard. And beyond these echoes, and through them, James could again auscultate the authoritative voice of Gibbon, who put an end to his chronicles of ancient revolutions right before the French broke out, providing its philosophical historians with abundant figurative material to fabricate their scenes of violent martyrdom. Although Susan holds the opinion "that all the Kate Croys in Christendom were but dust for the feet of her Milly" (248), the fact is that the latter will be somehow "sacrificed" (267) by Kate and Densher. The climactic scene in this sacrificial process occurs shortly after Kate acknowledges that Milly is not "easy to know" and that seeing is not knowing:

> The discrimination was interesting, but it brought them back to the fact of her success; and it was at that comparatively gross circumstance, now so fully placed before them, that Milly's anxious companion sat and looked—looked very much as some spectator in an old-time circus might have watched the oddity of a Christian maiden, in the arena, mildly, caressingly, martyred. It was the nosing and fumbling not of lions and tigers but of domestic animals let loose as for the joke.
>
> (246)

With this figuration of Milly as a Christian maiden martyred in the old-time circus, narrative fumbling with the figurative debris of pre-novelistic formulae reaches a peak of concretion. Drawing on the conventions of the life of the martyr, the subtextual romance is stabilized around the scene of her sacrifice. The princess, the novice, and the warrior are finally transmuted into a martyr, in the arena, surrounded by beasts:

> The huddled herd had drifted to her blindly—it might as blindly have drifted away. There had been of course a signal, but the great reason was probably the absence at the moment of a larger lion. The bigger beast would come and the smaller would then incontinently vanish.
>
> (247)

The qualified fierceness of the beasts (large lions or domestic animals) need not bother us here. We may recall, for instance, the case narrated by Eusebius, of the Christian martyrs Maturus, Sanctus, and Blandina, "led to the amphi-theater to be exposed to the wild beasts, and to give to the heathen public a spectacle of cruelty, a day for fighting with wild beasts being specially appointed on account of our people" (215). Blandina, in particular, was crucified on a stake before the animals and yet cast again into prison because "none of the wild beasts at that time touched her." Gibbon mentions her as the case of a Christian whose life was esteemed of "little value, and whose sufferings were viewed by the ancients with too careless an indifference." In footnote, he adds:

> Among the martyrs of Lyons, (Euseb. l. v. c. 1,) the slave Blandina was distinguished by more exquisite tortures. Of the five martyrs so much celebrated in the acts of Felicitas and Perpetua, two were of a servile, and two others of a very mean, condition.
>
> (*Decline* I.XVI.540 note 71)

The drifting away of the herd and the reticence of the wild beasts spell a related pattern of hesitancy that betrays the inconsistency of the martyr's social standing: it was Nietzsche who sarcastically deplored the fact that Christianity ethically enthroned those of mean condition. Despite the "imaginary value" of her prospective financial affluence, Milly's actual "little value" originates in her unwitting servility to such abundance. At any rate, the Christian servant-martyr—and Milly remains one—works structurally as the obscene supplement of jouissance that grounds (and sexualizes) the inconsistent edifice of Power (Žižek, *Plague* 90). The perverse logic of the masochistic spectacle may contribute to reverse the roles of the participants in the Hegel master-servant dialectics of recognition, yet—Marx would protest—ever so slightly. There remains also, moreover, the question whether Milly rejects or not the values of the social circus gathering around her. Gibbon states at one point that "the Christians, who with pious horror avoided the abomination of the circus or the theatre" (I.XV.460–461), but he later qualifies this assertion with ironic ambivalence:

> The pious Christian, as he was desirous to obtain, or to escape, the glory of martyrdom, expected, either with impatience or with terror, the stated returns of the public games and festivals. [. . .] Whilst the numerous spectators [. . .] resigned themselves to the enjoyment of pleasures, which they considered as an essential part of their religious worship, they recollected, that the Christians alone abhorred the gods of mankind, and by their absence and melancholy on these solemn festivals, seemed to insult or to lament the public felicity.
>
> (I.XVI.536)

For Saint Theresa, as George Eliot observes at the outset of *Middlemarch*, the Moors and the "domestic reality" that met her "in the shape of uncles" were alike inimical forces hastening her to "martyrdom" (*Middlemarch* 3). "That child-pilgrimage," Eliot enthuses, "was a fit beginning. Theresa's passionate, ideal nature demanded an epic life: what were many-volumed romances of chivalry and the social conquests of a brilliant girl to her? Her flame quickly burned up that light fuel" (3). In the logic of narrative compassion articulating her own novel, and also those of Turgenev, Theresa's only slightly figural martyrdom—she got herself into many nunneries and founded not a few of them—is transferred to those "later-born Theresas" who sink unwept into oblivion, (3) and "rest in unvisited tombs" (838). The analogy is tempting, but Milly probably never wanted to become one of those "later-born Theresas." It is the narrator, and Susan and Densher, who fantasize with her "ideal nature" and demand (this is Eliot's choice verb) from her and for her "an epic life"; it is they who postulate her *imaginary value* and set the fantasy she feels bound to traverse. A similar demand to *literary* (romance or epic) sublimation informs the famous night scene in *Daisy Miller* where the girl and Giovanelli, furtively conferring in the arena of the Colosseum, are spied by Winterbourne, who hears Milly say: "Well, he looks at us as one of the old lions or tigers may have looked at the Christian martyrs!" (*Daisy Miller* 60). James' intertextual fancy is here allusively drawn to Byron's *Manfred*, but it is obviously Gibbon who supplies most intimations of the physical setting, the historical atmosphere, and the ideological impregnation. James gives Daisy a second chance with Milly, but he ends up staging a similar sacrifice: we behold a young woman who is about to die like a Christian martyr, contemplated by her executioner and the public. The focus is again on spectatorial focus—on the act of (disinterestedly) contemplating what cannot be understood. The spiritual richness of the victim is opaque and intractable, it is "that within which passes show," an obscurely psychological—if not arcanely theological—mystery. Gibbon relishes in depicting the scenes of enthusiastic martyrdom that resulted from the clash of rival esoteric factions:

> The people of Constantinople was devoid of any rational principles of freedom; but they held [. . .] the color of a livery in the races, or the color of a mystery in the schools. The Trisagion [. . .] was chanted in the cathedral by two adverse choirs, and when their lungs were exhausted, they had recourse to the more solid arguments of sticks and stones. [. . .] The streets were instantly crowded with innumerable swarms of men, women, and children; the legions of monks, in regular array, marched, and shouted, and fought at their head, "Christians! this is the day of martyrdom: let us not desert our spiritual father."
>
> (IV.XLVII. 966)

## VIII

So Milly dies and becomes a dove. Or, more exactly, she is the living dove inside the woman who is about to die. This is Kate's exact persuasion: "you're a dove" (202). By incarnating the Christian symbol of the Holy Ghost, she is promoted from novice-martyr to goddess, an object of "worship" (277) waiting "to be adored" (329). Gibbon was not indifferent to the inherent ambivalence of the symbol of the dove. In his detailed narrative of the conversion of King Clovis, he makes ironic reference to the ceremony of baptism at the Cathedral of Rheims "with every circumstance of magnificence and solemnity that could impress an *awful sense of religion* on the minds of its rude proselytes" (*Decline* III.XXXVIII.458, emphasis added). His "warlike subjects" and some remaining "gentle Barbarians"—ever ready "to follow their heroic leader to the field of battle, or to the baptismal font"—imitate his example. In a footnote, he adds: "A vial (the *Sainte Ampoulle*) of holy, or rather celestial, oil, was brought down by a white dove, for the baptism of Clovis; and it is still used and renewed, in the coronation of the kings of France" (III.XXXVIII.458–459, note 29).[40] Second, he discusses the rise of a new cast of "ecclesiastical governors of the Christians" who were taught "to unite the wisdom of the serpent with the innocence of the dove; but as the former was refined, so the latter was insensibly corrupted, by the habits of government" (I.XV.483).[41] This corruption is further described as "tinctured with an additional degree of bitterness and obstinacy from the infusion of spiritual zeal" (483). The implication is that the innocence of the dove is not untainted by the related evils of metaphysical enthusiasm or political ambition. Matthiessen notes the necessary symbolic alliance, in James's novel, of dove and serpent, the former (Milly) being always informed by "the wisdom of the serpent" (*Major* 69), a Gibbonian phrase of scriptural origin (*Mathew* 10:16) that James literally reproduces in *The Wings of the Dove* (161). Finally, the symbol of the dove reappears in Gibbon's description of Rienzi's sumptuous sartorial and ornamental habits, which included "a dove with an olive branch [. . .] displayed over his head," probably in symbolic evocation of his reception of "the order of the Holy Ghost" from the hands of "a venerable knight" (VI.LXX.1032).

France, in *King Lear*, praises Cordelia, "that art most rich, being poor" (1.1.151). Milly's spiritual richness is similarly assessed by Kate and Densher as "something incalculable wrought for them—for him and Kate; something outside, beyond, above themselves, and doubtless ever so much better than they" (388). This sublime implication is beholden to the theological affordances of the trope, to the dove's Pentecostal bestowal of unlimited gifts. In Tacitus' *Annals*, Augustus is a tyrant mobilizing ex-army settlers through "gifts of money" (*The Annals* I.10, 9).[42] Likewise, Milly achieves her absolving ascension by means of (liberal) *donativa* and *largitionem*. But then, of course, the dispensation of the incalculable refers too to the material underside of the trope: " 'You have it all,' Kate said, 'from New York' " (496), and New York is shorthand for the "immoderate greatness" of Empire (Gibbon, *Decline* XXXVIII). Milly is not Cordelia. This "all" is the immensity, the infinite value, that is bestowed upon them in the dirty shape of money. The implication of a double axiological standard haunts the sublime trope from the outset:

> She has really been a perfect success—I mean of course so far as possible in the scrap of time—and she has taken it like a perfect angel. If you can imagine an angel with a thumping bank-account you'll have the simplest expression of the kind of thing.
>
> (253)

And more specifically: "She's a dove," Kate went on, "and one somehow doesn't think of doves as bejewelled. Yet they suit her down to the ground" (373). Densher's attempt to correct this view with the suggestion that although "that element of wealth in her" is a "power [. . .] only so far as one remembered that doves have wings and wondrous flights," they also have "tender tints and soft sounds" (373) reads like a sentimental concession made by someone who begins to resent the novel's symbolic sublimations because he is in love less with the ethereal dove than with the moribund girl. At any rate, what must be stressed is that James's attempt at subjectivating the girl is not checked solely by a constitutive gap (or excess) that bars her as a subject: her emptiness, her failure at character subjectivation—this is Leavis's astute reproach—originates in the way a real, material, excess overflows her symbolic construction. In Hegelian Lacanese, this is but a symptom of the intractability of the Real. It is the excess of money, larger than simple commodities, more abstract than tangible goods, but as objective and real as the *petit objet a*—the little nameless object, the commercial article—that haunts *The Ambassadors*. Moral luck turns into a makeshift lucky morality we may call occasionalism or even opportunism—more *seize the bounty* than *seize the day*, or more accurately, with Woody Allen, *Take the Money and Die*. Pippin's willingness to locate the yearning for a "free life" in the sense of "material independence, money" (174) at the very center of the moral network of questions and answers, challenges and solutions, predicaments and resolutions, would be correct if only he abstained from suggesting that money can be seen as an unproblematic answer, a solution, the resolution. To make, as Pippin quite often does without further sociological qualification or materialist afterthought, his entire theory of modern morality rest so closely upon the notion, formulated by Isabel Archer, but in part applicable to Milly, that "a large fortune means freedom" (*Portrait* 274; Pippin, *James* 136) appears to me hopeless. It is not enough to correct Isabel's delusive construal of romantic-transcendental freedom—her "fantasy of 'soaring away,' of choosing her fate, or willing her destiny" (Pippin, *James* 142)—with the alternative conception of a "dialectical problem of freedom" (136) based on Hegelian principles of social mutuality and interpersonal recognition. One must confront head-on the bearing that the obscene contingency (the material fact, the given) of inherited money has on the awkward configuration (the clinamen, the perversion) of the novel's moral issues, and especially on James's claim that there is, for the heroine of his novel, "a strong and special implication of liberty, liberty of action, of choice, of appreciation, of contact—proceeding from sources that provide better for large independence" (Preface to *Wings*, *LC II* 1290). I have already noted how damaging to the possibility of James's characterization of Milly is the fact that her (psychosocial and spiritual) interest can hardly be dissociated from the financial interest that encapsulates her "real conditions of existence" (Althusser, "Ideology" in *Lenin* 109). In his digression on inheritance and foreign debt, Derrida observes that

> with this name or with this emblematic figure, we are pointing to the interest and first of all the interest of capital in general, an interest that, in the order of the world today, namely the world-wide market, holds a mass of humanity under its yoke and in a new form of slavery.
>
> (*Specters* 117)

I am also trying to suggest that James's decision to victimize this interesting girl into a martyred slave gives rise to a very perverse fantasy. But Pippin likes it and has no interest in acknowledging not only that Hegel is the distant father of post-structuralism, but also that Marx fathered himself through the rewriting of that father. Surprisingly, no reference to Marx's ideas can be found in Pippin's book on *modern moral life*. Contrastively, Žižek argues that

> insofar as the paradigmatic case of the Marxist critique of the reification of an ideological abstraction mentioned above is money, we should not be surprised that the ultimate topic of Henry James's work is the effect of capitalist modernization on ethical life.
>
> (*Parallax* 126)

## VIII

Like Strether, another American expatriate, Milly is also, albeit disproportionately and in a life-changing manner, "elatedly finding in [her] pocket more money than usual" (*The Ambassadors* 2). Hers is too an "advantage snatched from lucky chances" (6), a condition that seriously endangers her entitlement to be called a lady, which in turn replicates James's and Gibbon's agonic bid at *gentlemanliness*. In his chapter on *The Golden Bowl*, Pippin examines a moral notion of freedom construed as "entitlement to treatment as a free subject." The nonchalance with which the American philosopher subsumes, and neutralizes, the signifi-cance of "money" in what he calls the "modern world" by placing it alongside other conditions of freedom is simply ingenuous: "James seems to understand the nature of such freedom, in all its relevant senses: independence, absence of constraint (or, in the Jamesian world, having money), autonomy, authenticity, self-determination, and even in a few works, political freedom" (30). What Pippin misses is the particular way in which the entire axiological and deontological (ethical, moral) struc-ture of the novel precariously rests not only on the primal cavity of *status inconsistency*—who or what is, socially speaking, Milly?—but also upon the mutual contamination between a restricted economy of fairness based on transparent and proportional relations and a non-restricted economy of excess based upon solipsism and misrecognition. The imbalance of such non-restricted economy is also visible in a feature of Gibbon's nar-rative persona that Womersley has carefully identified as that of "illu-sory confidingness" (57). The ironic disingenuousness of the figure of the narrator-as-historian lays no fertile ground for reciprocity. As with James, the reader lags always behind the writer. Passing moral judgement on this arrogantly flawed James is surely no part of our critical duty, but offhand absolution is also unacceptable:

> This acknowledgement of the necessary role of material independence and the acceptance of the benefits of chance does not amount to a pro-found answer on James's part to this aspect of the question. It accepts the injustices of luck quickly, almost indifferently, and moves on, and it constitutes no great political thought.
>
> (Pippin, *James* 175)

I would add that Pippin's acknowledgement of this acknowledgement is not enough, and it constitutes no great philosophical thought. When the social setting requisite for the interpersonal deployment of mutual recog-nition proves to be a mere superstructural proscenium erected upon the affordances of infrastructure-dependent financial affluence—"the money's his whole basis" (*Ambassadors* 42), says Strether of Chad—and when the dialogic exchanges that unfold therein—in *The Portrait of a Lady*, *The Golden Bowl*, *The Wings of the Dove*, and *The Ivory Tower*—turn almost exclusively upon the discrimination of degrees of affluence and shades of imaginary value, then we may well say that the Hegelian morality of reciprocal dependency unwittingly rests upon a bourgeois naturaliza- tion of deeply unfair social conditions. In this particular sense, describing James's sublimating attempts at constituting a Kantian sphere of artistic disinterestedness as an achievement of "transcendence, at least as a kind of trans-bourgeois independence" (175), is partly inaccurate. James indeed attempted such achievement, with no small reliance upon romantic ide- ologemes and Bohemian tropes, but he was simply unable to overpass bourgeois boundaries: his ideal of trans-bourgeois independence remained, to all intents and purposes, an *imaginary value*, i.e. a mystified affair of bourgeois dependence. According to Žižek,

> The fundamental lesson of the "critique of political economy" elabo- rated by the mature Marx in the years after *The Manifesto* is that *this reduction of all heavenly chimeras to brutal economic reality generates a spectrality of its own*. When Marx describes the mad self-enhancing circulation of Capital, whose solipsistic path of self-fecundation reaches its apogee in today's meta-reflexive speculations on futures, it is far too simplistic to claim that the spectre of this self-engendering monster that pursues its path regardless of any human or environmental concern is an ideological abstraction, and that one should never forget that behind this abstraction there are real people and natural objects on whose pro- ductive capacities and resources Capital's circulation is based, and on which it feeds like a gigantic parasite. The problem is that this "abstrac- tion" does not exist only in our (financial speculator's) misperception of social reality; it is "real" in the precise sense of determining the very structure of material social processes.
>
> (*Fragile* 12)

Although the infrastructural capacities of Capital produce the super- structural abstraction of the dove, these are in turn always-already *really* haunted by the dove. Granted. It may be far too simplistic to claim solely the former, and overlook the coda, but if you overlook the former you are doubly mystified, that is, twice bewitched by the Jamesian dove. Gibbon no doubt felt the charm, but he had penetration enough to imply a causal chain and denounce a contradiction:

> From Zurich we proceeded on a pilgrimage not of devotion but of curi- osity to the Benedictine Abbey of Einsidlen, more commonly styled Our Lady of the Hermits. I was astonished by the profuse ostentation of riches in the poorest corner of Europe.
>
> (*Memoirs* 101)

*Tessera*

To elucidate the trope or misprison of *tessera*, Harold Bloom resorts to Lacan's *Discourse de Rome* (1953):

> "This metaphor is sufficient to remind us that the Word, even when almost completely worn out, retains its value as a *tessera*." Lacan's translator, Anthony Wilden, comments that this allusion is to the function of the *tessera* as a token of recognition, or "password". The *tessera* was employed in the early mystery religions where fitting together again the two halves of a broken piece of pottery was used as a means of recognition by the initiates. In this sense of a completing link, the *tessera* represents any later poet's attempt to persuade himself (and us) that the precursor's Word would be worn out if not redeemed as a newly fulfilled and enlarged Word of the ephebe.
>
> (*Anxiety* 67)

In the *tessera*, insists Bloom, "the latter poet provides what his imagination tells him would complete the otherwise 'truncated' precursor poem and poet, a 'completion' that is as much misprision as a revisionary swerve is" (66). The completion involves the antithetical use of the precursor's primal words. In *The Wings of the Dove*, liberty is antithetically ascribed to barbarous religion. James furnishes what Gibbon refrained from giving, and he thereby sought to *ful-fill* him: he tells the tragic, sublime, near-heroic, Christian story of the (speculatively rich) girl's martyrdom. Milly is both dove and serpent, lady and plebeian, saint and whore of Babylon. James knows this redemptive restitution of the trope goes against the enlightened spirit of Gibbon's book, and that is the reason why he faults his precursor's whole with a missing link ("somewhere in Gibbon"): this affected disregard is an evasive misprision. The missing link is the absent piece in the mosaic, to which James readily alludes:

> The great ladies of that race—it would be somewhere in Gibbon— weren't, apparently, questioned about their mysteries. But oh, poor Milly and hers! Susan at all events proved scarce more inquisitive than if she had been a mosaic at Ravenna. Susan was a porcelain monument to the odd moral that consideration might, like cynicism, have abysses.
>
> (182–183)

But if Susan is imaginatively construed as the full mosaic and the intact porcelain monument, who or what is the crack signaling the abyss in the stellar vault (*considerare*, from *sidera*, stars) to which the dove is doomed to fly? Well, the missing *tessera* is the object she is there, in her capacity of symbolic Other, failing to inspect and oversee: the "mystery" of the refined, ironic, and over-tutored Milly.

Like Irma, Milly is a mystery, an open throat, an "empty container" (Žižek, *Parallax* 128), an abyss that is echoed, responded, and refracted in Susan's own *abysses of consideration*. One missing piece awkwardly corresponded by another missing piece. One *tessera* (in)consistently fitting into another *tessera*. If the mosaic tiles inconsist it is because the Real they seek to depict is ultimately *grundlos*. James once told Henry Adams that the past that was their lives "lies at the bottom of the abyss, if the abyss *has* any bottom" (qtd. in Tanner, "Henry James" 92).

## Notes

1 Robert Pippin and Slavoj Žižek have emphasized this Hegelian aspect of the Jamesian construction of social life. But only the latter makes room for systemic communicative failure. See Pippin, *Henry James*; Žižek, *Parallax View*, 124–144. See also my article, " 'Constructed to Revolve': Interest in Henry James."

2 According to Walzer in *The Revolution of the Saints*: "The activity of the gentleman acquired a new precision at the same time as his person became more difficult to define. The same can be said of the saint." Qtd. in McKeon, *Origins*, 194.

3 For James's "complex rhetorical derivatives" of the vocabularies of finance and economy, see Savoy, "Bad Investments."

4 See Cameron's analysis of the *indeterminacy* of bowl's value in *The Golden Bowl*: *Thinking*, 114–115.

5 The figurative identification of Milly with the dove is the outcome of a *symbolic* operation, and is therefore mediated by the grammar and lexicon of external ideology. For the relevance, to the reading of James, of the Lacanian transition from the imaginary to the symbolic, see Freedman, 213-214.

6 See also Žižek, *Parallax View*, 126–127, where he examines the "ideological abstraction" of money in *The Golden Bowl* and *The Wings of the Dove*.

7 In his edition of the novel, Peter Brooks detects a Milton echo in the repeated phrase "the world all before them": *Wings*, 520.

8 Gibbon considers Shakespeare as "my ancestor" who is "generally more attentive to character than to history" (*Memoirs* 46). Later he speaks of his passion for French theatre and the abatement of "my idolatry for the gigantic genius of Shakespeare" (103). Although Bowersock qualifies the intensity of his familiarity with Shakespeare, he concedes that the author of *Hamlet* and Milton are the two modern vernacular literary authors that Gibbon admired most. Gibbon held Fielding in great esteem and considered "the Romance of *Tom Jones*" an "exquisite picture of human manners" that "will outlive the palace of the Escurial [sic] and the imperial eagle of the house of Austria" (*Memoirs* 42). The reason why he will end up favoring "English writers since the Revolution" is that "they breathe the spirit of reason and liberty" (114). In his *Memoirs*, Gibbon confesses that "more than once I have been led by a novel into a deep and instructive train of thinking" (100). For Gibbon's admiration of Fielding, which also erupted in notes of *Decline and Fall* (III.XXXII.242 note 13), see Bowersock, 12, 39–50. See also Damrosch's sharp comment on the way both

Gibbon and Fielding exorcise fear, unlike Richardson, "by placing it in the past" (*Fictions* 112).

9 All quotations from Gibbon's *History of the Decline and Fall of the Roman Empire* are drawn from David Womersley's edition for Penguin: the first roman numeral indicates the volume of the Penguin edition, the second the chapter of the original edition, and the Arabic numeral corresponds to the page in the Penguin edition.

10 For an exhaustive examination of James's "Historiographical Model," of his interest in modern historiography (Niehbur, Mommsen, Guizot, Buckle, Ranke) and his attempt to orient the theory of the novel in the direction of history, see Jolly, *Henry James*, 19–35. In the preface to the edited collection, *Henry James: Fiction as History*, Ian Bell makes it clear that his use of "history" is narrowly tactical, something vaguely political or democratic to place in opposition to highbrow formalism: the book aims at "readings which attempt to re-structure [James's fiction] out of pure aesthetics in order to recognize the ruptures and difficulties of historical occasions" (*Fiction as History* 7). Bell's next book shows a firmer grasp of notions like "historical sense" or "historical imagination," but his discussion eschews far-ranging considerations of historiographic interpretation. See Bell, *Henry James and the Past*, i–xii. In an excellent book, Peter Rawlings argues that by the time he published *Italian Hours* (1909), James "had little interest in accommodating historians to the house of fiction." In his Italian travel-book, "the relics and documents on which history depends hover in the margins of the text as objects of irony, satire, and comedy" (*Henry James and the Abuse* xvi). Gert Buelens and Celia Ajmer speak of James's "distrust of grand narrative historical discourses" (197).

11 The relation between imperial "good manners" and the historical inevitability of "consenting victims" is briefly considered by Poole at the end of his essay: "James and the Shadow," 87–89.

12 The exact determination of Milly's literal and figurative disease (cancer, tuberculosis, financial consumption, capital) has become the object of much critical discussion: see the articles by Wenwen Guo, Adeline R. Tintner & H. D. Janowitz, Wibke Schniedermann, Thomas Constantinesco, and Richard Anker.

13 For the difference between a Classical and Roman-Republican (political) conception of liberty as the individual's being in her own power inside a given social-political milieu and a negative (mechanistic, legalistic) conception of liberty as the absence of obstacles to motion, see Skinner, *Hobbes and Republican Liberty*, 1–122.

14 Jolly also examines in depth James's critique of Trollope against the backdrop of developments in historiography: *Henry James*, 31–35. See also Zwinger's sophisticated reading of this very passage: *Telling*, 115–122.

15 Also worthy of consideration (especially with regard to the subtextual connections between *Daisy Miller* and *The Wings of the Dove*) is the section on the Roman Colosseum in Byron's *Manfred*.

16 In her edition of *The Education of Henry Adams*, Ira B. Nadel states that in this passage "Adams imagines Gibbon before Amiens Cathedral" (*Education* 477 n.323).

17 Adams explains that he was led to sit in the steps of the Ara Coeli church by Murray's providential use of the famous Gibbon quotation in his *Handbook for Travellers*: *Education*, 80. For the cultural implications of Adams's

repetition of Gibbon's gesture, see: Mark Schwehn; Edward Adams; and Luther Stearns Mansfield.

18  For this influence, see Pocock, *Barbarism II*, 177–257; and Womersley, *Transformation*, 20–38.

19  For Gibbon's absorbing and conflicted interest in Platonic and Neo-Platonic philosophy, see Pocock, *Barbarism and Religion I*, 5, 75; and Womersley, *Gibbon*, 130–139.

20  For the implications of the biographical episode of James's "obscure hurt," see Peter Rawlings's fascinating introductory essay to *Henry James and the Abuse of the Past*, ix–xviii.

21  For Gibbon's lifelong search for social-professional identity around the categories of *gentleman* and *man of letters*, see Womersley, *Gibbon*, 95–108, 148–150, 245–248. See also Craddock, 184 n21.

22  See Carnochan, *Gibbon's Solitude*, 14–15. Carnochan examines how in the three drafts of a paragraph of his *Memoirs*, Gibbon changes the account of his social-professional case, claiming "a station midway between that of 'gentleman' and that of 'author' or 'writer.'" Gibbon describes himself variously as gentleman, possessed of leisure and independence, of books and talents" and "Gentleman, possessed of leisure and competency" (qtd. 150). We may leave it as "Mr Edward Gibbon, gentleman, possessed." Carnochan concludes: "If anywhere in his autobiography, it is in this double role—Gibbon the writer, Gibbon the gentleman—that we catch a glimpse of his most consistent self" (150–151). Womersley has called attention to Gibbon's History's "simultaneously enlightened and well-bred holding in check of its necessary recourses to narrative, pinioning them with rewarding reflection" (*Transformation* 100). Well bred because in keeping with standards of genteel conversational behavior fitly summarized by Chesterfield in his advice to Philip Stanhope: "To have frequent recourse to narrative, betrays great want of imagination" (qtd. by Womersley, *Transformation* 100). Thus, "Gibbon satisfied the demands of both philosophy and politeness, and fulfilled the obligations laid on him by being both a gentleman and a historian" (100). In note 7, Womersley concludes: "In the 1760s Gibbon piqued himself on his gentility more than on his literary merits" (100).

23  Much ironic fooling around with the label *historian* in the lengthy meta-narrative asides and digressions in *The History of Tom Jones*. Also in *Amelia*: "but it is our business to discharge the part of a faithful Historian, and to describe Human Nature as it is, not as we would wish it to be" (424); "and consequently, whether we have, in this Place, maintained or deviated from that strict Adherence to universal Truth which we profess above all other Historians" (104). There is however a touch of irony in the way Fielding and other eighteenth writers use the category, and this irony appears lost in James' rather confident pronouncements on the seriousness and moral accountability of the novelist as historian: "The Art of Fiction" (*LC I* 46–47) and his 1883 essay on Anthony Trollope (*LC I* 1343).

24  Possibilities, in plural, is one of the concepts that define Milly, both in the novel and in the preface (xlv). Milly is her own *possibilities*.

25  "Hyacinth thought of her as some clever young barbarian who in ancient days should have made a pilgrimage to Rome might have thought of a Dacian or Iberian mistress awaiting his return on the rough provincial shore. If Millicent considered his visit at a 'hall' a proof of the sort of success that was to attend him (how he reconciled this with the supposition that she perceived, as a

ghostly irradiation, intermingled with his curly hair, the aureola of martyrdom, he would have had some difficulty in explaining)" (*Princess* 387). Also: "She evidently considered that in caring so much for them Hyacinth resembled the mad emperor who fiddled in the flames of Rome. European society, to her mind, was in flames, and no frivolous occupation could give the measure of the emotion with which she watched them" (476).

26  The very title of Richard Wilson's *Shakespeare in French Theory: King of Shadows* reveals our contemporary investment in this cultural problem. See particularly the chapter "Gothic Shakespeare: A Monster in the Latin Quarter," 29–74.

27  Susan and Milly are "braving the deeps" (144). Milly has a "view of the troubled sea" (319) and a vivid sense of Lord Mark "being so painfully astray, wandering in a desert in which there was nothing to nourish him" (333). Conventional formulae abound: "She affects one, I should say, as a creature saved from a shipwreck. Such a creature may surely, in these days, on the doctrine of chances, go to sea again with confidence. She has *had* her wreck—she has met her adventure" (254).

28  The same terms and even phrases ("gathered barbarians") reappears in *The Golden Bowl*, where a very similar interplay between civilization and barbarism is at work. See also James's story "The Pupil."

29  In the original: "Les nonnes sont malades./Malades à leur tour;/Les nonnes sont malades./Malades dans la tour" (11).

30  For the Maeterlinck echo, see Hannah, 1–2.

31  Led by the hint of the doctor's name (Luke), Anna Kventsel mentions the empress Eudocia: *Decadence*, 81.

32  For the notion of the *unrestricted economy*, see Derrida's essay on Bataille: *L'éctiture et la différence*, 369–408.

33  "But the armies of Rome, placed at a secure distance from danger, were enervated by indulgence and luxury" (I.XIV); "After the use of these internal garrisons had ceased with the civil war, the conqueror wanted either wisdom or firmness to revive the severe discipline of Diocletian, and to suppress a fatal indulgence" (I.XVII); "But the indulgence of ease and luxury had secretly nourished the principles of disease" (III.XXVII.68).

34  "Secrecy" and "mysteries" are alluded to in reference to Constantine's conversion. The term "mystery" is repeated in James' novel (189).

35  For Theodora, see Herrin, 26–32, 62–66, 100–144.

36  I explain the parallel between the "conceptual heiress" and the "conceptual Jew" in the first chapter of this book. They are both embodiments of the excluded other, and "in assuming that [jouissance] is there and that we are lacking it we generally attribute it to the Other" (Horner, *Lacan* 90).

37  For Theodora's nunnery, see Herrin, 142–149. According to Hugh Trevor-Roper, "hatred of social immobility made Gibbon particularly hostile to monasticism as the growing canker which, in the Middle Ages, gradually ate up the resources of [. . .] society" (672).

38  Reference is made, for instance, to "the warm and wealthy neighborhood of the Byzantine court, which already maintained in pride and luxury so many bands of confederate Goths" (IV.XXXIX.526).

39  James wrote about Lisa's going into a convent in *A Nest of Noblemen*, LC II 980–982.

40  For the political-genealogical significance of this legend to the narrative of origins of the French monarchy, see Gibbon, *Barbarism III*, 259.

41 The same formula is used to characterize Epiphanius, the bishop of Pavia (*Decline* III.XXXVI.396).

42 The regal bestowal of *pecunias* and *libertates* to slaves reappears in Tacitus, *Annales* 15.55. See *The Annals*, 9, 366. See also Hadfield, *Shakespeare and Republicanism*, 224.

# 5 Kenosis

## Friendly Hints, Tangled Clues: Rewriting Thackeray in *The Ambassadors*

I

In September 1899, James wrote a piece titled "Winchester, Rye, and 'Denis Duval,'" published later in *Scribner's Magazine* (January 1901) and included in *English Hours* (1905). Part travelogue, part autobiography, one may read it as an oblique review of Thackeray's unfinished novel *Denis Duval*. The essay's opening sentence alludes to an *adventure*. But the reader is soon disappointed: James refers to the paradoxical discovery that, although the "charming fragment" of Thackeray's novel proved, on rereading, devoid of "light" to illumine the two old towns of Winchelsea and Rye, the occasion of revisiting them has "quickened reflection on *Denis Duval*" and helped him "further to Thackeray" (*English Hours* 162). The *adventure*—possibly cued by the vogue of *home and haunts* tourism James did much to popularize—includes the realization that Thackeray's last novel is devoid of pictorial force, since it neither induces nor enhances the action of *seeing*.[1] James moves on to conjure the original serialization of the chapters of *Denis Duval*, which echoes an earlier evocation of the same editorial event in letter to P.S. Perry of 15 March 1864, where he writes: "I am *dying* to hear the end of *Denis Duval*: that is an earthly expression" (*Letters I* 49). This is the new evocation:

> I dare say I speak of "Denis Duval" as "old" mainly to make an impression on readers whose age is less. I remember, after all, perfectly, the poetry of its original appearance—there was such a thrill, in those days, even after "Lovel the Widower" and "Philip," at any new Thackeray—in the cherished *Cornhill* of the early time, with a drawing of Frederick Walker to its every number and a possibility of its being like "Esmond" in its embroidered breast. If, moreover, it after a few months broke short off, that really gave it something as well as took something away. It might have been as true of works of art as of men and women, that if the gods loved them they died young. "Denis Duval" was at any rate beautiful, and was beautiful again on reperusal at a later time. It is all

DOI: 10.4324/9781003199564-5

beautiful once more to a final reading, only it is remarkably different: and this is precisely where my story lies.

(162–163)

"The beauty," he explains, "is particularly the beauty of its being its author's." Then follows a defense of the durability of "feeling" over pleasures obtained with the help of criticism, an opinion that differs markedly from the position he advocated in 1884 in "The Art of Fiction." Here, "esteem" is made to depend almost exclusively on "deeper satisfactions." He admits to the relevance of the subjective factor, and adds that

> it is a matter [. . .] that belongs to the age of the loss—so far as they quite depart—of illusions at large. The reason for liking a particular book becomes thus a better, or at least a more generous, one than the particular book seems in a position itself at last to supply. Woe to the mere official critic, the critic who has never felt the man. You go on liking "The Antiquary" because it is Scott. You go on liking "David Copperfield"—I don't say you go on reading it, which is a very different matter—because it is Dickens. So you go on liking "Denis Duval" because it is Thackeray— which, in this last case, is the logic of the charm I alluded to.

(163)

The lineage that has been rapidly suggested—Scott, Dickens, Thackeray— is anything but casual. It includes writers who invariably provoke unaccountable *jouissance* on the faithful reader. The three are, we will see, unrepentant—though not unironic—storytellers. They *tell* so effectively that you don't need to *read* them: James's observation that you don't "go on reading" *David Copperfield* is extremely significant. Then follows a brief assessment of the novel's structure, plot, and subject. James is at a loss about how to deal separately with these three aspects, as the novel's structural dissipation renders them indistinct. His judgement becomes as gloriously circular as his *adventure*:

> The recital here, as every one remembers, is autobiographic; the old battered, but considerably enriched, world-worn, but finely sharpened Denis looks back upon a troubled life from the winter fireside and places you, in his talkative and contagious way—he is a practised literary artist—in possession of the story. We see him in a placid port after many voyages, and have that amount of evidence—the most, after all, that the most artless reader needs—as to the "happy" side of the business. The evidence indeed is, for curiosity, almost excessive, or at least premature; as he again and again puts it before us that the companion of his later time, the admirable wife seated there beside him, is nobody else at all,

any hopes of a more tangled skein notwithstanding, than the object of his infant passion, the little French orphan, slightly younger than himself, who is brought so promptly on the scene. The way in which this affects us as undermining the "love-interest" bears remarkably on the specific question of the subject of the book as the author would have expressed this subject to his own mind. We get, to the moment the work drops, not a glimpse of his central idea; nothing, if such had been his intention, was in fact ever more triumphantly concealed. The darkness therefore is intensified by our seeming to gather that, like the love-interest, at all events, the "female interest" was not to have been largely invoked. The narrator is in general, from the first, full of friendly hints, in Thackeray's way, of what is to come; but the chapters completed deal only with his childish years, his wondrous boy-life at Winchelsea and Rye, the public and private conditions of which—practically, in the last century, the same for the two places—form the background for this exposition.

(163–164)

The aborted state of the manuscript accounts for the abnormal impression that it is still a child who is telling the story of a complete life, whence comes the apparently unfocused quality of the whole affair. Four things demand our attention. First, the description of *Denis Duval* as "recital": the "story" is *told*—like *The Turn of the Screw*, by the fireside—in a "talkative and contagious way." Second, the idea that Denis's "possession of the story" amounts to the possession of "the object of his infant passion," the moral of which is that one is in possession of a story when one is in possession of a woman, or, less crudely stated, when one is capable of producing evidence of marital happiness. Otherwise, we may infer, one remains ambiguously *prepossessed*. James suspects that this is, in the case of *Denis Duval*, an ironic measure adopted precisely to cancel "the female-interest" and promote indeterminacy—thus opening the vacated story to preemption and repetition: I finish my story in the first paragraph so that we (you and I) can see the remaining chapters drift *à l'aventure* according to a logic of "repetition [that] is not grounded. (. . .) Each form of repetition calls up the other, by an inevitable compulsion" (Miller, *Fiction and Repetition* 9). The third idea is emphatically formulated: the story is empty, it has no "subject," no "central idea," "nothing" in the way of "intention." And yet, there are "friendly hints of what is to come." In Latin, what is to come is *ad venire*, whence comes the noun *adventure*. So *Denis Duval* is a story without a subject—*Vanity Fair* was, recall, *a novel without a hero*—but full of adventure. Such thematic destitution helps predetermine the hollowness of the "love-interest" or "female interest," the fourth important concern in the passage, which James construes as a consequence of the narrative precondition—of the fact that it is a happily married voice that tells the story. I guess what James is trying to say is that *the death of the author* is the least compelling way of leaving a novel unfinished. Before I move on to make my central claims, let me transcribe the succinct overview of the plot of *Denis Duval* as it appears in *The Oxford Companion to English Literature*:

> The story begins in Rye, in the second half of the 18th cent. The narra-tor, Denis Duval, grows up in a colony of French Protestant refugees. A French noblewoman, Mme de Saverne, escapes from the persecution of her husband and comes to England with the help of the sinister Chev-alier de la Motte, who was intended to become the villain of the novel. She takes refuge with her old nurse, Denis's mother, and Denis falls in love with her little daughter Agnes. Denis has to leave home and go to sea after he has exposed the smuggling activities of his grandfather and the treasonable behaviour of de la Motte, and the fragment ends at this point. Thackeray intended Denis to encounter a series of adventures at sea, and to return to rescue Agnes from the machinations of de la Motte.
>
> (267)

## II

My contention in this chapter is that *The Ambassadors* is a novel that rehearses through further *kenosis* the constitutive incompleteness—the indeterminacy—of *Denis Duval*.[2] In 1901, James began work in his new novel at Lamb House, in Rye, whose *genius loci* was the Victorian novel-ist who—alas—probably never set foot in Rye. Like Thackeray's, James's narrative is characterized by vocal prolixity, dissipating adventurousness, thematic vacuity, and the derogation of the female interest. Let me cite again James's epistolary phantasmagoria:

> I write with a pen snatched from my angel-wing. It is very pleasant up here but rather lonely, the only other inhabitants being Shakespeare, Goethe and Charles Lamb. There are no women. Thackeray was up for a few days but was turned out for calling me a snob because I walked arm-in-arm with Shakespeare. I am rather sorry, for I am dying to hear the end of *Denis Duval*: that is an earthly expression.
>
> (*Letters I* 49)

The ghostly ambience of the reverie is aggravated by impending irony: while James was figuratively dying to *hear the end* of what was to become Thack-eray's last, unfinished novel, the Victorian novelist was literally dying to *write* it. Also ironically circular is the way the closing trajectory of Thack-eray's literary career and the beginning of James's literary career intersect in the anomalous *scene of instruction* of a novelist-to-be who craves to *hear* (not read) the *end* of a story *without end*. The aural connotation (*hear*) may be a side effect of the fantasy where the masters (Thackeray, Goethe, Lamb) vocally address (interpellate, reprove) the pupils: "Thackeray [. . .] was turned out for *calling* me a snob" (emphasis added). A snob is originally a person of lower class, and a false but ingenious etymology reads the term as man without nobility (*sine nobilitate* > *snob*): Thackeray, who was probably intrigued by Hamlet's decision to defect from the ranks of the aristocracy and become the opposite of a snob—i.e. a Bohemian—wrote a book about snobs and spent his life exploring the stretching latitudes of Bohemia, the land where the *imaginary value* (Hamlet's noble mind and by extension the value of Continental tours, art studios, male comradeship) handed over by the vanishing aristocracy to the lower ranks had first imaginatively eventuated. It stands to reason therefore that the author of *Hamlet* should *call* Thackeray a *snob*. Althusser, who saw ideology as an "imaginary relationship" (*Lenin* 109), would describe this call as an ironic *ideological interpellation*—which unmasks Thackeray's social drama of pretense. Also Strether, the ambassador, the man without nobility (*ambassador* meant originally *servant*), gets drawn into the arc of the interpellation, steered toward the Bohemian space of homosocial recreation. The snob and the Bohemian are therefore two equidistant liminal *figures of status inconsistency*: whereas the Bohemian moves downward and out, the snob tries to move upward and in.[3] Inevitably, they end up meeting in a hinterland of outcasts. It is no accident that one of the fault lines of the gender system should break out somewhere around these interstices: the snob and the Bohemian preempt part of the structural middle ground where the homosexual will emerge. Strether is of course being interpellated from various quarters, most importantly from that of his employer, Mrs. Newsome, who pesters him with "communications." Hers is "the voice [. . .] of Woollett" (19). But he ends up giving in to other calls. First, to "the vague voice of Paris," described as "a far-off hum, a sharp near click on the asphalt, *a voice calling*, replying, somewhere and as full of tone as an actor's in a play (emphasis added)" (221); next, he responds to the promising call of the young men of the Boulevard, "the voice in which they had seemed then to speak to him" (354); finally, to the voice of their harbinger: "Chad's was the voice that, sounding into the night with promptness and seemingly with joy, greeted him and called him up" (423). Chad *calls* (addresses) Strether (as) an *ambassador*—he is actually the first one to impute Strether such role—and then calls for his "transformation" into a liminal *Bohemian*.

In parallel fashion, Thackeray *calls* James a *snob*. Beyond attesting to a major fact of status inconsistency, the phrasing may also betoken an admission of the mode of storytelling intimacy that James enjoyed with certain exclusive and uncanny narrative voices (Scott, Dickens, Thackeray). I use the Freudian adjective uncanny (*unhemilich*) because Thackeray's *dying voice* is very often invoked in association with the ghostly: Thackeray, he states, "went, I think, a greater way still, even if already, at the season I recall, to a more ghostly effect and as a presence definitely immortalized" (*LC I* 166). And commenting *The Thackerays in India*, he confesses that "we rejoice for him in this ghostly company of actors in a vast drama" (*LC I* 1398). *The ghostly company, the ghostly effect.*

In what follows, I will consider the four aspects mentioned previously: vocal prolixity, inconclusive adventurousness, thematic vacuity, and the derogation of the female interest.

## III

The Thackeray *evocation* (call) at Rye and Winchelsea was irresistibly strong. But there were other similar reminiscences prompted by reading-memory sites. In the "Preface" to *Lady Barbarina*, a walk through Picadilly (*LC II* 1220) induces an evocation of Becky's and Rawdon's house. And a sudden recollection of two lines from *Henry Esmond* gripped the young traveler during his first day in London in 1869. Passing under the Temple Bar, he looks at the statue of Queen Anne:

> "The stout, red-faced woman" whom Esmond had seen tearing after the staghounds over the slopes of Windsor was not a bit like the effigy "which turns its stony back upon St Paul's and faces the coaches struggling up Ludgate Hill." As I looked at Queen Anne over the apron of my hansom [. . .] it was a thrilling thought that the statue had been familiar to the hero of the incomparable novel. All history appeared to live again, and the continuity of things to vibrate through my mind.
>
> (*English Hours* 3)

Thackeray—from whose novel he imperfectly quotes, which makes sense because he doesn't *read* Scott, Dickens, and Thackeray: he *listens* to them—becomes the *manes* welcoming the young American artist into the traditional English world.[4] The evocation, prompted by a visual object, is aural, not visual: James recalls "things" that "vibrate through his mind," like the phrases and tones of a told story. The notion of "the continuity of things" lends a conservative, near-Burkean, coloration to his construal of history as genealogy. This is not just the continuity between an external (constitutional) past (Queen Anne's) and its present (Queen Victoria's), but rather the internal (vocal) continuity between a father (Thackeray) and his son (James). Such sense of vocal-aural *durée* also informs Milly's observation of Victorian London social life: what she *sees*—"the conscious sinking, at all events, and the awfully good manner, the difference, the bridge, the

interval, the skipped leaves of the social atlas"—gets soon reprocessed as
*legend* and *echo*:

> a mixed, wandering echo of Trollope, of Thackeray, perhaps mostly of
> Dickens—under favour of which her pilgrimage had so much appealed.
> She could relate to Susie later on, late the same evening, that the legend,
> before she had done with it, had run clear, that the adored author of *The
> Newcomes*, in fine, had been on the whole the note.
>
> (*Wings* 137)

For James, the adored author of *The Newcomes* was primarily a *story-
teller*, the author of stories to be told, recited, read once (*legend*), and
aurally remembered (*echo, note*).[5] *Storyteller* is a self-denomination that
James uses sparingly in his New York Prefaces, and it is revealing that he
should resort to it twice in the preface to *The Ambassadors*, the *tale* where
*Denis Duval* becomes *twice told*. James introduces himself as "the enlightened story-teller," a category that would have delighted Fielding. Thackeray was only second, in this capacity, to Walter Scott, "the first English
prose story-teller" (*LC I* 1201). "As a story-teller," James notes, Thackeray
"is well-nigh everything—as a preacher and teacher he is nothing" (*LC I*
225). This opposition is crucial. James often shunned Thackeray's shallow
moralism, which he imputed to his intellectual squalor. He inherited this
blemish from Richardson, whose " 'moralism" hangs about him as a dead
weight, obstructing the merits of his "realism." "The same may be said,"
he adds, "of Thackeray's trivial and shallow system of sermonizing" (225).
James regrets that the imposition of a moral vision on the reader limits the
psychological expansion of characters like Becky and Blanche Armory (*LC
II* 132–133). These are the costs, we could add, of adopting a capacious
narrator consciousness, like Fielding's. James constantly opposes this deficiency to the moral and intellectual accomplishments of George Sand and
George Eliot. Whereas Sand fills up her novels with "serious and passionate ideas," Thackeray holds merely "flimsy convictions" and "the lightest
and most superficial opinion." The English writer's "artificial posture," the
"superficial and materialistic quality of his mind" is measured up against
the "relative dignity of Madame Sand's religious attitude" (*LC II* 697). The
contrast is reinforced with the inclusion of Dickens on Thackeray's side.
Both writers, James points out, "express in a satisfactory manner certain
facts, certain ideas of a peculiar limited order," whereas "Sand expresses
with equal facility and equal grace ideas and facts the most various and the
most general." More specifically,

> The things which we can imagine Thackeray and Dickens attempting to
> *say* will be found on reflection, if we are not mistaken, to be so many
> variations of a small number of stock ideas and images. Thackeray will

*say* nothing that cannot be *said* humorously, colloquially, and lightly—in the light sentimental manner, at best. Dickens will *say* nothing that cannot be said specifically—applied to a particular person or thing. But the movement of Madame Sand's thoughts seems to us as free as the air of heaven.

(LC II 698; emphases added)

Note the implicit opposition between the celestial movement of Sand's *thoughts* and the humorous, light, and colloquial movement of Thackeray's *sayings*. A *colloquy* is, let me recall, a conversation. So, while Sand thinks, Thackeray chats—or story-tells. George Eliot, he urges in another essay, "is a thinker, -not, perhaps, a passionate thinker, but at least a serious one; and the term can be applied with either adjective neither to Dickens nor Thackeray" (*LC I* 926). Writing about Trollope's lack of penetration, James observes that

> he says things neither pictorially and grotesquely like Dickens; nor with that combined disposition to satire and to literary form which gives such a "body," as they say of wine, to the manner of Thackeray; nor with everything of the philosophic, the transcendental cast—the desire to follow them to their remote relations—which we associate with the name of George Eliot.

(LC I 1334)

This ad hoc differential diagnosis allows James to singularize "the manner of Thackeray"—just as Fielding had identified *the manner of Cervantes* in the original title page of *Joseph Andrews*—as non-philosophic and non-pictorial. Interestingly, in his review of *Thackerayana* he disagrees with those who praise Thackeray's pictorial talent, and elsewhere "sees" Thackeray's "light very much as the light (a different thing from the mere dull dusk) of rainy days in 'residential' streets" (*LC II* 126). When James opines that Thackeray is "world-worn," he means both that he had seen too much—socially more than other artists—and that he always lacked "virginity of perception" (*LC I* 1228).[6] So, while Dickens *paints*, and Eliot *thinks*, Thackeray barely *sees*, seldom *thinks*, but *speaks* inimitably, in *satirical* and *literary* form.[7] James spares no occasion to praise Thackeray's literary style and formal mastery of the English language.[8] Describing him as a novelist's novelist would not be a disservice, and James hints at the notion when he describes *Henry Esmond* as a "study in philology" (*LC II* 731). A study, that is, in the love (*philo*) of words (*logos*)—not of images or ideas.

This insistence on the oral and vocal quality of Thackeray's manner is only second to James's perseverance in proclaiming his admiration for the Victorian novelist. In light of his continuous professions of esteem, the lack of critical attention to James's indebtedness to Thackeray is something of a mystery.[9] When one of the characters in his conversational essay on *Daniel Deronda* announces that his "favorite novelist is Thackeray" (*LC I* 976), we know whose opinion is being voiced out. In another review, James observes that "a literary critic who does not enjoy Thackeray has certainly a limp in his gait" (*LC II* 807). James is aware that the appreciation of Thackeray's "inimitable pages" (*LC II* 64) is not completely accountable in critical terms and is to a large extent a matter of personal predilection. Thus, he appeals to "readers whose feeling for Thackeray is still a living sentiment" (*LC I* 1397). And yet, private predilection identifies a standard—*art, form, level*—that is central to the canon: "the exquisite art of Thackeray and Miss Austen and Hawthorne" (*LC I* 992), "the form of the novel as Dickens and Thackeray [. . .] saw it" (*LC I* 44), the "level" and "family" to which "Dickens, Thackeray and George Eliot" belong (*LC I* 1331). The private pantheon includes Scott, Austen, Dickens, Thackeray, Hawthorne, and Eliot.[10] The presence of Austen is rather unexpected, considering James's comparative lack of critical attention and allusion to the author of *Emma*, and it helps to secure the connection with the *manner of Fielding*.

## IV

James was in two minds about Thackeray's handling of his characters. Sometimes, an excess of narratorial "moral judgement" (*LC II* 132) limited their freedom. This contrasted with Balzac's and Trollope's ability to create independent characters (*LC I* 1356). Other times, he would combine satire and tenderness, "for the sake of his subject" (132), and put forward flexible characters, like Becky, whose "adventures" (*LC II* 191) he extols. It is as if the formal constraint of the *adventure*—a device he took from the picaresque tradition—in turn predetermined the narrator's liberal comprehension upon which the character's freedom is premised. Like Fielding and his narrators, Thackeray had, James concedes, "insight" (*LC II* 191), i.e. "a great conscience and a great mind" (*LC I* 47). This, he argued, connected him with Turgenev and George Eliot. Not, perhaps, a philosophical mind, but a great mind nonetheless. But what is a *great mind*? Discussing Trollope's limitations, James urged that "when a novelist's imagination is weak, his judgement should be strong. Such was the case with Thackeray." Trollope, by contrast, "is an excellent, and admirable observer; and as such he may accomplish much. But why does he not observe great things as well as little ones? It was by doing so that Thackeray wrote 'Henry Esmond'" (*LC I* 1314).[11] The inference is that Thackeray had no imagination but good judgement and a capacity to observe *great things*, whatever that means.

The resulting *great conscience* may explain why we don't believe Sand but "we believe [. . .] Thackeray" (*LC II* 713). He "produced with a freedom for which we are constantly grateful" (*LC I* 1331). A great conscience, for James, is a free conscience—free to experience and tell freely, in a "talkative and contagious way." This is not much in the way of normative criticism, but it helps explain James's insistence on the requirement that "the good health of an art which undertakes so immediately to reproduce life must demand that it be perfectly free" ("The Art of Fiction" 49). But *free* to do what? Well, free to remain open (*ad*) to what comes (*venire*). The novel, for Thackeray and James, is the free conversational telling of an adventure. Thackeray, we know, wrote *novels* like *Vanity Fair*, *histories* like *Henry Esmond*, but also *adventures*, from the start—*The Tremendous Adventures of Major Gahagan* (1838)—to the end of his career—*The Adventures of Philip* (1862). *Denis Duval* is also a book of adventures, and so is, I want to argue, *The Ambassadors*. Thackeray emulated *the manner of Fielding*, whose first important novel was *The History of the Adventures of Joseph Andrews*, prompting an ironic inflection (an introjection) of the picaresque that transpires also in the complete titles of novels by Scott (*Quentin Durward*) and Dickens (*David Copperfield, Martin Chuzzlewit*).

But how can the Master be placed in such a genealogy of puerile storytellers? Well, step by step. Let me start with the strong claim that everything that is significant in *The Ambassadors* is lodged in this early sentence:

> That note had been meanwhile—since the previous afternoon, thanks to this happier device—such a consciousness of personal freedom as he hadn't known for years; such a deep taste of change and of having above all for the moment nobody and nothing to consider, as promised already, if headlong hope were not too foolish, to colour *his adventure* with cool success.
>
> (1–2; emphasis added)

A definition of *adventure* breathes across the central terms: an *adventure* is the outcome of the *freedom* a *consciousness* has both to *change* and to *consider nobody and nothing*—which amounts to a Hamletian freedom to, presumably watching from behind the arras or the tree, consider potentially anything. It is the freedom of *indifference to difference*.[12] But what is Strether's "adventure"?[13] There are, the reader finds out, past "adventures"—"old ghosts of experiments" (*Ambassadors* 60)—registering the emotional aftermath of his family losses, his critical period, and the trail of failed projects he had embarked upon. But the reader only wants to know about his future ad-ventures. Is he, like Madame de Vionnett, "interested and prone to adventure" (161)? We feel that in speaking about "his adventure," James has perversely over-denoted the thing, just as he misrepresented the issues, in the essay on Winchelsea and Rye, when speaking about "a literary adventure." As perverse as comparing a day in the life of a Dublin advertising agent to the exploits described in the *Odyssey*. In *Denis Duval*, by contrast, when the protagonist refers to Agnes's cradle as the place "the adventures of her life began" (460), to "the Count's personal adventures" (463), and to his own "adventures" profusely—and qualifies them as "strange changes" or "dangers"—we know he is being as good as his word. Denis's life exploits appear lifted from a novel by Dumas *père*—a novelist revered by Thackeray and respected by James. They could also be read as a sentimental-bourgeois expansion of the sea-adventure story Hamlet tells Horace in a letter (*Hamlet* 4.6.11–25).

*The Ambassadors* swerves away from Thackeray's treatment of the central theme in *Denis Duval*: that the "affair of life" is to be found in one's external *adventures*. Strether believes, by contrast, that this affair is

> at the best a tin mould, either fluted and embossed, with ornamental excrescences, or else smooth and dreadfully plain, into which, a helpless jelly, one's consciousness is poured—so that one "takes" the form as the great cook says, and is more or less compactly held by it: one lives in fine as one can. Still, one has the illusion of freedom.
>
> (153)

The affair of life is here the inside jelly—the person, "one"—taking the form the external tin mold allows it to take. Denis gives us the tin mold instead, and the engrossing excrescences make up for the absence of jelly. Both novels signally share the necessity of the mold, that is, the form. Their central theme, i.e. *adventure*, is their very formal husk: they are stories about the form of stories—what Denis calls "zigzag journeys" (*Denis* 490)—even if James is resolved to pick up the spilled jelly. Let us consider the form.[14] Thackeray was almost unable to give up the heroic ideal of manly experience as a trial of adventures from which the individual subject must emerge either dead or more alive and wiser: the young men that matter in *Barry Lyndon*, *Vanity Fair*, *Henry Esmond*, and *The Virginians* are all entangled in military action. To this profession of warring masculinity, James responds with the postulate that real experience may accrue without adventure, "that a man may have [. . .] an amount of experience out of any proportion to his adventures" (160), which confirms Hegel's idea that the novel is the epic of the bourgeoisie, and anticipates the theory and practice of, respectively, Lukács and Joyce. And then he makes the perversely modernist claim, in the preface to the novel, that the composition of the novel is the real but "intimate adventure," the "adventure *transposed*" (xxxix). In this sense, *The Ambassadors* would read more like an amalgam of some of Thackeray's late narratives—*The Newcomes*, *Lovel the Widower*, and

*The Adventures of Philip*—than a rewriting of *Denis Duval*. I believe it is both things at once.

To be sure, the term *adventure* occurs as often in *The Ambassadors* as in James's other two "modernist" masterpieces—*The Golden Bowl* and *The Wings of the Dove*. But only *The Ambassadors* advertises in the title its ascription to secular-romance.[15] The novel is figuratively informed by the romance expectations of a "job" ("Preface") that Strether assumes with bonhomie. But he deplores the illiberal duties he is bound to discharge. Like the messengers Rosencrantz or Guildenstern, he is "sent" by domestic-political authorities who are intrigued by a young man's "transforma-tion" (*Hamlet* 2.2.5; *The Ambassadors* 97, 198) to "pluck out the heart of [Chad's] mystery," to "sound [him] from [his] lowest note to the top of [his] compass" (*Hamlet* 3.2.336–338). Note the geopolitical implica-tion: her American Majesty (Queen Mrs. Newsome) uses an ambassador to force one of his men (Chad, the original envoy) to withdraw from the French Court (of Madame de Vionnet), and then is obliged to send another ambassador (Mrs. Pocock) when she realizes there is an increase in the number of her revolted subjects. This spells a plot of gradual Anglo-Saxon revolution—Puritan, Glorious, American—confirming its freedoms against the decadent, absolutist, and Catholic, perversion of the French monarchy. James—who told a version of this story in *The American*—came across shreds of the narrative in *Denis Duval*:

> A post had come in that very evening from London, bringing intelligence of no little importance even to poor me, as it turned out. And the news was that his Majesty the King, having been informed that a treaty of amity and commerce had been signed between the Court of France and certain persons employed by his Majesty's revolted subjects in North America, "has judged it necessary to send orders to his Ambassador to withdraw from the French Court . . . and relying with the firmest confi-dence upon the zealous and affectionate support of his faithful people, he is determined to prepare to exert, if it should be necessary, all the forces and resources of his kingdoms, which he trusts will be adequate to repel every insult and attack, and to maintain and uphold the power and reputation of this country."
>
> (*Denis* 537)

Whereas in *Denis Duval* freedom is historicized as the religious freedom of the French protestants emigrated to England, as the traditional political freedom of the English people, and as the new freedom vindicated by the English colonies, in *The Ambassadors*, freedom is internalized as "the illu-sion of freedom" (*Ambassadors* 153). Still, echoes of the French Revolu-tion help Strether take full measure of his new liberty. The breaking down of his "moral scheme" is described as a "revolution" and it involves the intensification of his "lifelong trick of intense reflexion" (Preface to *The Ambassadors* xxxviii). It has "nothing to do with any *bêtise* of the imputably 'tempted' state," nothing to do with "the female-interest:" it is rather a Hamletian revolution to consider "more things than had been dreamt of in the philosophy of Woollett" (xxxviii). But this internal revolution—his sensorial-moral orientation towards the differential openness of the European experience—is accelerated by echoes of the French Revolution, still audible in the Paris streets:

> From beyond this, and as from a great distance—beyond the court, beyond the *corps de logis* forming the front—came, as if excited and exciting, the vague voice of Paris. Strether had all along been subject to sudden gusts of fancy in connexion with such matters as these—odd starts of the historic sense, suppositions and divinations with no warrant but their intensity. Thus and so, on the eve of the great recorded dates, the days and nights of revolution, the sounds had come in, the omens, the beginnings broken out. They were the smell of revolution, the smell of the public temper—or perhaps simply the smell of blood.
>
> (401)

Let me recall that Gibbon finished his masterpiece one year before this smell spread all over Europe, and that the Enlightenment narrative to which he so much contributed failed decisively to contain such event. In a certain sense, nineteenth-century realist fiction emerged to register the new excess and negotiate the disjuncture.[16] In *Denis Duval* we read that

> very sad times intervened between Denis and prosperity. He was to be taken prisoner by the French, and to fret many long years away in one of their arsenals. At last the Revolution broke out, and he may have been given up, or—thanks to his foreign tongue and extraction—found means to escape. Perhaps he went in search of Agnes, whom we know he never forgot, and whose great relations were now in trouble, for the Revolution which freed him was terrible to "aristocrats."
>
> ("Notes on *Denis Duval*" 567)

Chad is also taken prisoner by the French. Sad times intervene between himself and the economic prosperity that awaits him in America. He frets some long years in one of the arsenals in Paris. Also a foreigner, he too manages to escape, yet not so much *in search of* as *from* the French aristocratic lady that has taken him prisoner. And Strether somehow repeats the experience—he falls into the French aristocratic ladies' arms, throats, and minds—wrongly (or rightly) deluded by the thought that he is being "squared" at Woollett, i.e. that the "prison-house" is Elsinore and not the tin mold. In *Hamlet* we have the anachronic specter of the (London) City, where the prince enjoyed the luxury of a homosocial artistic fraternity, and of an anachronistically Protestant England, to which he decisively trave-led, confronting the inchoate backwoods absolutism of the Catholic Dan-ish monarchy. The underlying opposition between *barbarism and liberty* informs the (Gibbon's) Enlightened narrative of cultural development that *Denis Duval* and *The Ambassadors* will ironically handle. The French aris-tocratic Lady Miss Barrace tells the American Bohemian Mr. Bilham that he has come to France "to convert the savages" but "the savages simply convert *you.*" Little Bilham replies that the "cannibals" have "converted [him] into food. I'm but the bleached bones of a Christian" (144). The cannibals are here the sophisticated French aristocrats who both in *Denis Duval* and *The Ambassadors* are depicted in terms of scriptural evil: La Motte is a "serpent" whose "ill-omened eyes" glimmer upon Madame de Saverne, who stands for "Eve" (462), and Strether feels that little Bilham's amazing "serenity" is but "the trail of the serpent, the corruption, as he might conveniently have said, of Europe" (88). American Protestant hys-teria has been swallowed by decadent European serenity. Such dramatic reversal echoes the paradoxical volte-face in *The Wings of the Dove*—with the rich wasp girl, the condensation of capitalist modernity, turned mar-tyred dove in backward Italian soil. Similar inversions are at work in *Denis Duval*. Madame de Saverne converts to Catholicism and takes refuge in a convent with her child (466–467). The libertine Protestant Chevalier de la Motte becomes the inquisitorial persecutor of the Catholic convert, Mme. de Saverne. The boy Denis asks a good Papist priest if he has "burned any Protestants," and he replies that he has "roasted several and eaten them afterward" (*Denis* 472). Denis is helped by French aristocrats to escape from revolutionary France. The pointer of the enlightened compass oscil-lates wildly. In *The Ambassadors*, the Catholic Church is, for the American Waymarsh,

> the enemy, the monster of bulging eyes and far-reaching quivering grop-ing tentacles—was exactly society, exactly the multiplication of shibbo-leths, exactly the discrimination of types and tones, exactly the wicked old Rows of Chester, rank with feudalism; exactly in short Europe.
>
> (28)

And the epitome of this retrograde feudalism is less Miss Gostrey, styled "the Jesuit in petticoats" (28), as Madame de Vionnet. And yet, the novel reverses this valence by turning her into a liberal representative of revo-lutionary social modernity. On this logic, the multi-tentacular monster of bulging eyes is actually the Puritan, censorious, Mrs. Newsome. She has "plenty" of "money," the basis of "capitalism"—a term coined by Thackeray in *The Newcomes* (484)—and "the root of the evil" (40).

The ambassadors, in both novels, witness as well as mediate the reversals of these ideological transactions, thus helping to bring forth their "dense dialectical ironies" (Pippin, *James* 161). But there are more emissaries in stock. Maria, for instance, sees herself as the "supreme 'courier-maid'" (12), guiding compatriots through Europe. In *Denis Duval*, de la Motte calls Denis "my carrier-pigeon. Thou shalt carry no letter, but a message. I can trust thee now with a secret" (*Denis* 493). In both cases, an implication of clandestinity is at work. Part of Maria's job is sending back Americans after their visit to Europe. "Any port will serve in a storm," she observes, "I'm—with all my other functions—an agent for repatriation" (24). She elaborates:

> "What I attend to is that they come quickly and return still more so. I meet them to help it to be over as soon as possible, and though I don't stop them I've my way of putting them through. That's my little system; and, if you want to know," said Maria Gostrey, "it's my real secret, my innermost mission and use. I only seem, you see, to beguile and approve; but I've thought it all out and I'm working all the while underground. I can't perhaps quite give you my formula, but I think that practically I succeed. I send you back spent. So you stay back. Passed through my hands—"
>
> (25)

The report is laden with suggestions of furtiveness and surreptitiousness—*quickly, system, secret, innermost mission, beguile, underground, formula*—which evoke the smuggling activities across the English Channel of the central characters in *Denis Duval*. In both cases, business is conducted near ports (Rye, Calais, Liverpool) and across the sea: *The Ambassadors* is sustained by an underground figural thread of sea adventures, shipwrecks, and potential drowning.[17] But there are also "contraband gentlemen" (*Denis* 536) in James's novel. Notably, Chad's grandfather, who illicitly amassed the fortune the family still enjoys. When Strether suggests that the source of his wealth "was not particularly noble," Miss Gostrey demands more information. He speaks, vaguely, of "practices." "In business? Infamies? He was an old swindler?" she asks. "Oh," he said with more emphasis than spirit, "I shan't describe *him* nor narrate his exploits" (43). Let me insist: some of the most important *adventures* recorded in the fragment of *Denis Duval* are literally the exploits of old swindlers. Denis's relation to them (one of swindlers is his grandfather) is not unlike that of Chad to the "practices" of his grandfather. James refers in his essay to wealth "that had its roots in the malpractice of forefathers" (*English Hours* 166).

## IV

In both cases, moreover, a veil of indeterminacy covers the exact nature of the things (goods, commodities) that are being transacted in the clandestine business. Indeterminate (random, meaningless) are *ex definitione* the exploits performed in a context of adventure. They are formally determined, not substantially identified. Indeterminacy thus rules the compositional logic of a story of adventures, where adventure is arbitrarily determined solely for adventure's sake. When John Barth was asked to write about *The Adventures of Roderick Random*, he was hardly able to move beyond this flat realization.[18] The fate of Thackeray's reception is also marked by it.[19] In his review of Senior's *Essays on Fiction* (1864), James upbraided the author for not being able to identify why exactly Thackeray is "remarkable" (*LC I* 1204). But Senior was hardly to blame. The singularity of Thackeray's contribution to narrative art remains a vexed issue. While it seems easy to put the finger on the distinctive originality of other Victorian novelists like Dickens, Eliot, or Hardy, the reasons why we go on reading Thackeray—if we do: there is a *Cambridge Companion to Harriet Beecher Stowe* and none yet (2023) dedicated to Thackeray—have become increasingly abstruse. There seems to be no equivalent to what in the case of Dickens is a socially empathetic sensibility, in the case of Eliot a moral imagination, and in the case of Hardy a metaphysics of fate.[20] Indeed, one way of accounting for his exceptionality would be to argue that only Thackeray remained a storyteller in the genuinely traditional sense—the sense implied in the phrase *the manner of Cervantes*—and that while he aimed solely at telling good stories, other fellow writers like Charlotte Brontë, Emily Brontë, Elizabeth Gaskell, Charles Dickens, George Eliot, and Thomas Hardy were writing novels as a means to reach something else—be it personal salvation, social redemption, or moral regeneration. The fact that these admittedly extra-literary causes enjoy today great purchase in the academic industry may help explain the contemporary neglect of a novelist who was at his time regarded—often worshiped—as a novelist's novelist.

Discussing George Eliot's contribution to the novel, Harold Bloom distinguished between a "narrative tradition" and a "philosophical tradition," and suggested that, unlike Thackeray, she was far more interested in the latter (*Novels and Novelists* 139). To speak of a narrative *tradition* in the case of a cultural practice—the novel—that emerged against the normative field of neoclassical genres is disputable, and it raises again the issue of genealogy, for continuity in such tradition was achieved less through the compliant internalization of constituted norms than through the deviant introjection of deceased precursors. Technical guidance was limited to *imitatio*, and *delectare* (entertainment) overreached *prodesse* (teaching, instruction). Thackeray, it turns out, decided to imitate Fielding and the Dickens of *Pickwick Papers*, and he became this way beholden to a legacy of irresistible indeterminacy. When James argued in "The Art of Fiction" that the "form of the novel, as Dickens and Thackeray saw it, had no taint of incompleteness" (*LC I* 44), he was prevaricating. Almost twenty years earlier, in his review of *Our Mutual Friend* (1865), he had accused Dickens of overexertion, exhaustion, insufficiency. And in his preface to *The Tragic Muse* he famously wondered:

> There may in its absence be life, incontestably, as *The Newcomes* has life, as *Les Trois Mousquetaires*, as Tolstoi's *Peace and War*, have it; but what do such large, loose, baggy monsters, with their queer elements of the accidental and the arbitrary, artistically *mean*?
>
> (*LC II* 1107)

Two of these novels are war novels, and *The Newcomes* is presided by a colonel but is arguably about money. But is *that* (war, money) what they *mean*? Loose, baggy, and without a theme, a subject, an intention, a meaning: we have returned full circle to James's account of *Denis Duval*. It is as if the lack of a clear thematic-ideological instigation, a certain thinness in the context of reference, a paucity of strong doctrine, and the random, episodic, (non)form of the adventure novel were all features interrelated in overdetermined ways. Of course, with hindsight, referential ambiguity and thematic detachment presuppose the narrative irony characteristic of Cervantes's manner of calculated vacancy. What is *Don Quijote* about? And what does it "artistically *mean*"? I am not implying that *The Newcomes* is comparable to Cervantes's novel, but James's decision to place it alongside *War and Peace* is hardly a disservice, and it compounds further the ambiguity of his critique.

Thackeray's masterpiece is undoubtedly *Vanity Fair*, "a classic as compared with *The Newcomes*" (James, *LCII* 184)—and *Barry Lyndon* still enjoys a notorious late-modernist reputation. His loose baggy monsters (*Pendennis*, *The Newcomes*, *The Virginians*) were soon shelved as quaint objects of late-Victorian delectation, and the early fragmentary pieces gained some critical esteem after the publication of John Carey's influential *Thackeray: Prodigal Genius* (1977). Also, in the 1970s scholars began to pay new attention to other texts, like *Henry Esmond*, *Lovell the Widower*, *The Adventures of Philip*, all three paradigmatic for their ruthless ambiguity. Such *indeterminacy* was first brought to critical attention by Hillis Miller in a remarkable deconstructive reading of *Henry Esmond*. Following in his footsteps, other critics have examined the ideological effects of this indeterminacy, liminal thematic areas—Barbary Hardy spoke of *radical themes*—like the double-entendre of snobbery, sexual ambiguity, the fetishization of footmen and flunkeys, the axiological diffuseness of commodification.[21]

Chronologically, *Denis Duval* belongs to this body of late fiction characterized by ambiguity and indeterminacy, an odd corpus that probably fascinated James. Its unfinished status lent it a rare aura of aesthetic culmination—a climax of failure—and the first apologists of the novel could do little against the opinion that Thackeray's "vein is worked out; there is nothing in him left but the echoes of emptiness" (Greenwood, "Notes on *Denis Duval*," *Denis* 556). In his reading of the notes that Thackeray made during the composition of *Denis Duval*, John Sutherland contends that "it is hard to make out any underlying system" (229).[22] Both the notes and the letters written at the time show that he was tired and exasperated. This paralysis was not new. When writing *The Virginians*, Thackeray exclaims: "I hate story-making incidents, surprises, lovemaking" (Schacht liii). But if you reject those central devices of novelistic *poiesis* (making)—meetings, hinges, peripeties, recognitions, reversals of fortune—and you give up an "underlying system," what are you left with? Not much: you are left, at best, with adventures, and the sheer dissemination of *écriture*—an activity surely propped by the very unusual linguistic precocity of the polyglot Denis. Adventure is premised upon formal conditions, not substantial causes. It draws on the freedom inherent to indifference to difference, and this indifference is greatly urged by early linguistic acculturation. Indifference to meaning is urged by Denis's early exposure to reading—"I was so young that I could not understand all I read" (446)—by his premature and imperfect grasp of three languages (English and an Alsatian jargon of French and German), and by the related realization of the triviality of early mnemic impressions.[23] Thackeray's stylistic feat of writing another novel in "reconstructed eighteenth" is further proof that "his manner of thinking and feeling is quite as 'Roundabout' as his manner of saying" (James, *English Hours* 167). This critical aperçu leads James to his most dramatic assessment. The novel is marked by an "avoidance of picture" that raises questions about its subject. The reader who thought that my speculative excursions into the *form* of the empty adventure story were unwarranted should read carefully what James had to say about Thackeray's intentions when composing *Denis Duval*:

> For Winchelsea is strange, individual, charming. What *could* he—yes—
> have been thinking of? We are wound up for saying that he has given his
> subject away, until we suddenly remember that, to this hour, we have
> never really made out what his subject was to have been. Never was a
> secret more impenetrably kept. Read over the fragment—which reaches,
> after all, to some two hundred and fifty pages; read over, at the end of

the volume, the interesting editorial notes; address yourself, above all, in the charming series of introductions lately prepared by Mrs. Richmond Ritchie for a new and, so far as possible, biographical edition of her father's works, to the reminiscences briefly bearing on Denis, and you will remain in each case equally distant from a clew. It is the most puzzling thing in the world, but there *is* no clew. There are indications, in respect to the book, from Thackeray's hand, memoranda on matters of detail, and there is in especial a highly curious letter to his publisher; yet the clew that his own mind must have held never shows the tip of its tail. The letter to his publisher, in which, according to the editor of the fragment, he "sketches his plot for the information of" that gentleman, reads like a mystification by which the gentleman was to be temporarily kept quiet. With an air of telling him a good deal, Thackeray really tells him nothing—nothing, I mean, by which he himself would have been committed to (any more than deterred from) any idea kept up his sleeve. If he were holding this card back, to be played at his own time, he could not have proceeded in the least differently; and one can construct to-day, with a free hand, one's picture of his private amusement at the success of his diplomacy. All the while, what *was* the card? The production of a novel finds perhaps its nearest analogy in the ride across country; the competent novelist—that is, the novelist with the real seat—presses his subject, in spite of hedges and ditches, as hard as the keen fox-hunter presses the game that has been started for his day with the hounds. The fox is the novelist's idea, and when he rides straight, he rides, regardless of danger, in whatever direction that animal takes. As we lay down "Denis Duval," however, we feel not only that we are off the scent, but that we never really have been, with the author, on it. The fox has got quite away. For it carries us no further, surely, to say—as may possibly be objected—that the author's subject was to have been neither more nor less than the adventures of his hero; inasmuch as, turn the thing as we will, these "adventures" could at the best have constituted nothing more than its *form*. It is an affront to the memory of a great writer to pretend that they were to have been arbitrary and unselected, that there was nothing in his mind to determine them. The book was, obviously, to have been, as boys say, "about" them. But what were *they* to have been about? Thackeray carried the mystery to his grave.

(*English Hours* 168–169)

Robert Pippin's claim that *The Ambassadors* is characterized by a chronic lack of "determinacy of meaning and moral resolution" (154–155) could be applied to the unfinished novel of his precursor. Thackeray showed, at the beginning, some confidence: "I have a wild story in my mind which I might work into 100 pages of the Magazine" (qtd. in Schacht vii); it will be a "historical romance"; and it will have "no moral reflections and plenty of adventures" (vii). But the aplomb vanished, and he returned to old habits of compositional indolence: "When I am in labour with a book I don't quite know what happens. I sit for hours before my paper not doing my book but incapable of doing anything else, and thinking upon that subject always" (ix). What *subject*? Recall that James held serious doubts about "the specific question of the subject of the book as the author would have expressed this subject to his own mind." Thackeray knew, at least, that he wished to avoid "moral reflections" and to that end he replaced the detached hetero-diegetic first person he had originally conceived as the narrator for the first person of Denis Duval himself.[24] The success of this operation is disputable: James spoke of "the extremely talkative, discursive, ejaculatory, and moralising Denis" (*English Hours* 166). So he knew what he wanted, but little more: there would be a "course of true love," some "smuggling activities" culminating in de la Motte's "treason" and, finally, Duval's naval career (Schacht 21). But Thackeray knew nothing, for instance, about sailing and smuggling. In a letter to John Brown dated 23 September 1863 he protests "Instead of writing to you, why am I not writing the history of Denis Duval, Esq., Admiral of the White Squadron?" and answers himself: "Because I don't know anything about the sea and seamen, and get brought up by my ignorance every other page" (qtd. in Schacht xvii). This crisis of epistemic authority evokes the breakdown of visual knowledge in *The Turn of the Screw*. James, for instance, points out that "the fragment itself contains no positive evidence that Thackeray ever, with the mere eye of sense, beheld the place," a deficiency that might explain why its "charming fragment" failed to "say" much about "the little old towns" (*English Hours* 162).

So we have no subject, little thought, and less picture. Anything else? We have adventures, and the presumption of form. Let us reformulate the problem in James's own terms: although it would be an "affront" to Thackeray's memory to hold that the adventures are "arbitrary and unselected," one must assume that these adventures "constitute nothing" but the novel's "form," and that the novel is "about" them. They, in turn, are apparently about nothing. James is repelled by the insinuation that there is nothing in Thackeray's mind that "determines" the adventures, but the articulacy of his formulation betrays a secret fascination with this possibility. This is also part of the mystery, of James's mystery, which he took to his grave. In other words: what exactly *determines* Strether's adventures?

# V

Following Lacan, Žižek claims that we should "desubstantialize" sexuality. Far from being some "traumatic substantial Thing, which the subject cannot attain directly," sexuality "is *nothing but* the formal structure of failure which, in principle, can 'contaminate' any activity" (*Plague* 91).[25] This keen structural observation is bound up with the Lacanian formula that "it is qua Other that man desires," meaning that "what I desire is predetermined by the big Other, the symbolic space within which I dwell," but also that

> the subject desires only in so far as it experiences the Other itself desiring, as the site of unfathomable desire, as if an opaque desire is emanating from him or her. Not only does the other address me with an enigmatic desire, it also confronts me with the fact that I myself do not know what I really desire, with the enigma of my own desire.
>
> (*How to Read Lacan* 41–42)

On such libidinal logic, based on the inconsistency or decentering of the social Other, one may risk the following claims: 1) that Thackeray and James sought indeed to de-substantialize sexuality—not solely out of cultural priggishness or private perplexity, but also to denaturalize its prior dependence on genealogy and its modern reliance on science; 2) that they achieved this de-substantializing through the conscious adoption of "the formal structure of failure" that actually reveals sexuality; 3) that the formal nature of this structure transpires in the compositional indeterminacy and inconclusiveness that characterized both *Denis Duval* and *The Ambassadors*, forcing their sham ends (*nostos* followed by the survival of happy marriage in the former, and by the promise of unhappy marriage in the latter); 4) that such failed closure suggests an anxiety about "the enigma"—the diffuseness, ambivalence, and openness—of "desire," both of the narrator's and the hero's desire, which draws out the relevance of a homosocial spectrum already inhabited by the snob and the Bohemian; 5) that the resulting three figures, the snob, the Bohemian, and the "queer gentleman" (*Denis* 472) embody the fault lines of the inconsistent social Other upon which the whole mechanism rests.

So to the question, "What exactly *determines* Denis's and Strether's adventures?" we may tentatively answer: the formal structure of failure that constitutes both sexuality and society. This way, formal looseness (episodicity, accidentality), thematic diffuseness (doctrinal vacuity, referential indefinition), and ideological transgression (the exploitation of sites of sexual and status inconsistency) should be seen as equiprimordial, co-extensive, and co-implied.

*Denis Duval*, James noted, has no subject. It is about the nothing of its form. We are given the tin mold, but not the jelly. This vacuity contaminates the formal (w)hole with pervasive thematic indefinition, best visible in the constant resort to empty notions like *life* or *freedom*, concepts defined less by their actuality than by their future-gazing potential—life *for*, freedom *to*. Life and freedom are shorthand for experiential indeterminacy, openness, ambiguity. When reference is made to the need to "protect" Chad from "life," the implication is that he may fall into a domestic plot and forestall his experiential potential: "What you really want to get him home for is to marry him" (50). The tropes of life and freedom are the opposite of marriage. They are structurally used to sublate—to fight back and contain—the contamination of sexuality and society and to sponge (preempt, prepossess) the thematic overspill implicit in the story of adventures: they signal the structure of their failure.[26]

But thematic vacuity has other ways of expressing itself in the novel. One of them is epistemic impasse. When Madame de Vionnet suggests that, in order to keep Chad's mother patient, Strether should "tell her the truth," he retorts:

> "And what do you call the truth?"
> "Well, *any* truth—about us all—that you see yourself. I leave
>    it to you."
> "Thank you very much. I like," Strether laughed with a slight
>    harshness, "the way you leave things!"
> But she insisted kindly, gently, as if it wasn't so bad. "Be perfectly
>    honest. Tell her all."
> "All?" he oddly echoed.
> "Tell her the simple truth," Madame de Vionnet again pleaded.
> "But what *is* the simple truth? The simple truth is exactly what I'm
>    trying to discover."
>
> (178–179)

On sophistic logic, nothing exists; if anything did exist it could not be known; and if anything could be known it could not be communicated. This leads us to the next expression of the absence of subject (nothing exists): the referential indeterminacy lodged in the impossibility of communicating *it*. In *The Ambassadors*, James's notorious penchant for pronominal confusion (*him, her, them, it, nothing, anything, something*) develops into a compulsive oscillation between maximal determinacy (simply *the* truth, *the* simple truth) and maximal indeterminacy (*any* truth, *all*).[27] To an extent, Madame de Vionnet is also counting on the retroactive effect of Strether's inquest in order to fix (to determine) the nature of a complex relation (herself, her daughter, Chad) that is also a mystery to her. There is no sexual relationship, she suggests, except that there is (sexuality). There is something, she implies, there is this and there is all, and you, Strether, must fill it in, find it out, and name it—for us.

There is *this*, but what is *it*? Can we know it and communicate it? Madame de Vionnet succinctly formulates the epistemic nature of Strether's diplomatic task: "She sent you out to face the facts" (179). But he fails. Strether admits to Maria: "I haven't yet found a single thing." She concludes: "You've got at no facts at all" (85). In accordance with our Freudian analogy, these facts seem ultimately lodged inside a woman's throat. It may be worth noting that Althusser's first account of his life tragedy—he strangled his wife to death—was titled *Les faits* (1976). But structural Marxism teaches us that we must not expect the rewards of empirical certainty. Strether tells Maria: "I'm always considering something else; something else, I mean, than the thing of the moment. The obsession of *the other thing* is the terror" (13; emphasis added). Lacan and Althusser would have subscribed to the final sentence, which spells the formal structure of failure before the inconsistency and antagonism of sexuality and society. To consider always *something* else is to court the deferrals of *adventure* as "escritura desatada (unleashed writing)" (Cervantes, *Don Quijote* I.XLVII 550), and to condemn oneself to the absolutions of *everything* and *nothing*. Waymarsh questions Strether:

"But I thought you said you found out nothing."
"Nothing but that—that I don't know anything."
And what good does that do you?"
"It's just," said Strether, "what I've come to you to help me to discover. I mean anything about anything over here."

(73)

We later find him at a complete loss: "He had known nothing and nobody as he stood in the street; but hadn't his view now taken a bound in the direction of every one and of every thing?" (78). And on discovering the new Chad, he internally confirms that "everything was totally different" (105). Whatever that means. At this point of the novel, no reader actually cares. It is enjoyable enough to see how the empty signifiers (*anything, nothing, nobody, everyone, everything*) float adrift confounded in the eddies of the prose. These indeterminate pronominals cover the other side of a structural coin whose front are the speciously saturated tropes of *life* and *freedom*. Sexuality and society are the decentered, inconsistent, and contaminating forces that allow the novel to navigate by the Scylla and Charybdis of these pressing uncertainties. Only James could make a story flow out of similar inconsistencies: "Nothing was more natural than that these things should be the other things they absolutely were not" (*Turn of the Screw* 44).

Although *Denis Duval* is less undone by pronominal evacuations, some referential enigmas remain: the true extent of de la Motte's treason, the exact actuality of the injury Denis's forgives, and, especially, the nature of the contraband activities—the "smuggled goods" (*Denis* 502)—of the Mackerel Party. The inconclusiveness that surrounds this criminal business is signally transferred to *The Ambassadors*, where we never get to know the nature of the "article produced" at the family industry at Woollett (41). Strether refers to it, vaguely, as a "little thing" or "manufacture" (41). When Maria asks openly about the thing—"And what *is* the article produced?"—the answer, "I'll tell you next time," opens a cycle of incessant postponements. "In ignorance," Strether assumes, "she could humour her fancy, and that proved a useful freedom. She could treat the little nameless object as indeed unnameable—she could make their abstention enormously definite" (42). James reaches here a climax of speculative originality: *abstention* (the avoidance of determinate denotation, of referential determinacy, of specific naming) is transformed into something *enormously definite*. This is a dialectical operation: in accordance with the "law of the incalculable," a desire for definite information is satisfied through the higher-order *definition* of the very *indefinition* (the lack) that sets desire going in the first place. Interestingly, the determinate indeterminacy of this abstention—akin to the one that prompts the emergence of empty signifiers like *life* and *freedom*—presumes the (infrastructural) thing that is the cause of the (superstructural) family wealth. Indeterminacy contaminates the entire structural-causal chain of over-determination. Speculating about Chad's return to America, Strether notes: "He's glad enough of the *money* from *it*, and the money's his whole basis" (42). As we will see in the next chapter, this repeats the situation in Dickens's *Our Mutual Friend* of the young man returning to England in order to come into his inheritance. Maria asks Strether: "You say that if he does break, he'll come in for *things* at home?" Strether replies: "Quite positively. He'll come in for a *particular chance*—a chance that any properly constituted young man would jump at" (49; emphases added). A *particular chance* is like a *definite indefinition*, or an *unfree freedom*, or a *lifeless life*: it is the *unadventurous adventure* of marriage.

But will Chad break? Strether is sent to find out. Waymarsh describes him as "nosing round" (76)—inspecting faces, mouths, souls, minds, throats. But knowledge is doxal, indefinite, and the epistemic pursuit is bound to failure: "You can't make out over here what people do know" (75). In Vienna, Freud believed the same. Back in Paris, later, Lacan and Althusser agreed.

## VI

Let us now consider the miscarriage of what James called the "female interest." This consideration is premised on a central claim: James is not interested in society per se. Robert Pippin is, I believe, wrong. Through very vague references to "the faint murmur of the huge collective life" (*Ambassadors* 307) as something that happens outdoors, as an aural, sonic, backdrop ("the many sounds of the street" 308) to the psychomachia—the dialogue, the colloquium—where only an unhappy few are engaged, James reveals no interest in society as such. Connections and relations are relevant insofar as they determine personal behavior, but this determination is not regulated through processes of successful interpersonal recognition, reciprocity, and mutuality. James suggests that close interpersonal relation spells disowning and misrecognition, and that distant interpersonal connection compromises private life in impenetrable but indelible manners.

In his fictional memoirs, Denis speaks of

> a link in that mysterious chain of destiny which was binding all these people—me the boy of seven years old; yonder little speechless infant of as many months; that poor wandering lady bereft of reason; that dark inscrutable companion of hers who brought evil with him wherever he came.
>
> (475)

The list of relevant *dramatis personae* is complete. In *The Ambassadors*, the significant players are also four. This is Maria's superb synthesis of Strether's "business": "He's just a young man on whose head high hopes are placed at Woollett; a young man a wicked woman has got hold of and whom his family over there has sent you out to rescue" (37). A similar surface pattern governs both plots. In *Denis Duval*, a man (old Denis) tries to save a younger man (young Denis) from the deadly clutch of French connections (the men behind Madame de Saverne). In *The Ambassadors*, a man (Strether) tries to save a younger man (Chad) from the deadly clutch of French connections (Madame de Vionnet). In both cases, the aged man revisits his past and ponders alternative life courses and outcomes. In both cases, the aged man is compromised by his own ineliminable association with the feared connections (Denis is the grandson of an associate of de la Motte, Strether is an employee and prospective spouse of Mrs. Newsome). In both cases, finally, a girl is dismissed—whether to the inanity of prematurely revealed wedlock (Agnes) or to oblivion (Jeanne).

This parallel plot obscures the importance of a broader external schema, also present in both novels. It is a pattern of visual examination: just as in *Denis Duval*, the author (Thackeray) examines a French Catholic aristocratic lady (Madame de Saverne), in *The Ambassadors*, the narrator (James) examines a French Catholic aristocratic lady (Madame de Vionnet). Thackeray had personal motives to be engrossed with the figure of the mad Ophelia-like woman searching for a reclusive institution, but one cannot discount the Balzacian motive that drives James's interest in the French noblewoman.[28] In Balzac's urban society—which remains at some level that of the salons of Madame de Sévigné and Madame de Lafayette— women run the show and are primarily, if not exclusively, fascinated by women: men play a subsidiary role. This allows for a reformulation of the pattern in *The Ambassadors*, where, at bottom, Mrs. Newsome examines Madame de Vionnet, allowing for a further, more radical, readjustment of roles: there is a sense in which Mrs. Newsome—the mock-Puritan, closet liberal, wise, infinitely curious, manipulative, and detached observer—*is* Henry James.[29] And yet, the plot also conceals an inside patterning: the speculative inspection that one man conducts of another at the very core of each novel. Denis examines the younger Denis (and his dark male associates), and Strether examines Chad (and his Bohemian friends). This dialectical organization of narrative space into concentric frames confirms Peter Brooks's suggestion that Balzac's and James's textual surfaces are belied by the (atavistic, mythical, unconscious) realm of the "moral occult" (*Melodramatic* 2–9), which I would here reserve to the inmost scenario of male-to-male inspection.

To summarize, in both novels there is: 1) a mysterious woman who is being inspected at a distance, through delegation; 2) a girl who is negligible and exits the picture; 3) a Balzacian pattern of female-female curiosity organizing the whole; and 4) a clandestine relation between two defecting men hiding in the (w)hole. Note that the Balzacian formula, best exemplified in Rastignac's successive surveillance by Parisian ladies who are actually observing one another, determines the situation into which first Chad and next Strether, like the French provincial, fall. Strether senses the pull: "Was what was happening to himself then, was what already *had* happened, really that a woman of fashion was floating him into society" (28). The Balzacian *donnée* is therefore this situation called indistinctly "society" or "Europe" (29), whose emblem is Paris, where the aristocracy and the upper-middle-class people enjoy a "kind of freedom" (30).

But this situation centered around the social skills of a "woman of fashion" (the phrase occurs twice in the same paragraph)—the, for Strether, "unfamiliar phenomenon of the *femme du monde*" (150)—is displaced and in part replaced by the Thackerayan formula, where a retired gentleman— very possibly an erstwhile *gentleman of fashion*—supervises the survival of a young man trapped in fashionable society. Still, the Balzacian formula (*femme de monde* scrutinizes *femme de monde*) frames the Thackerayan formula. Henry James—who spent much time looking at the princess Casamassima—is now looking at Madame de Vionnet. But he transfers the homo-diegetic part to Mrs. Newsome, through a system of delegated inspection: Mrs. Newsome asks Strether to look after Chad because Chad has seen Madame de Vionnet. The sequence is further mediated by the presence of Maria Gostrey, who is somehow interposed between Strether and the Paris world in which Chad is engulfed.

James → [[Mrs Newsome → [Strether → (Maria) → Chad] → Madame de Vionnet]]

Placed at the very center, Maria vicariously stands for both external observers, James and his deputy Mrs. Newsome. At one significant point she describes herself as Strether's "brother in arms" (31), as if trying to invade his homosocial shelter. At this level of significance, Chad's role is negligible. If and when Strether reaches the femme de monde, the part of the American lady's son is over: "Mrs. Newsome *knew* in other words that very night at Woollett that he himself *knew* Madame de Vionnet and that he had conscientiously been to *see* her" (182; emphasis added). A mad logic of substitution organizes the structure of delegated inspection. When all the schemas and formulae blend, the result is a complex plot of declared intentions, assumed tasks, and hidden motivations. Mrs. Newsome wants to know who is the woman that keeps her son in Paris. The motif is traditional enough: *cherchez la femme*. She sends an ambassador (Strether) to find out. His finding out takes an examination of Chad's mind, and a vacancy is soon revealed. The content of his mind is to be filled in or played out by the surrounding inspectors, surveyors, inquisitors, confessing priests, doctors, just like Romeo's and Hamlet's interiorities are tackled by intrusive epistemic agents who seek to disclose their erotic secret (Benvolio, Montague, Lady Montague, Mercutio and Claudius, Gertrude, Polonius, Ophelia, respectively). Claudius, for instance, sends the "ambassadors" Rosencrantz and Guildenstern "to gather,/So much as from occasions you may glean,/Whether aught, to us unknown, afflicts him thus" (*Hamlet* 2.2.16–18).

The epistemic apparatus, which combines the judicial practice of *enquête* with the more scientific practice of *examen* (Foucault, *La vérité et les formes juridiques* 1409), is inherited from the Hamlet tradition. A limited number of people constitute a community of inspectors around a problematic human individual in order to violate his inside—to inspect the cavity of his throat—because at least one of them believes he holds a relevant secret or content. The problem in *The Ambassadors* lies in the indefinition that *ab origine* and of necessity plagues the identification and disclosure of such elusive content. This indefinition is so massive that it forces the pronominal denotation of the content to oscillate, brusquely, between the radical determinacy of a particular *something* and the inept absolution of *everything*. Not infrequently, therefore, this content is simply identified as *nothing* or *anything*. While Maria asks Strether, "Wasn't what you came out for to find out all?" (134) he wonders about how and when to "reach the truth of anything" (135).

This examination, in turn, gradually slides into Strether's "[spying] on Chad's proper freedom" (148), and, by extension, into an analysis of the small circle of women (Madame de Vionnet and her daughter) who apparently have cast an erotic spell on the promising American boy. Strether examines both women, inspects their contents, and meets a stark vacancy, a desert of indeterminacy. Strether is the doctor. Chad is his immediate patient, but diagnosis and therapy rest on mediation, on the further inspection of French women—Madame and Mademoiselle de Vionnet. These women, in turn, and other female Parisian observers, gather around the ambassador to (over)see—to know, and watch, and wait—in a manner that is nothing if not brutally clinical: "I don't want to turn the knife in your vitals, but that's naturally what you just meant by our being on top of you" (332), Miss Barrace tells Strether. An episode of transfer (from Chad to Strether, from patient to doctor) takes place. The latter seeks counsel, he needs the technical opinion of a board of males, led by little Bilham, and an attendant female, Maria Gostrey. This board is obviously the Fielding ideal of the "narrator" as "collective mind rising from the living together of men and women in a community" (Miller, *Form* 25). The pattern is viciously circular. Everybody in this "community of shipwreck" (*Ambassadors* 313) appears to lean over everyone else's backs, trying to inspect their chasms and gulfs. The narrator and Maria act as privileged supervisors.

## VII

Let us now consider in turn each of these three inset functions of inspection: first, the lady inspecting a more sophisticated, and freer lady; second, the mature man inspecting the sophisticated lady; third, the mature man and the younger man inspecting one another. Needless to say, the transition from the second to the third marks the derogation (the *epoché*, the disconnection) of what James called, in reference to *Denis Duval*, the "female-interest."

### Undistinguished Lady Inspects Sophisticated Lady

Fashionable French society, Balzac urged, was an affair of women surveying women. Critical emphasis on patriarchal authority has perhaps obscured the pervasiveness of female control over the public space. In the preface to his recent book *Our Henry James*, John Carlos Rowe rightly observes that "Isabel, Pansy, even Henrietta Stackpole are still [the male characters'] captives, angels in the house with little freedom" (xii), but this observation doesn't apply to their European equivalents—the free Valérie

Marnefes and Delphine de Nuncingens of Parisian society. From a distance, Mrs. Newsome presumes such freedom and raises the question *che vuoi?* (what is your desire?) but not to his son. She wants to penetrate the desire of free French women. Chad is the first ambassador, but he fails to report. That is the reason why Strether is sent. Chad's and Strether's ultra-ambiguous libidinal comportment—the formal structure of their (sexual) failure—is no doubt the novel's most impressive conception, but Madame de Vionnet's sexual infraction lies at its structural center. That an un-divorced woman who didn't marry out of love—"But being in love isn't, you know, here [. . .] thought necessary, in strictness, for marriage" (203), little Bilham tells Strether—can fall in love and fulfill her passion with a younger man is of course a fascinating cultural fact that combines the social archaism of unbreakable marriage with the moral wonderland of libertinage. Mrs. Newsome's curiosity honors her.

### Mature Gentleman Inspects Sophisticated Lady

The novel's framing schema is, we have seen, that of a male narrator gazing into a woman (Madame de Vionnet), with the help of another woman (Mrs. Newsome). For, in Balzacian logic, "there it was again—it took women, it took women" (408). But then Strether, the ambassador, steps in, and the pattern changes. His inspecting query to the French refined lady is predictable enough: *Che vuoi?* What do you want? What do you want of Chad, whom others—including me—also want? But there is no answer, only a vertigo of receding reference. As Adrian Poole observes, "the source of Madame de Vionnet's fascination is that there will always be more 'behind'" ("James and the Shadow" 86). And he illustrates this epistemic principle of *veritas a tergo* with a piece Strether's consciousness: "He felt what he had felt before with her, that there was always more behind what she showed, and more and more again behind that" (407).

The problem with Strether is that at one point he must relinquish his analytical position of observer—Chad calls him an "observer of manners"—and engage the plot. According to Pippin,

> Strether has now become, intimately, a part of the affair, however much he (and many readers) want to see him as ("tragically") a mere observer, a vicarious agent. He has become a part of the actual love affair, not just a part of the business of managing it.
>
> (*James* 164)

Unmistakably, he will take an interest in the sophisticated lady and fail to remain aloof. But only an interest. His Stoic indifference to *this* and *that* will be aggravated by the onrush of different particulars he will encounter at Paris. Whereas limited experience breeds passionate interest (the committed notation of difference) and by consequence the possibility of entanglement and emplotment—the Heideggerian fall (*Geworfenheit*) into plot—unlimited experience breeds critical-cynical disinterest (the uncommitted notation of difference). Commitment is the ethical prelude to decision: a committed notation of difference is a record of separate nonidentical singularity that elicits a libidinal response of attachment (fusion, in-separation, communion). Strether, by contrast, excels in the uncommitted or disinterested notation of difference: his is "the pure flame of the disinterested" (299).[30] And yet his sensorium is suddenly exposed to Madame de Vionnet's incontestably challenging difference (186–87). And he is invited by nearly everyone to scan it—largely in order, remember, to learn about the contents of Chad's elusive mind. This elusiveness, this vacancy, is transposed to her mind, and Strether must examine it. The board of male experts who will assist him in this task meet during "late sessions in the wondrous troisième, the lovely home, when men dropped in and the picture composed more suggestively through the haze of tobacco, of music more or less good and of talk more or less polyglot" (123). Strether is also assisted by Maria, but her role is rendered complex by her additional function as Socratic *eiron* and potential erotic partner. But suddenly a new directive is issued, and Strether is summoned, among others by Chad himself, to inspect the lady's daughter, Jeanne de Vionnet. She is, after all, Chad's most sensible match, and probably the reason why he tarries in Paris. *Cherchez la femme* now reads *Talk with Jeanne*. This is exactly what Chad asks Strether to do during a dinner at his house: "I should like so awfully to know what you think of her. It will really be a chance for you," he had said, "to see the *jeune fille*—I mean the type—as she actually is, and I don't think that, as an observer of manners, it's a thing you ought to miss" (181). What follows is described by Strether as "the collapse of the question of Jeanne de Vionnet's shy secret" (181). The *thing*, at bottom, that Jeanne *is*, is but a *miss*—a vacant mystery, a misleading hint. Jeanne is nothing to either. She is also the *miss*take of her genericity: Strether, the observer of manners, the indifferent recorder of proliferating differences, realizes, by virtue of his Paris experience, that the type (the genus, the universal, the form) fails to do justice to the *haecceitas* of the particular person.[31] In a sense, a sense also connected to the affordances of European freedom, the girl is also *different*:

> At the end of the ten minutes he was to spend with her his impression—with all it had thrown off and all it had taken in—was complete. She had been free, as she knew freedom, partly to show him that, unlike other little persons she knew, she had imbibed that ideal.
>
> (184)

Yet not sufficiently different to keep his or Chad's attention for too long. Predictably, she is sent to her nunnery.

### Mature Man and Young Man Inspect One Another

Strether tells Maria that "If I'm squared where's my marriage? If I miss my errand I miss that; and if I miss that I miss everything—I'm nowhere" (77). The panic driving these questions and mobilizing the empty determinants and pronominals (*that, everything, nowhere*) can hardly repress the reversal of its potential rationale—the fact that his *errand* is only *missed* when a *miss* interposes between himself and *that*. If *that* is a man then his is arguably a homosexual panic, or, less drastically, a homosocial shock. At the novel's center stage, as in so many narratives by Melville or Conrad, two males (Strether and Chad) are gazing at (into) one other.[32] In letter to Hugh Walpole, James noted that "the relation of Chad to Strether is a limited & according to my method only implied & indicated thing, sufficiently there" (qtd. in Bradbury, "Introduction" to *The Ambassadors* lxxviii). Implied, indicated, and sufficiently there, like the real *primal scene* that, according to Luckacher, the governess rightly attempts to see. As real a *thing*, in short, as the Lacanian Real.

The surface concern in *The Ambassadors* is the nature, degree, and complexity of Chad's entanglement, the extent to which he has allowed himself to be drawn into an erotic plot. This extent—the point to which he has let himself fall into some woman's hands—is the measure of his unfreedom. This is the novel's (Hamletian) problem: the predicament of a male spirit striving to elude the grasp of duplicitous women. "I say, we will have no more marriages" (*Hamlet* 3.1.146): so runs Chad's implicit defensive maxim. Also Hamletian is, of course, the male's resignation to the fact that "there's a special providence" (*Ambassadors* 163; *Hamlet* 5.2.157), a subtextual echo that is often sadly left unannotated by editors of the novel. Sadly, I say, for the novel chronicles the aborted *fall of* an American *sparrow*.[33] And the mystery, for there is an associated mystery, springs from the fact that this expectation—the supposition of his entanglement, which at Woollett is (quite correctly) taken for granted—runs counter to Strether's strong impression that Chad has become "so free and so strong" that he is just "inexcusable" (112). The correction of the Newsomes's expectation is James's unwitting homage to Puritan ethics—if they suspected unsimplicity (French complexity, moral duplicity, modern depravity), they were not *that* simple after all. Strether's quest consists in proving that Chad is "actually not entangled" (112). The simplicity of this epistemic adventure is however upset by unexpected intimations: "Do you think one's kept only by women?" Chad asks Strether. This subtle retort opens, for Strether, the window to a landscape of unpredictable, unclassifiable, difference.

The possibility of a difference so marked—not a radical alterity, for that belongs in a metaphysics of transcendence that is uncongenial to James— that is apt to dislodge the fixed taxonomies of status and gender consistency is best borne out in Strether's imaginative anticipation of Mrs Newsome's reaction to the *news of some*: " 'He says there's no woman. [. . .] What is there then?" (117) Short of a woman, the subject of their quest can only be an object, maybe an *abject*. Let me recall, in passing, that this obtuse line of inferential guessing is what characterizes the response of Hamlet's stage acolytes (Claudius, Gertrude, Polonius) to his enigmatic humoral particularity, his unmotivated melancholy. To prove, moreover, the hetero-erotic "cause of such *defect*" (*Hamlet* 2.2.102), Polonius promises to "find/Where truth is hid, though it were hid indeed/Within the centre" (2.2.157–159).

Around Chad gathers a homosocial community of fugitive Bohemians who seek to elude the grasp, hold, and purchase that the epistemic apparatus of surveillance-espionage-inspection has on them. And Strether is soon drawn into this community. The first member he meets is little Bilham, in an extraordinary scene that foreshadows similar moments in Hemingway (*The Sun also Rises*), Miller (*Tropic of Cancer*), Baldwin (*Giovanni's Room*), and of course Highsmith (*The Talented Mr. Ripley*). Later, Strether will interrogate little Bilham about the extent of Chad's freedom. He raises so many times the question "why isn't he 'free'?" (130) that the notion itself (the empty signifier *freedom*) becomes totally depleted, echoic, parodic. No clear reply is offered. Strether feels that "each of his remarks [. . .] seemed to drop into a deeper well" (130). This well is also a figure of Chad's interiority, the invisible jelly inside his tin mould of externals. At this point of the novel, Strether is beginning to feel that the two notions— *life* and *freedom*—that concentrated the gist of his emancipatory utopia (the recovery of *temps perdu*) are beginning to lose part of their pragmatic promise. What he can conceivably *do* with his freedom is a function of the particular actions that Chad may have managed to transform his own abstract freedom into. But what (the hell) is Chad doing? That is the question. Abstract *life* and *freedom* begin to disintegrate into the pool of indeterminacy—the mist of changing indistinct pronominals (*this, that, he, she, something, nothing, all, everything*)—that ends up swallowing the novel. His later explosion of confidence is compromised, on close inspection, by the resulting tropes of unspecified life—"Live *all* you can; it's a mistake not to. It doesn't so much matter what you *do in particular* so long as you have your *life*"—and delusive freedom—"Still, one has *the* illusion of *freedom*" (153; emphases added).

What is Chad doing in particular? He doesn't confess. Before such indeterminate and indefinite cavity the inspector who fails to discover the mysterious content is forced to imagine. Waymarsh's and Chad's colloquial expression to denote such activity is "to fill out" (20), and both wrongly expect Strether to be doing his homework:[34]

> "Still, you must have filled out." He had stopped, leaving his friend to wonder a little what point he wished to make; and this it was that enabled Strether meanwhile to make one. "Oh we've never pretended to go into detail. We weren't in the least bound to *that*. It was 'filling out' enough to miss you as we did." But Chad rather oddly insisted, though under the high lamp at their corner, where they paused, he had at first looked as if touched by Strether's allusion to the long sense, at home, of his absence. "What I mean is you must have imagined." "Imagined what?" "Well—horrors."
>
> (109–110)

When reading a story of adventures, including *The Heart of Darkness*, the attempt to "go into detail," the decision to bind oneself to "that," the resolve to concretize the horror, is merely pointless. When Strether delicately suggests that for Madame de Vionnet to care so much for Chad there must have been a predisposition of some kind on his part, little Bilham comes to his rescue:

> "I mean that originally, for her to have cared for him—" "There must have been stuff in him? Oh yes, there was stuff indeed, and much more of it than ever showed, I dare say, at home. Still, you know," the young man in all fairness developed, "there was room for her, and that's where she came in."
>
> (200)

There was *stuff* indeed, there was *jelly*. But what is *it*? What we find here is a plain illustration of the transitive structure of desire: desire is the desire of the other, and it is premised on the erotic jealousy (perhaps *jellisy*) before his/her *jouissance*.[35] Here is no longer the question of *What Maisie Knew*, which we have already examined as *What Miles and Flora Knew*. The question, here, for us, and with growing urgency for Strether, is *What Chad Liked*. The framing and the internal schemas meet at this juncture, for what Chad appears to like, at the surface level of the plot, is the object of Mrs. Newsome's secret desire, to wit, the sophisticated French lady. But this revelation comes to nothing before the shock formulated by Mrs Newsome in a letter Strether imagines she will write to her daughter: " 'He says there's no woman. [. . .] What is there then?"

## VIII

Material to the novel's significance is therefore the unanswered question of Chad's jouissance. When Strether asks little Bilham "*Is there some woman? Of whom he's really afraid of course I mean—or who does with him what she likes?*" he is not inquiring about some woman's desire, but rather about his: for what she likes is at bottom what he (the object of her desire) also likes. Desire is the desire of the Other. Before the collapse of life and freedom as sustainable moral fictions, Strether begins to sense the encroaching purchase of *jouissance*. During his walk through Chester with Miss Gostrey, he feels a sudden rush of delight. Questioned by her companion whether he believes he is doing something he thinks is "not right"—in fact, tellingly, he believes he should be sharing this experience with Waymarsh, not with Maria—he replies "Am I enjoying it as much as *that?*" (11) The expectation of guilt before an episode of excessive *jouissance* is ironic, and she speaks about his general "failure," which he rapidly identifies with "the failure of Woollett." She explains: "The failure to enjoy [. . .] is what I mean." He means the same: "Precisely. Woollett isn't sure it ought to enjoy. If it were it would. But it hasn't, poor thing," Strether continues, "any one to show it how. It's not like me. I have somebody" (11). *Jouissance* requires a witness—someone to show—for the perverse cycle of desire to persevere. But who is the person that Strether will "show it how"? Who is that "somebody"? Maria is of course a suitable candidate, but Chad is a more persuasive match. Strether wants to show Chad how much he endures the indefinite pleasure he has begun to realize Chad himself enjoys. The desire of the Other regulates too the doxal promptings of ideology, "the disposition to talk as 'society' talks" (28). But when society is free Parisian society, then shared *Gerede* and public manners are worth a try. Strether realizes that Chad has become "a man of the world" (106), that he has gained "experience" (108): "Yes, experience was what Chad did play on him, if he didn't play any grossness of defiance. Of course experience was in a manner defiance" (109).

In *Denis Duval*, this realization dawns on the mature storyteller as he reconsiders the stages of his life. At first, the investment of *jouissance* is confined to the luxuries of feminine domesticity: Denis looking back at his devoted mother's dedication with "thankfulness for the strange dangers from which I have escaped, the great blessings I have enjoyed," and Denis, reminiscing, after "a life of adventures and dangers, taking a last look at his dearest joy" ("Notes on *Denis Duval*," 568), i.e. his wife.[36] But soon the homosocial brotherhood of swindlers and sailors will offer an alternative escape route for his mimetic desire. But Denis's premature irruption into the realm of Scott's and Stevenson's male heroes is not devoid of reactionary value. It marks a reversion to the (reading) joys of domestic childhood. As I noted in the first chapter, James observed that

> what we see in [*Treasure Island*] is not only the ideal fable but, as part and parcel of that, as it were, the young reader himself and his state of mind: we seem to read it over his shoulder, with an arm around his neck.
>
> (*LC I* 1251)

In *Denis Duval*, the mature narrator is looking at the young Denis *living* his own novel, and reads it anew "over his shoulder, with an arm around his neck." The parallelism holds, for in *The Ambassadors* Strether reads over Chad's shoulder the chronicle of his own missed life, which is, incidentally, not dissimilar from Gray's "wasted life" (James, "Notes for *The Ivory Tower*" 246).[37] This may be the place to recall that Thackeray visited the James home in New York when James was nine, and that the first thing he noticed was his voice

> proceeding from my father's library, in which some glimpse of me hovering, at an opening of the door [. . .] prompted him to the formidable words: "Come here, little boy, and show me your extraordinary jacket!" [. . .] though he laid on my shoulder the hand of benevolence, bent on my native custom the spectacles of wonder [. . .] after asking me if this were the common uniform of my age and class, he remarked that in England, were I to go there, I should be addressed as "Buttons." It had been revealed to me thus in a flash that we were somehow *queer*.
>
> (*Small Boy* 74–75)

The passage, which I have unfortunately mangled, is simply magnificent. The motifs of status inconsistency, borrowed robes, male-to-male inspection, avuncular pressure, and consecutive queerness are all bound up in a *primal scene of eccentric individuation* that bears heavily on the arguments of my book. We now understand why Thackeray called James a snob, and why the latter disliked the dorsal laying of hands on his shoulder.[38] As Žižek has pointed out, "the ideological theme of the grown-ups' redemption through their infantilization [. . .] simultaneously produces a new subject position for the spectator" (Žižek, *Plague* 96). This theme sets the ideological pattern of the standard Dickens master narrative, whose archaizing romantic variation Thackeray explores in *Denis Duval*. Arguably, Strether is the infantilized grown-up who uses the signifier *life* (also *freedom* and *experience*) "as a kind of empty container for the multitude of mutually exclusive meanings." There is no ideology, Žižek argues, "without such a pullback from the signified content into the empty symbolic form" (*Plague* 95). By becoming the quiet spectators of their own juvenile vicarious selves, the mature Denis and Strether achieve symbolic alleviation of the real antagonisms of sexuality and society. They evacuate their fugitive contents into the mold of the empty symbolic form—the formal structure of failure—of the adventure story. Whatever consolation they obtain derives from watching the signifier they have enforced wander. Wander freely, that is, from gravitational pulls towards Oedipus or a plot. For there is always, as Sedgwick aptly noted, the vexing (Hamletian) question of maternal sexuality (*Between* 108). Is Chad in France because he cannot bear the prospect of his mother's engagement to Strether? Does he sexually fall for a mother because he is pathologically, and vicariously, attached to the maternal? Althusser reminds us that Oedipus is not about hidden meaning or concealed contents. Oedipus is rather

> la structure dramatique, la 'machine théâtrale' imposée para la Loi de la Culture à tout candidat, involontaire et forcé à l'humanité, une structure contenant en elle-même non seulement la possibilité, mais la nécessité des variations concrètes dans lesquelles elle existe, pour tout individu qui peut parvenir à son seuil, le vivre et lui survivre.
>
> (*Écrits sur la psychanalyse* 44–45)

Oedipus spells a thematic, dramatic, and theatrical interruption of the structure of failure. And the breakdown that is the Oedipal machine may occur anywhere, including the homosocial community that welcomes its fugitives. In *Denis Duval*, the escape from the domestic prison house takes the original form of subjection to alternative male tutorage. Denis is surrounded by vicarious fathers who belong to diverse fraternities (contraband, church, aristocracy, navy). One Papist priest, who strikes Denis as "a queer gentleman," is soon "amused by my simplicity and odd sayings. He was never tired of having me with him. He said I should be his little English master" (*Denis* 472). The pattern is recursively simple: an experienced gentleman *revives* in the enjoyable company of a younger male whom he maieutically coaches and instructs, exactly the position that the narrator and some characters of *Tom Jones* (Mr Allworthy, Thwackam, Square) occupy with respect to the young protagonist, whose formal *adventures* they vicariously experience. Although the direction of instruction has been in *The Ambassadors* ironically reversed (the young man teaches the mature man), Strether is this kind of "queer," experienced gentleman, and James could turn to late Thackeray to flesh out the type of the avuncular witness: *Lovel the Widower* and *The Adventures of Philip* are both told by the middle-aged friends, Mr. Batchelor and Arthur Pendennis, of the respective protagonists, Lovel and Philip.[39] Arthur Pendennis describes himself as "the perpetual speaker [who] must of necessity lay bare his own weaknesses, vanities, peculiarities" (Preface to *Pendennis*). Strether corresponds to the figure of the elderly character who guides and supervises a young character who is not necessarily a member of his family. The contract of homosocial bonding he renews very early with Waymarsh is prompted by their circumstantial unmooring from a nuclear family. Strether is a widower, and Waymarsh, married at thirty, "has not lived with his wife for fifteen years" (18).[40] Nothing but spleen and delay—an "impish deferring and deferring of climax" (Kenner, *Pound* 11)—stops them from reentering the matrimonial market—"You're a very attractive man, Strether" (21), Waymarsh compliments his friend.

In *The Ambassadors*, there are two allusions to Major Pendennis, uncle and advisor of Arthur, the protagonist of *The History of Pendennis*. Both Maria and Waymarsh are separately compared to this "wary and patient man of the world" (*Pendennis* 80), breakfasting, "like a gentleman," surrounded by morning papers, at the Megatherium Club (*Ambassadors* 23–24, 26), a living monument to the principle that "gentlemanly idleness is [. . .] more meritorious than hard work" (Carey, *Thackeray* 152). James must have been fascinated by the credentials of this seasoned snob, who "knew the name and pedigree of everybody in the Peerage" and was full of "stories of the fashionable world." This is the rapid account of his London routine:

> his newspapers and his mornings—his afternoons from club to club, his little confidential visits to my Ladies, his rides in Rotten Row, his dinners, and his stall at the Opera, his rapid escapades to Fulham or Richmond on Saturdays and Sundays, his bow from my Lord Duke or my Lord Marquis at the great London entertainments, and his name in the Morning Post of the succeeding day,—his quieter little festivals, more select, secret, and delightful.
>
> (*Kathleen Tillotson, Pendennis* 84)

More fascinating still is what is here left unsaid. According to Kathleen Tillotson, "Thackeray never tells everything; he leaves much to be read between the lines; the tone of intimate confidence often masks a real reserve" (*Novels* 254); John Sutherland argued that Thackeray's legendary omniscience cannot prevent his stage from showing *holes*.[41] Reading between the lines, let alone glancing at holes, is one of those things James could certainly do Hugh Kenner rightly spoke of "orgies of reticence" (*Pound* 23). Major Pendennis, his brother recalls, always boasted that he should "live and die an old bachelor" (*Pendennis* 13). Of Thackeray's memorable bachelors, Sedgwick has argued that they

> created or reinscribed as personality type one possible path of response to the strangulation of homosexual panic, their basic strategy is easy

enough to trace: a preference of atomized male individualism to the nuclear family (and a corresponding demonization of women, especially mothers); a garrulous and visible refusal of anything that could be interpreted as genital sexuality, towards objects male and female; a corresponding emphasis on the pleasures of the other senses; and a well-defended social faculty that freights with a good deal of magnetism its proneness to parody and to unpredictable sadism.

(*Epistemology* 192)

Strether is not exactly that kind of gentleman—if we aim at exactitude, the man is Hamlet—but he shares many traits with the type, especially the first three: male individualism, visible refusal to genital sexuality, and emphasis on alternative sensorial pleasures. We see them combine in Strether's conversion into a Parisian flaneur: "He fidgeted and wasted time" (15); "he was sated in fine with idleness" (65); "there were moments when he himself felt shy of professing the full sweetness of the taste of leisure" (27), looking, for instance, at shop-windows; he is "given over to uncontrolled perceptions" (34) and "his imagination roam" (35); he has internalized the Stoic and Hamletian "unattainable art of taking things as they came" (58); and he is haunted by "the question of what he was doing with such an exceptional sense of escape" (56). Whereas Waymarsh makes money, he has "never made anything" (30). And Maria conceives of herself and Strether as "beaten brothers in arms" marked by "futility" (31). Futile, impractical, idle: Strether is ready to pursue more consistently the path of homosocial bonding he has initiated with Waymarsh, and, to some paradoxical extent, with Maria. He makes substantial headway when he enters, through little Bilham, Chad's semi-Bohemian circle of friends in Paris. But the liminal space of Bohemia—an area of social reality open to snobs like Major Pendennis—contaminates, like sexuality, every new situation Strether encounters in Paris, all the way up to the crisis. The country meal that Strether shares with Chad and Madame de Vionnet right after their pastoral exposure is described as "a marked drop into innocent friendly Bohemia" (393). But echoes of Bohemia are already audible when Little Bilham, who had originally "come out to Paris to paint," accompanies Strether during a visit to the Louvre, and invites him afterward to his own studio,

his own poor place, which was very poor, gave to his idiosyncrasies, for Strether—the small sublime indifference and independences that had struck the latter as fresh—an odd and engaging dignity. He lived at the end of an alley that went out of an old short cobbled street, a street that went in turn out of a new long smooth avenue—street and avenue and alley having, however, in common a sort of social shabbiness; and he introduced them to the rather cold and blank little studio which he had lent to a comrade for the term of his elegant absence.

(89)

Much of this atmosphere is drawn from French novelists, but James was probably also taking *after* Thackeray. In his essay on Kemble, he refers to "that Newman Street which had a later renown, attested by Thackeray, as the haunt of art-students and one of the boundaries of Bohemia" (*LC I* 1074), a displaced recreation, imaginative evidence of which we can find in an essential passage in chapter 39, "Amongst the Painters," of *The Newcomes*, where old gentlemen, stirred by memories of Roman travels, join the company of Bohemian artists in city studios:

> When Clive Newcome comes to be old, no doubt he will remember his Roman days as amongst the happiest which fate ever awarded him. The simplicity of the student's life there, the greatness and friendly splendour of the scenes surrounding him, the delightful nature of the occupation in which he is engaged, the pleasant company of comrades, inspired by a like pleasure over a similar calling, the labour, the meditation, the holiday and the kindly feast afterwards, should make the Art-students the happiest of youth, did they but know their good fortune. [. . .] In every city where Art is practised there are old gentlemen who never touched a pencil in their lives, but find the occupation and company of artists so agreeable that they are never out of the studios; follow one generation of painters after another; sit by with perfect contentment while Jack is drawing his pifferaro, or Tom designing his cartoon, and years afterwards when Jack is established in Newman Street, and Tom a Royal Academician, shall still be found in their rooms, occupied now by fresh painters and pictures, telling the youngsters, their successors, what glorious fellows Jack and Tom were.
>
> (*Newcomes* 406)

Strether has temporarily become one of the gentlemen who never touched a pencil in their lives but who find the company of dilettanti and artists so agreeable that they are never out of studios. His entrance into an "aesthetic fraternity" (80) of sorts is obviously fraught with overt sexual implications:

> As a sort of reserve labor force and a semiporous, liminal space for vocational sorting and social rising and falling, bohemia could seemingly be entered from any social level; but [. . .] it served best the cultural needs, the fantasy needs, and the needs for positive and negative self-definition of an anxious and conflicted bourgeoisie. Except to homosexual men,

the idea of "bohemia" seems before the 1890s not to have had a distinctively gay coloration.

(Sedgwick, *Epistemology* 193)

Which means that for many a "queer gentleman" it *did* have a distinctively gay coloration. I am not trying to say that Strether, let alone Chad, are queer in any modern sense of the term. What I am implying is that in the dilated occasion of their pastoral renouncement of familial obligations and marital expectations, and of their gazing into one another to measure the extent of their productive vacancy, they seem to have temporarily halted "the routing of homosocial through heterosexual love" (Sedgwick, *Between* 160). I am also suggesting that their attempted flight testifies to "how pervasive, inescapable, and even ineradicable Thackeray considers the stain of worldliness to be" (Wheatly, *Patterns* 59). They compose their little "tableau of homosocial bonding" over "the sexually discredited body" of several women, notably Jeanne de Vionnet and Maria Gostrey. Their passionate friendship echoes that of Lord Castlewood and Lord Mohun in *Henry Esmond*, and that between de la Motte and Denis's grandfather in *Denis Duval*—relations of pragmatic but semi-romantic bonding established at the cost of discredited and banished women (Rachel, Beatrix, and Madame de Saverne). In the case of Strether and Chad, this relation remains asymmetrical, it is a "rapport de puissance," a non-relation if you wish, established, in the mode of a general disjunction, between "singularités distincts" and "insubstituables" (Badiou *L'immanence* 617).[42] James learnt to sketch this non-fusional homosocial relation between distinct male singularities by reading Thackeray, who in turn had been apprenticed to Fielding and Dickens. Cameron has rightly argued that in James's novels, "the effect of thinking is to disavow relation" and that "in the case of Strether, thinking leads to affectless disengagement" (*Thinking* 167).

### Kenosis

Denis's and Chad's existential exertions to attain experience in an emptied realm of adventure where both family business (contraband, commerce) and the female interest may be conveniently disconnected and bracketed paves the way to the liberatory fantasy of their elders—old Denis and Strether. Theirs is a fantasy of further evacuation:

> Poetic misprision, historically a health, is individually a sin against continuity, against the only authority that matters, property or the priority of having named something first. Poetry is property, as politics is property. Hermes ages into a bald gnome, calls himself Error, and founds

commerce. Intrapoetic relations are neither commerce nor theft, unless you can conceive of family romance as a politics of commerce, or as the dialectic of theft it becomes in Blake's *The Mental Traveller*. [. . .] The largest Error we can hope to meet and make is every ephebe's fantasia: quest antithetically enough, and live to beget yourself.

(78–79)

In *The Ambassadors*, James puts an end to his antithetical quest to redefine his own narrative voice over against the indefinition of Thackeray's story-telling voices. Poetry is a quest for discontinuity (79), for a poetic strength beyond the antinomies of thrown-ness (repetition) and extravagance (*Verstiegenheit* or madness, Error). But adventure is both, per definition, extravagance and the recollection forward that becomes, in uncanny Freudian logic, every repetition (82–83). James repeats Thackeray and discontinues him through enhanced indeterminacy and increased emptying out. Kenosis, Bloom argues, is an emptying out, an "act of self-abnegation" that "tends to make the fathers pay for their own sins, and perhaps for those of the sons also" (91). In the novels, it is the grandsons that pay for the commercial sins of their grandfathers. In the novel titled *The Haunting of James House*, the son cannot erase the sin inherited from the father—who was turned out, recall, for calling his son a snob. The pragmatic formula of kenosis is: "where the precursor was, there the ephebe shall be, but by the discontinuous mode of emptying the precursor of his divinity, while appearing to empty himself of his own" (91). Turning Thackeray out of the house is a way of emptying him further, no doubt. Dickens waits for him outside, knocking at the door. It is however unclear that James was ever inside. There are many ways of remaining enchanted, even divine—like Holly Golightly—in the open.

## Notes

1 For the "homes and haunts" genre, see the article by Alison Booth.
2 Nicola Bradbury doesn't include Thackeray in the "French and English Literary Contexts" she surveys in her excellent edition of *The Ambassadors*: "Introduction," lxix–lxxiv.
3 Late Thackeray was as ambiguous as James about the suitability of status consistency. John Carey argued that "class distinction was an enthusiasm he felt less chary about owning up to, and his eighteenth-century novels are full celebrations of it" (*Thackeray* 157). Barbara Hardy writes that Thackeray always appears to enjoy "showing a shift in the social and moral hierarchy [. . .] exposing [. . .] shiftingness and shiftiness of the mobility and hierarchy of *Vanity Fair*" (28).
4 Adrian Poole comments on the importance of this London evocation of "the shadowy presence" of Thackeray for the composition of *The Princess Casamassima*: "Introduction" to *The Princess*, LXVII–LXVIII.

5  Geoffrey Tillotson observed that Thackeray "was aware of the streamingness of experience. Not surprisingly, for he was one for those for whom narrative is as natural as the flow of the blood" (*Thackeray* 32).

6  Writing about Zola, he argues that "Thackeray, Dickens, George Eliot, have all had an eye to the innocent classes" (*LC II* 869). In the preface to *The Princess Casamassima*, he holds that "no 'story' is possible without its fools—as most of the painters of life, Shakespeare, Cervantes and Balzac, Fielding, Scott, Thackeray, Dickens, George Meredith, George Eliot, Jane Austen, have abundantly felt." Responsiveness to fools provokes both the artist's "moral reaction" and the "fine intensification and enlargement" of the "consciousness (on the part of the moved and moving creature)" (*LC II* 1092).

7  Despite the potential validity of my discrimination, the truth is that James hardly gives up the analogy that the novelist, including Thackeray, is primarily a painter: "[George Eliot] was a painter of *bourgeois* life as Thackeray was a painter of the life of drawing-rooms" (*LC I* 913).

8  George Eliot and Thackeray are masters of English, "great authorities" in the matter of "knowing English" (*LC I* 745). "Any quotation from Thackeray," he argues in another review, "anywhere, is sure to seem happy" (*LC I* 835). "There is no writer," in short, "of whom one bears better being reminded, none from whom any chance quotation, to whom any chance allusion or reference, is more unfailingly delectable. Pick out something at hazard from Thackeray, and ten to one it is a prize" (*LC I* 1289).

9  In 1954, Geoffrey Tillotson devoted five fine pages (296–301) to this connection in *Thackeray the Novelist*. Significantly, Philp Horne's 2017 article "Henry James, Winchelsea, Rye, and Thackeray's *Denis Duval*" doesn't include in the bibliography one single essay or book on the influence of Thackeray on James. He could have mentioned Rowe's 1984 book, where the American scholar argues twice, very much against the grain, that Thackeray—alongside other predecessors like Hawthorne, Trollope, and Flaubert—contributed greatly to the "constitution" of Henry James (*Theoretical* 67, 74).

10  In an essay on George Sand, he inventories again "the leading English novelists": "Miss Austen and Sir Walter Scott, Dickens and Thackeray, Hawthorne and George Eliot" (*LC II* 724). Unlike Sand, they "have all represented young people in love with each other," but no one has represented a passion.

11  The fact that he never granted Trollope the distinction of having organized some critical principles about the art of storytelling in his book on Thackeray, let alone the merit of having written it in the first place, can only be explained in terms of rivalry between disciples. There is a Trollopean school of Thackeray as much as there is a Jamesian school of Thackeray, and Rowe's decision to focus on the Trollope-James relation bespeaks extraordinary cunning. But this is not our concern here. What matters is that James is keen to acknowledge the fact that a consummate novelist, an artist whose foremost call is to picture reality, can draw half of his resources of inspiration from the pictures of another novelist.

12  This is implied in Derrida's overall deconstructive project and is also visible in the liberal program of thinkers like Finkielkraut, *L'identité malheureuse*, 46.

13  Peter Brooks describes Strether's "adventure of consciousness" as "less a happening, a set of events [. . .] than a perceptual experience": *Henry James* 51–52.

14  For formal circularity in *Denis Duval*, see Harden, *Thackeray the Writer: From Pendennis to* Denis Duval, 215–216.

15 The other two titles bear connection with religious epic-visionary stories about the Holy Grail, the Ascension of the Virgin, or The Parliament of Birds.
16 See Moretti, *The Way of the World*, 5–35.
17 Strether was described as bewildered by novel circumstances, as being "so often at sea" (81). Something easy (like Chad marrying the daughter) is described as "plain sailing" (130); there is reference to "a final impulse to burn his ships" (93); and also very unusual allegorical developments, redolent of scenes of immersion in *Richard III*: "Waymarsh himself, for the occasion, was drawn into the eddy; it absolutely, though but temporarily, swallowed him down, and there were days when Strether seemed to bump against him as a sinking swimmer might brush a submarine object. The fathomless medium held them— Chad's manner was the fathomless medium; and our friend felt as if they passed each other, in their deep immersion, with the round impersonal eye of silent fish" (122). Recall too the phrase: "a quaint community of shipwreck" (313).
18 See his afterword to an edition of Smollet's novel included in *The Friday Book*, especially his analysis of formal accidentality at pp. 33–34.
19 Trollope held that the story of *Vanity Fair* was "vague and wandering, clearly commenced without any idea of an ending" (*Thackeray* 95). Geoffrey Tillotson argued that Thackeray "was at home in vastness and never-endingness" (*Thackeray* 12), and praised his "method of delaying the completion of what is to be said of a thing" (32).
20 For an elaboration of this point, see Hardy, *Exposure*, 11.
21 See in particular the work of Brian McCuskey and Andrew Miller.
22 See also Sutherland, *Thackeray at Work*, 110–123.
23 "I learned to speak English like a Briton born as I am, and not as we did at home, where we used a queer Alsatian jargon of French and German" (446); "What trivial things remain impressed on the memory" (471).
24 See Schacht's Introduction to his critical edition of *Denis Duval*, x–xi.
25 Žižek's account is notably more Lacanian than Foucauldian. I believe, however, that Foucault's theorization of the power-discursive *dispositif de sexualité* can be reconciled with Žižek's adoption of Lacan's more naturalized, less constructivist, take on sexuality. The fact that power-related discourses on sexuality aimed at the constitution of a homogenous sex are neither homogeneous nor compatible is a matter to ponder, for it may well betoken the (Lacanian) bankruptcy of symbolization before the Real. For the tension between the Lacanian and the Foucauldian models, see Copjec. For the impossibility of formalizing the sexual relationship, see Reinhard's remarkable Introduction to Badiou's and Cassin's *There is No Such Thing as a Sexual Relationship*, XIV–XV.
26 Eric Haralson speaks of a "continual dispersion trather than a concentration of the novel's sexual/textual energies": *Henry James*, 131.
27 For the ambivalence of the expletive "it" in James, see Chatman, 72–76. For the "queer formalism" of "trope and syntax" in James, see Savoy, "The Jamesian Thing."
28 Thackeray's farewell to the mad woman who has been sent to a nunnery, an attic, or an institution, places *Denis Duval* under the auspices of *Hamlet*: "She often rambled about this ball and play, and hummed snatches of tunes and little phrases of dialogue which she may have heard there" (*Denis* 846).
29 James notes that "Several English romancers—notably Fielding, Thackeray, and Charles Reade—have won great praise for their figures of women; but they owe it [. . .] to a meaner sort of art [. . .] to an indefinable appeal to

masculine prejudice—to a sort of titillation of the masculine sense of difference" (*LC I* 962).

30  The notion of *disinterestedness* appears often in the novel: Mamie is "disinterestedly tender" (316). The going on of Chad and the French women is described as "beautiful," "innocent" because "disinterested" (188). For the relation between delegated representation and openness to difference, see Rivkin's excellent reading of *The Ambassadors*, 57–81.

31  The ontological thematic of difference, central to the novel, is bound up with the problem of social types, also material to it.

32  In his remarkable reading of the novel, Haralson favors Strether's potential infatuation with Bilham over the Strether-Chad homoerotic relation: *Henry James*, 125–126.

33  Metaphorical references to *traps* laid by French women to catch aerial men are common in the novel, especially in the opening section of Book III.

34  For Strether's reconstructive examination of Chad, cued by pragmatic openness, see Hocks, 160–168.

35  For the shocking omnipresence of *pleasure* in *The Ambassadors*, see Hadley, 86–112.

36  The "Notes on *Denis Duval*," written by Frederick Greenwood, were published in 1864 as "a tail-piece to the novel's incomplete serialization in the *Cornhill*" (Sutherland, *Genesis* 226).

37  Kevin Ohi sees into this relation a realization of *belatedness*: "the regret for the life one missed *is*, paradoxically, the life one missed" (156).

38  Thackeray visited the family again in Paris in 1857: see Kaplan, 30.

39  For the use in James of the bachelor to tell another man's story, see the section "Gender, Genre, and the Airplane of First-Person Narration" in Snyder, *Bachelors*, 107–117. In his reading of *Pendennis*, Harden speaks of "the ironic relationship between Pen's hopes and enthusiasms and the narrator's more mature perspectives": *Thackeray the Writer: From* Pendennis *to* Denis Duval, 3.

40  Strether escapes from his event horizon, trying to disconnect all his future spatiotemporal points from other points in the past: "the period of conscious detachment occupying the centre of his life, the grey middle desert of the two deaths, that of his wife and that, ten years later, of his boy" (35).

41  Discussing the critical commonplace that Thackeray is an omniscient narrator, John Sutherland argues: "But just has with the historical backdrop, the front of the stage has its holes. The reader is again teased by what this allegedly omniscient novelist would seem not to know, will not acquaint himself with, or declines to impart. Omniscient he may be; omnidictive he is not" ("Introduction" to *Vanity Fair* xx).

42  Badiou singles out *The Ambassadors* as an instance of the conventional handling that art makes of the problem of love, in this case as an illustration of the notion "que c'est dans le renoncement sexuel que l'amour preserve son essence, parvenant au passage à rien de moins qu'au sublime" (*L'immanence* 615). I guess he fails to consider the "love non-relation" between Strether and Chad.

# 6  Clinamen

## Swerving from Dickens: Henry James in *The Ivory Tower*

I

On 21 December 1865, Henry James publishes in *The Nation* a review of Charles Dickens's *Our Mutual Friend*. James is twenty-two and has only published two novellas. Dickens is fifty-three and this is his fourteenth novel, the last he completed. The young critic reads the mature novelist. The review is impressively overconfident. James makes three tightly related claims:

1. Dickens's creative *exhaustion* tells in the *forced* quality of all his writing since *Bleak House* (1853): "the present work," he denounces, "is dug out as with a spade and pickaxe." In the same figurative vein, James adds that "to say that the conduct of the story, with all its complications, betrays a long-practised hand, is to pay no compliment worthy the author." The implication is that an excess of labor—*working, forcing, digging out, practicing* the "manufacture of fiction"—is bad per se, and doesn't absolve other faults. "Seldom," he concludes, "had we read a book so intensely *written*, so little seen, known, or felt" (*LC I* 853).
2. The novel's occasional humor can be extolled, but only that. Of his "old humor" only "the letter" remains, "without the spirit," and this letter is a "fancy" whose movement is "lifeless, forced, mechanical." This becomes evident in his treatment of "character" as "a bundle of eccentricities animated by no principle of nature whatever." Dickens's characters have neither "nature" nor "humanity." They are not "characters," only "figures," not "types," only "exceptions," not generalities prompting "generalizations," only particulars leading nowhere. Society, "maintained by natural sense and natural feeling," vanishes from his world: "a community of eccentrics is impossible" (855).
3. Because "he has created nothing but figure," Dickens lacks "insight." His "conception is weak." When he tries to fly above the particular oddness of his characters, and reach the breath of a moralist, he fails.

DOI: 10.4324/9781003199564-6

He shows no "intellectual superiority" to the "passions" of his characters. The moralist, the philosopher, "must know *man* as well as *men*," but Dickens is "unable to prosecute those generalizations in which alone consists the greatness of a work of art." One of the "chief conditions of his genius" is "not to see beyond the surface of things." He is "the greatest of superficial novelists" (856). *Our Mutual Friend* is, in conclusion, not a good novel, for, as he will argue in "The Art of Fiction," "no good novel will ever proceed from a *superficial* mind" (*LC I* 64; emphasis added).

The review is written in a spirit of controlled iconoclasm, and it owes whatever authority it has to the manners and principles of neoclassical criticism: the reliance on abstractions (*nature, humanity, society*), the calculated counterpoising of alternatives ("the habitual probable of nature and the habitual impossible of Mr. Dickens"), the taste for chiastic paradox ("This may sound like very subtle talk about a very simple matter; it is rather very simple talk about a very subtle matter"), the confidence in the moral priority of nature. But one senses, behind the apparent poise, an apprehensive posture. One senses James's anxiety. Killing a father takes time, especially when the motive is unclear. In the Oedipus story, the motive is always unclear. Parricide is just a contingent compulsion, an error. But James had additional reasons to expedite the crime and move rapidly forward. He felt deeply uncomfortable with the idea that someone who was only "a great observer and a great humorist," a man "most at his ease" in the "quarter of society" where "villainous" characters like Rogue Riderhood thrived, a man who could not "understand what he was talking about" (857), someone, in short, like Mark Twain, could have, at some point in James's childhood and youth, so rashly forced his way into the vacant throne of artistic paternity. The young James was aiming at a more genteel descent—responsible romancers like Nathaniel Hawthorne or George Eliot. But, like Balzac, he was doomed to *parents pauvres*.

   In general, James's critical appraisal of Dickens is less enthusiastic than his valorization of Thackeray. This apparent lack of estimation is caused by an excess of exposure. Whereas Thackeray seemed a luminous choice, Dickens was an infection and a fatality.[1] In his autobiography, James comments extensively on his very premature susceptivity to visual information, in New York, of "arrangements of Dickens for the stage" (*Small Boy* 97). He recalls the figures of actors and actresses of dramatic adaptations of *Dombey and Son, David Copperfield*, and *Oliver Twist*, and also his infantile perusal of the "illustrations of Phiz." A particular production of *Nicholas Nickleby*, and especially the stage characterization of Smike, stuck in his memory with "ineffaceability" and "sharp retention" (*Small Boy* 101). Then comes this amazing confession:

> Such at least was to be the force of the Dickens imprint, however applied, in the soft clay of our generation; it was to resist so serenely the wash of the waves of time. To be brought up thus against the author of it, or to speak at all of the dawn of one's early consciousness of it and of his presence and power, is to begin to tread ground at once sacred and boundless, the associations of which, looming large, warn us off even while they hold. He did too much for us surely ever to leave us free—free of judgment, free of reaction, even should we care to be, which heaven forbid: he laid his hand on us in a way to undermine as in no other case the power of detached appraisement. We react against other productions of the general kind without "liking" them the less, but we somehow liked Dickens the more for having forfeited half the claim to appreciation. That process belongs to the fact that criticism, roundabout him, is somehow futile and tasteless. His own taste is easily impugned, but he entered so early into the blood and bone of our intelligence that it always remained better than the taste of overhauling him. When I take him up to-day and find myself holding off, I simply stop: not holding off, that is, but holding on, and from the very fear to do so; which sounds, I recognise, like perusal, like renewal, of the scantest. I don't renew, I wouldn't renew for the world; wouldn't, that is, with one's treasure so hoarded in the dusty chamber of youth, let in the intellectual air. Happy the house of life in which such chambers still hold out, even with the draught of the intellect whistling through the passages. We were practically contemporary, contemporary with the issues, the fluttering monthly numbers—that was the point; it made for us a good fortune, constituted for us in itself romance, on which nothing, to the end, succeeds in laying its hands.

(101)

At the dawn of consciousness, the arrival of Dickens as something "at once sacred and boundless" produces a traumatic "imprint," leaving the victim "free of judgement," without "the power of detached appraisement." Liking or disliking becomes a meaningless choice when one has "forfeited half the claim to appreciation." Dickens is already inside—he has "entered so early into the blood and bone of our intelligence"—before one can even begin to measure his presence. Under these conditions of *absolute prepossession*, there is no point in trying to "overhaul" him. And yet Dickens tried in his review of 1865 to do exactly that. Note that what was originally a surplus of visual exposure—watching the figures of actors and actresses and the illustrations of Phiz—has now become a systemic failure of reading: *take up, hold off, stop, hold on, don't renew.* The same will happen with Cruikshank's "vividly terrible" illustrations of *Oliver Twist*.[2] Dickens cannot be *reread* because he was never *read* in the first place. He was always-already internalized before he could reach James as a meaningful external object: he was the "treasure hoarded in the dusty chamber of youth." And this was so for two reasons. One, implicit: like Denis Duval, "[he] was so young that [he] could not understand all [he] read" (*Denis* 446). The other, explicit: James *heard* Dickens before he *read* him. In Joycean terms, the author of *David Copperfield* was for him an *ineluctable modality of the audible* before he could become an *ineluctable modality of the visible* (*Ulysses* 37–38). This covers a related reminiscence in the memoirs. He is sent to bed one evening, in Fourteenth Street, "as a very small boy," when one of his cousins from Albany begins to "read" to his mother the first installment of *David Copperfield*. He feigns to withdraw, but is actually there, listening. The description of the pleasurable moment is distinctively Proustian. He is then discovered and banished, "but the ply then taken was ineffaceable."

> I remember indeed just afterwards finding the sequel, in especial the vast extrusion of the Micawbers, beyond my actual capacity; which took a few years to grow adequate—years in which the general contagious consciousness, and our own household response not least, breathed heavily through Hard Times, Bleak House and Little Dorrit; the seeds of acquaintance with Chuzzlewit and Dombey and Son, these coming thickly on, I had found already sown. I was to feel that I had been born, born to a rich awareness, under the very meridian; there sprouted in those years no such other crop of ready references as the golden harvest of Copperfield. Yet if I was to wait to achieve the happier of these recognitions I had already pored over Oliver Twist—albeit now uncertain of the relation borne by that experience to the incident just recalled. When Oliver was new to me, at any rate, he was already old to my betters; whose view of his particular adventures and exposures must have been concerned, I think, moreover, in the fact of my public and lively wonder about them. It was an exhibition deprecated—to infant innocence I judge; unless indeed my remembrance of enjoying it only on the terms of fitful snatches in another, though a kindred, house is due mainly to the existence there of George Cruikshank's splendid form of the work, of which our own foreground was clear. It perhaps even seemed to me more Cruikshank's than Dickens's; it was a thing of such vividly terrible images, and all marked with that peculiarity of Cruikshank that the offered flowers or goodnesses, the scenes and figures intended to

comfort and cheer, present themselves under his hand as but more subtly sinister, or more suggestively queer, than the frank badnesses and horrors. The nice people and the happy moments, in the plates, frightened me almost as much as the low and the awkward; which didn't however make the volumes a source of attraction the less toward that high and square old back-parlour just westward of Sixth Avenue (as we in the same street were related to it) that formed, romantically, half our alternative domestic field and offered to our small inquiring steps a larger range and privilege. If the Dickens of those years was, as I have just called him, the great actuality of the current imagination, so I at once meet him in force as a feature even of conditions in which he was but indirectly involved.

(*Small Boy* 102–103)

This is a narrative of mistimed reception and premature mis-cognition—*contagious consciousness*, dim *recognitions, imagination*—the story of something that is (aurally, aerially, visually, imaginatively) apprehended-before it is actually comprehended, or, and this is the *awkward* implicature in James's *indirectly involved* chronicle, of something that cannot be apprehended (heard, seen, imagined) because it has always-already been traumatically comprehended. This tale of *ply* and *pleasure*, drive and dread, is, indeed, "subtly sinister" and "suggestively queer." Dickens, for James, is not exactly an influence. He is rather an unavoidable given, a prepossession, an inexorable *fatum*, an astrological visitation, a childhood disease: less an ephemeral influence than a chronic *influenza*.

If we juxtapose the review of *Our Mutual Friend* and this powerful autobiographical evocation, we obtain a dialectical version of a *scene of instruction*. At that point in life in which the adolescent realizes that the ways of the world are opening before him, and discerns in the "book of my memory, after the first pages, which are almost blank, there is a section headed *incipit vita nova*" (Dante, *Vita Nuova* I.1), he sees himself compelled to "wipe away" the "little" that is faintly written, the "trivial fond records" (*Hamlet* 1.5.99) and cope with an inscriptive "commandment" (1.5–103) that threatens to paralyze his life. This commandment is the injunction to comprehend a set of *intensely written* graphs (*characters, faces, figures*) that have overtaken and prepossessed the table of his memory. Unable to comprehend them, he will try to *efface* the *faces* and *surfaces*. The early review is a first attempt to undo their *ineffaceability*. The final attempt is the writing of *The Ivory Tower*, James's last, unfinished, and widely unread, novel, which reads as a tentative swerving away (a *clinamen*) from the *ply* prematurely *taken* towards Dickens.[3] Neither attempt proved successful. In his beginning is his end.

## II

In the review of *Our Mutual Friend* James implicitly accuses Dickens of not being a moralist. But should the novelist be a moralist? Is that James's belief?

In 1864, James wrote about Walter Scott's fiction in a review of Nassau W. Senior's *Essays on Fiction*, published in the *North American Review*. James praises the Scottish writer's lack of moralism, his indifference to instruction, his exclusive interest in entertainment and the fireside pleasures of storytelling. "There are," James observes, "some busy men that have read more romances and verses than twenty idle women" (1197). Criticism is important, of course, but the common reader has a right to relieve "the great pressure of reason" aside by drawing, by the evening lamp, "a long breath in the fields of fiction" (1197). Writing about early Dickens, Steven Marcus rightly speaks of "the important place [. . .] that the ability *not* to think often occupies in art" (*Dickens* 19), but it is hard to see James conceding so much. And yet, the "moral effects" the common people are concerned about are, James holds, legitimate and spring from a writer's "fertility of invention" (1198), not from his intelligence. Let me insist: neither claim—the temporary *epoché* of reason, and the legitimacy of imaginative, not natural, moral effects—could have been made in his review of Dickens. James was defending exactly the opposite. Curiously, however, Scott is "the inventor of a new style" (1201) whose distinct heirs are Dickens and Thackeray. Scott was, moreover, the "first English prose story-teller [. . .] the first fictitious writer who addressed the public from its own level, without any preoccupation of place" (1201). By contrast, earlier novelists of the eighteenth century were "emphatically preachers and moralists. In the heart of their production lurks a didactic *raison d'être*" (1201).[4] *Waverley*, James begins his crescendo, "was the first novel which was self-forgetful. It proposed simply to amuse the reader, as an old English ballad amused him. It undertook to prove nothing but facts. It was the novel irresponsible" (1202). An imagination so "vast and rich" (1202) expressing itself in prose was unprecedented. The quantity and quality of his lifelike portraits were unmatched since Shakespeare. The "indifference to historic truth" (1203) of his works, "written without pretense," turns them "emphatically" into "works of entertainment" (1203). "Scott was a born story-teller: we can give him no higher praise." Because of his "wondrous improvisation" (1203), he is "identical with the ideal fireside chronicler" (1204), a phrase that brings to mind the narrative frame in *The Turn of the Screw*.

According to these criteria, the novelist is not only decidedly not a moralist. He is not even a thinker, and his commendable taste for invention and indifference to "historic truth" places him in an awkward relation to character, to humanity and, ultimately, to nature. Dickens too, including very late Dickens, was, in a sense, this kind of improvisational storyteller, this *novelist irresponsible*. But James used the same set of criteria differently, altering the valence, in order to appraise his work. He could be volatile, we know, when it came to matters of personal taste. His comments on Scott endorse the prejudice that James will ten years later ridicule as the "comfortable, good-humoured feeling [. . .] that a novel is a novel, as a pudding is a pudding, and that our only business with it could be to swallow it" ("The Art of Fiction," *LC I* 44). His earlier allusion to *naïveté* of "the form of the novel as Dickens and Thackeray (for instance) saw it" seeks to reinforce an idea of critical immaturity and creative irresponsibility with which the maturing James takes issue. Ten years earlier, Scott, and his heirs (Dickens and Thackeray), were being extolled for producing "the novel irresponsible." Ten years earlier, too, Dickens was being reproved for precisely such fault: for failing on the moral side, for seeking solely "moral effects" of *face* and *surface*, for not being responsible enough, responsive enough, that is, to nature and humanity. James probably never changed his mind about Scott.[5] Thackeray's shallow moralism always irritated him. In the case of Dickens, there is no constancy of critical judgement. His viewpoint oscillates brusquely, in an inexplicable manner. He was, yes, very anxious about Dickens.

This anxiety is also connected with the problematic emergence of an idiom of morality and ethics in the epistolary and critical writing of the novelist-to-be called Henry James. This is a fascinating question that lies beyond the scope of this chapter. Suffice it to say that James sought to adapt neoclassical and enlightened (universalist) principles of morality to the new postromantic and post-transcendentalist (individualist) horizon in which his work was to unfold, and that the strain told in various ways, most evidently in the lavish, unthinking promptitude with which he resorted to the adjective *moral*. Writing on Stevenson, he often alludes, rather un-specifically, to "the perpetual moral question" (*LC I* 1252), and the question of "the moral sense" reemerges, with equal imprecision, in his essay on D'Annunzio (*LC II* 930). The question became so relevant for him that sympathetic critics and friends tended to give him a taste of his own medicine. Edith Wharton opined, for instance, that "for him every great novel must first of all be based on a profound sense of moral values and then constructed with a classical unity and economy of means" (qtd. in Matthiessen xi).

Morality can be construed *descriptively* in a pre-Kantian manner, as a mere jumble of cultural norms, religious maxims, behavioral rules, social principles, and communal habits, or *normatively*, as a code of conduct accepted by all rational people. In a post-Kantian sense, Robert Pippin argues that

> A moral phenomenon is usually characterized by some sort of experi-
> ence of a tension or conflict between one's own advantage or interest and
> either the advantage or interests of others or the rights and entitlements
> of others to consideration (most controversially, to equal consideration).
> (*James* 24)[6]

And he concludes that "the moral point of view" is therefore necessarily "distinguished by its assumption of individual agency and individual
responsibility and by an assessment of such responsibility by attention
to the intentions or motives of the agent" (25). Such focus on "personal
accountability and universal entitlement" (25) finds its perfect expression
in the Hegelian conception of society, an avatar of the objective spirit
premised upon reciprocity, recognition, and mutual un-separateness. But
Bertrand Russell rightly said of Hegel that "from his early interest in mysticism he retained a belief in the unreality of separateness" (*History* 662).
In fact, the un-amenability of *Our Mutual Friend* and *The Ivory Tower* to
the Hegelian conception of morality championed by Pippin springs from
the fact that both novels presuppose, represent, and examine the *reality of
separateness*. Not only are their protagonists and secondary characters separate from one another: they are invariably deprived from the "assumption
of individual agency" and "personal accountability." They try, to be sure,
to become moral in the modern sense, but their stories allow them scarce
room for the operations of "individual responsibility" and a very mar-
ginal access to claims of "universal entitlement." The reader could rightly
protest that this is the case with all stories, but not in all stories are the
central characters presented as not only separated from the rest, but also
separated from themselves, split between their (sur)faces and their under-
skins, consistently without depth. Not only are the characters "eccentrics"
(with respect to the center of *natural humanity*): they are also "a bundle of
eccentricities," i.e. composites of parts without center.

## III

In the preface to *The Princess Casamassima*, James complained that

> the picture of an intelligence appears for the most part, it is true, a dead
> weight for the reader of the English novel to carry, this reader having
> so often the wondrous property of caring for the displayed tangle of
> human relations without caring for its intelligibility.
> (36)

This charge is germane to the accusation of lack of compositional-theoretical awareness that James levelled against the standard English romancier (Scott, Thackeray, Trollope), and is somehow parallel to the charge of prudery we have examined in the chapter on *The Turn of the Screw*. The possible association between moral effrontery and intellectual perspicuity is one we should not discount, for although we may not be able to formulate the positive rationale of the conjunction, James soon realized its critical potential. Thus, for example, as an artist, Dickens defaulted on both counts: he was unintelligent and a prude. He was, in other words, unable to intelligibly disentangle "the displayed tangle of human relations," of which, we have seen, status and sexual inconsistency make so large a part. Still, it was Dickens's distinctive merit to take stock of the complexity and intractability of the tangle. Other writers either registered less or registered more tractably. When in *Our Mutual Friend* a satirical glance is cast on high-class people who boast of their "high moralities" (5) and "moral being" (12), the implication is that they fail to see the "moral sewage" running "down by where accumulated scum of humanity seemed to be washed from higher grounds, like so much moral sewage, and to be pausing until its own weight forced it over the bank and sunk it in the river" (21). Another skeptical assault on the sentimental pieties of bourgeois morality can be found in Mortimer's and Eugene's parodic debate about "the moral influence" of kitchen furniture (284–285, 295) on humans. In this late novel, Dickens seems to have reached a peak of despair.

Interestingly, James follows a similar path of disenchantment. In the *The Ivory Tower*, Gray appeals to his "life" as that of a "moral consciousness" (162), and Rosanna is described in the "Notes" as "*morally* elephantine [. . .] morally most massive and magnificent" (223). But both are forced to factor in financial considerations whose disruptive effect on moral calculus proves unfathomable. Gray speaks of *insuring* his "moral consciousness" for the "advantage" (162) of Horton, his temporary financial associate. He confesses that he decided to come over to America in part "to know so far as possible where I am and what I'm about: morally speaking at least, if not financially" (169). The correlation (morally = financially) is abyssal. When he was young, he was forced to act as a true moral agent. He was summoned by his mother "to decide and to settle it that way for both of us. She has put it all upon me, he said—and how can I choose, in such a difficulty" (31). And he chose, following Rosanna's indirect advice. Now Gray tries to avoid becoming again this decision-making moral agent. He much prefers a Hamletian withdrawal into inaction and quietism. Like Harmon in *Our Mutual Friend*, it seems as if fate (external circumstances, chance, providence) has decided for him by way of the incalculable provision of inheritance. To be sure, Harmon acts more than Gray, but he does it against a backdrop of confirmed affluence, a prospect of abundance predetermined by fate. James swerves from Dickens in the way he deepens the inaction of his hero. No genuine obstacle prevents him from coming into his fortune. The only real complication arises later, when the money has to be taken care of, and what follows is a fable of *moral* misrepresentation—in a comic reversal of the international story, the American ingénue misrecognizes Americans—and social corruption. Dickens, by contrast, forces his hero to endure a test of character before coming into his fortune.

The role of fate also compromises Rosanna's potential to remain a moral agent. In the past, she took responsibility and "settled it. I was fate" (32). But now she knows "the readiness is all" (*Hamlet* 5.2.160). She tells Gray that "there's nothing you can stop now [. . .] for your fate, or our situation, has the gained momentum of a rush that began ever so far away" (100). Gray protests: "When you talk of my 'fate' [. . .] you freeze the current of my blood" (100). They look back at the earlier decision as a possible "mistake" and consider the need to face answerability. Rosanna is adamant: "Well, I took my responsibility years ago" (101). The upshot of this conversation is that *morality*, like art for Hegel, has become *a thing of the past*. Perhaps also—and this is my strong claim in this chapter—humanity has become a thing of the past. In *The Ivory Tower*, James reconciles himself with Dickens's dystopian vision of a moribund community of separate humans miraculously kept alive by the timid glow of moral disinterestedness that some very exceptional characters are able to emit.

In his preface to *Stories of artists and writers*, Matthiessen argued that "James's recurrent use of the word 'morality' has a residue, quite foreign to Pater, of the values of James' transcendentalist father" (3), and he cited a "nutritive or suggestive truth" from the preface to *The Portrait of a Lady* about "the perfect dependence of the 'moral' sense of a work of art on the amount of felt life concerned in producing it" (*Portrait* 45). Translated into Marxian terminology, the moral sense is like the surplus value of a manufactured *work*, which depends on the amount of labor force (*spent life*) invested in *producing* it.[7] Obviously, the notion is not that intensive production—or the production of texts "intensely written" (James's characterization of *Our Mutual Friend*)—secures the moral sense of what is being produced. James' insistence, in a letter of early 1895 to Howells, on his need to "produce again—produce, produce better than ever" (*Life in Letters* 277) holds therefore little moral promise per se. And it proves that *becoming Dickens*—the title of Douglas-Fairhurst's excellent book—was not a privilege or a curse reserved exclusively to the author of *Great Expectations*. It sufficed to produce *separate* reserves of *exclusive* characterization (faces) within a given social field made of surfaces to take a distinctively Dickensian *ply*. *The Ivory Tower* may prove nothing, but it surely disproves James's axiom that "a community of eccentrics is impossible."

## III

The central characters in *Our Mutual Friend* (Moran, Lizzie) and *The Ivory Tower* (Gray, Rosanna) are *eccentric* because they are unmoored from a social center and eccentric to themselves, i.e. made up of *eccentricities*. They inconsist both internally and externally. The moral sense in both novels has inexorably declined because the amount of communal life concerned in producing them is minimum. Both stories are condemned to the moral death of social entropy. Organic symbolic figuration, frequent in the initial writing of both novelists, has been replaced by an allegorical diction that wrests its energy from the inorganic aggregation of inanimate parts. And yet both stories presume a totality of which they are the "reflector as vast as a natural lake" (*LC II* 1030). Such implication of totality, which James attributes to Tolstoy, takes moral courage. In "The Art of Fiction," he argued that "the essence of moral energy is to survey the whole field" (*LC I* 63). The idea that the *whole field* (totality, reality) is reflected in the vast, natural lake suggests both the workings of inconsistency—of the (w) hole—and the inevitability of surfaces. In other words, the narrative truth of the particular is beholden to a surface-ridden presumption of riven totality. Maybe this is what James implied when he stated, in *Daisy Miller*, that "Geneva is the most moral city in Europe." Not Calvin, not Rousseau, but the reflecting lake—later transposed to Bly. But this is only one condition for the moral novel. For the moral sense, in a romantic standpoint, to obtain, a certain communal life must get reflected in the surface, which should in turn spell an implication of living depth. As it happens, in *Our Mutual Friend* the waters reflect nothing and send up only corpses. In *The Ivory Tower*, Rosanna's coming in for millions is compared to her sitting, "like Truth, at the bottom of a well" (155). It is likely that James, who was interested in the work of Jean-Leon Gerome, had seen his paintings titled "The Truth at the bottom of a well" and "Truth Coming out of her Well."[8] Or maybe Frances McDonald's watercolor, "Truth Lies at the Bottom of a Well" (c. 1912–1915). The romantic, anti-pragmatic belief that truth is revealed and comes out of a well may be based on a saying by Democritus, and finds an eloquent pictorial representation in Gerome's second painting, which resembles Lizzie escaping along the Thames. But it is Frances McDonald's watercolor, painted at the time James was writing his unfinished novel, that speaks more to the significance of both novels. The well resembles a tower, on whose battlements three naked women stand, holding their fingers to their lips, looking at another who lies, asleep and naked, at the bottom. That woman could be Rosanna, but also Harmon, spectrally biding his time under the Thames. There is also a sense in which Gray is the dead American girl returning to the fiction (*Daisy Miller*, *The*

*Wings of the Dove*) from which she was originally sacrificed. At any rate, none of the three paintings invests on the implication of depth.

I have just evoked the image of Lizzie walking "alone by the water," which I read as an emblem of potential separateness. Her flight along the river outlines a trajectory of moral freedom. She shares this temporary eccentricity with Rosanna, also a strong moral agent. The male protagonists of the novels are less inclined to decisive action, especially erotic action. Harmon's explanation to Bella, "Because I am truly, deeply, profoundly interested in you, Miss Wilfer" (375), is merely mystifying. Socially alienated from the rest of the characters, Lizzie and Rosanna appear transitorily entitled to the *principle of individuation*, though not perhaps in the radical sense stipulated by Deleuze, for whom "individuation is a relation conceived as a pure or absolute between, a between understood as fully independent or external to its terms—and thus a between that can just as well be described as 'between' nothing at all" (Hallward, *Deleuze* 154).⁹ In this radical sense, only Jenny qualifies as a full individual. In his review of Dickens's novel, James went out of his way to explain how much he disliked her:

> What do we get in return for accepting Miss Jenny Wren as a possible person? This young lady is the type of a certain class of characters of which Mr. Dickens has made a speciality, and with which he has been accustomed to draw alternate smiles and tears, according as he pressed one spring or another. But this is very cheap merriment and very cheap pathos. Miss Jenny Wren is a poor little dwarf, afflicted, as she constantly reiterates, with a "bad back" and "queer legs," who makes dolls' dresses, and is for ever pricking at those with whom she converses, in the air, with her needle, and assuring them that she knows their "tricks and their manners." Like all Mr. Dickens's pathetic characters, she is a little monster; she is deformed, unhealthy, unnatural; she belongs to the troop of hunchbacks, imbeciles, and precocious children who have carried on the sentimental business in all Mr. Dickens's novels; the little Nells, the Smikes, the Paul Dombeys.
>
> (*LC I* 854–855)

Note the categorial oscillation: she is "the *type* of a certain *class* of *characters*." This means that she belongs in a *class*, after all, which is the very claim the whole review aspires to refute. For James, the *genus* humanity does not include the *species* Jenny; or better, the *species* humanity does not include the *specimen* Jenny:

> The word *humanity* strikes us as strangely discordant, in the midst of these pages; for, let us boldly declare it, there is no humanity here.

Humanity is nearer home than the Boffins, and the Lammles, and the Wilfers, and the Veneerings. It is in what men have in common with each other, and not in what they have in distinction. The people just named have nothing in common with each other, except the fact that they have nothing in common with mankind at large. What a world were this world if the world of *Our Mutual Friend* were an honest reflection of it! But a community of eccentrics is impossible. Rules alone are consistent with each other; exceptions are inconsistent.

(855)

The question is: can "exceptions" make up a type or a class? In a radical sense, they cannot. First, if they are real exceptions, they should also be exceptions to the *class* of exceptions. Second, if they are always inherently in excess of the set that seeks to comprise them, they become liable to intensive instantiation. Whereas the first condition evokes Russell's set-theoretic paradox (*Mathematical* 188–192), the second brings to mind Badiou's take on inconsistent multiplicity and explosive eventuality (*Being* 38–48). Jointly, both conditions submit the odd anti-Leibnizian notion that because Jenny is impossible (*inconsistent*) she must exist.[10] Harold Bloom rephrased this "antithetical formula" as "the motto for post-Emersonian American poetry: *Everything that can be broken should be broken*" (*Wallace Stevens* 1).

Let me clarify. Exceptions, James rightly argues, are—like status in our modern world—*inconsistent*. They are therefore part of humanity (men, women) and *not* part of humanity (man, woman). One would need a paraconsistent logic in order to account for this contradiction without the risk of *explosive* consequence relations, i.e. arbitrary conclusions.[11] One such explosive relation is the odd character herself—the little monster. In Badiou's ontology, the presentive force of the event is made to depend upon the mathematical paradox of a part of a set that is larger than the set to which it belongs (*Being* 38–48). This is also the odd character. Dickens is indeed a master of the monster, the explosive, intensive character in excess of her situation. In *The Varieties of Religious Experience*, William James reports the following vision of an anonymous correspondent:

Simultaneously there arose in my mind the image of an epileptic patient whom I had seen in the asylum, a black-haired youth with greenish skin, entirely idiotic, who used to sit all day on one of the benches, or rather shelves against the wall, with his knees drawn up against his chin, and the coarse fray undershirt, which was his only garment over them inclosing his entire figure. [. . .] This image and my fear entered into a species of combination with each other. *That shape am I*, I felt, potentially.

(*Writings 1902–1910* 149–150)[12]

Epilepsy, we know, appears often in Dickens's novels: Monks, Guster, and Bradley Headstone are all subject to epileptic seizure. But the vision evokes the description of Smike in *Nicholas Nickleby*:

> It induced him to consider the boy more attentively, and he was surprised to observe the extraordinary mixture of garments which formed his dress. Although he could not have been less than eighteen or nineteen years old, and was tall for that age, he wore a skeleton suit, such as is usually put upon very little boys, and which, though most absurdly short in the arms and legs, was quite wide enough for his attenuated frame. In order that the lower part of his legs might be in perfect keeping with this singular dress, he had a very large pair of boots, originally made for tops, which might have been once worn by some stout farmer, but were now too patched and tattered for a beggar. Heaven knows how long he had been there, but he still wore the same linen which he had first taken down; for, round his neck, was a tattered child's frill, only half concealed by a coarse, man's neckerchief. He was lame; and as he feigned to be busy in arranging the table, glanced at the letters with a look so keen, and yet so dispirited and hopeless, that Nicholas could hardly bear to watch him.
>
> (*Nicholas* 79)

What little Dick, Smike, Jenny, and many other Dickens eccentrics have in common is that they have nothing in common with the rest of humanity, and perhaps not even with themselves as parts of the exclusive, explosive set of little monsters. This is Henry James, again: "The people just named have nothing in common with each other, except the fact that they have nothing in common with mankind at large." And he bitterly remonstrates: "What a world were this world if the world of *Our Mutual Friend* were an honest reflection of it! But a community of eccentrics is impossible. Rules alone are consistent with each other; exceptions are inconsistent." But what is, in set theory, a set of parts that are not—cannot be—parts of a set? Dickens's response to this question is always the same: if a community of eccentrics is impossible, it is the idea of the community—its stipulations of reciprocity, conditions of recognition, and assumptions of commonality— that is to blame, not the eccentrics. The eccentrics are a fact, the community merely a wish.

## V

*Our Mutual Friend* and *The Ivory Tower* share much of what James, in his "Notes for *The Ivory Tower*," called "the essence of the Situation" (203). Two estranged younger relatives (son and nephew) of two capitalist predators reject the marriage-related conditions first stipulated for securing their rightful inheritance only to, in the last instance, on the death of their elders, return from overseas (South Africa, Europe) to family places (London, Newport) where they must face a moral trial of recognition before coming into a fortune they at bottom despise. Both novels describe an "adventure" (*Ivory* 179) of misrecognition and identity. Because the protagonists are, like Hyacinth and Milly, "the very children of accident" (*Ivory* 193), their moral agency is seriously compromised from the outset. They try to measure the freedom they can count on in their present situation the more effectively to display a strategy of retention and withholding—if not of downright abstention. Not only do they want to procrastinate their access to an immense amount of stained money. They yearn for a freedom to withhold—via delay (Harmon) or repudiation (Gray)—the apparent necessity of marriage.[13] Neither has "sexual presence" (Poole, "Introduction" to *Our Mutual Friend* xix). They are, in fact, as "sexually innocent" as Pickwick (Marcus, *Dickens* 27). Their moral tepidness is characteristically foiled by young energetic women (Lizzie and Bella in *Our Mutual Friend*, Rosanna in *The Ivory Tower*) who are very capable of rejecting proposals of marriage. Only in Dickens's novel, and only very timidly, does effective marriage suggest a future of domestic regeneration. Both novels invest much of their thematic and figurative force in adumbrating the moral death of society at the hands of pervasive moral disorder. And both test the desire to recoup lost energy, with the aid of specters, in an age of waste and decadence, decline and fall.

The basics of the social situation in both novels derive from one single factor: "The enormous preponderance of money. Money is their life" (*Ivory* 84). Gray differs from the rest of "our people" (84) because he is a "perfect clean blank," ignorant of the world of money. The rest are all "full of poison" (85). Whereas he marks an extreme of total ignorance— "I understand so little and like so little as the mystery of the 'market' and the hustle of any sort" (85)—his uncle stands at the other end of the spectrum, as a man alienated into money: "I was business. I've been business and nothing else in the world. I'm business at this moment still—because I can't be anything else" (86). Whether openly or indirectly, social life turns around it: " 'That's what we mean,' said Rosanna, 'when we talk of anything at all—for of what else but money *do* we ever talk?' " (105) Everything hinges upon reciprocal "attestations of value" (10) in a mesh of "personal relation" (11) whose patterns of reciprocal recognition—"a relation is exactly a *fact* of reciprocity" (173)—are immorally vitiated by calculus. Conversation is driven by a mode of interest that is unashamedly financial. Mr. Betterman, for instance, has "an absolute interest" in "his own private facts, which were facts of numerical calculation altogether" (7). Gray turns out to be one of his facts, but everybody is "interested" in him (13, 19).

Reciprocally, their interest amounts to "the question of what Gray's 'interest', in the light of his uncle's intentions, might size up to" (70). *Disinterestedness* (194) is by contrast predicated on separation, on unrelation, and this only Gray and Rosanna pursue, although in different directions.

In a strategy of ironic contamination, the narrator deploys various financial tropes like *credit, account, value, interest,* and a number of polysemous verbs like *owe, pay, gain, cheapen* (40), in order to reinforce the mercantile ethos internalized by most characters. Gray's present and future is described by the narrator, with a figurative literalness that can only be called ironic, as "an extraordinary blank cheque" (179). When Cissy and Horton *speculate* about the amount that Gary may have inherited, phrases like "first-rate value" and "speculation for speculation" (129) gain a distinctly ironic ambivalence. As Hillis Miller demonstrated in a crucial 1964 essay, money lies too at the centre of the moral vision in Dickens's *Our Mutual Friend.* In the part of the story dedicated to Lizzie Hexam's courtship by two rivals, "Dickens is acutely conscious of the difference in people made by class distinctions" (Miller, *Subjects* 69), and yet distinctions of class and status are

> to be closely intertwined with the power of money. [. . .] In the England of *Our Mutual Friend* inherited rank is in the process of giving way to the universal solvent of money, and most of the characters set their hearts on "money, money, money."
>
> (69)

The same point has been made by Wendy Graham apropos of *The Ivory Tower.*[14]

The poor clerk Reginald Wilfer capitulates to the fact that "money and goods are certainly the best of references" (39), and his daughter grudges "this money going to the Monster that swallows up so much, when we all want—Everything" (41). Bella at first believes that *everything* can be "smoothed away by the money, for I love money, and want money" (37). When she shows interest in what Miss Wilfer is reading, a brief but revealing exchange follows: " 'A love story, Miss Wilfer?' 'Oh dear no, or I shouldn't be reading it. It's more about money than anything else.' 'And does it say that money is better than anything?' " (205). The waterman Gaffer Hexam puts it in metaphysical terms that apply to both novels: "What world does a dead man belong to? 'Tother world. What world does money belong to? This world" (*Mutual* 4). But in a world that Thackeray already labelled *capitalist*, money had the power to edit sharp distinctions and reawaken dead souls: "The market was 'rigged' in various artful ways. Counterfeit stock got into circulation. Parents boldly represented themselves as dead, and brought their orphans with them. Genuine orphan-stock was surreptitiously withdrawn from the market" (196).

The notion that financial accumulation is achieved at irreversible moral cost is central to both novels. Rosanna, overwhelmed at becoming the recipient of her father's "whole fortune," elaborates on the causes of his death:

> "He's dying, at any rate," she explained, "of his having wished to have to do with it on that sort of scale. Having to do with it consists, you know, of the things you do *for* it—which are mostly very awful; and there are all kinds of consequences that they eventually have. You pay by these consequences for what you have done, and my father has been for a long time paying. . . . The effect has been to dry up his life."
>
> (*Ivory* 105)

The fortune Gray will receive from his uncle is no cleaner than hers. Both suffer the consequences of an evil—"vagrant parenthood" (Marcus 32)—that haunted Dickens's narrative unconscious. When the expression "a most monstrous fortune" (146) is later used, the adjective implies both grotesque quantitative exorbitance and sublime evil. As we will see, Gray's and Rosanna's attempts to respond to their respective inheritance in a *moral* way will deepen the complications of dialogized psychomachia the novel consists of. But their response echoes closely Harmon's extraordinary moral solo on inheritance, a rhetorical piece inspired in Edgar's tribulations in *King Lear*. In fact, Edgar's "I nothing am" (*King Lear* 2.3.21) reverberates in Harmon's admission that "I cannot possibly express it to myself without using the word I. But it was not I. There was no such thing as I, within my knowledge" (369). And both realizations of personal misrecognition are also rehearsed in the words of William James's correspondent, facing the epileptic patient: "*That shape am I*, potentially." What I am trying to say is that Harmon's determination to supplement his own identitarian and moral rebirth with the grotesque shadow of his own corpse has consequences. And that these consequences (barred subjectivity, exceptionality, oddness, chronic superficiality) will surely endanger his bid at moral resurrection and communal recognition.

Harmon moves on to reconsider the way he turned

> the danger I had passed through, to the account of being for some time supposed to have disappeared mysteriously, and of proving Bella. The dread of our being forced on one another, and perpetuating the fate that seemed to have fallen on my father's riches—the fate that they should

lead to nothing but evil—was strong upon the moral timidity that dates
from my childhood with my poor sister.

(370)

James's protagonist is also afflicted by "moral timidity" before the awareness of an "evil" necessarily joined to the "fate" of inherited "riches." Gray
too would like to expose those riches to a process of hygienic absolution, to
"[efface] the old rust and tarnish on the money" (*Ivory* 372).[15] But in neither novel, faces, including the rusty faces of coins, bear effacement. Harmon plans to wait until "the great swarm of swindlers under many names
have found newer pray" (373). In *The Ivory Tower*, the old swindlers—
Betterman covets the "fruits of his swindle" (9) and he "swindled"
("Notes" 211) Rosanna's father, who was no less a swindler—are being
replaced by a new generation of scoundrels, best represented by Horton,
who practices "swindle" and "absolute theft" ("Notes" 217) on Gray. The
bourgeois domestication of the heroic profession of smugglers heralded
in *Denis Duval* is no longer possible. This is a world, Harmon realizes,
where people "speculate" in people (*Mutual* 377). No wonder he decides
to become an exceptional face, and considers—like Kent and Edgar in the
tragedy—schemes of withdrawal and transformation:

> When in the distrust engendered by his wretched childhood and the
> action for evil—never yet for good within his knowledge then—of his
> father and his father's wealth on all within their influence [. . .] "This is
> another of the old perverted uses of the misery-making money. I will let
> it go to my and my sister's only protectors and friends."
>
> (379)

From such self-righteously abstentious (Hamletian) standpoint, "coming to life and accepting the condition of the inheritance" (380) appears
too risky a prospect, although he will end up accepting it. But Harmon
is not the only character to prefigure Gray's moral paralysis before the
obscenity of money. Boffin is also overwhelmed: "I don't know what to
say about it. . . . It's a great lot to take care of" (89). The motives driving
old Harmon to leave him and his family so large a fortune also reemerge
in *The Ivory Tower*. What we learn of old Harmon, that he "mistrusted all
mankind—and sorely indeed he did mistrust all who bore any resemblance
to himself—he was as certain that these two people, surviving him, would
be trustworthy" (*Mutual* 102), applies word by word to Mr. Betterman.

The pervasiveness of money simultaneously promotes and elides the differences of *status inconsistency*, thus aggravating "fears of social unpre-
dictability" (Douglas-Fairhurst, *Becoming* 201). Upper-class predators are
only different from low-class beasts of prey in that the money they both

covet has the power to displace them up and down *the ladder of dependence* (Fielding)—up and down the dust mountains, up and down the ivory
tower—and broaden further the gap between both. A devoted reader of
Balzac, James acknowledged the social relevance of "the power to climb
the ladder, to wriggle to the top of the heap, to clutch the money-bag" (*LC
II* 48). In *Our Mutual Friend*, Bradley Headstone embodies the resentments of "obscurity" and rank-and-class inequality (*Mutual* 293). His
reproach to his sister brings to mind Hyacinth's frustration in *The Princess
Casamassima*:

> "Upon my soul," exclaimed the boy, "you are a nice picture of a sister!
> Upon my soul, you are a pretty piece of disinterestedness! And so all my
> endeavours to cancel the past and to raise myself in the world, and to
> raise you with me, are to be beaten down by *your* low whims; are they?"
> (*Mutual* 401)

To cancel the past and raise to themselves is what, for apparently opposite
reasons, Harmon, Gray, and Rosanna would like to do, but they can't.
The Lizzie subplot is also marked by recursive considerations of "station" and "class" (395–396). Yet in the new realm where the action of
money, as Hillis Miller points out, supersedes the operations of a social
field based on rank and class—Bella's sudden rise to gentility and property
is a case in point—there are errors of attestation and calculation. James
was particularly attracted to the consequences of such axiological shift.
Rosanna, for instance, is speculatively drawn to reflect on "certain anomalies of ignorance and indifference as to what" the elder accumulators (Mr.
Gaw and Mr. Betterman) actually "stood for" (11). This means that the
consideration is no longer one of rank or class oscillation, but rather one
of oscillation of quantity within the rank-less class of businessmen. Some
old reflexes remain, of course. Mr. Northover, for instance, is a "perfect
Englishman, of great taste and thoroughly a gentleman" (27), a description that betrays the survival of the imaginary value (taste). Still, a society
where nurses address doctors in the way doctors used to address nurses
(65) is no longer a consistent social field. This very inconsistency allows an
*unlikely gentleman* as Gray to shine through as someone placed above and
beyond all inherited forms of organic togetherness, i.e. rank society, class
society, and money society. (124).

*Shine through* may not be the best figurative choice, for Gray—like
Hamlet—returns from the sea. He swims through, not as literally as Harmon, emerging semi-drowned from the Thames, but James's investment
in nautical imagery and sea mythology turns "the great sea spaces" into
something more than a scenic prop.[16] Both Gray and Harmon come back as
revenants from "the great ocean, Death" (*Mutual* 71), only to get caught,

like the protagonist of *The Bride of Lammermoor*, in the deadly *lime* (150, 161) of waterside social existence. The original situation of Harmon and Gray is very similar to Milly's—at bottom, in James's imagination, to Miranda's in *The Tempest*. New York, London, Naples, you name it:

> It was New York mourning, it was New York hair, it was a New York history, confused as yet, but multitudinous, of the loss of parents, brothers, sisters, almost every human appendage, all on a scale and with a sweep that had required the greater stage; it was a New York legend of affecting, of romantic isolation, and, beyond everything, it was by most accounts, in respect to the mass of money so piled on the girl's back, a set of New York possibilities. She was alone, she was stricken, she was rich, and, in particular, she was strange.
>
> (*Wings* 75)

Both Harmon and Gray will somehow cultivate this romantic isolation, this loss of human appendage, this "detachment" (*Ivory* 7), in their cases from Society as "the business world." When Vinty challenges Gray with the question, "Well, what are affairs but life?" he replies: "You'll make me feel, no doubt, how much they are—which would be very good for me. Only life isn't affairs—that's my subtle distinction" (175). The subtle distinction is literally the cause of his own distinction, which the community of swindlers both admire (as a form of imaginary value) and despise (as a lack of real value). Gray's inclination to distance himself from "the rumour of the world, the voice of society, the harmonies of possession" (185), leads him to consider the symbol of that which gives the novel its title. He asks Rosanna: "And doesn't living in an ivory tower just mean the most distinguished retirement?" (109) The etymology is stubborn and suggests a formula: since Gray seeks *distinction* and a *distinguished* retirement, he is *distinct*—which, in the neoclassical logic of the early James, is the opposite of common, natural, and human. Interestingly, Gray is distinguished enough to register the dialectical-materialist fact that the little ivory tower "was a remarkable product of some eastern, probably some Indian, patience" (110). By thus denouncing "the perfect dependence of [. . .] a work of art on the amount of [. . .] life concerned in producing it," Gray reveals a *moral sense* that is lacking, for instance, in Milly and in so many Victorian readers bewitched by Ruskin's celebration of Gothic art. If the tower is a "wonder of wasted ingenuity," (110) the dust mounds (mountains, volcanos) in *Our Mutual Friend* are merely wonders of waste. The (moral) sense of a misused labor force and squandered human life is powerfully implied in both related tropes.

## VI

Gray also enjoys sudden feats of elation that place him above the surrounding waste, in a position of distinct absolving freedom. This distances him from his precursor, Harmon, and connects him with Milly. Like the American heiress, Gray manages to survive, with the help of a friend, a risky rock-climbing accident that makes him "slid down to a scrap of a dizzy ledge" and leaves him hanging "helpless over a void, unable to get back" (170). In the "Notes," he refers to "the holiday cours among the mountains, when Horty has fished Gray out of a hole, I don't mean quite a crevasse, but something like, or come to his aid in a tight place of some sort" (214). What counts in these parallel incidents is the dialectical dependence of the sublime position of *total* surveillance afforded by the mountain upon the sustaining *hole* or *void* that stands for the inconsistency of the (never total) surveyed reality. And recall that reality is never complete because the observer is either an abstraction (the conceptual heiress) or a concretion (the distinct particular) that per definition cannot belong. In addition, this void is precisely "that part of Davey's abysses of New York financial history" that is also "his own, their own, but his in particular" ("Notes" 242). Superstructure and substructure are secretly connected through the hole—at the very bottom, "the abyss of consciousness" (Bloom, *Anxiety* 40)—that makes them both inconsistent with the structure of reality that is symbolic ideology.

Gray feels his "consciousness making also more at each moment for an uplifting, a fantastic freedom, a sort of sublime simplification" (83). In the case of the New York heiress, I pointed out that James was unable to separate the girl's apparent distinction (moral freedom) from the mathematical sublime (big money) that infrastructurally constituted her. Indeed, the "sublime simplification" is also a function of their calculated ignorance, their not knowing not only *how much* (the amount of their fortune) but also *how* (the logic of its accumulation, the laws of the market, the moral cost, the human waste). James's resolve to register, in his "Notes to *The Ivory Tower*," his total ignorance of these matters—"my total absence of business initiation" (216)—stretches further the chain of "responsibility" (211, 212).

When Gray is unsure about his course of action, he says: "I think I must just *like* to drift" (163). James pointed out in his "Notes" to the novel that he always wanted "to do an out and out non-producer" (245). This appetite for Bohemian abstention and indifference is at one with the Hamletian taste for withdrawal shown by Harmon. Shakespeare's tragedy is an important subtext of both novels. In *Our Mutual Friend*, the echoes of the play thicken when the ironies controlling the father-daughter relation are exposed, when Bella says that "A happy and a chatty man was Pa in his new clothes that day. Take it for all in all" (318), or when Lizzie addresses her dead father: "Father, was that you calling me? Father! I thought I heard you call me twice before! Words never to be answered, those, upon the earth-side of the grave" (174). In James's novel, the original situation is a context of repeated mourning, with the ghosts of an uncle and a father haunting every single conversation that occurs in anticipation and preparation of the funeral proceedings. The difference between young characters like Gray and Rosanna who cared, and those "who weren't up at the cool of dawn" (192), can be traced back to the loyalty of Horatio and Hamlet, who will wait, if necessary, until they hear "the trumpet of the morn" (*Hamlet* 1.1.149). Gray's Horatio is Horton, who evokes how their Pasteur at Neuchatel recommended them "La lecture et la promenade" (122), an advice never lost on the Danish prince. Gray in mourning is explicitly compared to "a happy Hamlet" (144). His *imaginary value* depends on his belonging to the set of "subjects tremendously educated, tremendously 'cultivated' and cosmopolitanised" (144). But Gray tells Horton he is afraid of social relations: " 'You see "people" are exactly my difficulty—I'm so mortally afraid of them' " (149). His friend pretends to be shocked: "I seem to remember you, on the contrary, as so remarkably and—what was it we used to call it?—so critico-analytically interested in 'em." Gray admits to being in fact "beastly interested" in people, and adds, signally: "Don't you therefore see [. . .] how I may dread the complication" (149). To dread the complication is to abhor plot entanglements. By stepping out of the *field of complication*—by hiding behind the tree—he seeks to gain, like Hamlet, critico-analytical distance over it.

But his destiny forces him to engage in "the tangle of human relations" that makes up the plot. Complete withdrawal is not possible, delay has limits, only a temporary reluctance is due. Confronted with this impasse, the only solution is the Hamletian expedient of *choosing your assigned fate*. Gray tells Horton: "I *want* [. . .] to like my luck. I want to go in for it, as you say, with every inch of any such capacity as I have" (152–153). He must learn to place desire and moral decision under the authority of Stoic resignation. "Hamlet returned" (4.7.102) from the sea is a transformed Hamlet, the *revenant* as pragmatic avatar.[17] This transformation is complete when he discovers that Ophelia is dead. He becomes a new man who has internalized the external fate of his disinheritance. "This is," he can at last say, "I,/Hamlet the Dane" (5.1.241–242). His fate is symbolically embodied in the cherub he sees before abandoning Elsinore. When King Claudius asks Hamlet if he knows his purposes (sending him to England), the prince replies: "I see a cherub that sees them" (4.3.50). The keen-sighted cherub is a symbol of heavenly knowledge or pro-*vidence*. Hamlet thus begins to entertain ideas of transcendent foreknowledge and predetermined fate when his trip to England is decided. On his return, he salutes providence, the "divinity that shapes our ends" (5.2.10–11), and praises for the first time the benefits of acting upon impulse—"let us know/our indiscretion sometime serves us well/When our dear plots do pall" (5.2.7–9). This closely echoes Gray's difficulties at making decisions, and Harmon's speculative, methodical, soliloquizing way of dealing with his course— or, better, *dis-course*—of action. Like Hyacinth, they both hesitate before the *passage à l'acte*, the only true *Aktus der Freiheit* that may absolve them (Zupančič 11).

Hamlet's return to Elsinore is marked moreover by an episode of providential liberation from his real captors (the Danish embassy)—a "seafight" (5.2.55) complete with forged letters and pirates—that foreshadows much in *Denis Duval* and *Our Mutual Friend*. The subdued, clandestine irony of Hamlet's letter to his uncle infuses Harmon's sophisticated plan, and it gives shape to some of Gray's inarticulate thoughts:

> High and mighty, you shall know I am set naked on your kingdom. Tomorrow shall I beg leave to see your kingly eyes: when I shall, first asking your pardon thereunto, recount the occasion of my sudden and more strange return.
>
> HAMLET (4.7.42–45).

Reacting to the letter, the king exclaims: " ' "Naked"! And in a postscript here, he says/"Alone" ' " (*Hamlet* 4.7.50–51). *Naked* and *alone*: the conjunction of these adjectives provides, literally and metaphorically, a fit account of the Adanic pretense that informs the characters of Harmon and Gray. It is a pretense because the ghosts have complete dominion. Bloom portended that "the strong dead return, in poems as in our lives, and they do not come back without darkening the living" (*Anxiety* 139), but he also conceded that "the mighty dead return, but they return in our colors, and speaking in our voices, at least in part, at least in moments, moments that testify to our persistence, and not to their own" (140). Whether and how such persistence can be deemed a moral fact is of course our problem. But I can only approach it through subtextual detours. The obsession in *Our Mutual Friend* with the uncanny persistence of the dead is but a symbolic outlet for the ideological energies that concentrate around the sociosexual inconsistency of personal singularity: not only do eccentrics exist, and only them exist, but they tend to reappear and/or to repeat themselves among the living. The question—"What world does a dead man belong to? T'other world?" (*Mutual* 4)—is a question about the *persistence of singularity*. The "dismal house" the Boffins inherited is "haunted" (191) by "the faces of the old man and the two children" (189). This is Mrs. Boffin's description of the apparition:

> A face growing out of the dark. [. . .] For a moment it was the old man's, and then it got younger. For a moment it was both the children, and then it got older. For a moment it was a strange face, and then it was all the faces.
>
> (190)[18]

There are also the steps of the "haunting Secretary" shaking Mrs. Wilfer's poor house, "stump—stump—stumping overhead in the dark, like a Ghost" (208). And the school where "spirits" of different hues "jumbled jumbled jumbled jumbled, jumbled every night" (215). The cumulative effect of these Gothic overtones reaches a climax of uncanny intensity in Jenny's conversation with Fledgeby about the sensation of strange elation that overpowers you when you feel "as if you are dead":

> Oh, so peaceful and so thankful! And you hear the people who are alive, crying, and working, and calling to one another down in the close dark streets, and you seem to pity them so! And such a chain has fallen from you, and such a strange good sorrowful happiness comes upon you!
>
> (281)

This is not far from Gray's "sublime simplification," his "consciousness making also more at each moment for an uplifting, a fantastic freedom" (*Ivory* 83). That such moral elation should be foreshadowed by a crippled teenager who fantasizes with an old Jew coming out of his grave is profoundly paradoxical and is a lesson in the limits of imaginative freedom.

## VII

The decay of the "standardised face" (185) of the "business world" in James's novel is prefigured by the way the facades and surfaces of old London houses are fallen into "desuetude" (183). The rest of the faces emerge into this already constituted world of standard appearances (faces) and unfathomable sham depths (quantities). The "bad infinity" (Hegel) of the incalculable works to multiply the surfaces. The novel opens with Rosanna's difficulty at "the constitution of a 'figure' " (5), a term that in French means *face*. In both novels, figures and faces are mutually exchangeable. Rosanna arrives at a florid villa "as if to put a question to its big fair foolish face" (5). If human beings are *figures* with *faces*, houses are *facades* with *faces*. She glances at the "blank windows" and compares them to "so

many showy picture-frames awaiting their subjects" (6). Her consideration is meta-narrative, for a frame awaiting its pictorial subject is a form
awaiting its subject matter, a mould awaiting its jelly, a surface awaiting
its depth, or a superficial novel—like *Our Mutual Friend*, according to
James—awaiting its subjects, i.e its real human being.[19]

Douglas-Fairhurst has observed that the "lively confusion between people's insides and outsides" is something "central to Dickens's imagination" (58), and brings James to task for his critical attack on *Our Mutual
Friend*. "James was mistaken," he opines, "to think that Dickens's interest
in people was limited to their surfaces" (59). Still, some of his comments
elsewhere evince the hold James's points have on his critical imagination:
Dicken's "writing is an unflagging celebration of the unique, the freak-
ish, the stubbornly eccentric" (182). There is reason to believe that in his
last unfinished novel James was also celebrating the uniqueness of humans
conceived as picture-frames, as facades, as little more than faces. In a long
conversation between Cissy and Horton about Gray's face, the crucial
question is raised: "what are photographs, the wretched things, but the
very truth of life?" (132) If the bidimensional framing of the human face
reveals the truth of the subject—the truth, recall, that sits at the bottom of
a well—then this explains the time these two characters spend in examining their impressions of the hero's face. The conversation closes with the
set of neat oppositions that informed James's review of Dickens's novel,
oppositions between *men* and *man*, the *universal* and the *particular*, the
*natural-social-human* and the *eccentric*:

> "I won't have him subject to the so universally and stupidly applied
> American law that every man's face without exception shall be scraped
> as clean, as *glabre*, as a fish's—which it makes so many of them so much
> resemble. I won't have him so," she said, "because I won't have him so
> idiotically gregarious and without that sense of differences in things."
>
> (133)

So Cissy rejects the *universal law* and favors the *exception*, shuns the
*gregarious* and urges a *sense of difference in things*. Is Cissy here James's
mouthpiece?

Also critical to our matter at hand is the conversation between Horton
and Gray about the extent of one's openness to women if one is to have
a place in the marriage market. Horton slips into the trope of the man as
house:

> "Every man's life is full of them that has a door or a window they can
> come in by. But the question's of yourself," said Haughty, "and just

exactly of the number of such that you'll have to keep open or shut in the immense façade you'll now present."

(154)

When Gray, surprised, replies that he "shall present an immense façade?" Horton hesitates:

"You've great ideas if you see it yourself as a small one." "I don't see it as any. I decline," Gray remarked, "to *have* a façade. And if I don't I shan't have the windows and doors." "You've got 'em already, fifty in a row"—Haughty was remorseless—"and it isn't a question of 'having': you *are* a façade; stretching a mile right and left. How can you not be when I'm walking up and down in front of you?"

(154)

The ontological invitation of the trope—"you *are* a façade"—is unmistakable, and its rationale harkens back to the tendentially depthless universe of *Our Mutual Friend*, a novel that "characterizes the willed self as the erection of a façade" (Costell, "Introduction" to *Our Mutual Friend* xvi). Gray later revisits the congruence of the trope from a related figurative perspective: " 'Every one among us—I mean among the moneyed—*isn't* a monster on exhibition.' In proof of which he abounded. 'I know people myself who *aren't*' " (155; emphases added). The same truth was in order many years earlier, when James reviewed Dickens—only the charity was missing: "Like all Mr. Dickens's pathetic characters, she *is* a little monster" (155; emphasis added). Who speaks for James in this near-Socratic exchange, the cynical Horton or the guileless Gray? Is Gray too a *little monster*?

When Horton sarcastically suggests that Rosanna "sits, like Truth, at the bottom of a well," Gray denies that Rosanna can be called a "façade": "She loathes self-exhibition; she loathes being noticed; she loathes every form of publicity" (155). To make his point clear, he shifts the ground of the evolving trope (from *well* to *façade*):

"Well then if what I have is a molehill beside her mountain, I can the more easily emulate her in standing back." "What you have is a molehill?" Horton was concerned to inquire. Gray showed a shade of guilt, but faced his judge. "Well—so I gather."

(155)

Although the tenor of this allegorical exchange concerns the quantity of his fortune, the figures (molehill, mountain) obtain a phenomenal life of their own. It is in the logic of the rhetorical figure to embody the un-phenomenal, to lend a sensible aspect to an idea. But a *figure* is also a *face* (individual) and a *number* (quantity). Hence the resulting circularity of designation. In *Our Mutual Friend* the mathematical figures implied in the inheritance are phenomenalized through the actual existence of the dust mounds and the speculation about the treasure—in the form of wills and "properties" (85)—concealed inside them. The reader *sees* Harmon's fortune in the dust mound. The extraordinary description that opens chapter 12 of Book II, with the grating wind making the "sawdust" whirl about the streets, blinding and choking every passenger, and the "mysterious paper currency which circulates in London when the wind blows" (*Mutual* 144), suggests a tropological correlation between money and dust. This rhetorical strategy is less effective and continuous in *The Ivory Tower*. The figural suggestions are more intermittent, but they *are*, and they owe much of their existence to Dickens's novel. James swerves away from the grotesque phenomenality of *Our Mutual Friend* largely because he admits to his cognitive failure before the new financial realities. He fails to see the new quantities—the sublime "enormities of expenditure and extravagance" ("Notes" 245). By contrast, Mr. Betterman can only think through those figures, he is "incapable of thought save in sublimities of arithmetic" (9): "If he hadn't thought in figures how could he possibly have thought at all?" (7) The infinity of the mathematical "sublime" (29) originates of course in "the fruits of his swindle" (9) and it only poses "mysteries of calculation" (71) to the unknowing. To save appearances, James recycles shreds of an old romantic jargon: "conditions incalculable" (99), "uncharted infinite" (99), "enormity," "quantities inconceivable" (105), "quite immense things" (185).

Throughout the novel, a distinction is suggested between a *mathematical sublime* and a *dynamic sublime*. The latter has to do with our considering nature as a dangerous power that however has no complete dominion over us: the episode in the overhanging cliff is a fit illustration, but we could also consider the water-and-sea imagery that informs so many speculative descriptions in the novel. The mathematical sublime, by contrast, devoid of phenomenal expression, appears to rule over the market and business world. But James, I insist, tried hard to make us *see* the obscenity of the mounds, mountains, and amounts. Gray construes the arrival of Mr Betterman's lawyer as a revelation of dryness:

> and yet the dryness was of a sort, Gray soon apprehended, that he might take up in handfuls, as if it had been the very sand of the Sahara, and thereby find in it, at the least exposure to light, the collective shimmer of myriads of fine particles. It was with the substance of the desert taken as monotonously sparkling under any motion to dig in it that the abyss of Mr. Crick's functional efficiency was filled.

(180)

What is "the collective shimmer of myriads of fine particles" if not the *society of eccentrics* that James rejected in his review? The grains of sand that Dickens gathered together in mounds, creating a "range of dust-mountains" (*Mutual* 15), are now the lone and level sands of the Sahara, stretching far away. The possibility of a formal gradation— *desert, molehill, mound, mountain*—implies that both novelists are aiming at the same dialectical impossibility: the phenomenal visualization of infinity. And this attempt hinges upon the likelihood of *seeing a figure* (shape, trope, number, written character, personal character), which in turn depends on the possibility of distinguishing, with Wallace Stevens, between *nothing that is not there* (the insubstantial Newport people) and *the nothing that is* (the potentially explosive character, like Gray and perhaps Rosanna). *Our Mutual Friend* opens with two "figures" (1) in a boat: we see them. *The Ivory Tower* opens with the "constitution of Rosanna's ponderous 'figure'" (5): we also see her. The problem with the second novel is that very soon we stop seeing *because* we *only* see the *figures* (faces, façades, surfaces). Gussy, described as a "woman [. . .] who had no depth" (35), appears to Rosanna "as an advertisement of all the latest knowledge of how to 'treat' every inch of the human surface and where to 'get' every scrap of personal envelope" (39). The supplement or *petit objet a* furnishes the individual with the "scrap of personal envelope" that secures her successful individuation. Not only is Cissy little more than a stretch of human surface: she is a stretch that can be treated (computed) in inches. Not only does the human character lack depth: the surface that remains can be decomposed into parts and particles, like the grains of sand in a desert. The eccentric, to use James's vocabulary, is made up of eccentricities. The reader may protest that Cissy is not, in the novel, a paradigmatic James character, but I would reply that if he was aiming at depth in Gray and Rosanna he certainly fared no better. Are they any *different* from Cissy?

## VIII

But what is *difference*? What do we mean when we say that a person is different from another person? I noted previously that individuation can be seen as a non-relational relation or absolute between, "a between understood as fully independent or external to its terms—and thus a between that can just as well be described as 'between' nothing at all" (Hallward, *Deleuze* 154). Jenny is exactly that, but also Riderhood, whom Deleuze singles out in his last published essay, "Immanence: A Life . . ." (1995) as an instance of *radical separate individuality*. The French philosopher reads the scene where the dead waterman's "spark of life" becomes "curiously separable from himself" (*Mutual* 442): it is the appropriate occasion (*Ereignis* or *événement*) when, between his life and his death,

> there is a moment that is only that of a life playing with death. The life of the individual gives way to an impersonal and yet singular life that releases [*dégage*] a pure event [. . .] a "Homo tantum" with whom everyone empathises [*compâtit*] and who attains a sort of beautitude.
>
> ("L'immanence" 361)[20]

Something similar happens with Barnardine, the dissolute condemned prisoner in *Measure for Measure* (4.3). Few Shakespeare characters are more alive than him. Few cling more strenuously to their *spark*—or, like Hamlet, to their *story*. Commenting on Deleuze's reading of the episode in *Our Mutual Friend*, Peter Hallward describes the spark as "perfectly unique, perfectly singular—it is this spark, and no other—yet fully 'separable' from the object it sustains" (25) and moves on to propose a definition of literary writing as "a process that sweeps individual characters up in intensive movements that explode their constituted limits," carrying them off, in Deleuze's terms, "into an indefinite [*un indefini*]" (25). This in turn forces the individual character to bear an internal *indefini*, an infinite within—which is also, in my reading, the hole that bars the subject and makes society inconsist. The rule is simple: one is only separate if empty within. Only then can one become a *between nothing* at all. If this sounds to you like the kind of abstruse idea that, according to Eliot, never violated James's fine mind, read carefully Gray's musing over the American elegance of his cool bedimmed room in section one of book second of the novel, where he expresses his desire that "things should be different, should positively glare with opposition," to the point of obtaining "character," on a range and scale permitting "each object or effect" to "[disown] connections"— his "cherished hope" that "the fresh start and the broken link" would allow "its measure filled to the brim" (59). The *separation* of the *broken link* is the condition of indefinite explosion, and the singular individuation of character is pitted against other infinite climaxes. *Character*, in *The Ivory Tower*, is the opposite of "type" (62). In Jamesian terminology, *men* are opposed to *man*. At bottom lies the scholastic debate over individuals and particulars, and Heidegger's reactivation of the question of ontological difference. And my point is that, however critically James responded to Dickens's passion for the disconnected particular, in his unfinished novel, following a passion for "concentrated difference" (*Ivory* 67) that is already present in *The Ambassadors*, he reconsidered the *possibility* of his precursor's "society of eccentrics," of characters moved by an "inward energy or necessity" (67). Mr. Betterman, for instance, praises Gray's separate individuality:

> "Because you are different," Mr. Betterman considered. "But different from what?" Truly was Gray interested to know. It took Mr. Betterman a moment to say, but he seemed to convey that it might have been guessed. "From what you'd have been if you had come."
>
> (79)

The uncle insists on the seriousness of his ontological penetration—"I see you are, I see *what* you are" (80)—and concludes, dramatically: "you are different from *anything*" (80). Gray rightly takes *different* here to mean "alien from what I feel surrounding me" (81) and accepts the thrust of his uncle's dialectical discrimination: "My point isn't so much for you are as for what you're not" (82). The broken link (Gray) is being valued for its ability to disconnect from the general chain. The singularity of this *between* is that it can connect, like Eliot, *nothing with nothing*. And only from the standpoint of this separate *homo tantum*, only from the eccentric supplementation his radical difference introduces, can the community of lesser faces be ideally redeemed: "We require the difference that you'll make," Mr. Betterman tells him, and adds: "the question isn't of your doing, but simply of your being" (84). Gray replies that "I don't know that I came out so very much for myself" (87). Coming out to become oneself, for oneself, the doing of becoming someone, is exactly what Hyacinth attempts in imitation of Hamlet: "This is I,/Hamlet the Dane." "To make a difference" (102) is therefore a passive action the novel keeps enforcing, in two related senses: the singular human making a *difference from* the human community and the human part making a *difference from* the human (w)hole. The former action we have already considered. The second, involving the mechanical autonomy of body members or parts like the face or the mouth, is implied in the first aspect of the novel pointed out by James in his review of *Our Mutual Friend*:

> Who but Dickens could have written it? Who, indeed? Who else would have established a lady in business in a novel on the admirably solid basis of her always putting on gloves and tieing a handkerchief round her head in moments of grief, and of her habitually addressing her family with "Peace! hold!"
>
> (*LC I* 853)

James emphasizes not only the autonomy of the gloves and the handkerchief, which highlights the potential separateness of, respectively, the hands and the head, but also the independence of the *repeated phrase*. Mrs.

Wilfer becomes the mechanical—almost Beckettian—aggregate of a pair of gloves, a handkerchief, and a phrase. His critique betrays a romantic-organicist, tendentially symbolist prejudice against the mechanical risks of allegorical diction:

> The movement of Mr. Dickens's fancy is, to our mind, a movement life-less, forced, mechanical. It is the letter of his old humor without the spirit. It is hardly too much to say that every character here put before us is a mere bundle of eccentricities, animated by no principle of nature whatever.
>
> (854)

This principle of mechanical movement animating a part (a member, an organ) of the body without the actual animation of its spirit is what psychoanalysis calls *drive*: "drive is fundamentally the insistence of an undead 'organ without a body,' standing, like Lacan's *lamella*, for that which the subject had to lose in order to subjectivize itself in the symbolic space of the sexual difference" (Žižek, *Organs* 154). But Žižek obviously implies what James is unwilling to accept: that every subject, to emerge as such, is obscenely supplemented by one of its (autonomized) organs. In 1954 Geoffrey Tillotson rightly argued that Dickens's "creatures are bits of human beings wonderfully exaggerated and coloured" (*Thackeray* 110), and four years later the great Anthony Burgess observed, recapitulating an inveterate critical tradition, that Dickens's "characters are really 'humours'—exaggerations of one human quality to the point of caricature" (183). In the case of James—especially the late, proto-modernist, James—this *humor, organ* or *bit* is his emancipated *voice*—"the undead vocal drive, the immortal life, going on" (*Organs* 150).[21] This voice is his narrative persona, the narrator, a modernized version of the ancient Chorus or Prologue, described by Žižek as effectively functioning as the Freudian *Vorstellungs-Repräsentanz* (representative of representing), placed within the "diegetic reality of representation," and yet introducing "the moments of distance, inter-pretation, ironic comment" (152). Moretti sees this Chorus as vanishing in psychological tragedy, and Žižek as disappearing "with the victory of psychological realism" (152). The first fully fleshed, totally successful Prologue voice in modern English narrative is of course that of Fielding, with Thackeray as distinguished heritor, and both profit from Hamlet's triumphant internalization of the censuring choric voice-over: the solilo-quy opening with the lines "Now I am alone./O, what a rogue and peas-ant slave am I" (*Hamlet* 2.2.484–485) exemplifies the mechanical auton-omy of the disciplinary super-egoic voice that was once the Chorus's. For good or bad, James's narrators and mouthpiece characters belong too in this tradition, and they are accordingly exposed to the logic of the organ-based compulsive drive.

## IX

Let me return to James's disdainful remarks on Jenny. I have suggested that the mechanical iterative principle (*constantly reiterates, for ever pricking*) that is therein identified as governing the personality of this monstrous character, visible in the autonomous drive of her hand and mouth, is bound to reappear in all of James's novels, especially in the final ones, where voluptuously spiritual girls are placed against a backdrop of vicious "tricks" and "manners," and narrative opinion flows deformed, unhealthy, unnatural. In *The Ivory Tower*, we have seen, the part of the body that embodies the drive is not exactly an organ, but rather a bidimensional representative of the body-mind admixture that is the *person*: it is the metonymy of the πρόσωπον (prosopon) or *face*. James' judgement of Jenny is echoed in Leavis's assessment of Nelly, the protagonist of *The Old Curiosity Shop*: "to suggest taking Little Nell seriously would be absurd: there's nothing there. She doesn't derive from any perception of the real, she's a contrived unreality" (qtd. in Bowen 133). Like the grotesque, absurd name, the odd, unreal face is a recurrent motif in Dickens's fiction, particularly in *Oliver Twist*. His "literary writing" lends faces and names a bizarre independence. But James is not immune to these faults. A novelist who decides to call one of his central characters Mr. Betterman cannot claim (realistic, naturalistic) superiority over the novelist who calls his social climbers the Veneerings. Isolated names and separate faces make up the puppet show of salient surfaces and façades that Thackeray speaks about in his prologue, "Before the Curtain," to *Vanity Fair*—another unforgettable story of "monsters on exhibition."

In his excellent book on Deleuze, Žižek glosses Diderot's text on the female mouth and vagina:

> A woman speaks with two voices. The first one, that of her soul (mind and heart), is constitutively lying, deceiving, covering up her promiscuity; it is only the second voice, that of her *bijou* (the pearl which, of course, is vagina itself), which, by definition, *always* speaks the truth—a boring, repetitive, automatic, "mechanical" truth, but truth nonetheless, the truth about her unconstrained voluptuousness. The notion of the "talking vagina" is not meant as a metaphor but meant quite literally: Diderot provides the anatomical description of vagina as instrument *à corde et à vent* capable of emitting sounds. (He even reports on a medical experiment: after excising the entire vagina from the body, doctors tried to "make it talk" through blowing it and using it as a string). This,

then, would e only one of the meanings of Lacan's *la femme n'existe pas*: there are no talking vaginas directly telling the truth: there is only the elusive, lying, hysterical subject.

(*Organs* 152)

This brings to mind Hamlet's reluctance to have his recorder (his flute, his instrument) played upon by others, by meddlers, envoys, ambassadors and spies who seek to produce his truth, and also Gray's exposure to rapacious characters keen on extracting his intentions. One may, analogically, suggest that the *truth-telling vagina* is systemically built (as a possibility) into the wistful uncommitted male hero of the Western narrative tradition. I already noted in the first chapter that James tends to refrain from giving the floor to the female heroine—perhaps because, as Žižek suggests, "the male gaze endeavors to counter the fundamental hystericity (lie, lack of a firm position of enunciation) of the feminine speech" (*Organs* 152). But it is not only James who senses this cultural inconsistency: although, for instance, *Wuthering Heights* is chiefly the handmaid's tale, Nelly's tale, Emily Brontë found it necessary to place a sober male character at the supporting edges of her tale, to play the role of judiciary Prologue. I want to retain the scene of the doctors gathering around the girl for their medical experiment, trying to make her vagina talk. This scene is almost identical to that of Freud's colleagues helping him to examine the vocal cavity of Irma. What is so tantalizing about this primal scene is the resolve to make the invaginated surface reveal a depth that is simply not there. Such Leibnizian insight was soon adopted by psychoanalytical hermeneutics, and it became post-structuralist in a broad sense:

what is concealed may just as easily lie on the surface. Lacan [. . .] like Foucault, believes there is nothing but surface, but he maintains, nevertheless, that the corpse, the private "self", the purloined letter are not simply fictions; they are real.

(Copjec 170)[22]

The failed revelation of depth is a constant motif in *Our Mutual Friend*, where characters resurface from the river water, peep under bedsteads, and poke into limehouse holes, in search of a secret, or a treasure, or a future.[23] In *The Ivory Tower*, revelations don't fail because there are *no implications of depth*. There are only Baroque convolutions of inferential folds leading to delayed assessments of depth and unlikely disclosures of truth. But, if the doctors nevertheless assemble, who or what is the *talking head* in *The Ivory Tower*? What mouth is separated from whose body? How much "ventriloquism and thrown voice" (Ohi 120) is James willing to admit as constitutive of his and his characters' narrative personae?

Whose face storms and surfs the novel's surface? Whose vagina treasures what and whose truth? In his reading of *The Old Curiosity Shop*, John Bowen diagnoses an episode of failed introjection and forced incorporation of the lost object in a crypt, "an inaccessible psychic space distinct from the unconscious" (Bowen 142), which evokes the separateness of Riderhood's living spark. The *petit objet a* that supplements such individuation—the obscene and talking organ—is, in the case of the earlier novel, little Nell's wooden leg. The mechanical prosthesis is her accompanying corpse and private self, and so are Gray's and Rosanna's more or less standardized faces, immense façades, and elephantine talking heads.[24] We may connect this insight with the modernist afterlife, in *Hamlet*, of the Hegelian " 'hollowing out' of allegorical subjectivity," which coincides with the mechanistic drive of the "puppet" (Halpern, *Shakespeare* 236) that de Man examined in his essay on Kleist (*Rhetoric* 263–290). It is in this historical context of accelerating modernization—capitalism, embourgeoisement—that Halpern's claim that "the fulness of the bourgeois heart and its metaphysical interiority" is replaced by "the literal interiority of a stuffed subject" (232) makes full sense. The literal interiority of James's central subjects in *The Ivory Tower* is also stuffed by "every scrap of personal envelope," commencing with the person itself as prosopon, mask, or face. This lends a scriptural, near-emblematic force to this fragment of late writing that we could term litteral as both disposable and "intensely written," to use the predicate James reserved for Dickens's "literary writing" in *Our Mutual Friend*. The unlikelihood of meaningful reading—of, among other books, Gibbon's *History of the Decline and Fall of the Roman Empire*, which Wegg reads to Boffin—is a constant concern in Dickens's novel, and this manifestly bears on the parallel strain (the effort, the sheer material impossibility, the interdiction) of writing.[25] In "A Note on the Text," Cotsell mentions how, in the version of 1867, Dickens cut off long passages of the original version "because of overwriting." The difference with James is that the American novelist lived long enough to waive those scruples: he had discovered that *the condition of writing is overwriting*—and that "a complex text" like *Our Mutual Friend* or *The Ivory Tower* "can speak beyond the control of its author" (Poole, Introduction to *Our Mutual Friend* xx). Otherwise put, he learnt, with Dickens, that the condition of life is death, the condition of living man is semi-dead humans, the condition of a body is its parts, the condition of ideally organic society is materially separate character, the condition of presumed depth is assumed surface. In *The Ivory Tower*, James turns doggedly to the conditions. This should come as no surprise. If Dickens was a necessary condition for James, it was predictable he should try to settle accounts with the father of Smike, Monks, and Lizzie before he abandoned himself to "the great ocean, Death" (*Mutual* 71).

# X

Žižek rightly points out that consciousness and the unconscious are utterly incommensurable (*Bodies* 123). On this logic, narrative can be seen as an attempt to render consciousness (the face, the surface) commensurate with the unconscious (the bottom of the river, the tower, or the well), to make the Unconscious more readable inside and across the scripts of the conscious. If James' novels are experiences of consciousness, then this attempt generates a tension that is also part of the experience. If "what does not become conscious gets inscribed into a memory trace," then consciousness is a "defense-formation, a mode of repression: we become conscious of something so that we can directly forget it" (123). A tower, even an ivory tower, is admittedly a defense-formation, and James's novel betrays the traces of his conscious attempt to erase earlier (and other) memory traces. But, as Žižek argued in his critique of Habermas, the retranslation of latent dream-thought (Dickens's world) into the language of intersubjective communication (Fielding's world) is never accomplished without tropological leftovers (de Man) and inassimilable remainders (Adorno): "meaning as such [always] results from a certain distortion" (Žižek, *Metastases* 26–27), or deviation (*clinamen*), and literary meaning, in the Western cultures, "is a history of anxiety and self-saving caricature, of distortion, of perverse, willful revisionism" (*Anxiety* 30). James wanted, needed, to forget Dickens, his talking heads, his figures, his faces. Arriving at Gloriani's house, Strether had an uncanny "sense of names in the air, ghosts at the window, of signs and tokens" (*Ambassadors* 137). Evocative of a "convent," these were not the tokens of his Parisian new life. James spent his life trying to forget some tokens of an earlier life, his life—certain names, signs, and ghosts at the window. He needed to forget the brutal and indelible precision of Dickens's narrative diction, which appeared to materialize at the verge of an abyss, as a "wild and naked intensity that often sputters into inarticulateness" (Marcus 41), as the phrase *dug out* at "the limits of articulacy" (Bradbury, "Henry James and Britain" 411). He needed to wipe out the *imprint* of Cruikshank's illustration of Monks and the Jew behind the window, but also the surfacing faces in the river of *Our Mutual Friend*. He wanted to un-remember whatever and whomever was not properly *membered* in Dickens's last novel, and to give its elusive hero a new chance. Whereas Dickens wanted fragmentary people to reunite in consistent plots, James preferred to see apparently compact people to freely inconsist in withdrawals from communal plot. Tellingly, Harmon is only mentioned *once* in his review of the novel, and he is *only* mentioned. James probably fancied the character. Harmon repeated Pickwick and Nickleby, unlikely gentlemen—free, idle wanderers across the theatre of life, prototypes of the Dickens flaneur—whose social rehabilitation caused him great anxiety.

The comedic fact that Harmon's transoceanic travels, subaqueous troubles, and underground trials leads him—upon coming to his *damnosa hereditas*, to the disciplinary domestication of the marriage plot—is the tragic outcome that James set out to correct. And he wrote *The Ivory Tower*, presumably to offer his alternative hero something both firmer and less concrete than a dust-mountain wife.

In his Introduction to the novel, Michael Costell holds

> the landscape of *Our Mutual Friend* is hugely "preliterated": it is as much an evocation of a tradition of texts as a representation of the objective world. Similarly, the novel's theme of waste recycled can be read as a declaration of "intertextuality", of how the new text is built up out of the pieces of the old.
>
> (xx–xxi)

This *preliterated* condition accounts for its "rich linguistic textuality," redolent, according to the same scholar, "of modernist writing" (xxi). James, recall, opined that the novel was "intensely written," and little seen, known, or felt. But writing is also a perceptive-cognitive mode of experience, and experience, James gradually realized, tended to be already written, scripted, preliterated. Or prepossessed by other voices who also—perhaps—failed to see in the right way. Trilling wrote that "what James saw he saw truly" (60). What did he mean? Can truth apply to visual perception? Isn't it rather an affair of conceptual constitution and transcendental apperception? Can one see with a voice? Perhaps what we call "moral" is precisely the ability to see truly without recourse to a narrative voice, to accountability, to the account of the tale. Clinamen is vocal revision, for a voice revises—etymologically, sees (vised) again (re)—and revoices. Clinamen is to see again, with a deviant voice—a separate voice.

The review of *Our Mutual Friend* is James's first attempt to bring to consciousness Dickens's narrative world in order to forget it. *The Ivory Tower* is a final, desperate, unfinished attempt. The novel is a "picture of detachment" ("Notes" 246)—Gray's *detachment*. Hence his "exalted queerness," his "prodigious queerness" ("Notes" 236), otherwise known as *eccentricity*: in Low German, "queer" meant oblique, off-center. It is paradoxical that James should urge this figure of eccentric separation in a text, the "Notes" for the novel, that hinges upon the capacity of narrative "Joints" (224–235) to make "the Whole" (231) cohere. For only what is made of joints can become (w)hole or *out of joint*. Thackeray's Becky, for instance, was "uncommonly flexible in the joints, and lively on the wire" (Preface to *Vanity Fair* 2). If Jenny Wren is less flexible, less lively on the wire, it is because she is also made of wires, and joints. And so is Gray. If "a relation is," in his view, "exactly a *fact* of reciprocity" (173), how can he relate exactly to whom when his prodigious queerness turns him into a part of parts, a separately parted particle, organized less as a bundle of universals (Russell) than as a "bundle of eccentricities." Whereas the shared assumption of rational commonality (Arendt), ethical reciprocity (Pippin), and communicative reason (Habermas) is the *discernibility of identicals*, of what is identical (common) in the self to other selves, the assumption of an aleatory-materialist ontology is that if subjective individuation is predicated upon the "stain which is the 'subject'" (Zizek, *Metastases* 33), then *identicals are indiscernible*—for universals may recur, and should recur, but no two stains are the same. In other words, the separate self is unreadable, indiscernible, unexaminable, because it is identical with its supplementary spark or paradoxical object, i.e. identical with itself. Irma is identical with her "white spot," Amelia with her broken nose, Jenny with her "bad back" and "queer legs," Gray with his "face."[26] They are *what*—not *who*—they are. But they at least *are*. By contrast, other surfaces and figures hardly manage to open the intensity of their existence to the transcendental indexation characteristic of *evental individuation*.

## Clinamen

Gray is a relation from nowhere to nowhere. He dwells in a realm where faces misgive, and surfaces blink in blankness. Not much to relate with or to. But he is also a face and a blink, a name and a spark, for Dickens and his heritor have "created nothing but figure" (James, "On Our Mutual Friend," *LCI* 852), but also figures that *are* nothing. Gray's *haecceitas* or singular identity rests on his determination to become a different face, a more resilient spark. Like strong poets, he "opts for *clinamen* as freedom" (*Anxiety* 44). Separateness is clinamen as swerve, and swerve is freedom—because "discontinuity is freedom" (39). Awkward freedom, perverted freedom, queer freedom, strange freedom. Steven Marcus has noted that "for Dickens, the intrusion [. . .] of the past into the present must inevitably bring with it a diminution of integrity and self-sufficiency" (38), and the name James gives to our resolve to consider the *contraction* of selfhood induced by the mysteries of the past is that of "desolate freedom" (*Ivory* 180).

Dickens's being outside in our primal scene, knocking at the door of the *House of Jamesian fiction*, stipulates a pre-ontological condition of exteriority from which the *new man* must further separate himself: "The poem is *within* him, yet he experiences the shame and splendor of *being found* by poems—great poems—*outside* him" (26).[27] Dickens is simultaneously outside and inside James, an aural persona (*prosopon*) that constitutes the latter from the interiority of his outside-sensitive childhood. Bradbury rightly speaks of a shared "thematic interest in vulnerability, particularly in the treatment of the child" ("Henry James and Britain" 412). According to John Bowen, James "reads by not reading Dickens, possessing him without possession" (33). But, Poole questions in deManian perplexity: "What does it mean to read, or be able to read?" (Introduction to *Our Mutual Friend* xx) Hard to tell, but what appears to me indisputable is that "passive, mechanical reading" cannot be opposed, in Dickens's novel, as Poole suggests, to "active performative reading" (xxi). Dickens's relevant figures perform their readings of the scripts of experience, and even of books, always in a compulsively mechanical manner, as a dynamic drive allowing these figures to swerve into their distinct contraction and separate distinction. At any rate, "the stronger the man, the larger his resentments, and the more brazen his clinamen" (Bloom, *Anxiety* 43). But Dickens's original strength affords little room for creative deviation. Young James decided to obviate the fact that in the world of literary authors, "all regularities are [. . .] 'regular exceptions': the recurrence of vision is itself a law governing exceptions" (*Anxiety* 42). Pitting Dickens's eccentrics against the regularities of nature and humanity was a hopeless move, for James needed in turn to segregate himself both from his society *and* from Dickens in order to store up meaningful experience. To be one of those on whom nothing is lost is to be an exception, and if nothing is lost on them, it is precisely because they fail to relate and to reciprocate. They may be open on one side, but closed on the other, whence the concentration and the (ontologically explosive) gain. The Dickensian "sense of differences in things" (*Ivory* 133), the pull toward "concentrated difference" (67) ran counter to James's more urbanely moral compositional exigency "to keep the door open always to something *more* right and *more* related" ("Notes" 254). Both requirements were fundamentally incompatible. Something had to give. Eventually, it was James who gave up.

## Notes

1 Follini has provided an excellent account of the impact of Dickens in James's authorial and autobiographical *personae*: see "Indirections"; and also "Temporality," 224–226. Also very astute is John Bowen's reading of this episode of influence, which he describes as "infection": *Other Dickens*, 31–34. See also Bradbury's remarkable meditation on a "creative struggle that persisted throughout James's life, generating enormous energy": "Henry James and Britain," 410–413.

2 See the third chapter in *The Turn of the Screw*, and also my article on *Julia Bride*, another narrative strongly prepossessed by Dickens.

3 Jonathan Freedman's description of "the James of *The Ivory Tower*" as a person "whose energies have turned wholly inward, consuming themselves in writing fables about fable-making" (248) is baffling, since they apply more to the "Notes for *The Ivory Tower*" than to the novel proper. In structure, theme, and

style, what remains of the book is no different from *The Wings of the Dove* and *The Golden Bough*.

4 All are aiming to instruct. The minister in *Tom Jones* is described as "awful, impersonal Morality" (1202).

5 For the Scott-James connection in the light of "moral fiction," see the article by Lawrence Berkove.

6 See also Greg Zacharias's succinct clarification of the meaning of morality in James as the ethical problem of "choices made by characters and human beings and [. . .] the consequences of those choices": *Henry James*, xi–xii.

7 For the relation between economic surplus and the verbal surplus of meaning in *The Ivory Tower*, see the excellent essay by Wendy Graham, especially 68–71.

8 Gerome's painting of Rachel may have inspired *The Tragic Muse*. James wrote from Paris about the purchase of Gerome's paintings by American wealthy people. For the connection with *The Tragic Muse*, see Rowe, *The Other Henry James*, 212, n.25. Rowe cites Adeline Tintner's study *Henry James and the Lust of Eyes* (1993).

9 This quote is used by Žižek in *Bodies*, xi.

10 Just as societies exist in their inconsistency, with hegemonic parts totalizing, and even sublating, the whole in their claims to generic universality: see the essays in Judith Butler, Ernesto Laclau and Slavoj Žižek in *Contingency, Hegemony, Universality: Contemporary Dialogues on the Left* (2000). Societal inconsistency is already an issue in Mill's examination of civil liberty: he stresses that a part of the people, claiming to represent the totality, may repress a part of their number (*On Liberty* 6).

11 For the notion of explosion and paraconsistent logic, see Graham Priest et al.

12 Matthiessen attributes the vision to William himself in *Henry James: The Major Phase*, 142.

13 Horton insists that part of the solution to Gray's troubles is "marriage" (152), but Gray "absolutely [doesn't] want a wife" (153).

14 "Money begins to figure as the overweening measure of class and caste in American life, even where the elites are concerned. For James, modernity in all its facets revokes the authority of the past through new economies of scale and the infusion of difference" ("Signifying" 71).

15 In "Repairing Injustice," Paul B. Armstrong connects Gray's inherited wealth with the Rhode Island slave trade.

16 There are references to Rosanna sailing (*Ivory* 16) and mythological sea creatures (184).

17 For the *revenant* in *Hamlet*, see Lawlor, *Derrida and Husserl*, 216–220.

18 "No ghost should trouble Mr and Mrs Boffin's peace; invisible and voiceless, the ghost should look on for a little while longer at the state of existence out of which it had departed, and then should for ever cease to haunt the scenes in which it had no place" (*Mutual* 379).

19 See Derrida, *La vérité en peinture*, 109–113.

20 I use the translation of the passage as quoted by Hallward. In the French original there is no footnote explaining the meaning of *homo tantum*, a phrase Deleuze probably lifted from Boethius *De trinitate*: "sed homo tantum magnus, deus vero ipsum magnus exsistit." The gestural dimension of the individualizing spark of life reminds us of the distinctive *style* of Jenny's individuation, made of bodily intensities, vocal iterations, and gesture. Ohi invokes Deleuze's analysis of gesture in his study on James's queerness of style: *Henry James*, 20.

21  Raymond Williams pointed out that "Dickens was creating [. . .] a world in which people had been deprived of any customary identity and yet in which, paradoxically, the deprivation was a kind of liberation, in which the most fantastic and idiosyncratic kinds of growth could come about": *The English Novel*, 54.

22  For monadic surfaces, see Deleuze's study on Leibniz, *Le pli*, 5–37, 113–132.

23  Consider the extraordinary description, which closes Book 1 of *Our Mutual Friend*, of the wooden-legged Wegg peeping under the bedsteads, hopping up ladders, poking and prodding into dust mounds.

24  The adjective "elephantine" is applied in the "Notes" to Rosanna. For a sophisticated reading of her characterization as an individual prone to corporal excess, overspill, and eventually waste, see Daniel Hannah.

25  There is, in Dickens's novel, a constant reference to reading, writing, literacy, grammar-books (55–52). Mr. Wegg shows "deep acquaintance with [the] eight volumes of *Decline and Fall*" (53–55, 58), whose contents are briefly summarized at one point (59). "Professionally," moreover, we are told, Mr Wegg "declines and he falls" (98) like characters in Evelyn Waugh's eponymous novel. And as a friend he drops into "poetry" (98), and reference is made to the decline of the Boffin House, like that of the "Roman Empire," which "usually declined in the morning" (296).

26  The critical debate over the incident of Amelia's broken nose—the intolerance of readers and reviewers to countenance this facial accident (Sabor 95–99)—speaks to the taboo connotations that accrue around the anatomically eccentric, possibly, in my interpretation, because it comes as a reminder of deeper antagonisms and inconsistencies—in the Real. Fielding's determination to place the scar at the center of her virtuous heroine testifies to his moral courage, as does Polanski's similar brilliant decision in *Chinatown*.

27  For the connection between the primal scene, the ghostly, and the pre-ontological, see Luckacher, *Primal Scenes*, 119–121.

# Bibliography

Adams, Edward. "Gibbon, Virgil, and the Victorians: Appropriating the Matter of Rome and Renovating the Epic Career." In *The Call of Classical Literature in the Romantic Age*. Eds. K.P. Van Anglen and James Engell. Edinburgh: Edinburgh UP, 2017.313–338.

Adams, Henry. *The Education of Henry Adams*. Ed. Ira B. Nadel. Oxford: Oxford UP, 1999.

Adorno, Theodor and Marx Horkheimer. *Dialectic of Enlightenment: Philosophical Fragments*. Ed. Gunzelin Noeri. Stanford: Stanford UP, 2007.

Althusser, Louis. *Écrits sur la psychanalyse: Freud et Lacan*. Paris: STOCK, 1994.

———. "Ideology and Ideological State Apparatuses." *Lenin and Philosophy and Other Essays*. Trans. Ben Brewster. New York: Monthly Review, 2001.85–126.

Anesko, Michael, ed. *Letters, Fictions, Lives: Henry James and William Dean Howells*. Oxford: Oxford UP, 1997.

Anker, Richard. "Materiality Without Matter in *The Wings of the Dove*." *Revue française d'études américaines* 172.3 (2022): 93–107.

Armstrong, Nancy. *Desire and Domestic Fiction*. Oxford: Oxford UP, 1987.

———. *How Novels Think. The Limits of British Individualism 1719–1900*. New York: Columbia UP, 2007.

Armstrong, Paul B. "Repairing Injustice: The Contradictions of Forgiveness and *The Ivory Tower*." *The Henry James Review* 30 (2009): 44–54.

Ashbery, John. *Self-Portrait in a Convex Mirror*. New York: Penguin, 1976.

———. *Other Traditions*. Cambridge, MA: Harvard UP, 2001.

Austen, Jane. *Northanger Abbey*. Ed. Marilyn Butler. London: Penguin, 1995.

Badiou, Alain. *Being and Event*. Trans. Oliver Feltham. London: Continuum, 2006.

———. *Conditions*. Trans. Steven Corcoran. London: Continuum, 2008.

———. *Logics of Worlds. Being and Event 2*. Alberto Toscano. London: Continuum, 2008.

———. *L'immanence des vérités. L'être et l'événement 3*. Paris: Fayard, 2018.

Badiou, Alain and Barbara Cassin. Formulas of L'Étourdit. *There Is No Such Thing as a Sexual Relationship*. Introd. Kenneth Reinhard. New York: Columbia UP, 2017: 45–62.

Barthes, Roland. *Le Plaisir du texte*. Paris: Seuil, 1973.

Batsaki, Yota. "*Clarissa*; or, Rake versus Usurer." *Representations* 93 (2006): 22–48.

Battestin, Martin C. "The Problem of Amelia: Hume, Barrow, and the Conversion of Captain Booth." *ELH* 41.4 (1974): 613–648.

Bell, Ian F.A., ed. *Henry James: Fiction as History*. London: Vision Press, 1984.

——. *Henry James and the Past: Readings into Time*. London: Macmillan, 1991.

Bell, Millicent. "Class, Sex, and the Victorian Governess: James's 'The Turn of the Screw'." In *New Essays on Daisy Miller and The Turn of the Screw*. Ed. Vivian R. Pollak. Cambridge: Cambridge UP, 1993.91–119.

Belleforest, François de. *Le cinquieme tome des Histoires Tragiques*. Ed. Hervé Thomas Campagne. Droz: Genève, 2013.

Bellow, Saul. *More Die of Heartbreak*. New York: William Morrow, 1987.

Belsey, Catherine. *Shakespeare in Theory and Practice*. Edinburgh: Edinburgh UP, 2010.

Benjamin, Andrew. *Working with Walter Benjamin: Recovering a Political Philosophy*. Edinburgh: Edinburgh UP, 2013.

Benjamin, Walter. *The Origin of German Tragic Drama*. Trans. John Osborne. London: Verso, 1998.

Berkove, Lawrence. "Henry James and Sir Walter Scott: A 'Virtuous Attachment'?" *Studies in Scottish Literature* 15.1 (1980): 43–52.

Bloom, Harold. *The Anxiety of Influence: A Theory of Poetry*. Oxford: Oxford UP, 1973.

——. *A Map of Misreading*. Oxford: Oxford UP, 1975.

——. *Wallace Stevens: The Poems of Our Climate*. Cornell: Cornell UP, 1977.

——. *Novelists and Novels*. New York: Chelsea, 2005.

Booth, Alisa. "The Real Right Place of Henry James: Homes and Haunts." *The Henry James Review* 25.3 (2004): 216–227.

Bowen, John. *Other Dickens: Pickwick to Chuzzlewit*. Oxford: Oxford UP, 2000.

Bowersock, G.W. *From Gibbon to Auden: Essays in the Classical Tradition*. Oxford: Oxford UP, 2009.

Bradbury, Nicola. "Henry James and Britain." In *A Companion to Henry James*. Ed. Greg W. Zacharias. Chichester: Wiley, 2014.400–416.

Brodhead, Richard H. *The School of Hawthorne*. Oxford: Oxford UP, 1990.

Brooks, Peter. *The Melodramatic Imagination: Balzac, Henry James, Melodrama, and the Mode of Excess*. New Haven, Yale UP, 1976.

——. *Henry James Goes to Paris*. Princeton: Princeton UP, 2007.

Buelens, Gert, ed. *Enacting History in Henry James: Narrative, Power, Ethics*. Cambridge: Cambridge UP, 1997.

——. *Henry James and the "Aliens" in Possession of the American Scene*. Amsterdam: Rodopi, 2002.

Buelens, Gert and Celia Aijmer. "The Sense of the Past: History and Historical Criticism." In *Palgrave Advances in Henry James Studies*. Ed. Peter Rawlings. London: Palgrave, 2007.192–211.

Burgess, Anthony. *English Literature: A Survey for Students*. Burnt Mill: Longman, 1974.

Burke, Edmund. *Reflections on the Revolution in France*. Ed. Conor Cruise O'Brien. London: Penguin, 2004.

Butler, Judith, Ernesto Laclau and Slavoj Žižek. *Contingency, Hegemony, Universality: Contemporary Dialogues on the Left*. London: Verso, 2000.

Butterworth-McDermott, Christine. "James's Fractured Fairy-Tale: How the Governess Gets Grimm." *Henry James Review* 28.1 (2007): 43–56.

Byron, Lord. *The Major Works*. Ed. Jerome McGann. Oxford: Oxford UP, 1986.

Cameron, Sharon. *Thinking in Henry James*. Chicago: The U of Chicago P, 1989.

Cargill, Oscar. "*The Princess Casamassima*: A Critical Re-appraisal." *PMLA* 71 (1956): 97–117.

———. *The Novels of Henry James*. New York: Macmillan, 1961.

Carnochan, W.B. *Gibbon's Solitude: The Inward World of the Historian*. Stanford: Stanford UP, 1987.

Castle, Terry. *Clarissa's Ciphers. Meaning and Disruption in Richardson's Clarissa*. Ithaca: Cornell UP, 1982.

Cervantes, Miguel de. *Don Quijote*. Ed. Francisco Rico. Barcelona: Crítica, 1998.

Charnes, Linda. *Hamlet's Heirs: Shakespeare and the Politics of a New Millennium*. London: Routledge, 2006.

Chatman, Seymour. *The Later Style of Henry James*. Oxford: Blackwell, 1972.

Constantinesco, Thomas. "The Matter with Milly Theale: The Logics of Consumption." *Cycnos* 36.1 (2020).

Copjec, Joan. *Read My Desire: Lacan Against the Historicists*. London: Verso, 2015.

Coulson, Victoria. *Henry James: Women and Realism*. Cambridge: Cambridge UP, 2007.

Craddock, Patricia B. *Edward Gibbon, Luminous Historian 1772–1794*. Baltimore: The John Hopkins UP, 1989.

Critchley, Simon. *Ethics-Politics-Subjectivity: Essays on Derrida, Levinas and Contemporary French Thought*. London: Verso, 1999.

Damrosch, Leo. *Fictions of Reality in the Age of Hume and Johnson*. Madison: The U of Wisconsin P, 1989.

Dante. *La vita nuova*. Trans. Barbara Reynolds. London: Penguin, 2004.

Davidson, Guy. "'Almost a Sense of Property': Henry James's 'The Turn of the Screw', Modernism, and Commodity Culture." *Texas Studies in Literature and Language* 53.4 (2011): 455–478.

Davis, Colin. "Hauntology, spectres and phantoms." *French Studies* 59.3 (2005): 373–379.

Deleuze, Gilles. *Différence et répétition*. Paris: P.U.F., 1968.

———. *Le pli: Leibniz et le baroque*. Paris: Minuit, 1988.

De Man, Paul. *The Rhetoric of Romanticism*. New York: Columbia UP, 1984.

Derrida, Jacques. *L'écriture et la différence*. Paris: Seuil, 1967.

———. *Marges de la philosophie*. Paris: Minuit, 1972.

———. *Positions*. Paris: Minuit, 1972.

———. *Glas*. Paris: Galilée, 1974.

———. *La vérité en peinture*. Paris: Flammarion, 1978.

———. *La carte postale. De Socrate à Freud et au-delà*. Paris: Flammarion, 1980.

———. *Margins of Philosophy*. Trans. Alan Bass. Chicago: The U of Chicago P, 1982.

———. *The Postcard*. Trans. Alan Bass. Chicago: The U of Chicago P, 1986.

———. *Spectres de Marx*. Paris: Galilée, 1993.

———. *Specters of Marx*. Trans. Peggy Kamuf. London: Routledge, 1994.

Dickens, Charles. *David Copperfield*. Eds. Andrew Sanders and Nina Burgis. Oxford: Oxford UP, 1997.

———. *Our Mutual Friend*. Ed. Adrian Poole. London: Penguin, 1997.

———. *Our Mutual Friend*. Ed. Michael Cotsell. Oxford: Oxford UP, 1998.

———. *Nicholas Nickleby*. Ed. Paul Schlicke. Oxford: Oxford UP, 1999.

———. *Oliver Twist*. Ed. Philip Horne. London: Penguin, 2003.

Doody, Margaret Anne. *The True Story of the Novel*. New Brunswick: Rutgers UP, 1997.

Douglas-Fairhurst, Robert. *Victorian Afterlives: The Shaping of Influence in Nineteenth-Century Literature*. Oxford UP, 2002.

———. *Becoming Dickens. The Invention of a Novelist*. Cambridge, MA: Harvard UP, 2011.

Duckworth Jr, William C. "Misreading Jane Austen: Henry James, Women Writers, and the Friendly Narrator." *Persuasions: The Jane Austen Journal* 21 (1999): 96–105.

Duperray, Max. "'Déjà vu' in 'The Turn of the Screw.'" In *Henry James's European Heritage and Transfer*. Eds. Dennis Tredy et al. Cambridge: Open Books, 2011.1147–1157.

Eliot, George. *Middlemarch*. Ed. Rosemary Ashton. London: Penguin, 1994.

Eliot, T.S. *Selected Prose of T.S. Eliot*. Ed. Frank Kermode. London: Faber and Faber, 1975.

Eusebius Pamphilus. *Church History*. Eds. Philip Schaff and Henry Wace. Grand Rapids: Ethereal, 1890.

Everett, Barbara. *Young Hamlet: Essays on Shakespeare's Tragedies*. Oxford: Clarendon Press, 1989.

Felman, Shoshana. "Turning the Screw of Interpretation." *Yale French Studies* 55/56 (1977): 94–207.

Fielding, Henry. *Tom Jones*. Ed. John Bender. London: Oxford UP, 1996.

———. *Joseph Andrews* and *Shamela*. Ed. Douglas Brooks-Davies. Rev. Thomas Keymer. Oxford: Oxford UP, 1999.

———. *Amelia*. Ed. Linda Bree. Peterborough: Broadview Press, 2010.

Filmer, Robert. *Patriarcha and Other Writings*. Ed. Johannn P. Sommerville. Cambridge: Cambridge UP, 1991.

Finkielkraut, Alain. *L'identité malheureuse*. Paris: Folio, 2015.

Fish, Stanley. "Interpreting the Variorum." *Critical Inquiry* 2.3 (1976): 465–485.

Follini, Tamara. "James, Dickens, and the Indirections of Influence." *The Henry James Review* 25.3 (2004): 228–238.

———. "A Geometry of His Own: Temporality, Referentiality and Ethics in the Autobiographies." In *Henry James Studies*. Ed. Peter Rawlings. London: Palgrave, 2007.212–238.

Foucault, Michel. *The History of Sexuality*, Vol. 1. Trans. Robert Hurley. New York: Pantheon, 1978.

———. *La vérité et les formes juridiques* in *Dits et écrits I 1954–1975*. Paris: Gallimard, 1994.

Freedman, Jonathan. *Professions of Taste. Henry James, British Aestheticism, and Commodity Culture*. Stanford: Stanford UP, 1990.

Freud, Sigmund. *The Interpretation of Dreams*. Trans. Joyce Crick. Oxford: Oxford UP, 1999.

Fussell, Edwin Sill. *The Catholic Side of Henry James*. Cambridge: Cambridge UP, 1993.

Gaddis, William. *A Frolic of His Own*. New York: Simon & Schuster, 1994.

Gallagher, Catherine. "The Rise of Fictionality." In *The Novel*. Vol.1. Ed. Franco Moretti. Princeton: Princeton UP, 2006. 336–363.

Garibaldi, Korey. "Sketching in an Age of Anxiety: Henry James's Morganatic Baroness in *The Europeans*." In *Reading Henry James in the Twenty-First Century: Heritage and Transmission*. Eds. Dennis Tredy, Annick Duperray and Adrian Harding. Cambridge: Cambridge Scholars, 2019.317–328.

Gibbon, Edward. *Memoirs of my Life*. Ed. Betty Radice. London: Penguin, 1990.

———. *The History of the Decline and Fall of the Roman Empire*, 3 volumes. Ed. David Womersley. London: Penguin, 1995.

Golding, William. *Rites of Passage*. London: Faber & Faber, 1980.

Gorra, Michael. *Portrait of a Novel. Henry James and the Making of an American Masterpiece*. New York: Liveright, 2012.

Graham, Wendy. "Signifying in *The Ivory Tower*." *The Henry James Review* 30 (2009): 68–74.

Greenblatt, Stephen. *Shakespeare's Freedom*. Chicago: The U of Chicago P, 2010.

Griffin, Susan M. *Anti-Catholicism and Nineteenth-Century Fiction*. Cambridge: Cambridge UP, 2004.

Guo, Wenwen. "Disease and Desire in the Dove." *ANQ* 32.2 (2018): 1–5.

Habegger, Alfred. *Henry James and the 'Woman Business'*. Cambridge: Cambridge UP, 1989.

Hadfield, Andrew. *Shakespeare and Republicanism*. Cambridge: Cambridge UP, 2005.

Hadley, Tessa. *Henry James and the Imagination of Pleasure*. Cambridge: Cambridge UP, 2002.

Hägglund, Martin. *Dying for Time: Proust, Woolf, Nabokov*. Cambridge, MA: Harvard UP, 2012.

Halpern, Richard. *Shakespeare among the Moderns*. Ithaca: Cornell UP, 1997.

Hannah, Daniel. "'Massed Ambiguity': Fatness in Henry James's *The Ivory Tower*." *Twentieth Century Literature* 53.4 (2007): 460–487.

———. "Hearing Henry James's Poetry." *The Henry James Review* 42.1 (2021): 1–8.

Haralson, Eric. *Henry James and Queer Modernity*. Cambridge: Cambridge UP, 2003.

Harden, Edgar F. Thackeray the Writer: *Pendennis* to *Denis Duval*. London: Palgrave, 2000.

Hawthorne, Nathaniel. *The Scarlet Letter*. Ed. Thomas E. Connolly. London: Penguin, 1970.

———. *Young Goodman Brown and Other Tales*. Ed. Brian Harding. Oxford: Oxford UP, 1987.

Heffernan, Julián Jiménez. "'Lying Epitaphs:' *Vanity Fair*, Waterloo, and the Cult of the Dead." *Victorian Literature and Culture* 40.1 (2012): 25–46.

———. "Pamela's Hands. Political Intangibility and the Production of Manners." *NOVEL: A Forum on Fiction* 46.1 (2013).

———. "Togetherness and Its Discontents." *Community in Twentieth-Century Fiction*. Ed. Paula Martín et al. London: Palgrave, 2013.1–47.

———. "Two New Sources for *The Tragic Muse*," *ANQ* 29.3 (2016): 149–152.

———. "'Constructed to Revolve': Interest in Henry James." *The Henry James Review* 38.2 (2017): 188–206.

———. "'On the Outer Edge': The Temptation of Bohemia in Henry James." *Studies in American Fiction* 44.1 (2017): 53–86.

———. "'The Stamp of Rarity': Ancestrality and Extinction in *Daniel Deronda*." *Representations* 144 (Fall 2018): 90–123.

———. *Limited Shakespeare: The Reason of Finitude*. London: Routledge, 2019.

———. "'The Hard Worldly Basis': History and Infrastructure in Henry James's 'Julia Bride'." *Arizona Quarterly* 77.4 (2021): 1–30.

Hegel, G.W.F. *The Encyclopedia of the Philosophical Sciences*. Ed. William Wallace. Oxford: Clarendon, 1894.

———. *Aesthetics. Lectures on Fine Arts*. Trans. T.M. Knox. London: Clarendon Press, 1975.

———. *Phenomenology of Spirit*. Trans. A.V. Miller. Oxford: Oxford UP, 1979.

———. *Aphorismen aus Wastebook 1803–1806. Werke 2*. Eds. Eva Moldenhauer, Karl Markus Michel et al. Frankfurt am Main: Suhrkamp, 1986.

Herford, Oliver. "Henry James and the Habit of Allusion." In *Henry James's European Heritage and Transfer*. Eds. Dennis Tredy et al. Cambridge: Open Books, 2011.179–189.

Herrin, Judith. *Unrivalled Influence: Women and Empire in Byzantium*. Princeton: Princeton UP, 2013.

Hillman, David. "Philosophical Sex." In *Shakespeare's* Hamlet. *Philosophical Perspectives*. Ed. Tzachi Zamir. Oxford: Oxford UP, 2018.72–104.

Hobbes, Thomas. *Human Nature and De corpore politico*. Ed. J.C.A. Gaskin. Oxford: Oxford UP, 1994.

———. *On the Citizen*. Eds. Richard Tuck and Michael Silverthorne. Cambridge: Cambridge UP, 1998.

Hocks, Richard A. *Henry James and Pragmatic Thought*. Chapel Hill: The U of North Carolina P, 1974.

Höfele, Andreas. *No Hamlets: German Shakespeare from Nietzsche to Carl Schmitt*. Oxford: Oxford UP, 2016.

Horne, Philip. "Henry James among the Poets." *The Henry James Review* 26 (2005): 68–81.

———. "Henry James, Winchelsea, Rye, and Thackeray's *Denis Duval*." *The Henry James Review* 38 (2017): 219–230.

Jackson, Shirley. *Novels and Stories*. Ed. Joyce Carol Oates. New York: The Library of America, 2010.

James, Henry. *The Sense of the Past*. London: W. Collins Sons & Co., 1917.

———. *Stories of Writers and Artists*. Ed. F.O. Matthiessen. New York: New Directions, 1944.

———. *Letters. Vol I 1843–1875*. Ed. Leon Edel. Cambridge, MA: Harvard UP, 1974.

———. *The Notebooks of Henry James*. Ed. F.O. Matthiesen and K.B. Murdock. Chicago: The U of Chicago P, 1974.

———. *Letters. Vol II 1895–1916*. Ed. Leon Edel. Cambridge, MA: Harvard UP, 1984.

———. *Literary Criticism*, Vol. I. Ed. Leon Edel. New York: The Library of America, 1984.

———. *Literary Criticism*, Vol. II. Ed. Leon Edel. New York: The Library of America, 1984.

———. *The Portrait of a Lady*. Ed. Geoffrey Moore. London: Penguin, 1986.

———. *Roderick Hudson*. Eds. Geoffrey Moore and Patricia Crick. London: Penguin, 1986.

———. *The Princess Casamassima*. Ed. Derek Brewer. London: Penguin, 1987.

———. *Italian Hours*. Ed. John Auchard. London: Penguin, 1992.

———. *The Wings of the Dove*. Ed. Peter Brooks. Oxford: Oxford UP, 1998.

———. *Complete Stories 1864–1874*. Ed. Jean Strouse. New York: The Library of America, 1999.

———. *A Life in Letters*. Ed. Philip Horne. London: Penguin, 1999.

———. *The Turn of the Screw*. Ed. Jonathan Warren. New York: Norton, 1999.

———. *The Ivory Tower*. Introd. Allan Hollinghurst. New York: NYRB, 2004.

———. *The Ambassadors*. Ed. Christopher Butler. Oxford: Oxford UP, 2008.

———. *English Hours*. Foreword by Colm Tóibín. London: TTP, 2011.

———. *Notes of a Son and Brother*. Ed. Peter Collister. Charlottesville: U of Virginia P, 2011.

———. *A Small Boy and Others*. Ed. Peter Collister. Charlottesville: U of Virginia P, 2011.

———. *Daisy Miller* and *An International Episode*. Ed. Adrian Poole. Oxford: Oxford UP, 2013.

———. *The Ambassadors*. Ed. Nicola Bradbury. Cambridge: Cambridge UP, 2015.

———. *The Princess Casamassima*. Ed. Adrian Poole. Cambridge: Cambridge UP, 2021.

James, William. *Writings 1902–1910*. Ed. Bruce Kuklick. New York: The Library of America, 1984.

———. *The Letters of William James*. Ed. Henry James. New York: Atlantic Monthly Press, 1920.

Jameson, Fredric. *Sartre: The Origins of a Style*. New Haven: Yale UP, 1961.

———. "Magical Narratives: Romance as Genre." *New Literary History* 7.1 (1975): 135–163.

———. *The Political Unconscious. Narrative as a Socially Symbolic Act*. Ithaca: Cornell UP, 1982.

———. *Valences of the Dialectic*. London: Verso, 2009.

Jolly, Roslyn. *History, Narrative, Fiction*. Oxford: Clarendon Press, 2001.

Jones, Ernest. *Sigmund Freud: Life and Work, Vol 2*. London: Hogarth Press, 1953.

Joyce, James. *Finnegans Wake*. Ed. Seamus Deane. London: Penguin, 1992.

———. *Ulysses*. Ed. Jeri Johnson. Oxford: Oxford UP, 1993.

Kaplan, Fred. *Henry James: The Imagination of Genius*. Baltimore: John Hopkins UP, 1992.

Kenner, Hugh. *The Pound Era*. Berkeley: U of California P, 1971.

Keymer, Thomas and Peter Sabor. *The Pamela Controversy. Vol 1: Criticisms and Adaptations of Samuel Richardson's Pamela*. London: Routledge, 2001.

———. *'Pamela' in the Marketplace: Literary Controversy and Print Culture in Eighteenth Century Britain and Ireland*. Cambridge: Cambridge UP, 2005.

Kventsel, Anna. *Decadence in the Late Novels of Henry James*. London: Palgrave, 2007.

Laclau, Ernesto. *Emancipations*. London: Verso, 2006.

Lamb, Charles. *Tales from Shakespeare*. Intr. Marina Warner. London: Penguin, 2007.

Lawlor, Leonard. *Derrida and Husserl: The Basic Problem of Phenomenology*. Bloomington: Indiana UP, 2002.

Leavis, F.R. *The Great Tradition: George Eliot, Henry James, Joseph Conrad*. New York: George Stewart, 1950.

Lesser, Zachary. *Hamlet After Q1: An Uncanny History of the Shakespearean Text*. Philadelphia: University of Pennsylvania Press, 2014.

Leyburn, Ellen Douglas. "Virginia Woolf's Judgement on Henry James." *Modern Fiction Studies* 5.2 (1959): 166–169.

Lukacher, Ned. *Primal Scenes: Literature, Philosophy, Psychoanalysis*. Cornell: Cornell UP, 1988.

Lupton, Julia Reinhard. *Thinking with Shakespeare*. Chicago: The U of Chicago P, 2011.

McCuskey, Brian. "Fetishizing the Flunkey: Thackeray and the Uses of Deviance." *NOVEL* 32.3 (1999): 384–400.

Macpherson, C.B. *The Political Theory of Possessive Individualism: Hobbes to Locke*. Oxford: Oxford UP, 1962.

Maeterlinck, Maurice. *The Plays of Maurice Maeterlinck: Princess Maleine. The Intruder. The Blind. The Seven Princesses*. Trans. Richard Hovey. Chicago: Stone & Kimball, 1895.

———. *La princesse Maleine*. Paris: Georges Crès, 1918.

Mansfield, Luther Stearns. "Henry Adam's Longest Journey: From Santa Maria di Ara Coeli to Notre Dame de Chartres." *The Centennial Review* 20.3 (1976): 197–218.

Marcus, Steven. *Dickens from Pickwick to Dombey*. New York: Simon and Schuster, 1965.

Markovits, Stefanie. *The Crisis of Action in Nineteenth-Century English Literature*. Columbus: Ohio State UP, 2006.

Marx, Karl and Friedrich Engels. *The German Ideology: Introduction to a Critique of Political Economy*. Ed. Christopher John Arthur. London: Lawrence & Wishart, 1970.

Matthiessen, F.O. *Henry James: The Major Phase*. Oxford: Oxford UP, 1944.

———. *The James Family: A Group Biography*. 1947. New York: The Overlook Press, 2008.

McGinn, Colin. *Shakespeare's Philosophy*. New York: Harper, 2006.

McKeon, Michael. *The Origins of the English Novel 1600–1740*. Baltimore: The John Hopkins UP, 2002.

———. *The Secret History of Domesticity: Public, Private and the Division of Knowledge*. Baltimore: John Hopkins UP, 2006.

McWhirter, David Bruce. *Henry James in Context.* Cambridge: Cambridge UP, 2010.

Mill, John Stuart. *On Liberty and Other Writings.* Ed. Stefan Collini. Cambridge: Cambridge UP, 1989.

Miller, Andrew H. *Novels Behind the Glass: Commodity Culture and Victorian Narrative.* Cambridge: Cambridge UP, 1995.

Miller, D.A. *The Novel and the Police.* Berkeley: University of California Press, 1989.

Miller, J. Hillis. *The Form of Victorian Fiction. Thackeray, Dickens, Trollope, George Eliot, Meredith and Hardy.* Notre Dame: The University of Notre Dame Press, 1968.

———. *Fiction and Repetition: Seven English Novels.* Cambridge, MA: Harvard UP, 1982.

———. *Victorian Subjects.* Durham: Duke UP, 1990.

———. *Literature as Conduct. Speech Acts in Henry James.* New York: Fordham UP, 2005.

Momigliano, Arnaldo. "Gibbon's Contribution to Historical Method." *Historia: Zeitschrift für Alte Geschichte* 2.4 (1954): 450–463.

———. *Studies in Historiography.* London: Weidenfeld and Nicolson, 1966.

Moretti, Franco. *Signs Taken for Wonders: On the Sociology of Literary Forms.* London: Verso, 1983.

———. *The Way of the World: The Bildungsroman in European Culture.* London: Verso, 1987.

Münz, Sigmund. "Ferdinand Gregorovius." *The English Historical Review* 28.7 (1892): 697–704.

Murdoch, Iris. *Sartre: Romantic Rationalist.* London: Vintage, 1999.

———. *The Bell.* Intr. A.S. Byatt. London: Vintage, 1999.

Nietzsche, Friedrich. *Unzeitgemässe Betrachtungen.* Ed. Peter Pütz. Berlin: Goldmann, 1992.

Nussbaum, Martha. *The Fragility of Goodness: Luck and Ethics in Greek Tragedy and Philosophy.* Revised edition. Cambridge: Cambridge UP, 2001.

O'Brien, Karen. "Introduction" to *The Cambridge Companion to Edward Gibbon.* Eds. Karen O'Brien and Brian Young. Cambridge: Cambridge UP, 2018.1–19.

Ohi, Kevin. *Henry James and the Queerness of Style.* Minneapolis: The U of Minnesota P, 2011.

Parker, Fred. "Gibbon's Style in *The Decline and Fall.*" In *The Cambridge Companion to Edward Gibbon.* Eds. Karen O'Brien and Brian Young. Cambridge: Cambridge UP, 2018.167–183.

Parrington, Vernon Louis. "Henry James and the Nostalgia of Culture." *The Question of Henry James.* Ed. F.W. Dupee. New York: Henry Holt, 1945.128–130.

Peterson, M. Jeanne. "The Victorian Governess: Status Incongruence in Family and Society." In *Suffer and Be Still: Women in the Victorian Age.* Ed. Martha Vicinus. Bloomington: Indiana UP, 1972.3–19.

Pippin, Robert. *Henry James and the Modern Moral Life.* Cambridge: Cambridge UP, 2000.

———. *Hegel's Practical Philosophy: Rational Agency as Ethical Life.* Cambridge: Cambridge UP, 2008.

———. "Back to Hegel?" *Mediations* 26.1 (2012–13): 7–28.

———. "On Maisie's Knowing Her Own Mind." *A Companion to Henry James.* Ed. Greg W. Zacharias. Chichester: Wiley, 2014.121–138.

Pocock, J.G.A. *Barbarism and Religion*, Vol. I. *The Enlightenments of Edward Gibbon. 1737–1764.* Cambridge: Cambridge UP, 1999.

———. *Barbarism and Religion*, Vol. II. *Narratives of Civil Government.* Cambridge: Cambridge UP, 1999.

———. *Barbarism and Religion*, Vol. III. *The First Decline and Fall.* Cambridge: Cambridge UP, 2003.

———. *Barbarism and Religion*, Vol. IV. *Barbarians, Savages and Empires.* Cambridge: Cambridge UP, 2005.

———. "An Overview of the *Decline and Fall*." *The Cambridge Companion to Edward Gibbon.* Eds. Karen O'Brien and Brian Young. Cambridge: Cambridge UP, 2018.20–40.

Poole, Adrian. "James and the Shadow of the Roman Empire: Manners and the Consenting Victim." In *Enacting History in Henry James.* Ed. Gert Buelens. Cambridge: Cambridge UP, 1997.75–93.

———. *Shakespeare and the Victorians.* London: Thomson Learning, 2004.

———. "The Romance of Certain Old Texts: Henry James and Shakespeare." *Archiv für das Studium der neueren Sprachen und Literaturen* 254.1 (2017): 1–15.

Posnock, Ross. *The Trial of Curiosity: Henry James, William James and the Challenge of Modernity.* Oxford: Oxford UP, 1991.

Pound, Ezra. "Notes for *The Ivory Tower*." In *The Ivory Tower*. 261–266.

Priest, Graham, Richard Routley and Jean Norman, eds. *Paraconsistent Logic: Essays on the Inconsistent.* München: Philosophia Verlag, 1989.

Purton, Valerie. "Henry James's The Turn of the Screw and Fielding's Amelia." *The Explicator* 34.3 (1975).

Racine, Jean. *Bajazet.* Paris: Gallimard, 1995.

Rawlings, Peter. *Henry James and the Abuse of the Past.* London: Palgrave, 2005.

———, ed. *Palgrave Advances in Henry James Studies.* London: Palgrave, 2007.100–125.

———. *Great Shakespeareans: Emerson, Melville, James, Berryman.* London: Bloomsbury, 2011.

———. "Henry James." In *Emerson, Melville, James, Berryman: Great Shakespeareans.* Ed. Peter Rawlings. London: Bloomsbury, 2011.95–132.

Rawson, Claude, ed. *The Cambridge Companion to Henry Fielding.* Cambridge: Cambridge UP, 2007.

Reinhard, Kenneth and Julia Reinhard Lupton. *After Oedipus: Shakespeare in Psychoanalysis.* Ithaca: Cornell UP, 1993.

Richardson, Samuel. *Clarissa.* Ed. Angus Ross. London: Penguin, 1985.

Rivkin, Julie. *False Positions. The Representational Logics of Henry James's Fiction.* Stanford: Stanford UP, 1996.

Robbins, Bruce. *The Servant's Hand: English Fiction from Below.* Duke UP, 1993.

Rowe, John Carlos. *The Theoretical Dimensions of Henry James.* Madison: The U of Wisconsin P, 1985.

———. *The Other Henry James.* Durham: Duke UP, 1998.

———. "Ghostly Visitations in Henry James's *Daisy Miller*." *Rivista di studi vittoriani* 22.43 (2017): 63–81.

———. *Our Henry James in Fiction, Film and Popular Culture*. New York: Routledge, 2022.

Rowe, John Carlos and Eric Haralson, eds. *A Historical Guide to Henry James*. Oxford: Oxford UP, 2012.

Royle, Nicholas. *How to Read Shakespeare*. New York: Norton, 2005.

———. *In Memory of Jacques Derrida*. Edinburgh: Edinburgh UP, 2009.

Russell, Bertrand. *Introduction to Mathematical Philosophy*. London: Routledge, 1993.

———. *History of Western Philosophy*. London: Routledge, 2004.

Ryburn, May L. "*The Turn of the Screw* and *Amelia*: A Source for Quint?" *Studies in Short Fiction* (1979): 235–237.

Sabor, Peter. "Amelia." *The Cambridge Companion to Henry Fielding*. Ed. Claude Rawson. Cambridge: Cambridge UP, 2007.

Salmon, Richard. *Henry James and the Culture of Publicity*. Cambridge: Cambridge UP, 1997.

———. "Henry James in the Public Sphere." In *A Concise Companion to Henry James*. Ed. Greg Zacharias. Oxford: Blackwell, 2008.456–471.

Santner, Eric. *The Royal Remains: The People's Two Bodies and the Endgames of Sovereignty*. Chicago: The U of Chicago P., 2011.

Savoy, Eric. "The Queer Subject of 'The Jolly Corner.'" *The Henry James Review* 20.1 (1999): 1–21.

———. "The Jamesian Thing," *The Henry James Review* 22 (2001): 268–277.

———. "Bad Investments." *Henry James's European Heritage and Transfer*. Eds. Dennis Tredy et al. Cambridge: Open Books, 2011.51–57.

Schacht, John Hammond. *A Critical Edition of William Makepeace Thackeray's Denis Duval*. Thesis. Urbana: University of Illinois, 1950.

Schniedermann, Wibke. "Illness as Capital in *The Wings of the Dove*." *Journal of American Studies of Turkey* 40 (2014): 75–94.

Schwehn, Mark R. "Henry Adams: An Intellectual Historian's Perspective Reconsidered." In *Introspection in Biography. The Biographer's Quest for Self-Awareness*. Eds. Samuel H. Baron and Carl Pletsch. London: Routledge, 1985.

Sedgwick, Eve Kosofsky. *Epistemology of the Closet*. Berkeley: U of California P, 2008.

———. *Between Men: English Literature and Male Homosocial Desire*. Foreword by Wayne Kostenbaum. New York: Columbia UP, 2015.

Shakespeare, William. *Hamlet: The Texts of 1603 and 1623*. Eds. Ann Thompson and Neil Taylor. London: Bloomsbury, 2008.

———. *The Norton Shakespeare*. Eds. Stephen Greenblatt et al. New York: Norton, 2008.

Skinner, Quentin. *Liberty before Liberalism*. Cambridge: Cambridge UP, 1998.

———. *Hobbes and Republican Liberty*. Cambridge: Cambridge UP, 2008.

Snyder, Katherine V. *Bachelors, Manhood, and the Novel, 1850–1925*. Cambridge: Cambridge UP, 2004.

Sprinker, Michael, Ed. *Ghostly Demarcations: A Symposium on Jacques Derrida's Specters of Marx*. London: Verso, 2007.

Spurgeon, C.F.E. *Shakespeare's Imagery and What it Tells Us.* New York: Cambridge UP, 2005.

Stern, Tom. "Schopenhauer's Shakespeare: The Genius of the World Stage." In *Shakespeare and Continental Philosophy.* Eds. Jennifer Ann Bates and Richard Wilson. Edinburgh: Edinburgh UP, 2014.56–75.

Sussman, Henry. *The Hegelian Aftermath: Readings in Hegel, Kierkegaard, Freud, Proust, and James.* Baltimore: The John Hopkins UP, 1982.

Sutherland, John. *Thackeray at Work.* London: The Athlone Press, 1974.

———. "The Genesis of Thackeray's *Denis Duval.*" *The Review of English Studies* 37.146 (1986): 226–233.

Tanner, Tony. "Henry James and Henry Adams." *TriQuarterly* 11 (1968): 91.

———. *The American Mystery: American Literature from Emerson to DeLillo.* Cambridge: Cambridge UP, 2000.

Taylor, Andrew. *Henry James and the Father Question.* Cambridge: Cambridge UP, 2002.

Taylor, Charles. *Modern Social Imaginaries.* Durham: Duke UP, 2003.

Tennyson, Alfred. *The Complete Works of Alfred, Lord Tennyson.* New York: Frederick Stokes, 1891.

———. *The Major Works.* Ed. Adam Roberts. Oxford: Oxford UP, 2009.

Thackeray, William. *Vanity Fair.* Ed. John Sutherland. Oxford: Oxford UP, 1983.

———. *The Adventures of Philip.* In *Complete Works* 20. New York: Harber & Brothers, 1904.

———. *Denis Duval.* In *Complete Works* 23. New York: Harber & Brothers, 1904.

———. *English Humorists of the Eighteenth Century.* In *Complete Works* 14. New York: Harber & Brothers, 1904.

———. *The History of Pendennis.* In *Complete Works* 3. New York: Harber & Brothers, 1904.

———. *The Newcomes.* In *Complete Works* 15–16. New York: Harber & Brothers, 1904.

Tillotson, Geoffrey. *Thackeray the Novelist.* 1954. New York: Methuen & Co., 1974.

Tillotson, Kathleen. *Novels of the Eighteen-Forties.* Oxford: Clarendon Press, 1954.

Tintner, Adeline R. "Henry James's Hamlets: 'A Free Rearrangement'." *Colby Quarterly* 18.3 (1982): 168–182.

Tintner, Adeline R. and H.D. Janowitz. "Inoperable Cancer: An Alternate Diagnosis for Milly Theale's Illness." *Journal of the History of Medicine and Allied Sciences* 42.1 (1987): 73–76.

Trevor, Douglas. *The Poetics of Melancholy in Early Modern England.* Cambridge: Cambridge UP, 2009.

Trevor-Roper, Hugh. "Appreciation." Afterword to *The Decline and Fall to the Roman Empire.* Ed. H. Trevor-Roper. London: Phoenix, 2005.

Trilling, Lionel. *The Liberal Imagination.* New York: NYRB, 2008.

Trollope, Anthony. *Thackeray.* London: Macmillan, 1912.

Warner, William Beatty. *Reading* Clarissa. *The Struggles of Interpretation.* New Haven: Yale UP, 1979.

Watt, Ian. *The Rise of the Novel: Studies in Defoe, Richardson and Fielding.* Harmondsworth: Penguin, 1966.

Williams, Raymond. *The English Novel. From Dickens to Lawrence*. London: Chatto & Windus, 1970.

Wilson, Edmund. *The Triple Thinkers*. London: John Lehman, 1952.

Wilson, John Dover. *What Happens in Hamlet*. Cambridge: Cambridge UP, 1951.

Womersley, David. *The Transformation of* The Decline and Fall of the Roman Empire. Cambridge: Cambridge UP, 1988.

———. *Gibbon and the 'Watchmen of the Holy City': The Historian and his Reputation, 1776–1815*. Oxford: Clarendon Press, 2002.

Woolf, Virginia. "Modern Fiction." *Selected Essays*. Ed. David Bradshaw. Oxford: Oxford UP, 2009.

Young, Brian. "Gibbon and Catholicism." In *The Cambridge Companion to Edward Gibbon*. Eds. Karen O'Brien and Brian Young. Cambridge: Cambridge UP, 2018.147–166.

Zacharias, Greg W. *Henry James and the Morality of Fiction*. New York: Peter Lang, 1993.

Žižek, Slavoj. *The Sublime Object of Ideology*. London: Verso, 1989.

———. *The Metastases of Enjoyment: On Women and Causality*. London: Verso, 1994.

———. *The Plague of Fantasies*. London: Verso, 1997.

———. *The Fragile Absolute, or Why Is the Christian Legacy Worth Fighting For?* London: Verso, 2000.

———. *How to Read Lacan*. London: Faber & Faber, 2006.

———. *The Parallax View*. Cambridge: The MIT Press, 2009.

———. *Organs without Bodies: Deleuze and Consequences*. With a new introduction by the author. London: Routledge, 2012.

Zupančič, Alenka. *Ethics of the Real: Kant and Lacan*. London: Verso, 2000.

Zwinger, Lynda. *Telling in Henry James: The Web of Experience and the Forms of Reality*. London: Bloomsbury, 2017.

# Index